SPRING *for*
SUSANNAH

$\mathcal{S}$PRING *for*
SUSANNAH

CATHERINE RICHMOND

THOMAS NELSON
Since 1798

NASHVILLE   DALLAS   MEXICO CITY   RIO DE JANEIRO

To my folks.
A house full of books is a launching pad for life.

Published in Nashville, Tennessee, by Thomas Nelson. Thomas Nelson is a trademark of Thomas Nelson, Inc.

All scripture quotations are taken from the King James Version of the Bible.

ISBN-13: 978-1-61129-847-5

Printed in the United States of America

Chapter 1

Please, Lord, let my Susannah be on this train.
And give me some fancy talking so she'll stay.

"Fourth Siding," the conductor yelled as he trundled down the aisle. "Your stop, miss."

Susannah peered through the soot-covered window. Nothing. No false-fronted buildings, no hardy pioneer families riding in wagons, no tented gatherings of fur trappers and gold miners. Just drab brownish-green grass waving all the way to the horizon, as it had since Fargo this morning. Dakota Territory had to be the emptiest place on earth.

She pulled the letter from the pocket of her traveling suit. "Fourth Siding" was scrawled beneath his name, but no further directions. "I'm needing a wife," he'd written in bold, angular letters, a mix of cursive and manuscript. The second page, folded with it for safekeeping, was written by Reverend Mason in precise script, round letters all slanting right.

Surely this Mr. Jesse Mason would be like his brother the minister—a kindly gentleman with a placid temperament. Susannah stowed the letter.

The engine swung onto the sidetrack. This was it. Time to

make a good first impression. She patted her chignon, tucked in hairpins, straightened her bonnet and veil. She shook out her skirt, smoothed her jacket, and pulled on her gloves.

Her fluttering drew the attention of the other passengers, two soldiers and a civilian. The civilian, a grizzly bear of a man, shot a stream of tobacco juice in the general vicinity of the spittoon, then swabbed the dregs on the sleeve of his checked shirt. His beard parted, showing a raw space where an upper incisor should be. Susannah shuddered. Poor dentist.

Please let my husband have all his teeth. And let him be free of the tobacco habit.

Susannah stopped herself. It was no use praying. If God listened, she wouldn't be in this predicament. The Almighty wasn't going to help her, that much was clear. She'd just have to manage in her usual way, without divine intervention.

With a squeal and jerk of the brakes, the Northern Pacific westbound run pulled up to a small platform. Late summer sun baked the new wood of a locked shed. No sign of Mr. Mason or anyone else to meet her. No town, no depot, no hotel. Susannah's heart sank. Well then, she'd ride on, wherever the train went.

The tobacco spitter stood and stretched, filling the aisle with his bulk. "I'll fetch your grip." His bristly paw engulfed the handle of her satchel, which contained her change of collars and cuffs, handkerchiefs, and towel, all in desperate need of laundering.

"But . . ." She followed, not knowing what else to do.

He deposited her bag on the platform and handed her down. "Begging pardon, miss, but you're looking mighty peaked. You all right?"

As much as she'd paid for her breakfast toast, she would not lose it. "I'm fine, thank you."

At the freight car door, the conductor hauled out two trunks, all that was left of her life in Detroit. Susannah needed to inform

2

the train crew she wouldn't be staying; please put her luggage back on. But the grizzly wouldn't let go.

"If it don't work out with Jesse," he said in a phlegm-thick voice, "you're welcome over to my place. Across the river at the next siding. Name's Abner Reece."

How did he know she was here to meet Jesse Mason? And was he *proposing*? Surely she'd done nothing to encourage his attention. She'd avoided even glancing his way. "If you'll excuse me—"

The train whistle split the air, and the conductor hustled Mr. Reece back into the passenger car.

Susannah raised her voice and her arm, abandoning all pretense of ladylike behavior. "Wait! Pardon me, sir. There's no one—"

But the pounding steam engine drowned out the conductor's reply. He pointed north, over her shoulder, to a telegraph pole. When Susannah turned back, the locomotive had *huff-huff*ed west with its two cars.

"Wait!"

A shower of red-hot cinders rained down. She jumped, shaking her black serge skirt. When she looked up, the train had grown smaller. It crested the earth and disappeared.

A bone-deep ache pressed down on her, heavy as the August sun. Her knees shook. A tear slipped out. It wasn't like she'd answered an advertisement in a hearts-and-hands publication. No, her pastor's brother had written to her, had asked her to marry him. He should be here.

Susannah knew what they said about her at Lafayette Avenue Church. With her plain looks and her family's limited means, she could hardly expect to attract a husband. Her shyness made others uncomfortable. And her interest in her father's veterinary surgery was highly inappropriate.

She hadn't been invited to parties, hadn't had a proper coming out, hadn't been courted, not even by the battle-scarred soldiers limping home from the War. Becoming a mail-order bride seemed like her best chance, her only chance, for a home and family of her own.

Susannah removed her veil, wiped her cheeks, and drew in a breath. As she stuffed her gloves into her pockets, her fingers brushed the handkerchief knotted around the last of her funds. After paying for train tickets, hotels, and restaurant meals, she was left with $3.72.

Not much. Not enough. She had no choice. She would simply take the next train, wherever it went, whenever it came.

After four days on the train and three nights in noisy, smelly hotels, the platform was a fine place to wait. Fresh, quiet, like a raft floating on a sea of grass.

A loud thump shook the boards beneath her feet. Susannah spun around, her mind conjuring images of stampeding buffalo, cattle rustlers, Indians on the warpath. Her heel caught on her satchel and she fell.

As she lay there breathless, she heard heavy boots cross the planks and caught a glimpse of a wide-brimmed straw hat and broad shoulders covered by a faded blue shirt. His open hands carried no weapons. He must have been hiding under the platform, holed up like a bandit. But Susannah didn't have a derringer in her pocket or a bowie knife in her boot or even a next-door neighbor with a fireplace poker.

"Are you all right?" His low voice cut through the wind.

Due to the current fashion of bustles and petticoats, Susannah could fall on her backside without injury, but standing was another matter. Gathering the fragments of her dignity, she straightened her back and lifted her chin. "Have we been introduced?"

The man wiped his palms on his pants and reached for her. "Miss Susannah Underhill?"

Susannah planted her hands as far down as she could reach, trying to keep the wind from blowing her skirts over her head.

She'd lived anonymously her entire life in Detroit; now all the inhabitants of Dakota Territory seemed fully informed of her identity and intentions. "How do you know my name?"

The man sat on his heels. One corner of his mouth curved as if he couldn't manage a full smile. "I'm Jesse Mason. Your husband."

She looked up into a face that seemed oddly familiar. Then the image changed, like a stereopticon picture coming into focus. The high forehead, prominent nose, and mouth that tilted to the right were the same as his brother's, but this man was a few years older, his skin weathered. His face was rounder, the cleft in his chin more pronounced. Deep-set eyes—hazel, not blue— inspected her.

"Guess I gave you a scare. Sorry about that." He grinned, and she was glad to see he did indeed have all his teeth.

His wide hands, clean for a farmer's, enveloped hers, and the touch of his skin reminded her she'd removed her gloves. So much for a good first impression. The only thing worse would be bursting into tears, making her nose run and her eyes red. Or losing her breakfast. She clamped her lips together, squeezed her eyes. A small hurt sound, accompanied by a tear, got away from her.

"You're crying. Hurting from your spill?"

She fumbled in her pocket, but her least dirty handkerchief was wrapped around the evidence of her poverty, and she wasn't ready for him to find out about that just yet.

He removed his neckerchief, then frowned and stuffed it in his back pocket. "Can't use a sweaty bandanna on a lady." One warm, calloused finger skimmed her cheek. "Got you shaking like the cottontail my dog brought me last week." The planks creaked as he sat beside her. For a moment, they were eye to eye.

Susannah wanted to say how relieved she was that he came for her, to explain she was crying from nervousness. A word scraped up her throat, past the dry lump of her breakfast. "Hotel?"

"Closest is a tent with bunks, ten miles west. Half-dollar more fare and no place for a lady. Nearest one with real rooms is fifty miles back in Fargo. You stayed there last night." His thumbs rubbed her palms. "I got your trunks down below."

"You live here?"

"No, I—*we*—have a house south of here a few miles."

"You knew I'd arrive today?"

"Matt sent a telegram, and here you are, right on time! Welcome to Fourth Siding, Dakota Territory."

"Is this the town?" Her voice betrayed her with a squeak.

"Northern Pacific built the siding this spring. Us New Yorkers want to call it Buffalo. Expect naming will have to wait until we get a few more people."

What New Yorkers? she wondered.

"Here, let me help you up." He pulled her to standing, bringing her level with the tuft of brown hair curling from his collarless neckline. "Hey, you're a little bit of a thing." He gave her an extensive perusal, a farmer inspecting livestock. She might as well have opened her mouth so he could figure her age by her teeth.

"Gets pretty cold and lonesome out here." He shook his head, his jaw set in the "not buying" mode.

Panic shot down her spine. Was he going to send her back before he'd even given her a chance? "I brought warm clothes." Susannah rose on tiptoes to look taller. "Ellen thought—"

But she'd already lost his attention. He squinted over her head and whispered, "Dear Lord." In one swift move he spun away, kicked the shed door, and broke inside. He jerked the pump handle, working it furiously. Water sputtered into a bucket. "Cinder sparked the grass!"

A tiny puff of smoke spiraled alongside the tracks half a block west. "Fire! Fire!" Susannah yelled. "Where's the nearest fire department?"

6

"Fargo, maybe. Or St. Paul." He grabbed the sloshing bucket and dashed off the west end of the platform. "Fill the other!"

Smoke rose above her, tainting the air. A line of flames slithered toward the platform. He swung. Water hit its target, but the fire grew, chewing through the dry grass. At this rate, the whole territory would go up within minutes, taking them with it. Susannah grabbed the pump handle.

"Hurry!"

Arms aching, she hauled the full bucket and he swapped it for the empty one. The blaze raced toward them. This time she made it to the edge of the platform before him.

"One more!"

He disappeared into grass taller than his head, then popped out nearby, both arms raised. "Hallelujah! Who needs a fire department? I got you!"

Susannah leaned against the shed, wheezing like a horse with the heaves. Her bonnet hung on her ear, her chignon drooped on her neck, and her skirt sagged with water. She had passed the glowing allotted to ladies and dripped sweat like a horse.

With one hand he vaulted onto the platform and landed with another loud thud. As their handwriting predicted, this man was nothing like his brother. In spite of the heat, a shiver ricocheted through her, shoulders to toes. "Forgive me for raising my voice."

"Shouting is warranted when facing an inferno." He rinsed his bandanna under the pump, wrung it out, then reached for her.

What a mess she must be. Susannah raised her hand. "It's all right. You don't have to—"

"I promised God I'd take care of you." He moved so close she had to shut her eyes. The cool cloth brushed her forehead, wiping from hairline to jaw, then down the other side. "You shouldn't wear black in summer."

"I'm in mourning."

"I know," he said, his tone patient. "But you'll melt with this sun. Take off your hat and coat."

Undress in public? Her corset inexplicably tightened. Her heart beat against her ribs in protest. What kind of man had she married? She had kept her jacket on the entire trip, in spite of the heat, so strangers wouldn't stare.

A twitch of a smile crossed his face. "Queen Victoria will never find out. Guaranteed."

This stranger was her husband. She'd promised to obey him. Susannah nodded. He helped her out of her redingote. She untied the ribbons from her neck and lifted off her bonnet. The breeze wove cool fingers through her hair.

"Better?"

"Fine, thank you." Truth was, she felt exposed. Without the protection of her hat's brim, her words vanished on the wind. Her blouse flapped in an unseemly manner. She crossed her arms to maintain some particle of modesty and hide her frayed cuffs.

He looked her up and down. "Prettier than I thought." He made a sound in the back of his throat, somewhere between a groan and a cough, then glanced at the sun. "We'd best head for home."

Chapter 2

Help me not to judge on appearance, Lord.
I trusted You for a wife, the right wife
for me, so I'm leaning on faith here.

Susannah considered herself far too practical to believe in love at first sight. All she wanted was a small miracle, that she would feel something other than overwhelming shyness.

Too much to hope for, she supposed. At least he didn't chew tobacco.

Jesse led her into the draw where his ox waited in the shade of the platform. He stowed her bag, then lifted her to the seat. With easy, efficient movements, Jesse swung up and took the reins. He sprawled, his knee brushing hers. She scooted to the edge and dug her fingers into the plank seat. They bumped over the tracks and headed south along two lines of bent stems.

"Guess this old wagon doesn't ride as smooth as the train."

"It's fine." She glanced over her shoulder as the shed disappeared behind a curtain of tall grass.

"What're you looking for?"

"Is there a grocer's?"

"General store at Fifth Siding, but we'll grow most of our food." Jesse reached under the seat behind her feet.

Susannah flinched as an unwelcome memory surfaced, an arm clothed in finely woven wool. She pushed the image aside. The future was frightening enough without the past intruding.

He handed her a pail. "I fixed biscuits for you. Sourdough, seeing as how there's no milk or eggs. Plums from down by the crick." He hefted an earthenware jug. "From the beautiful Sweetwater Spring. Finest-tasting water anywhere. Being first out here, I claimed the quarter section with the best spring."

"Is there a cup?"

His shoulders drooped. "Guess I forgot how to treat a lady."

Susannah's arms trembled under the weight of the jug. Water splashed her linen shirt. So clumsy.

"Don't worry, you'll dry off quick in this wind. It never stops. Feels good in the summer when you work up a sweat, but freezes your nose off in winter. 'Course that might be an improvement with a snout the size of mine."

She took a tiny bite of biscuit, then realized he wasn't eating. "I'm sorry. Would you like some?"

"Nope. Ate mine watching for your train. Go ahead."

"Did you have long to wait?"

"My fault. I left home too early. Heard some brides cash in their ticket to cheat the husband. Not that you'd do such a thing, but changing trains in Chicago isn't easy. Your luggage might be stolen. Some sharper might see a woman traveling alone and try to swindle her out of her tickets, her money, or her honor. Or maybe you'd catch the eye of a Beau Brummell who'd smooth talk you into marrying him instead of this dirt man." He bent to retie his brogan. "Then I worried you wouldn't like me, or the house, or the territory." He straightened. "So, what do you think of Dakota?"

Explorer Stephen Long had labeled this the Great American

Desert. What could she add? "The grass is so tall. It makes me feel like planting trees."

"Scratch a city girl, find a farmer." He chuckled. "Yes, ma'am, we'll need a shelterbelt around our house to keep it from blowing away. And an orchard sure would be nice. Newspaper says some fellows are selling trees east of Fifth Siding. We'll see about buying a few saplings, if this harvest pays. This is real good land, the best. No stumps to plow around. No digging rocks every spring like back east. The soil here is so rich, wheat's shooting up in spite of the drought."

Over her shoulder, the telegraph poles sank behind the swell of the land. "Do you ever get lost?"

"I steer for a spot on the horizon. See that little dip? We'll go to the right of it, then there's another spot to hunt for farther on." A half smile twitched his mouth. "Guess this old ox could find his way home without me."

Grass slapped against the wagon. Unlike Michigan's soft emerald lawns, it grew dusty and dry, bleached tan in places.

"How far is your"—what was the proper term?—"your claim?"

"We'll be home before dark."

A shudder vibrated through her. No. Best not to worry about that which cannot be changed.

He shifted in the seat to face her. "Tell me about your train ride. Guess you met some interesting folks."

Did he think she was so ill bred she'd encourage such familiarity? "No," she said.

He took a deep breath. "All right. Five states and one territory. What's the most curious thing you saw?"

"Chicago. They've rebuilt from the fire."

"Anything happen on your trip?"

Her mind went blank. "No."

"Not a thing?" He drew back, shoulders drooping. He expected something from her, and she had disappointed him.

She swallowed against the constriction in her throat and hunted for something to say. "Have you seen Indians here?"

"Not a one. Army moved them west after the Sioux Uprising. The nearest post, Fort Ransom, closed last spring due to lack of hostiles."

"The *Detroit Free Press* reported General Custer sent his wife and the other officers' wives back east from Bismarck. Does he expect trouble from the Sioux?"

"Nope. Like the rest of the territory, Bismarck suffers from a lack of accommodations. The ladies won't have anyplace to stay until Fort Abraham Lincoln is finished this fall. Say, isn't Custer from Michigan? Know him?"

"Father met him during the War."

"Hear tell he's quite the character." He waited for her to say something, but she couldn't imagine what. "Guess your pa had some stories about our youngest general."

"He kept dogs in his tent."

"So your pa was a man of few words and you take after him." He propped his forearm on the seat back.

"I'm sorry."

"Well then, how's my little brother?"

"Oh yes, Reverend Mason told me to give you this right away." Susannah retrieved the marriage certificate from her pocket. "He married us before I left, by proxy, since there're so few pastors out here. I won't hold you to it if—"

"Yeah, Matt said something about this in his last letter. Hey, got a witness at my wedding I never heard of. Who's this?"

"Homer Ferguson. The organist's father."

"All right." He stretched, taking up most of the bench. "Since I couldn't make it to my own wedding, you tell me about it. Everything. All the details."

"Well, the usual—"

The certificate tapped against the hand holding the reins. "Start from the beginning. You got all dressed up."

"No, I had on my brown—no, my blue calico."

"And you went over to the church."

She shook her head. "Miss Ferguson was practicing the organ. Reverend Mason had us stand in his parlor."

"He crammed everyone in his front room?"

"It was only the Reverend, Ellen, Mr. Ferguson, and the children." *"Courage,"* Ellen had told her. *"Be brave."*

One eyebrow arched. "Just because my friends couldn't be there doesn't mean you couldn't invite yours. Then what?"

"Reverend Mason read the ceremony."

"And this Ferguson said my part?"

"No, he hasn't spoken since the War. The Reverend said the vows on your behalf. If you'd rather not—"

"No, this is great. We're married, all legal and official, and didn't have to spend a dime. No preacher's fee, no extra train fare for me to ride to Fargo." He folded the certificate into his pocket. "Well, much as I respect my brother, I'd just as soon have God hear it straight from me."

He dropped the reins. The ox slowed to a stop. Now what? He stood, pulled her up, and lifted his face to the clear sky. "Dear Lord, I come before You today to marry this woman." He smiled down at her. "I, Jesse, take you, Susannah, to be my wife, to love, honor, and cherish, as long as I live."

A long minute passed. His thumbs pressed her palms. She whispered, "I, Susannah, take you . . . Jesse, to love, honor, and obey, as long as I live."

"What God has joined together, let no man put asunder." He grinned at her. "Now we'll put it in writing." They sat. From under the bench, Jesse brought out a worn Bible, a metal ink bottle, and a pen. He opened the book to the first blank page. "Let's see: 'United in Holy Matrimony, August 26, 1873, Dakota Territory.' Now sign your name and I'll add mine."

Her hand shook so hard, her signature was unreadable. His marched across the page, past the allotted line. Duty complete, he replaced the book and snapped the reins. "Seems kind of short. What else?"

"Ellen read some verses."

"'Though I speak with tongues of men and angels . . .'" He went on and recited the whole thirteenth chapter of First Corinthians. "'And the greatest of these is love.' And now, music. What's your favorite hymn?"

"You pick."

"How about one of Wesley's?" He sang "Love Divine, All Loves Excelling."

Susannah leaned against the backrest. His deep voice flowed over her, easing a particle of tension from her shoulders.

"Sing with me," he directed, starting "Amazing Grace." Susannah took the alto part.

"You sing so well," she said when they finished. "Did you consider going into ministry too?"

"Susannah, we can't talk about that in the middle of our wedding. I still have to kiss the bride!"

She clutched the seat. As a girl she'd dreamed of a first kiss, the dream fading through years without suitors. Now, here it was, a first kiss on her wedding day, no less. His lips, warm and soft, brushed hers. She opened her eyes. He tilted his head, eyebrows drawn together. She'd disappointed him again.

He stared off into the distance. After a while, he cleared his throat. "Yeah, I did consider the ministry, but God didn't call me. Matt's better at bookwork anyhow. I need to be outside, moving around. Can't sit still. Could've stayed to help my little sister and her husband run the old farm, but I wanted somewhere new, a challenge, a chance to build a place all my own."

He leaned toward her, his head inches from hers, and wiped his brow with his bandanna. *Breathe,* Susannah reminded herself.

"So I took the train as far west as the tracks were laid."

He was a talker. Good. He spoke in staccato phrases, drawing out the last word, punctuating with easy movements of his wrists. His voice sounded half an octave lower and rougher than his brother's polished speech. He paused and looked at her. Her mind had wandered, and she hadn't the faintest idea what he was saying.

"Do you have neighbors?"

"Ivar and Marta Vold."

Susannah looked where he pointed. No smoke from a woodstove, no plowed field, no path. Just empty prairie.

"Ivar showed up my first fall. Couldn't speak a word of English, but I talked his ears off anyway. Helped me get the first harvest in, then we built his soddy. Wouldn't stay in it, though. 'Round about Christmas, he made skis and hiked over from his place. About choked on my grub when he banged open my door—I sure wasn't expecting any visitors. He looked like Saint Nicholas himself, his beard and eyebrows crusted with snow, nose bright red. Must have decided I wasn't all that good of company. First sign of spring he sent for his wife."

A low chuckle rolled from deep in his chest. He unbuttoned his cuffs and folded up his sleeves. Dark brown hair curled across his forearms and lay flat over the back of his hands. His skin was work-worn, ruddy from the sun. "Last winter Ivar stayed over at his place. He couldn't leave his wife, what with a baby on the way."

Two veins formed an x before his third and fourth knuckles. The fingers of his left hand twitched and his right wrist moved side to side for no apparent reason. His ox ignored the oscillations of the reins.

"Don't know if winter was so much worse, or I'd just had enough of my own company, but soon as the weather broke, I wrote Matt asking if he knew anyone he'd like as a sister-in-law. Sure am glad I won't have to face another winter alone." His warm hand pressed Susannah's. "I'm talking too much. Your turn."

"What should I say?"

"Anything. Tell me about you. Ever been out of the city?"

She'd never been farther from home than Detroit's outlying farms, making calls with Father. She'd never visited New York City or Washington City or even Toledo. "No."

Enthusiasm drained from his voice. "Sidestepping all my questions, like your letters: 'The weather has been pleasant.' Susannah, I want to know you, what you like, what you want."

What she wanted? Since when was that important?

Susannah's throat tightened. She'd spent days on those letters—composing drafts, searching for words that were not too forward or self-serving, then feeding her poor efforts to the fire. Finally she had copied samples from a correspondence book, using the fancy pen and stationery she'd received for graduation. "I'm sorry."

He groaned. "All right, back to talking about my brother."

Ah, a safe topic of conversation. "He's well. The Reverend preached my parents' funerals. Ellen packed for me."

The prairie dissolved. Back in Michigan, Ellen and her husband tucked their children into bed. She could see Reverend Mason, with his Lincolnesque stature, bent almost double under the rafters. The two oldest girls had given up their bed for Susannah and were curled on a pallet, covered with quilts. The Reverend listened to their prayers, which included entreaties for traveling mercies for Susannah. Smoothing their hair, he kissed them good night. Ellen sat by the stove, rocking the baby's cradle with her foot, hemming a shirt for the older boy.

"Where did you go?" Jesse broke into her reverie.

"I'm sorry. I was thinking about the children." And wondering if she'd ever have a family.

"How many nieces and nephews do I have these days?"

"Four and one on the way. They may have to change churches if the congregation doesn't add on to the parsonage. It's only four rooms, same as ours. I mean, same as Father's."

"Five children! We've got some catching up to do." He winked.

Susannah swallowed and looked away. This couldn't be real. Not this man. Not this place. The wagon lurched and a splinter dug into her finger. It was real. She had better get used to it.

"Susannah." He touched her chin, bringing her to face him. His stare dissected her, cutting to the core. She focused on the brim of his hat, fighting the urge to put space between them.

"Your eyes are the same color as the sky right now," he said. "Best part of the day. Time to stop work, look over all you got done."

He let go. She inhaled, her breath sounding like a gasp, and turned away from him. A gray animal darted out of the draw ahead. "Wolf!" Susannah tightened her grip on the seat.

"It's a dog. Norwegian elkhound. From Ivar's first litter."

The animal bounded into the wagon box. He hopped over the luggage and stuck his wet nose into Susannah's neck. His frame was more compact, with shorter legs and a wider chest than the wolf specimen mounted in her father's office. Unlike his wild counterpart, the dog's tail curled tightly over his back.

"Handsome boy." Susannah rubbed his soft fur.

"Sit, Jake."

The dog complied.

"You've trained him well."

"He's all I've had to talk to until you."

"Well, please don't stop talking to him on my account. I don't want him mad at me."

Jesse grinned. "Jake, let's give Susannah the grand tour. On your left is the spring." Sunlight reflected off a narrow band of water edged by saplings. "On your right, the barn, then our mansion."

A stovepipe and black barrel marked the roof of the sod house. A plank door was set deep in walls over two feet thick, centered between a pair of six-pane windows. A sod stable with a woven willow enclosure abutted the east side. To the west a sapling vibrated in the wind, red knobs decorating its branches.

"You have an apple tree."

"You didn't know Johnny Appleseed made it this far west?" Jesse leaped down. "Brought it out on the wagon with me. Thought it'd died by the time I got here, but it's growing good now."

Susannah gathered her skirts.

"Wait." He held up a palm. "We may not live in a castle, but I'll treat my bride like a queen." He put an arm under her legs and another around her back. Before she could figure out what to do, he lifted her off the seat and carried her inside. "Welcome home."

Afraid he might kiss her again, Susannah twisted out of his arms. With a glance she took in his house: one room, dark. Fried pork and wood smoke odors mingled with the overriding damp-earth smell. His letter said he'd built it from sod bricks, but she hadn't expected it to resemble a cave. She averted her face, trying to hide her shock.

"I'll unload the wagon."

She followed him out. "If you'll tell me where those plum trees are, I'll pick more."

"Try the thicket along the crick." He stepped close and whispered, "The outhouse is behind the apple tree."

Chapter 3

*Lord, I know You don't make mistakes, but maybe
Matt made one. Well, we're married, so I'm asking
for a heavy dose of wisdom. Don't hold back.*

J esse unhitched Pa Ox and sent him into the stable with his
supper of grain. Then he ran to the south field for Ma Ox,
who'd gained weight this summer and wasn't inclined to move.

"C'mon, slowpoke." He clapped his hands behind the beast.
"Got my new bride to take care of."

A new bride. Who brought to mind—well, she bore no re-
semblance to the laundress, wife of the big galoot with a big name,
from down Binghamton way. Van Valkenburg. That's it. Probably
weighed more than two of Susannah. So why think of her?

Antietam.

Corporal Van Valkenburg hadn't come back when the shooting
stopped, so the missus set out hunting him. When she didn't return,
the other laundresses raised a fuss and sent Jesse to find her. She'd
left a trail, rolling over each casualty, folding hands on chests, even
those who'd been blown to bits. Even the Rebs. Even the wounded.
Sometime in the night, she'd found her husband and managed to
get him laid out. But instead of stopping, instead of coming back to

camp, she'd kept on, working her way through the cornfield, down Bloody Lane, along the fences. Jesse caught up to her by one of the bridges. The hem of her dress dragged with blood and her hands were covered with offal. When he called her name, she kept going. Finally, unable to stand the smell, he'd grabbed her elbow. She'd flinched and screamed, more afraid of him than the dead.

Jesse could understand Mrs. Van Valkenburg being afraid. But why would her look, eyes wide and staring through him, show in Susannah's face? Susannah hadn't been to war. No battles had been fought in Michigan. Nothing happened on the train, she'd said. So then where'd she get her case of cannon fever?

While Jesse's mind wandered, Ma Ox had stopped to chew a clump of big bluestem. "Get along now," Jesse said to the cow and to himself. The last place he should let his mind go was the War. Lord Almighty. Anywhere but the War.

Back at the stable he settled Ma in, then unloaded the wagon. The cabin was empty. Where'd his scared little rabbit bride run off to?

He lit the lantern and checked his reflection in the window. He was overdue for a barbering but otherwise presentable. And ready for supper. When he pulled a chunk of meat from the brine barrel, the smell brought Jake in. "Hey, she seems to like you all right," he said to the dog. "Go find Susannah!" Jake licked his chops, then loped out.

Why was she so skittish? Was it the soddy? It was built solid, plumb and true. He had tidied up the best he could.

Maybe she was used to fancy. But no, she'd had the shakes from the very beginning, back at the siding.

A twig snapped in the clearing as Jake led Susannah back. The set of her shoulders, the way she held her elbows close, her measured steps, was like she was heading for the hangman.

"Lord," he whispered, "I don't know what's wrong, but I sure hope You'll show me how to fix it."

She stepped inside just enough to set the pail on the table. "Is the dog allowed . . ."

"It's your house now." Jesse kept his voice quiet. "You make the rules as you see fit."

Jake went into begging mode, complete with wagging tail.

Susannah fell for it. "It's all right. You can stay."

He plopped next to the bed, watching for dropped food.

"Shouldn't I be doing the cooking?"

Jesse wiped his palms on the seat of his pants. He was sweating up a storm, not a real attractive quality in a bridegroom.

"Do you know how?" He twisted the dish towel. "I mean, you probably had a cook."

"She quit at the beginning of the War. I can prepare meals."

"Well, supper's about ready. You can start tomorrow. Here's the fixin's: baking powder, cinnamon, cocoa, salt, and—" His brain gave out. "Sally Ann, the other salty stuff."

"Sodium bicarbonate? Saleratus?"

"Yep, that's it." He tried to focus. "Next shelf: coffee grinder, mixing bowl, colander, cook pot. There's salt pork in the barrel, molasses in the firkin, cornmeal in the sack, and that bag hanging from the ceiling is a side of bacon. Root cellar in the back corner. Guess it's not as fancy as you're used to."

"It's fine." She nodded at the shelves. "We never kept much food in the house."

"What was your pa's rank?"

"Sergeant Major."

"Seventy-five dollars a month."

"No, it wasn't—" She stopped suddenly and bit her lip as if she'd said something inappropriate.

"Seventy-five. I was paymaster for a time. From the shock on your face, I'd guess not much of that made it home."

"It was just Mother and me. We didn't need much."

"You're not used to fancy living. Reckon that's a good thing for being out here." He served the side pork and biscuits. "We'll use your trunk as a chair for now."

Susannah perched on the edge and looked around. "You don't have room for more furniture." She stopped and gave him a nervous look. "Sorry."

Well, she was right. Jesse had never really noticed how small the place was; now he bumped her legs when he settled on the stool.

He reached across the table and she shrank back. *Patience,* he told himself. "In my family, we hold hands when we ask blessing."

Susannah hesitated and then at last extended a hand in his direction. He caught hold of her cold fingers. "Thank You, Lord, for answering my prayer for a wife, for bringing Susannah home safe, and for this food. Amen."

She pulled away and stared down at her plate, avoiding his eyes.

Now what? When he'd thought about taking a wife, he imagined they'd have enough to say to each other that they wouldn't run out of words until 1875 or so. Instead, here she was, silent as a stone, and he had to carry the conversation. "Got to get back to the wheat in the morning."

She picked at her food. "What do you want me to do?"

"Whatever you'd be doing back in the States."

"Laundry."

She must have gotten a whiff of the mess under the bed. "Diving right in to heavy work. I haven't had time to wash in ages. It'll probably take a couple days. I'll fill the tub in the morning."

That gave him an idea. He straightened and grinned. "I know what you'd like after all that train riding—a bath!"

She choked. "Heating the water's so much trouble—"

"Not at all. You saw that black barrel on the roof? The sun does the work. It's great!" He brought in the washtub, set it under the pipe running down the back wall, and pulled the bung. Water gurgled into the tub. "I built this out of stuff the railroad threw away. Hop in and enjoy!"

She stared at her half-eaten food and didn't move.

Jesse could have kicked himself. Did he expect Susannah to drop her drawers right here and now? He was an idiot. "I'll go check the oxen," he said. "Yell when you're done."

The door slammed behind him.

Susannah stared at the tub. Actually, she'd love a bath but wasn't about to bathe in front of him. No one had seen her undressed since she learned to wash herself at the age of four. She glanced at the dusty windows but saw only the reflection of the lantern's flame. She'd have to make curtains as soon as possible.

She dimmed the wick, dropped her clothes, and folded herself into the tub with a sigh. The unscented soap lifted away the sticky layer of perspiration and coal dust, and the warm water helped take the knots out of her sore, tense muscles. For a while she drifted, and her memory brought up an image of Ellen Mason's boy, racing around the kitchen table, dripping wet and giggling. His equally naked little brother toddled after him. Ellen chased the little ones and ordered the girls out of the bathtub.

This girl needed to get out of the tub too. Before *he* returned.

She stood and squeezed the water from her hair. Since she'd started wearing it up half a lifetime ago, no man had seen it loose. Not that it was much to see—dirt brown, with enough wave to keep it from being silky, but not enough curl to hold a style without a dozen hairpins. She slipped on her muslin nightdress, tied the ribbons at her neck, wrapped a shawl around her shoulders.

At the door, she hesitated. She had written "Dear Mr. Mason" on her two letters, but that greeting sounded even more stilted aloud.

Using his first name seemed presumptuous. Finally she announced, "I'm done." He bounded in from the direction of the stable.

"You smell sweet as an apple blossom."

She wove her fingers through the fringe of the shawl. "I feel cleaner. Thank you."

"Water's still warm. I'll take one too."

"I'll wait outside."

"No. Your wet hair will call all the mosquitoes in the territory." He shut the door, closing off her escape. "Susannah, I'm your husband," he said in a low voice. The lamp flame cast deep shadows on the planes of his face. He unbuttoned his shirt.

Susannah sank onto the stool with her back to him and brushed her hair. Two splashes. He must be in the tub. She needed to think about something, something besides the fact that a man was bathing in the same room. Her head bobbed, heavy and dull, unable to catch thoughts hovering at the edge of the light.

"Let me help you."

Susannah jerked upright and stared at this stranger who was her husband. She must have dozed. He was done with his bath and stood over her wearing only a nightshirt.

What did he want? To consummate the marriage, of course. It was to be expected. She had hoped fatigue would dull her senses for the procedure, but his touch affected her in the opposite direction.

"You were asleep! Susannah, you're all played out." He took the brush and worked at the tangles. "What a week you've had, leaving your old stompin' ground, riding the train a thousand miles, getting married, new home. It's enough to—"

He stopped and raised the wick in the lamp. "What's this?"

"Nothing." She covered her neck with her shaking hands.

"Looks like someone tried to strangle you." He pried her fingers away. His face darkened. "What happened? Who did this?"

Her heart gave a feeble flop, and a chill frosted her all the way to her bones. She should have explained, should have told him when she first got off the train.

Through her fingers, she watched him take two steps to the door, turn, and pace back, clenching his fists and exhaling with each step, a bull in a stall. At last he sat on the trunk, scowling out the window. Susannah remained frozen in place. A sign from the Wells Fargo shipping office hung in her mind: "Damaged Goods Returned upon Receipt." He had every right to put her out right now, in the dark of night. After several minutes, he gave a deep sigh and crossed the room. With an unsteady breath, he went down on one knee beside her.

"Tell me."

Air caught in her chest. She choked out, "He said he was from the bank. He said Father owed money, a dreadful amount. Unless I—" She couldn't say it. She couldn't think it, even. "He grabbed the yoke of my apron. I fainted. Ellen struck him with the fireplace poker and he ran away."

"My sister-in-law was your guardian angel? Did he . . . hurt you . . . anywhere else?"

"No." She was crying in earnest now. Where was her handkerchief? "It's my fault. I didn't lock the door when I brought in the mail."

"Only one person's to blame. And you're not him." He wiped her tears away with a work-calloused thumb.

"I'm so sorry. All I've brought you is a ruined reputation."

"Reputation? Who's out here to gossip? I found a fresh start here and you will too."

"He threatened me. The Reverend said it wasn't safe to stay in Detroit."

"So that's why you came out here so suddenly." He squeezed her hand again and gave her a crooked grin. "I thought it was all those fancy letters I wrote."

"I'm sorry."

"Stop apologizing. I'm glad I know. Explains why you're so skittish." He exhaled heavily. "Susannah, you're my wife. God put you in my care. I would never hurt you. And I'm not going to rush you into something you don't want. You let me know when you're ready."

Was he offering a reprieve or looking for a way to send her back? She pulled in a breath. "Best just get it over with."

"Susannah, Susannah." His words came out soft and slow. "It's not a tooth-pulling."

"There's only one bed."

"I'll build you a fence." He made a barrier with a quilt, then steered her to the bed. "Get some sleep now," he whispered. "I've got to . . . check the oxen."

Dirt walls. Dakota Territory. Her . . . husband, Jesse, snored inches away on the other side of the rolled quilt. He hadn't woken her, and neither had the nightmares. Maybe the doctor had been right, the change of scenery would do her good. This marriage, on the other hand . . .

Sunrise showed a house about the size of her parents' parlor, dug into the hillside and finished with sod bricks. Loosely woven branches webbed with the roots of prairie grass formed the ceiling. She bit her lip. Best not to look up there. It was probably home to several dozen species of insects and spiders.

Susannah had never shared a bedroom, much less a bed, with anyone. What was proper: to arise and start breakfast or wait for him to wake up? Mother always dressed before leaving her room. The way Susannah's luck ran, he would rouse while she was changing. If she slid forward—

The rhythmic breathing ended with a snort and the mattress shifted, setting off an odd vibration in her midriff.

"Good morning, Mrs. Mason." Propped up on one elbow, he peered over her shoulder. "You have a line of freckles running just below your eyelashes and across your nose."

She pulled the corner of the sheet up to her shoulders. "I should have worn a sunbonnet yesterday."

"Susannah."

Here it comes. She braced.

"Guess I acted like a big galoot last night. I'd been praying for your safety on the trip, never thinking anyone would assault you in your own home. Scum, attacking a helpless woman. I should have gone back east to get you, if I could have sprung for train fare." His fingers curled into a powerful fist.

"There's nothing you can do; best to put it out of your mind." She clung to the bed frame to keep from sliding closer.

"No, I don't suppose there's anything I can do about him." He opened his hand and laid it on her hip. "The question is, what can I do about you?" He gave her a little shake, breaking her stiffness.

"I don't know." Was he considering sending her back and wanted her to broach the subject?

He flung off the quilts and clambered over the footboard. His arms spanned the width of the bed when he stretched. This was the first time she had seen him in daylight without a hat. Dark copper waves rambled back from his broad forehead and straggled around his ears.

"You have red hair," she blurted out. The words came out blunt and harsh, in her mother's critical tone. "Uh, I mean—red hair is fine. It's handsome."

"Hope our children look like you." With a grin, he slid his feet into moccasins and headed out. "Be right back."

"You're going outside in your nightshirt?"

"Don't tell anybody." He winked.

Susannah raced into her navy calico. As she fastened her boots, the moccasins reappeared in the doorway. And stayed.

"Forgive me for staring, but you—you're like a bur oak in a field of big bluestem. A much welcome sight."

She fumbled with her shoelaces. "I'll pick more plums for breakfast."

He chuckled. "How will you go to the outhouse when the plums are gone?"

"Then it will be time to pick apples." Her face burning, she made her escape into the quiet morning.

The temperature rose while she picked. Without the softening of rising dew, each blade of grass stood in sharp relief on the horizon.

"He'll be expecting breakfast. I'd better get moving." She forced her feet back to the soddy but found it empty. Ah. The washtub had been dumped. Coffee simmered over the stoked fire. She sliced salt pork and potatoes into the cast iron skillet, then set the table. The dog bounded in, sniffing for scraps. He positioned himself by the bed; his coffee-bean eyes tracked her every move.

"So now you're going to stare at me, just like your master." Susannah scratched behind his ears and stroked his spine. A cloud of fur covered her hand. Examining him, she discovered countless tufts falling out of his coat.

"Mmm, breakfast!" Jesse said from the doorway. Susannah stepped back, pressing her hands together. "What've you got? Jake's hair? Every spring he loses enough to make a second dog. Birds love it, makes good nesting material."

"Yet he's otherwise healthy."

"Yep. Ivar's hounds are walking fur factories too."

Susannah squeezed together the tufts she had collected. When she opened her hand, the hair puffed back into a ball shape. "Do your neighbors use this? For quilts or sweaters?"

"You can ask next time we see them." He reached around her and she scuttled to the door, letting the fur blow away.

He said "we." Apparently he had no immediate plans to ship her back. Although if he had to serve himself breakfast like he was doing now, he might reconsider. Susannah hurried to pour his coffee. "When might that be, when we see the neighbors?"

"After the harvest is finished. We'll go to the store with them. If you think of any supplies we need—"

What didn't he need? She'd better start small, in case his lack of necessities was due to a shortage of money. "Perhaps jars for canning? I'd like to put up some plums. No, that won't work; they'll be gone by then."

"I've got canning jars in the root cellar. Brought them out on the wagon but didn't know how to use them. Plum preserves! Can't wait! Anything else?"

"Many recipes call for eggs."

"Yep. Bought wood for a chicken coop this spring. Know much about birds?"

Susannah nodded. "I've raised Rhode Island Reds."

"What a team we'll make!" He stood and reached for her. She stepped back, bumping the shelves. For a moment or two he held his arms out, then finally let them slap down against his legs.

"Guess I'd better get moving." He washed down the last of his breakfast with coffee, watching her over the rim of his cup.

"What are your instructions regarding dinner?"

"Laundry'll keep you hopping, so fix something easy, something you can tote. Jake'll know where I am."

"What time?" She scanned the room. "There's no clock."

"I'm ready when you are."

Susannah winced. Would she ever be ready for him?

Chapter 4

Is this going to be a lesson in forbearance,
God? I asked for wisdom, not patience!

J ake, stay. Watch over Susannah for me." Jesse's voice carried from
the yard, and then he was gone. The dog's toenails clicked on the
threshold.

Susannah dropped her breakfast into his bowl. "You finish
this. I can't eat a bite. Feels like I swallowed a sparrow."

Jake inhaled the meal and then rested his head in Susannah's
lap. She stroked his velvet ears. "So how did Reverend Mason make
your master agree to this arrangement? I'm not wealthy, not pretty,
and not trained for any work. So there you have it, the sorry tale of
my life. What do you think?"

Jake seemed to grin as he panted.

"I suppose I'd best earn my keep." Susannah got up, put two
more logs on the fire, and set water to boil. The stove was a basic
four-lid model, without the water reservoir and warming oven considered essential in Detroit's kitchens. Water had to be hauled from
the spring instead of a pump.

This city girl would manage.

She sorted the laundry. A sleeve from his undershirt, tacked with a running stitch, covered a rip in his sheet. The hem of his pillowcase had come undone. From under the bed Susannah pulled shirts with torn shoulder seams and threadbare elbows, canvas pants with frayed knees, socks with missing heels. He'd worn his best yesterday.

"I feel like a burglar, rooting through this man's possessions." Susannah shook out a wad of yarn, finding a moth-eaten sweater. "Except he has nothing worth stealing."

Jake plopped his head to the floor and looked up with sorrowful eyes.

"Present company not included." She stroked his head.

As she lifted the pile, she jostled the crate next to the bed and knocked off a couple of books. She let the laundry drop. Books were too precious to leave on the floor. What did he read? The Bible, of course.

"Here's the real problem," she confided to the dog. "God doesn't consider me worthy of His attention, so I stopped praying." She returned the book to its place. "I asked God to heal my mother and He didn't. I asked Him to spare my father and He didn't. And I asked for a husband—"

Now she had one. Had God remembered her after all this time? Not likely. She was here and married, but there was no guarantee she'd stay that way for long.

The second book was a ledger. Neatly penciled entries showed every penny spent for the past three years.

Flour $6/100 pounds
Dried apples $25/barrel

Prices seemed high, but then, so were the quantities.

Lamp chimney 30c
Black thread 10c
Guitar string 15c

Guitar? She looked around. There it was, propped in the southwest corner, protected by a canvas bag. Maybe he wasn't such an ascetic after all.

While the whites soaked, Susannah looked for a shovel. She found it on the manure pile, its handle cracked. The wood was dark gray-brown, smooth from use, but the splinters were clean, fresh. He'd broken it last night, after he'd learned about her. If only she could mend it for him and mend herself into the wife he needed.

Using the pitchfork, she broke the dirt in front of the soddy and planted the limp shoots from her mother's garden.

"Now, I know you've had a rough week," she told the seedlings as she patted the dirt around the roots. "I have too. And this is the wrong time of year to transplant you, and you probably won't like your new soil, but I want you to grow anyway."

She brought a bucket of springwater and gave them a drink. "See that apple tree? It rode for weeks on a wagon. You can survive four days on a train."

Susannah sat back on her heels. "Here less than a day, and I'm babbling to a dog and some half-dead plants. How did Jesse survive two years alone?"

The nervous flutter in her stomach returned as she prepared dinner. Jake led her past the spring, where she refilled the jug, then up the slope. At the crest of the hill, hot wind surged out of the clear sky, erasing yesterday's wagon tracks.

On a speck of cultivated land in the wilderness, Jesse cradled golden-brown wheat to the rhythm of "The Man on the Flying Trapeze." Jake raced to him. The man waved his bandanna.

Susannah faced the wind and felt it pull at her hair as if she were riding. She had always loved being on horseback. When the gardener enlisted for the Union cause, she had eagerly taken on the exercise of her father's patients. Even at a walk or slow trot, she reveled in equine power. More than anything, she wanted a horse of her own. The Underhills, in a rare showing of parental unity, explained that their daughter had no need for such frivolity. But the wanting didn't stop.

Now here she stood on open grassland all the way to the horizon. A rider could go on forever—

"Susannah, what are you thinking?"

She flinched and her stomach churned. No use mentioning her spendthrift wish. "N-nothing."

"Your face was all soft and pretty." He raised a skeptical eyebrow. Finally he marched to a cleared spot on the edge of the field. "Mrs. Mason, your table."

"Thank you." She laid out the food.

"Got company up here today."

"Where?" Susannah scanned the horizon.

He pointed northwest. "See that smudge? Ivar. All the dust he's raising, guess he's hired a cutting machine this year. He'll probably finish a week ahead of me."

"Why didn't you do that?" Susannah examined a strip of beef jerky, looking for a ladylike way to eat it.

"If this harvest pays off, maybe I will next year. Got to get chickens this year." He took three giant swallows from the jug. "And how was your morning?"

"Fine, thank you. Except I couldn't find your clothesline, or bluing, or washboard . . . or flatiron."

He shook his head. "Remember, I've been baching it."

"I'm sorry. I don't mean to complain." She choked down a bite of cornmeal biscuit. In the list of matters never to be discussed, money held first place. Yet if she had known something of her father's finances, she might have been able to fend off the banker's attack.

The big question loomed over her: could this man afford a wife? She glanced up, making eye contact for only a second. It was enough.

"Guess you're wondering if you landed in the poorhouse. No, I'm not having money problems—" He grinned. "Unless you count lack of money a problem." He gazed at the horizon. "Susannah, when this farm gets going, I'm going to build you a two-story house with bay windows, a swing on the porch, a fancy six-lid stove in the kitchen, a piano in the parlor so you can teach our children to play."

Another strike against her. "I don't know how to play the piano," she said. "I'm sorry."

"Then we'll hire a piano teacher." Her eyebrows must have shot up, because he added, "He can sleep in the bunkhouse with the hands. There'll be a big barn out back, a smokehouse so we can have meat besides sowbelly and salt horse. Cows, sheep, chickens, horses, a buggy, and a sleigh. There's a banker in St. Paul who'd loan me the money in an eye blink, but I won't borrow. Too many times I've seen some farmer go in over his head. One bad crop later, he's thrown out, nowhere to go, nothing to start over with."

Jesse chewed on his beef jerky and took a bite of biscuit.

"Back in '57, the neighbors just south of us lost everything. Here it is, fifteen, sixteen years later, and I can still see the faces of those boys as the bank sold their beds, the milk cow, their schoolbooks. Pa gave them a ride into Buffalo so they could look for work. Just the clothes on their backs." He shook his head. "Guess God has all those verses in the Bible about the perils of debt for a reason. My brother ever preach on the subject?"

"Yes." Susannah picked crumbs off her skirt.

"What happened with your pa? He get in pretty deep?"

Susannah cut her gaze away. "Last week was the first I'd heard of any difficulty. He paid his bills on time. A few people in the area were behind on their veterinary accounts, but he never seemed too concerned. Mother ran our house by Mrs. Child's book."

"My ma swore by *The Frugal Housewife* too. See, we do have something in common." His smile held a hint of challenge. He quoted, "'The best economy is to do without.' Mrs. Child would sure be impressed with this little farm."

"It's fine."

"Matt said your pa was busy. Must have been good at doctoring animals."

"He was busy because he was one of the few college-educated veterinary surgeons in the state. Perhaps he was better with animals than money." She polished a plum with the corner of her apron, then took a deep breath and delivered the rest of her bad news. "I hope Reverend Mason can raise enough from the sale of the house to clear the debt. I didn't bring a dowry—"

"You brought yourself. Don't need anything more." He put his hand over hers. "I'm taking care of you now."

It was a lovely thought. All those years caring for Mother, Susannah wished for someone to care for her. But this man hung on by a frayed thread. She nodded to show she'd heard him.

He stood and stretched. "Best get back to the wheat so I can come home early."

"I suppose that's as clean as a dirt house can be." Susannah set the broom in the corner and dabbed perspiration from her forehead. Late afternoon sun painted indigo shadows across the packed-earth floor. Jake stretched beside the bed, his ears twitching to her words. "Dirt house. Mother would have said I married down but at least I'm married."

Susannah sliced a carrot into the stew. "As for Father, he never concerned himself with the house or its appointments. He never voiced an opinion about the conduct of others, including me and my lack of a social life. Except"—she added a turnip—"when I was twelve, I won the school award for orthography. All he said was, 'You're missing a button on your sleeve.'" A lump rose up in her throat. "Foolish of me to hang on to that hurt, isn't it?"

Jake seemed interested, in the food, if not in the story.

"Ah, but if Father had not died, I would be in Detroit, drying herbs for medicines, accompanying him on calls, serving as his second pair of hands. I knew the names of his instruments and could thread needles faster than any heavy-handed farmer. I would have helped him every day if Mother hadn't intervened."

Next, a few leaves of parsley. "Do dogs think about their parents? I failed both of mine. Father wanted a son. Mother wanted a daughter who would marry well." Susannah frowned at her own brooding. "Enough. They're gone and buried. Moping won't help. Besides, if I was in Detroit, I wouldn't have met a good dog like you."

Jake raised a hopeful eyebrow at the stew. Susannah gave it a good stirring. Celery or peas would make it better, but she didn't have either.

Jake lifted his head, listened, then dashed out. Moments later a shadow filled the doorway. Susannah startled and dropped the ladle. *Jesse.*

"Hey!" Two steps brought him to the bed made with a new quilt and white sheets. "I thought you didn't have a dowry."

Susannah wiped the dipper with a dish towel. "Ellen packed some linens I sewed."

Damp, clean hands lifted the edge of a pillowcase. "Look at all this fancy stitching. Must have taken years—" He ducked his head. "Sorry. Guess I put my foot right in it."

"It's all right. I know I'm an old maid. I turned thirty last spring." She filled the bowls.

"Well, you're not an old maid any longer. Look here, a little *S* stitched on this pillowcase!"

"A girl is supposed to embroider her future husband's initials next to hers while she's engaged." Susannah sat on the stool and sliced a loaf of sourdough. "Supper is ready."

His voice deepened. "This isn't the engagement you were planning when you did all that fancy stitching."

"Thank you for taking me in."

"Thanks for coming." He took her hands and said grace. His thumbs rubbed her wrists. "So soft."

She pulled away, skin tingling. "Your food is getting cold."

"Laundry and a hot meal. You're a hard worker." He tried the soup. "You've added some different flavors."

"I'm sorry. I should have asked first."

"Best I've had in years. What is it?"

"It's parsley from Mother's garden."

"Ah, what you planted by the door."

"With peppermint, rosemary, sage. I told them to grow like the apple tree."

"Good."

"Good?" For the first time that evening she met his gaze. "You don't think it's odd, talking to plants?"

He shook his head. "No. All these years I've been talking to God, my crops, Jake. And you."

"How could you talk to me?"

"I figured if God provided a wife for Adam in the Garden of Eden, He'd surely provide for me. I'd talk to you, tell you to hurry home. Don't girls dream about a handsome prince on a white horse?"

"If you've been dreaming about a princess, I'm afraid I've disappointed you."

He cupped a hand at his mouth, announcing in heraldic fashion, "Presenting Susannah, Princess of Plums on the Plains." He winked, then leaned forward, serious again. "Tell me what happened with the banker."

Susannah chased a chunk of potato around her bowl and tried to keep her voice steady. "Nothing. Ellen stopped him."

"Did the two of you talk about it?"

"There was nothing to talk about. Nothing happened."

"And 'nothing' makes you jump every time I get near you." He tipped his bowl, mopping up with a biscuit. "You know he can't find you here. I'll keep you safe."

"It's not a problem."

"Well then, what is? I've promised never to hurt you. I've promised not to go in debt. I'll build you a decent house soon as I can pay cash. I'll get a haircut the minute there's a barber within a hundred miles."

His thumb slid under the cuff of her sleeve. "Say, you're not pining away for some poor soldier who didn't make it back from the War, are you? My older brother's sweetheart moped around for two years. They weren't even engaged. Or maybe there's someone else you'd rather marry, maybe someone who didn't ask in time."

"There's no one."

"So what is the problem? Are you homesick? Miss your folks? Just tell me what's got you so fidgety, and I'll fix it."

"It's nothing."

He dropped her hand, almost pushing her away. "I'm going to check on the oxen." Lighting the lantern, he flung open the door. The dog rushed in, wolfed down her leavings, then plopped next to the bed. He panted, contented and relaxed.

"Jake, you're going to get fat off my nervous stomach." Susannah's voice wobbled as she scoured the kettle with sand.

"Why does this soddy feel like plenty of room when it's just you and me, but when there's one more person, it's filled to over-crowding? I don't know where to stand, how to move, what to say. You seem pretty happy here; you probably don't have any idea what I'm talking about." Her hands paused in midair over the dishpan. "Maybe I should have put his sheets back on the bed. What if he thinks—"

"Susannah—" The door banged open. Jesse paused on the threshold to catch his breath. "Don't suppose your pa said much about cows."

Chapter 5

Yes, Lord, she's got a secret. And it's a good one!

S usannah's father had, in fact, said quite a lot about cows, all of which her mother forbade her to repeat in polite society. But the look on Jesse's face told her this was no time to think about propriety. "What seems to be the problem?"

"C'mon. Quick." With a tip of his head, he rushed back into the night. Susannah caught up with him at the stable door. She inhaled the strong bovine odor, a welcome change from the emptiness of Dakota's air. Jesse hooked the lantern on a low-hung rafter. "Two years I've had this pair, and now . . ."

The bull gave them a glance, then turned his attention back to chewing his cud. The cow lay on the straw, abdominal muscles rippling with strain, trumpeting her distress.

"I can't afford to lose her. If you know anything, tell me. Please."

"Your Ma Ox is about to drop a calf. They must be Milking Devonshires. There's hot water on the stove. We'll need soap and rags."

"I'll get it." He returned in a moment. "Thank God you're here! What else?"

Susannah had watched her father and assisted him often enough to know what needed to be done. She remembered how Father would calm the anxious farmer by asking questions. "You've never seen a cow drop a calf before?"

"We raised pigs. They pop out." He made the noise with his mouth.

Susannah rolled her sleeves up and lathered her arms. "What did your family do for milk?"

"My uncle had a large dairy across the road. Used to be one big farm until Grandpa Mason divided it between his sons." The cow moaned again and he mopped his brow. "Is she dying?"

"I'll do what I can, but she may not be receptive to my help. There's no way to tie her up. You still have your boots on? If you could, please sit on her shoulders. Slow and easy. Put your heels on her horns. Steady, now."

The cow protested with a long high-pitched moo. Holding the tail with her left hand, Susannah knelt behind the animal and reached into the birth canal. Wet. Good. The bag of waters hadn't been broken long; the cow should have enough energy left to do her job, once the calf was in position.

Jesse glanced over his shoulder, his face pale. "What are you doing?"

"Checking the position of the calf—or I should say calves. Congratulations. You've got twins."

"Two?"

"Yes. She's struggling because both are trying to come out at once. I'll untangle them and give one a head start."

The pressure increased. Susannah pulled back. Too late. Her wrist caught between the first calf's head and the cow's pelvis. Her bones ground together and she bit down on a scream.

Jesse turned. "Susannah?"

"Stay-right—where—you-are." Susannah's words came out in gasps. "Contraction. Over soon."

"No sense you getting hurt. Get out of there. I'll buy another cow."

"I can't. I'm stuck."

"How much longer?"

"Don't know." She exhaled. "Easing up. There. It's over." She pulled her arm out, gritting her teeth as circulation prickled back into her fingers. "We need to switch places."

"You're hurt?" He stood.

"No, my reach isn't long enough, which is one of the reasons they don't let women into veterinary school. Wash up." She moved her hand above the cow's rump, demonstrating the necessary motions. "You'll go in, push the head down, unfold two legs forward. You'll feel a third leg on your right. It belongs to the twin. Push that back. It takes a fair amount of force, more than you might expect. Any questions?"

Soap glistened on his long well-muscled arms. "What if she has another contraction?"

"Work fast." Susannah straddled the neck. "Ready."

"Lord, help us."

"Straight in," Susannah said. "What do you feel?"

"Nose. An ear. She's fighting me."

"That's normal. Put your palm between the ears and push. Easy there, Ma. Reach down the neck and find the knees."

His grunt turned into a yell, then he hushed himself.

"Contraction?"

"Not exactly." The unmistakable smell of fresh manure filled the stable.

"You probably compressed the intestine. Did you unfold the legs? Be sure the other is out of the way."

"Yes. Got it."

"Switch places with me again." She glanced at him as he stepped past. "Father always carried an extra set of clothes."

42

He shrugged out of his shirt. "You might have warned me."

"Sorry." Susannah checked the calves. "Leg, leg, head. Good."

"I have some rope if you think we should pull them."

"No. She'll deliver on her own." She washed. "Why don't you get some sleep? I'll stay and keep an eye on her."

He nodded and shuffled out. She dimmed the lantern and settled into the straw to wait.

The cow groaned, waking Susannah. Sometime in the night Jesse had returned, covered them both with a blanket, then fallen asleep next to her.

Susannah slid away from his warmth and resumed her position behind the cow. Two pointed hooves peeked out, then slipped back. When they made a second appearance, she grabbed and held on. "C'mon, Mama. You can do this," she whispered. A nose came next, then the whole head. Susannah wiped the steaming membranes from its face. Another spasm and the body squeezed out. The calf's head bobbed on its slender neck, ears flapping.

"Perfect." She rubbed him with a handful of straw, admiring the swirl of hair between his eyes, the curve of his ears, the triangle of his head. "So strong. And here comes your twin."

Susannah cleaned the second. When Ma Ox took over, she sat back on her heels. "Absolutely beautiful."

"I couldn't agree more."

She jumped. Jesse was awake and watching her, his hair tousled and lit with red from the sunbeam coming through the door. She looked down. Her bare arms and apron were covered with mucus and blood. She'd discarded all decorum, showing off and ordering her husband about. He would surely send her back. "Please forgive me." She washed off in the bucket.

He pulled her into the warm circle of the blanket. "What for? I write away for a wife and get a veterinary surgeon. Best bargain ever." He pulled a piece of straw from her hair. "Here I thought you were too little, too city-girl, to be a farmer's wife. Never been so happy to be proved wrong."

He aimed for a kiss, but she tucked into his shoulder. "I didn't do anything. You got them into position."

"If you hadn't been here telling me what to do, I'd have lost them all." The calves made it to their feet. "Twins. What a deal!"

"You have one of each. The female might be a freemartin, sterile. They should stay in here today, at least until the afterbirth—" She paused and ducked her head. "Mother would wash my mouth out with soap."

"Us farmers pay good money to hear someone spout big veterinary words." He cradled the back of her neck, his thumb rubbing her tense muscles. "I'm so glad to hear you talk, you can say anything to me."

"But it's not ladylike."

"Susannah, you'll be a lady whatever you say. Starting with, 'Fix me breakfast, farm boy!'"

Susannah could hardly believe Jesse would allow, even appreciate, her veterinary skills. The thought lightened her steps as she carried dinner to the field.

Jesse opened the dinner basket and inhaled appreciatively. "Calves and fresh bread, all in the same day." He grinned. "Can you pull a chicken out of your hat?"

Was he joking? Criticizing? His face raced through expressions faster than she could read them, and he stared at her until she couldn't help but squirm. Finally he blinked and straightened. "You've never been teased before."

"No." She changed the subject, tipping her head toward the wheat. "You've done a lot since yesterday."

"Should have this cut by tonight. I'll start on the south field tomorrow. It's larger. Takes two weeks to cut. And I've got to check the garden, see what the rabbits left us."

"I could help with that. Where is it?"

"Other side of the spring. Thought I'd be taking care of you, but you're taking care of me." He reached toward her.

She put a plum in his hand. "How many acres have you cultivated?"

Fatigue lined his face. "Too many to harvest by hand but not enough to hire a cutting machine. It's a big help having you bring dinner." He finished the water and stood. "I'll be back early this evening."

"You should have slept in the bed last night."

He tipped her straw hat and planted a kiss on her forehead. "Married men don't sleep alone." Then he sauntered across the field, whistling "Buffalo Gals."

Chapter 6

My very own veterinary surgeon! What a blessing!

Five-year-old Susannah Underhill nestled into the cook's cushiony lap. The woman murmured soft words, removed the bee's stinger, dried her tears. An unfamiliar feeling of security warmed the little girl and supplanted the pain in her finger.

Mother's steps tapped into the kitchen. "Mrs. Schiller! My instructions regarding the child were clear: no mollycoddling."

"But, ma'am—"

"Mother, I was stung by a bee." Susannah displayed her wound.

"Ladies do not interrupt. Go to your room."

Susannah left the comfort of Cook's arms and dragged herself upstairs, but the warm heaviness around her waist remained.

The contradiction dissipated her dream. She opened her eyes. Jesse's arm stretched across her; his hand rested on the mattress in front of her face. His index finger and thumb alternately twitched, tendons flickering under work-hardened skin. In her exhaustion last night, she had forgotten to reassemble the blanket fence. Susannah lay close enough to absorb his warmth, to hear his deep breathing.

Was she safe here? Maybe. If he just wouldn't expect so much. But his questions unnerved her like an oral examination at school: the topic was a surprise, the timing abrupt, and a passing grade uncertain. Even in the midst of his long-winded monologues, he wanted more than clichés and platitudes from her. If only he'd stop prying and be more easygoing like his minister brother.

Did Reverend Mason have any idea how Jesse lived? He knew about the lack of a church; he'd performed the proxy wedding. But of course, that wasn't enough for Jesse. He insisted on repeating the vows—with only an ox for a witness.

The thought of the ox brought Susannah's attention around to Ma Ox and her newborn calves. When they were bucket trained, milk and butter would be added to the menu.

A deep voice whispered, "Good morning," in her ear.

She inched away. "Sleep well?"

"Like a log. Don't remember you coming to bed."

"Those calves tired me too. Speaking of which, I'd better go check on them." She slid from his grasp.

The noise from the back of his throat sounded like the ox's moan. "I'll go out so you can get dressed."

The calves moved steadier on their legs today. Susannah helped Jesse guide them to the field. On the walk back, he reached for Susannah's hand. She crossed her arms. His fingers wormed under her elbow. She loosened, moving his hand away.

"So what's on your calendar this fine morning, Mrs. Mason?"

"I should make preserves before the plums overripen."

"All right. I'll bring more water. Save some jam for me."

When Jesse returned at sundown, Susannah was still canning. Three kettles boiled on the stove. Fruit, jars, and the sugar tin sat on the table. Every utensil was in use. She fought a losing battle with flies lured by the sweet smell.

"I'm so sorry," she said. "I didn't realize canning would take so long. I've never made preserves by myself." She tensed. Would he beat her? Yell? Send her back?

Much to her amazement, he did none of those things.

"I'll help. Tell me what to do."

As Susannah poured the fruit mixture into the jars, Jesse sealed them with the three part lids. When he closed the last one, she apologized again. "I'm sorry about supper."

"Plenty of times I've worked too late to fix a hot meal. In fact, let's picnic." He packed a basket and tucked the buffalo hide under his arm. "Mrs. Mason, bring the canteen, please."

Jake circled around her as she followed Jesse out and up the hill into fading light. "What's wrong with your master?" Susannah whispered to the dog. "He doesn't get angry, doesn't lecture, doesn't shout. I'll do better tomorrow. If he gives me another chance."

A mourning dove called its five-note song, accompanied by a cricket chorus. The high winds of the afternoon had calmed to a soft breeze, enough to keep the mosquitoes at bay.

At the top of the hill, Jesse rolled out the hide and spread his arms. "The heavens declare the glory of God!"

All across the horizon, a magnificent sunset lit the sky with orange and purple and pink. Above them, the stars began to come out one by one.

Susannah watched as the panorama unfolded above her. "So many stars! The North Star, Milky Way, Big Dipper. Look—a falling star! Did you see it?"

"Nope. Missed it. Where?"

"To the north. There's another!"

"Two in less than a minute. Just for you!"

"Could they be part of the Perseid meteor shower? No, it's over by mid-August. Next year—" The words slipped out before Susannah could call them back. She glanced at Jesse, but he seemed not to notice.

"Supper and a show. Wonderful!" He passed her a cracker sandwich. "Hmm, good jam." His finger squeaked against the bowl. "You'd better have a taste."

His silhouette blocked the starlight. She turned her head and a sticky kiss landed below her ear. She tried to relax, but her arms wouldn't move from their defensive position on his shirtfront. His next kiss grazed her cheek.

"Jesse."

"You remembered my name."

"This is not—"

"I know." He whispered, "It's your time of the month."

Was nothing private? Susannah twisted away, grateful the darkness hid her blush. "Men aren't supposed to know . . ."

"Didn't Matt tell you we have four sisters?" The canteen gurgled. "Anyway, you need more courting time."

She gulped in a breath. "Thank you."

"You get a better view lying down." He rolled onto his back, pulled her beside him, and settled her head on his shoulder.

"I've been thinking—" His voice came out muffled. "About marching through the woods in Virginia, near the Shenandoah. Rumor said Jeb Stuart hid there, that behind every rock itched a Reb wanting to take us out. Turns my guts to ice thinking of it. We'd try to be quiet, but someone'd swat a fly, step on a twig, cough. Those Rebs watched us sneak through their woods. I'd have given a month's rations to know where they were." His words came clearer. He must have turned toward her. "I know what it's like to be afraid. Susannah, we're on the same side, you and me."

She tried to respond, but the words wouldn't come.

"If someone hurt you, if you tell me, then I won't do the wrong thing, and we'll be easier with each other."

"I'm fine."

"I thought it might not be so difficult to talk out here in the dark." He paused for three long breaths. "Guess not."

Susannah had been shy her whole life. Perhaps she wasn't cut out to be a wife. She had often thought she would have been better off alone. By herself, perhaps, she could open her Pandora's box of thoughts, sort through them, make peace with them. In front of this stranger who pried at her with a crowbar? Impossible.

"Guess not," he said again, his words so slow and heavy they hung in Susannah's ears instead of blowing away.

Susannah jerked awake and sat up. "We fell asleep outside."

"Good morning," Jesse said. He stretched toward the rosy glimmer in the east. "What's wrong? Weren't you warm enough?"

"What will people think?"

"What people? Jake had a good time. Didn't you, boy?"

The dog's curly tail wagged in agreement.

The sky turned the color of peach skin. "What a sunrise," Susannah murmured. "And last night's stars—"

"God's beautiful creation." He wrapped an arm around her and kissed the top of her head. "Like you."

With her hair matted and dress wrinkled? Did he need spectacles? "If you'll let go, I'll fix you a hot breakfast to make up for last night's supper."

"Breakfast isn't what I'm hungry for, Miss Susannah." His eyelids lowered. He drew a line down her neck.

Oh, this man! Susannah grabbed the food basket and marched

down the hill. Jesse followed, serenading the dawn with a jaunty rendition of "Little Old Sod Shanty."

When they reached the front door, Susannah bent to examine three purplish-white flowers planted among her herbs. "Asters?"

"They grow wild hereabouts. Fellow's supposed to bring flowers when he's courting." He tipped his head, a question in his eyes.

"Thank you."

Jesse finished his morning chores all too quickly and came back to roost on the trunk while Susannah finished cooking breakfast. The cornbread would be a minute yet. She served bacon onto plates and put them on the table along with salt, pepper, forks, knives. The smell of cornbread filled the room. She jerked open the oven door. One corner had burned to charcoal.

Susannah's shoulders drooped. He might as well know: he'd married a half-wit.

Jesse said grace, then served himself the scorched corner without commenting. "Could use your help with the wheat today."

"If I bound the sheaves, you could keep cutting."

"Exactly. We'll get caught up on this harvest."

"You lost a whole day fetching me."

"Can't count it a lost day, when I gain a wife."

"I'll pack dinner."

"You could borrow a pair of my pants."

Susannah had never worn hand-me-downs or borrowed clothes. Wearing men's pants, *this* man's pants, seemed indecent. "No, thank you."

He shrugged. "Some women take to wearing them out here. Seems like it'd be easier, but it's up to you."

"I'd best stay in my skirt."

"Then at least take off your corset."

Susannah felt herself flush. How could he talk about undergarments at the table? "I'll meet you at the field."

Jesse sang with the rhythm of the swinging cradle, but Susannah had no extra energy for harmonizing. Every muscle in her city-girl body howled with pain. The constant wind blessed and cursed: drying her perspiration, keeping the flies from lighting, blowing dust in her eyes.

A cloud, she wished. Just a little shade. Memory summoned trees: tall elms lining the streets, the backyard apple fragrant with good fruit, the cool pines fringing Michigan's lakes. The only trees she'd seen in Dakota were back in Fargo, along the Red River. Perhaps the harsh wind or lack of rain kept the rest of the territory a barren grassland.

The sun simmered low on the horizon when Jesse called a halt. "Three acres! Beats my usual two a day." He tugged the work gloves off her limp hands, flinching at her blisters. "I won't always work you like this. If those grasshoppers hadn't wiped me out, I'd have hired help." Long fingers kneaded her shoulders. "A bath'll feel good tonight."

"I didn't think people on the frontier bathed this often."

"Don't know about the rest of the neighborhood, but I try to get a bath every Saturday night, for church tomorrow."

"Church? I thought you said—"

"There's no preacher or building. Just Ivar and me. We sing, pray, share a few verses. Nothing fancy."

"Sounds like a first-century church."

"That's the idea. Congregation's growing. Marta last year, baby Sara this spring, and now you."

Marta. All week loneliness had dragged at Susannah, making her wish for Ellen. She missed their easy confidences, her friend's blunt good sense and droll worldview. Exchanging correspondence would take months. Besides that, her letter would be passed around; much of what she'd like to write would have to go unsaid. Surely Marta had been lonely too, and would welcome her friendship.

Just the thought made Susannah's heart a little lighter.

Chapter 7

All-wise God, please . . . why won't she talk to me?

A re you in love with Matt?"

Susannah choked on her coffee. "Pardon me?"

Jesse leaned across the table. "You asked if I'd thought of going into the ministry. Maybe you're in love with Matt, hoped I'd be just like him. It's not unheard of for a woman to fall in love with her pastor."

Her appetite vanished under his scrutiny. "He's married."

"What if he hadn't been?"

"Ellen is a much better pastor's wife than I would ever be."

"Why do you say that?"

Susannah picked at a fried potato slice. "She's a 'blessed peacemaker.' At the first sign of discord she jumps right in, not resting until it's resolved."

"Where are you when the doctrines fly?"

"Hiding under the pews."

Jesse chuckled. "Guess we're different there. My family likes nothing better than a good old brawl. Ma would even change sides to keep it going, though she drew the line at defending slavery."

"I was under the impression your family got along well."

"We did. No suffering in silence for us. We enjoy the debate too much." He thumbed his whisker stubble. "So, what'd you see in my brother that made you think I'd be a good husband?"

Susannah served him a wedge of plum pie. "Why do you ask?"

"I'm trying to puzzle you out. Figure out why you married me." He raised his hands, palms toward her. "Yes, Matt and Ellen threw you on the train because you weren't safe alone, and they didn't have room for you, and you didn't have any money. But you wrote me before all that, before your pa died. Why?"

Why? Because Ellen told her to. No one refuses Ellen.

Susannah remembered the exact afternoon, eight days after her mother's funeral. The thrumming of a spring rain framed the uncharacteristic quiet of the parsonage. The boys napped and the girls were still at school. Bread in the oven filled the house with a welcoming yeasty smell. Ellen served tea at the kitchen table, and she had that look on her face, the expression that told Susannah she wanted something. As it turned out, she wasn't recruiting a Sunday school teacher or a women's circle leader, merely someone to write to the Reverend's brother, alone on the frontier.

Susannah agreed. After all, writing came easier to her than talking. Even when Ellen got around to the subject of marriage, Susannah wasn't too worried. She couldn't leave Father. And surely Mr. Mason would write to several women and choose someone else.

Ellen's eyes brightened with a zealot's flame. Didn't Susannah realize? This was their chance to become sisters. With a hug, Ellen welcomed her to the family.

Now Susannah rolled up the corner of the oilcloth, studying the neat hemming her mother had stitched. With his blunt question, Jesse had nipped at the heels of the truth. In marrying the minister's brother, she hoped in some way to become more like Ellen: confident, outspoken, at ease with people.

But how could she explain that? "Reverend Mason is a good

man. He's gentle with his children, well respected in the community, doesn't indulge in tobacco or alcohol."

"Guess he didn't tell you about my drinking habit."

"You have nothing stronger than coffee here."

Jesse rubbed his temples. "When I first came home from the War . . . well, let's just say I don't remember '66 at all. Except maybe waking up in an alley in Buffalo, hands frozen to a whiskey bottle."

Ah, that explained the deep lines carved in his face, the sadness tugging the corners of his eyes. What horrors he must have seen to resort to drink in a family of teetotaling Methodists. Susannah reached across the table. "Plenty of men despaired of the War. You're to be commended for conquering it."

"I had help—strong hands lifted in prayer and reaching down to me." He caught her wrist, his thumb overlapping the last joint of his middle finger. "Aren't you going to have some pie?"

"I'm not hungry."

"You're too jumpy to eat. What were we talking about? Oh yes, how you wrote to me because my brother doesn't drink. I'll just hold this hand of yours until you tell me the rest."

She pulled. His grip held. "What do you want me to say?"

"What's in your head, in your heart." His other hand worked a fork through the pie. "Hmm. You're a better cook than my ma."

"Cooking for such a large family must have been a challenge." She waved a fly away from the open pan. Jesse flicked it out of the air with a one-handed snap of his napkin.

"Susannah—"

"All right." She worked a thread loose from her apron. "It's not so much what I thought of the Reverend, but my admiration for the way he and Ellen work together. They support each other."

His grip loosened into a caress. "I'd like our marriage to be like that."

Susannah stood to clear the table.

"Did Ellen ever take on your folks?"

Her plate dropped back to the oilcloth. "Pardon me?"

"You said she dove into conflicts."

"Whatever gave you the idea my parents had conflicts?"

"So I'm wrong. Tell me about Mr. and Mrs. Underhill."

Father's college education earned him no financial reward or respect in a country where any farmer could call himself a veterinary surgeon. Yet he refused to return. Mother pined away for her beloved England. Susannah had never wanted to involve herself in the conflict; she feared their bitterness might infect her. If she understood her parents' feelings, she might feel the need to take sides, so she stayed out of the line of fire. She took care not to draw their attention, not to give them a focus for their anger.

"They never raised their voices," she said. Not often, anyway.

"Did they talk?"

She scoured the cook pot. "Of course."

"More than 'How's the weather, what's for dinner, and guess whose horse went lame today?'" Jesse slid his plate into the dishwater. "Did your pa hug your ma? Did she run to kiss him when he came home? Why are you an only child?"

She wiped the plate. "That's hardly—"

"Hear me out. I've been chewing on this. Seems like people tend to follow the roads they know, without thinking where they want to go." He reached around her for the coffeepot and refilled their cups. "Guess your folks' marriage was quite a bit different from Matt and Ellen's."

Susannah scrubbed harder.

"Looking at other marriages, I see a lot of unhappy people. Guys in my regiment signed up to get away from their wives, if you can imagine. I don't want us to be like that." Grasping her arms, he turned her toward him. "I want this marriage to work for both of us. I want you to be glad to see me when I walk in the door."

He slid his hands up to her shoulders, rubbing in circular motions. "See how wound up you are, how you pick at your food. Susannah, you don't want to live like this forever."

She bit her lip and focused on the empty pie pan. What choice did she have?

He sighed. "Guess I need to back off, give you more time. Will you think about what road we should take?"

She nodded.

"I'll bring in the tub. Want me to scrub your back?"

Her midriff quivered. "No, thank you."

One finger moved to the top hook of her bodice. "Or help you undress?"

She backed away. "I believe I hear your oxen calling you."

Jesse sighed. "Some other time."

This broad-shouldered man was her husband. She had to get used to the idea. Closing her eyes, she gave a quick nod.

"I'll take that as a promise, one I won't forget." He sauntered to the door. "Holler when you're done."

Although the warm water soothed her aching muscles, Susannah bathed quickly, not trusting the man to wait.

"Jesse!" she called out the door, then sat with her back to the washtub. While he took his turn, she mended his shirt. She heard the rustling of clothes, the splashing as he entered the water, then turned her thoughts to church tomorrow. They would sing and read Scripture, Jesse said. She hoped to talk privately with Marta.

"Don't suppose you'd scrub my back?"

Susannah started toward the tub, then caught herself. "You'll sing tomorrow? I forgot, the Reverend sent a hymnbook." She rummaged through the trunk by the table.

"A hymnbook? Tune up the piano!" Jesse splashed out.

"Must be in the other one." Using her hair to shield her vision, Susannah sidestepped to the other. "Yes, here it is."

Jesse reached around her, his nightshirt flapping. "*Protestant Episcopal Hymnal.* Guess the Methodist songbook isn't out yet."

"Reverend Mason said it could be another year or two."

"Well, let's sing! Teach me a new one."

While he tuned his guitar, Susannah set aside the hymnal and pulled a copy of a magazine from the trunk. "Here's Fanny Crosby's latest, 'Blessed Assurance.'" She passed the magazine to Jesse. "Page 36."

"Palmer's *Guide to Holiness and Revival Miscellany*?" he asked. "That's a mouthful."

"Ellen gave it to me," Susannah said. "It was just published in July." She stood behind him as he propped it on the table with the cracker tin and two potatoes. His fingers picked out the melody, adding chords as she sang. Heat rose off him in a steam. They'd used the same soap, yet he smelled so *different.*

Midway through the first verse, he stopped. "You're breathing through your shoulders, like the other day on the wagon. Come here." He did not raise his voice, but it was a command just the same. He set the guitar down. "Sing the last line again, without moving your shoulders." He shook his head when she inhaled. "Corsets. They make you huff and puff even when you're not wearing one." He spread his palm across her lower rib cage. "Breathe so you move my hand."

How could she, with all that fluttering going on inside?

"Better. You'll have air to sing a whole line on a breath."

Her heart raced and her legs had all the stability of a newborn calf's. Surely he could feel it. She could barely breathe, let alone sing.

Jesse raised a speculative eyebrow in her direction. "Let's try again." He picked up the guitar and resumed playing. On the next verse, a yawn interrupted Susannah's singing.

"I've worn you out with this fieldwork." His face softened with an apologetic smile. "Lie down. I'll join you soon."

Susannah nodded, then, just for a second, touched his elbow. She dropped off to sleep during his next song.

Morning found Susannah face-to-face with a snoring man. *Husband*, she corrected, as if the word might offer some comfort. Why did this man affect her so? Jesse had an aura of command, perhaps from his time in the army. He took charge, issued orders, while his brother let life unfold around him. He had an edge to him, a wildness absent in the civilized Reverend. Where the minister saw good, this man seemed too aware of the dark side of people, including herself. His critical eyes could pierce any armor. She had the feeling he could see beyond her mask of respectability to her worst self, the self she couldn't face, and it terrified her.

Susannah had once called on Ellen and happened upon the Reverend Mason. He had fallen asleep stretched out on the braided rug in the parlor, the baby napping on his chest. His expression had relaxed and, except for the full mustache, he looked like a larger version of the little boy.

Here in Dakota, the sleeper on the other side of the bed was no little boy. He had a rugged face, with a nose that ran straight down from his wide forehead; deep eye sockets, high cheekbones, jutting chin. Even a big smile. Smile? How long had he been awake?

"What's good for the gander . . ." His early morning voice rumbled. "I've been studying you enough, you're welcome to take a peek at me."

"I'm sorry." She attempted to roll away, but her muscles cramped in protest.

"You're hurting. Lie on your stomach and I'll rub your back." He tried to look innocent, businesslike. The attempt was only partially successful.

She eased upright. "I'll be fine once I get moving."

"You should have soaked in the tub longer." Jesse clamped a warm hand on her shoulder, kneading the base of her neck, loosening each knot of pain. It felt entirely too good. "Where are you going? I'm not done yet."

Susannah slipped off the bed. "Thank you. I feel much better, but I must—"

"The outhouse. Have to figure that out before winter hits."

"Pardon me?"

"When it's bad, I use a bucket. Not comfortable for you."

"I'm used to cold weather."

"Not this cold. When the wind kicks up you won't be able to find the outhouse. It's all I can do to get to the stable and back. We'll buy a chamber pot when we're in town."

"Where—?" Susannah glanced around the soddy.

Jesse sat up and rubbed his chin. "Good question. We could tie a clothesline between the rafters, hang a sheet over it."

Susannah hurried out. How would she manage, cooped up with this man for months on end? How did anyone survive out here? And how would she get even a tiny portion of the privacy she craved?

Marta. She would ask Marta.

Only another woman would know how to endure winter with a husband. Only another woman would be able to answer her questions.

"Ahh, just what these sourdoughs have been crying for." Jesse spooned plum jam onto a biscuit. "Until I tasted this, I used to think apple butter was—" He frowned. "Susannah!"

"What's wrong?" She smoothed the bombazine dress. Had she spilled on her skirt, missed a button on her basque?

Jesse shoved the spoon into the jam, tipping the jar. "Black? You're wearing black?"

"This has been my Sunday dress since my mother's death."

"I hoped celebrating our marriage would outweigh mourning your folks."

The hurt in his voice pierced though her social conventions. "I'll change."

"Appreciate it." He touched a work-roughened finger to her cheek. The door closed with a soft click.

Susannah pulled on her dark red dress and buttoned it. When would she learn how to please him?

Chapter 8

Susannah is a new song in my heart.
Teach me to sing her.

D o you know anything about this church?" Susannah asked
Jake as she packed dinner into the basket. "They're not going
to ask for a testimony, are they?"

The dog tipped his head to one side, then the other. He was a
wonderful listener, but he didn't have many answers.

Jesse stuck his head through the doorway. "Ready, Susannah?"
He nodded his approval and came to her to touch the lace decorating her neckline. "Oh yes. Very nice. Prettier than ever in red."

Morning sun heated their shoulders as they crossed the wheat
field and plunged into the prairie. Big bluestem grass shimmered
silver overhead. Insects scattered before them. Hindered by her
petticoats, Susannah stopped to shift the basket and pull her skirts
close. When she looked up, she was alone.

"Jesse?"

He couldn't be far ahead. She took a step forward. Wait a minute. Which way was forward? She ought to see a path, a line of
bent stalks, but the grass grew equally dense in every direction.
Susannah stood on tiptoes but saw only seed heads vibrating above

her. She was lost. No, not quite lost. She could return to the wheat field. Except . . .

She couldn't tell which way they'd come.

Her mouth went dry. They'd been heading west. The sun shone almost directly above her. No help there. Wind whipped the stems, slapping her face. She turned, but the grass beat her from a different direction. Flowered spikelets pressed close, shutting off the air. What was that rustling noise?

The sound moved closer. A snake? Her heart raced. Or a fox or a badger? With a gasp, she pulled her skirts higher. She whirled right. No escape. It could be a wolf, inches away, watching, waiting for an opportunity to pounce. Or an Indian.

"Jesse?" Her voice quavered.

He emerged on her left. "Yes?"

Her knees buckled and she almost threw herself into his arms. She swallowed hard. "I was wondering . . . what sort of animals live in this grass."

He shifted the guitar to his other shoulder, then brushed a bead of perspiration from her temple. "The big-eared sort. They heard us and are miles away by now." He took the food basket from her, then hiked on, whistling "The Campbells Are Coming."

With hands free, Susannah managed to keep Jesse in sight. Thank God he'd come back for her. Could she thank God for Jesse?

The land ascended to the west, opening to a valley cut more than a hundred feet into the plain. Hills and draws rippled along the bluffs. A stream flowed south through a ravine filled with cotton-woods, elms, box elders, willows, and scrub oaks.

"The Sheyenne River." Jesse pointed.

"Trees," Susannah sighed. After six days of nothing but grass, the wooded slopes seemed like a paradise.

"This is where we get our firewood."

"Why don't you live here?"

"Our claim's got the best spring in the territory. Soil's not so good here." His boot scraped at a patch of gravel between clumps of grass. He glanced from her face back to the valley. "I suppose we could build our real house here."

Jesse headed for the nearest cottonwood where two people sat on a blanket. Susannah tucked a stray lock of hair under her hat and brushed seeds off her skirt. What if Marta didn't like her? What if she thought Susannah's worries were foolish?

"You're looking mighty fine." He tucked her hand onto his arm.

"Jesse!" A stocky man jumped up and sprinted toward them. "You old dog! You half a wife and not tell us!" His accent sounded German—no, Jesse said they were Norwegian. He hugged Jesse, pounding him on the back, then held him at arm's length. "Look at you! No beard. You shave now you half a wife?"

"Sure! Don't want to scratch when I kiss her. And by the way, this is no half-wife. You won't believe all she can do."

Ivar faced her. "He's always making fun of how I speak. All his fault; he taught me English." Susannah stepped back, but to her horror, he lifted her. "I don't know, Jesse. She may be half-wife if you don't start feeding her."

When her feet reached the ground, Susannah stumbled. Jesse steadied her with an arm around her shoulders. "Susannah, this is our neighbor, Ivar Vold. Ivar, my wife, Susannah Mason."

How odd to be introduced as a wife, with a new last name. Ivar pumped her hand. Strawlike hair stuck out from his hat and the lower half of his apple-cheeked face. She glanced at Jesse. His neck and jaw were a shade lighter than the rest of his face.

Ivar motioned toward the blanket. "This is Marta and our baby, Sara."

A woman with a thick braid of light brown hair sat cross-legged, nursing a baby. To Susannah's surprise, she showed no sign of embarrassment. Ellen had nursed her own infants, but Susannah had never seen her do so in mixed company.

Ivar addressed his wife in Norwegian, and Susannah's heart sank. Marta didn't know English. Susannah turned away and pretended to cough, struggling to compose her face.

Marta spoke.

"She says, will you help her learn English?"

Susannah blinked. "Oh. Yes, of course. I would be glad to."

Marta returned her smile.

"Good news!" Jesse tuned his guitar. "Susannah brought a copy of Fanny Crosby's brand-new hymn. We'll have a new song this morning."

"But I was just learning your old song." Ivar winked.

Jesse passed the magazine to Ivar, who sat by Marta and interpreted. Their voices joined together in "Blessed Assurance." In her good-sized Detroit congregation, no one noticed if Susannah sang or not. On the banks of the Sheyenne, she comprised the entire alto section.

"Marta says she is thinking of the book of Ruth," Ivar began, pausing for his wife's words. "Like Ruth, Susannah has traveled far to marry a man she did not know. Like Ruth, may you find great joy in your new family."

Blinking away tears, Susannah extended her hand to Marta.

"I am thinking of the first man, Adam." Ivar opened his Bible to the beginning. "He walked and talked with God, yet he was lonely. God saw this and made Eve. Susannah, your husband walks and talks with God, but he has been lonely. So God brought you here. Genesis says, 'A man shall leave his father and mother and cleave to his wife, and they shall be one flesh.'"

Susannah felt the heat rise to her face and looked down at her hands. She was a married woman; she shouldn't blush.

"I cannot say welcome to Paradise," Ivar continued. "I don't think it snowed much in the Garden of Eden. So I say welcome to Dakota. I hope you and Jesse will be as blessed as Marta and me." He smiled at the baby sleeping in his wife's lap.

There was an interminable pause. Susannah stared at her clenched hands, afraid to look up. Was she expected to say something? She'd never spoken in church. Throughout years of Sunday school, her sole contribution was reading a lesson. Itinerant evangelists, with their habit of calling on the congregation for testimonies, struck fear in her heart. She always hid in the pew behind the large Goodman family, each child an advertisement for their father's confectionery.

"Thank you." Jesse nodded at the Volds. "Susannah's folks recently passed on. She's left her home and friends to come out here. This song, from Psalm 30, is for you, Susannah.

"'Thou hast turned my mourning into dancing for me—'"

Sunlight flickered through the cottonwood leaves, the same sun that glistened through the stained glass windows at Lafayette Avenue Church. Susannah could almost hear Miss Ferguson embellishing the final chords of the postlude with glissandos. She could see Reverend Mason bent over Mrs. Griswold's hand, inquiring about the health of her cats. The congregation, their escape blocked, would mill helplessly around as Ellen homed in on a soloist for the next service, an assistant for the boys' Sunday school class, someone to sit with Susannah's mother.

No longer . . .

"'Oh Lord my God, I will give thanks unto Thee forever.'" Jesse finished the song and strummed the final chord.

"Your husband half a song for everything," Ivar said. "And a prayer."

They joined hands and Jesse began, "Dear God, thank You for friends, old and new." He squeezed Susannah's fingers. "Watch over us during this harvest season. Grant us fair weather and good health. Forgive our sins and help us grow. All these things we ask in Your name. Amen."

"Does he do as good a job as his brother?" Ivar asked.

"He doesn't take as long," Susannah blurted. Jesse grinned and seemed to take no offense.

After dinner, Marta settled her sleeping baby on a blanket and stood. With a graceful turn of her wrist, she beckoned Susannah to follow. Arm in arm they strolled the riverbank, collecting plums. Marta pointed out canes of wild raspberry bushes and vines of other fruits, next summer's harvest.

Marta didn't walk, she glided. She had wide cornflower blue eyes like her husband, but instead of his ruddy complexion, Marta's skin was smooth and white like the inside of an oyster shell. She wore an embroidered bodice and white blouse over a sapphire blue skirt. The Norwegian style seemed more feminine than the fitted basques and unwieldy bustles in fashion of late, and more comfortable too.

When they returned they found Ivar stretched out, snoring. Jesse carried on a deep conversation with the baby in his arms.

Marta smiled. "Is good man."

At the sound of her voice, he turned. "Sara really listens, like she knows what you're talking about."

Ivar rose on one elbow, rubbing his face. "You will half one of your own soon, then you'll see how much work it is."

"I'm looking forward to it." Jesse winked at Susannah and passed the baby back to Marta.

The Volds headed north, along the bluff. Susannah followed Jesse east.

"I need your help with the wheat this week," Jesse said as they swished through the grass. "Ivar says the crew'll be by Friday, to thresh what we've got cut. They take bags of wheat in payment. Save us a couple weeks' dusty work, give me time to build a chicken coop before we go to town. Ivar will help me pitch sheaves. Marta can give you a hand with cooking. She makes the best lefse—it's like a thin pancake made from potatoes. You can make sourdough and baked beans. Use up whatever's in the brine barrel. I'll go hunting Saturday; I'm hungry for fresh meat. How's the coffee holding out?"

Jesse turned and stopped. Susannah dipped her head and motioned for him to continue walking. Too late. He'd noticed her tears. He set down the lunch basket and guitar and opened his arms. Closing her eyes, she steeled herself for his touch. One hand rubbed her back, the other pushed her hat off and guided her head to his shoulder.

"Go ahead, cry it all out." He kissed the top of her head.

The wind wrapped her skirt around his legs. She gulped. "I'm sorry. I'm not usually like this."

"You're upset because Marta doesn't speak English."

This man. Could he read her thoughts?

He continued, "Ivar learned pretty quick. We got along fine. So will you and Marta."

She nodded. "Foolish of me to assume she'd already know."

"Guess you've missed Ellen." His warm fingers rubbed a knot in her neck. "Know what Dakota means? It's Sioux for 'friend.' All this week I've talked until my throat's sore, but you've hardly said a word. I'll be your friend, if you'll talk to me."

She shook her head. "I don't know what to say to you. I've never had a male friend before." Truth be told, making friends with women wasn't easy either.

"Well, start with what you were planning to say to Marta."

She tried to pull away, but he held on. She condensed her thoughts to the briefest answer possible, a statement she hoped would make him retreat. "Just woman things."

The mere suggestion of "woman things" would be sufficient to deter most men. Not Jesse. "Like what? With my pack of sisters, I got more than a passing acquaintance with woman things."

"It's nothing."

"You're all wound up, and I want to know why." He leaned down to look her in the eye, but it seemed safer to burrow into his shoulder. "Going to make me figure it out on my own, are you? I'm guessing it's marriage, what a husband and wife do in bed."

She flinched.

"Bull's-eye. Now, what were you going to ask Marta?"

Might as well tell him. He'd figure it out soon enough. "My mother . . . maybe she didn't think I'd ever get married. I don't know . . . what to do."

"I've never done this before either, if that's what you're asking. Sometimes parents explain spooning in funny ways, based on their own experiences. So maybe you're better off not talking with your ma about this." He rested his cheek on her forehead. "Judging by the number of people on this planet, I'd say plenty of men and women have figured it out just fine. We will too."

He didn't release her. "Susannah, one of the reasons I like living out here is getting away from the 'shoulds.' Back east, you should be wearing mourning clothes, I should be sitting in your parlor a couple nights a week. But reality is, the sun would bake you if you wore black, and there is no parlor. There's just us. So let's leave behind the 'shoulds' and enjoy what we've got."

"But I'm asking so much of you. Patience, self-control—"

He sighed. "With the threshers coming Friday, we'll be lucky if we do any sleeping, much less anything else in bed this week."

This week, Susannah thought. *But what about next?*

Chapter 9

Lord Jesus, were You ever too tired to pray?

Bang! Bang, bang!

Susannah sat up in bed, her heart pounding. The banker!

No, it was the door of the soddy in Dakota. She covered her mouth, stopping a scream.

Jesse's warm palm squeezed her shoulder. "It's the Volds."

From the other side of the door, a hoarse voice yelled, "You spend all day in bed now you half a wife?"

"It's still dark. How did they get here?" Susannah groaned. The week had flown by in a blur of cutting wheat, binding wheat, stacking wheat, without even time to change clothes. She tugged at her waist where stale perspiration had stuck her drawers to her skin, and her neckline where chaff formed a crust. "At least we don't have to worry about getting dressed."

Jesse grunted in agreement, lit the lamp, and opened the door.

"Threshers on their way," Ivar announced. He carried in an armload of firewood. "Coffee will get you moving." He sounded far too cheerful for this early in the morning, but then, he already had his crops harvested.

In the light of the lamp, Ivar caught sight of Susannah's

windburned face. "You half worked outside!" He stomped to the doorway and spit out a Norwegian word, drawing a hiss from Marta.

Susannah shrank into the corner. She hadn't minded the hard work. At home, she took care of her mother, managed the house and garden, and helped with her father's patients. Here, harvesting the wheat kept Jesse too tired to talk and Susannah too tired to worry about his staring.

"Just this one time." Jesse rooted under the bed for dry socks. "Next year I'll buy a reaper, hire a man."

Ivar snorted. "If you married Norwegian—"

"Too late. The only one she knows is already hitched." Jesse knocked off his neighbor's hat on his way out.

Susannah followed. Stars twinkled in the dawn air. A sliver of pink glimmered on the eastern horizon.

"Isn't it early for frost?" Their breath puffed white.

"We usually get a light freeze this time of year." Jesse handed down Marta and the sleeping infant.

Susannah settled Sara in the middle of the bed. "Oh, to be a baby and sleep all day."

At least threshing day meant variety in the menu. To free her time for fieldwork this week, Jesse had started a kettle of beans on Sunday. Every dinner since featured them: beans with corn cakes, beans with sourdough, beans with crackers. Fieldwork made her so hungry not even last night's dinner, bean mush, went to waste.

The four adults crowded into the soddy, bouncing off each other like croquet balls.

"*Ut!*" Marta pointed to the door. Jesse complied. Ivar continued to rifle the food baskets. Marta repeated her command, swatting him on the seat of his pants. Slinking out, he mumbled two words from the corner of his mouth. Countering with a remark of her own, Marta flicked her apron at him and sent him howling into the yard.

Susannah busied herself with unpacking and tried to conceal her shock. Marta had touched her husband—on his buttocks! How could she be so familiar, so relaxed, playful? Had she known Ivar a long time, perhaps growing up on neighboring farms, perhaps marrying him before she came to Dakota? Susannah could not imagine bantering like that with Jesse.

Marta handed Susannah a sack of potatoes. Donning her cleanest dirty apron, Susannah sat on the trunk to work while Marta unpacked and started a second pot of coffee. The Norwegian woman moved efficiently, never hurried, pausing only to hold up an object for Susannah to name. She was a quick student, but it would be a long time before meaningful conversation would be possible.

Jake's bark proclaimed the arrival of the threshing crew. Ivar assembled a table from the soddy door and a pair of sawhorses. Marta set it with muffins, sausage, a kettle of oatmeal, and the coffeepot. Susannah tended the stove while Marta served. The men devoured the meal, then hurried to their machine. Setting the dishes to soak, the women ate breakfast. When Susannah reached for the dishrag, Marta motioned for her to wait, then held up a mirror.

Susannah groaned. "No wonder you kept me inside." She covered her rat's nest with her hands. In Michigan, neighbors gossiped about women who neglected their appearance. Only ten days into her marriage, Susannah had joined the ranks of the slovenly. Why didn't Jesse say something? Father certainly would have.

Marta seated Susannah on the stool and brushed the tangles, hairpins, and wheat chaff from her hair. Then she wove a long braid and secured it with a thread. The simple plait running down Susannah's back fit this land better than her chignon. Even a dozen hairpins were no match for Dakota's wind. "Thank you," she told her new friend.

Susannah started dinner, then joined Marta in the doorway where she nursed the baby. The breeze carried the low cadence of the threshing machine.

Baby Sara cooed from her mother's lap. The infant had given Jesse a smile. Would she smile again?

Marta touched Susannah's waist. "Baby?"

"No." She shook her head, then took a deep breath. "Who helped you . . . when the baby came?"

Marta shrugged. Susannah asked again, with pantomime.

"Ivar help. Marta help Susannah."

"Did it hurt? Ow?"

Marta nodded. "Ow. Marta help Susannah."

Susannah knew a good deal about breeding stock and, as with Ma Ox's twin calves, had midwifed the delivery of animals. Her knowledge of human birth, however, was less complete, cobbled together from vague medical texts and whispered horror stories. Every girl in school knew about boys and babies, but the information was hidden behind a veil of giggles and hints. The sisters next door had been present at the arrival of their last sibling, and they claimed knowledge about how babies started.

No, Susannah decided, if it had not been for the language barrier, she would have set aside her manners and asked questions.

Marta reached an arm around her and murmured a quiet word. The Norwegian woman's peace highlighted her own nervousness. Could Susannah ever find such tranquility?

Jake's barking heralded the arrival of the men at midday. The women loaded the table with pork and beans, sliced sourdough, cookies, coffee, and the Norwegian potato flatbread called lefse, which was rolled out with a large grooved rolling pin and cooked on a griddle.

The crew sprawled on the grass to eat. They were a scraggly lot, dusted in wheat grit, a mix of ages, national origins, and attire.

One wore an entire Union cavalry uniform. Jesse caught her eye and winked. After ten days, his was the familiar face.

Jake wandered under the table, foraging for scraps. Susannah leaned over to scratch behind his ears.

"Know something, Jake?" she whispered. "He might not be so bad after all, that master of yours."

His curly tail wagged in agreement.

Late afternoon a shout came from the field, indicating the end of threshing.

Marta sliced the corned beef, and Susannah set out the rest of the meal. After supper, Jesse brought out his guitar.

"'Jeanie!'" the men shouted. "'Oh, Susanna!'"

Jesse honored a few requests, then launched into a railroad ballad with the crew joining in on the chorus. Despite the grueling harvest, Jesse reveled in the gathering. Between songs he told jokes and absurd stories, many about the War. To the delight of the men, Jesse stopped a song in the middle to try to find a note the crew chief could sing in tune. Calling each by name, he divided the men, lining out harmonies and counterpoints for the halves. Now he resembled his brother, Jesse the minister and the crew his congregation, exhorting, encouraging, directing.

Susannah drifted to the creek where a boy watered the team. The horses stood with straight backs, weight even on all four legs. At her approach, first their ears, then their heads turned, eyes bright and curious.

"Watch yerself, ma'am," he said. "Them are ornery cusses, not family pets."

Susannah stroked the withers of the buckskin, feeling his ribs and an adequate layer of fat. Dust and hair stuck to her hand; the horse needed a bath as much as she did. Chipped hooves and long toes showed they were overdue for a visit to a farrier. "Hardworking foursome you've got here."

"Boss gets his money out of the brutes, for certain."

Susannah brushed flies from a wound. "What happened here?"

"Them all have it, from turning power for the thresher."

Susannah threaded her way between the animals, finding identical lesions on each right shoulder. "I have some gall remedy." She hurried to the soddy. When she returned, the boy was gone. The driver blocked her way.

He planted his feet shoulder width apart and rocked back on his heels. "Don't mess with the horses." He scowled, his jaw lifted high and his eyes narrow.

In Detroit, her father's reputation had buffered her from this sort of resistance. But Father was dead. The name of Charles Edward Underhill, veterinary surgeon, carried no weight with this barbarian. Flies buzzed around the horses' wounds. Susannah held out the tin. "They have open sores—"

The driver stepped closer, menacing. "I said, don't mess with the horses."

The music stopped.

These days, keeping an eye on his wife was Jesse's favorite occupation. The threshing crew seemed a decent sort, but knowing how rarely they saw women and how easily Susannah spooked, Jesse had been extra vigilant. He noticed she had fixed her hair like Marta's, only Susannah's braid had escaping curls and ended in a twist.

After supper, he watched her inspect the horses, running her tiny hands down their thick legs, poking her fingers near their big choppers, at ease with the four-leggeds of this world. She hurried inside, only to be waylaid by the driver on her return.

Hang on. Reinforcements are on the way.

The driver stuffed his thumbs in his belt loops. "Don't need no woman telling me how to care for these nags."

Over her head, Jesse gave the driver his best gunslinger's glare. No one messed with his wife. "Mrs. Mason's pa doctored Custer's mounts during the War."

The threshing crew circled for the best theater they'd seen in months.

The crew chief took the tin from Susannah's hand. "What is this?"

"Gall salve," she said. "My father's remedy. It heals sores and wounds."

The driver continued to glare at Susannah. She raised her chin at him and glared right back. Jesse grinned. *Atta girl. Back off, you old goat.*

The chief pried off the lid and took a sniff. "I understand our boy general's mighty particular about his equine friends." He returned the tin to Susannah. "Don't see any harm in trying."

"I'd never harm an animal."

The driver stomped off. The chief escorted Susannah to the shoulder of the buckskin, who tolerated her ministrations without flinching. Then he followed her to the sorrel. "How often should the salve be used?"

"Morning and evening until healed." Susannah moved to the first chestnut. "If the straps could be padded with sheepskin or adjusted to rub in a different place, they would heal faster." She proceeded to the last. "Is there any way to change the power so the horses walk clockwise instead of counterclockwise?"

Jesse's chest swelled with pride. An excellent suggestion from his brilliant wife.

"Clockwise, eh? Then the pull would come from the left shoulder. Yeah, we can do that." The chief scratched the stubble on his jaw. "I'd better see if I can get some of that gall salve."

"Why don't you take this?" Susannah handed him the tin.

"Mrs. Mason, you've been most helpful." He shook her hand, then turned to the crew member in the cavalry uniform. "We'll be leaving one more bag of wheat here."

"That's really not necessary."

"I'm sure your father charged for his services, ma'am. You deserve no less." He pumped Jesse's hand. "Mr. Mason, you got yourself a fine woman here. Thank you for your music and hospitality, but we've got work waiting on us up the river."

He rounded up his men and set off, while Jesse launched into "Shoo Fly." Laughing, the crew joined him. All but the driver, who still looked like he was chewing nails.

The Volds, too, drove off into the red sunset. "See you Sunday!"

Susannah took a deep breath. "I'm sorry about interfering with the horses. I didn't mean to make a scene."

"Are you kidding? We got an extra bag of wheat out of the deal." Jesse pulled her close and planted a kiss on her temple. "And I'm so proud of you, I could burst."

Chapter 10

Brave enough to battle the driver but scared
of me. Lord, I just don't understand.

L et's go home," Jesse said to Jake. A whole day's hunt and only a
prairie chicken to show for it. He would have been better off,
surely less footsore, had he brought his fishing pole instead of his
gun. The valley was hunted out, like an army had tromped through.

Jesse knew something of foraging armies. Since they were both
fairly good shots, the lieutenant had sent him out with Sellers, a
fellow from Elmira way. But Sellers, an expert in marriage after
twenty-two months of wedded bliss, had been more interested in
bending Jesse's ear than securing venison for dinner. To hear him
tell it—and every deer in the county had—he'd caught his girl's
eye during the sermon, courted her as the congregation shuffled
out, and proposed before her family loaded the wagon for home.

So, Lord, how can I win Susannah's heart?

An army on the march or huddled around the campfires had
no interest in the next day's battle. The talk was all about wives,
sweethearts, and anyone else of the female persuasion. Jesse, being
unattached, had been served an ample ration of advice.

A bouquet of posies? Yep, planted in front of the soddy. A book

79

of poetry? Guess he could send off for one. Dancing? Might be able to find a couple musicians in the territory, but they'd all want to twirl his wife. As little time as Susannah had spent in his arms, he surely wasn't ready to see her in anyone else's.

As he crested the bluff, the soddy came into view. Susannah gathered laundry from the slope behind the draw.

Jake galloped to her. She paused to scratch his ears, then scanned the horizon. Ah, she'd been watching for him. She started toward him with a smile, like she might be thinking of hugging, then stopped and clasped her hands in front of her.

"Seems the threshers scared away the big game." He handed her the bird. "Prairie chicken. Not much meat."

"How odd." Susannah inspected it like the veterinary surgeon she was, examining the orange pouches on either side of its neck and the feathers shooting up from its head like horns. "Exotic markings."

"Apparently birds have as much trouble courting as men do." Jesse caught her braid. "I like coming home to you."

She wiggled away. "Is it all right for me to wear my hair in the Norwegian style?"

"Of course. Your hair is pretty every way. Especially loose on the pillow."

Susannah hung the chicken by its feet at the end of the roof. "It's our odor scaring the animals away."

Was that why she was keeping her distance? Jesse motioned toward the stack of clean clothes. "Everything's washed but us. I'll bring in the tub."

"It's early yet."

"Did my little brother ever mention the Hebrew people started their Sabbath at sundown the night before?" He rested a hand on her shoulder, rubbing the stiff muscles at the base of her neck. "I'm ready for a day of rest. How about you?"

She nodded, tired enough to let him touch her.

He worked both hands across her shoulders. "So, what do you think of your new life?"

"I keep wondering, what would you do without Ivar and Marta? How can they be repaid?"

"When Ivar arrived, I helped him build his soddy and put in his first crop. He gave me pick of the litter when Freya whelped. We've been swapping work ever since." He pulled the thread off her braid, loosening her hair. "I keep thinking, what would I do without you?"

"You've done just fine."

He slid his hands down her arms. "Two lonely years, no one to share good or bad times. I used to dread winter, not seeing another person for months. But I'm looking forward to it this year. It'll give me time to get to know you."

"Shall we bring in the oxen?"

"I already know how practical you are," he said. "I'll get the wash-tub, then the oxen, and you can start your bath." He closed the door, then opened it again and grinned at her. "Laundry on a Saturday? What will the neighbors think?"

And then Susannah surprised him. Taking a lesson from Marta, she snapped her apron at him. "Out."

"What are you working on?" Jesse finished his bath and climbed out of the tub.

"I thought I should write to Ellen." The cut glass inkwell sparkled in the lantern's light as she stirred the dark powder and water together. "But I can't think what to say."

"Thank her for sending you to this handsome husband who waits on you hand and foot and lives in a mansion with running water and a scenic view."

"She'd think I'd disembarked at the wrong station."

"I'm not handsome?" He leaned over her shoulder.

"You're dripping." She blotted the paper with her sleeve, then shot a glance up at him. Yes, he'd put on his nightshirt.

He rubbed his head with the towel. "We should work on the list for the store too. How are you set for winter clothes?"

"Ellen packed my cold weather gear." Susannah exchanged her pen for a pencil, stationery for scrap.

"We take winter seriously out here. Let's see what you have." Jesse opened her trunk.

Susannah squirmed as he rooted through her trunk. He seemed bent on destroying every last particle of her privacy.

"Add yarn for more socks, another pair of long johns, and a greatcoat. Your cape may be the latest fashion in Detroit, but a coat with sleeves will keep you warmer in the wind."

"I could remake it so it has sleeves."

"Great! That will save some money." Jesse unwrapped tissue paper, revealing a light gray garment. "Hey, what's this?"

Susannah gasped. "I didn't know Ellen had packed—"

"The dress you were supposed to get married in." He lifted it up. Heavy satin shimmered in the lamplight. "Let's see it on you."

"Now?"

"Yes, ma'am." Eyes twinkling, he handed her the gown and turned his back.

Susannah stepped out of her muslin nightgown and slid the dress over her head. It was a waste of trunk space, entirely too fancy for a farmer's wife. She would have told Ellen not to pack it, had it not been for the laudanum . . .

No, she must not think about Detroit, only about Jesse. He took her in when no one else would. He'd been so kind and patient. Her fingers fumbled with the buttons behind her, an unusual design. "It's supposed to be worn with a bustle and petticoats."

He turned and inhaled, eyes wide. "Susannah."

What was he staring at? She looked down. Without undergarments, the fabric accented every curve.

He took her hands. "We should have had a big church wedding to show you off, except I wouldn't want to share you. Mrs. Mason, may I have this dance?" Humming "The Blue Danube" waltz, he guided her around the small space between the table and the bed.

The room spun. "You dance quite well for a Methodist."

"Episcopalian ancestry. Might I say the same for you?" Jesse bowed over her hand.

"Church of England." She curtsied in return.

Starting another Strauss waltz, he lifted her left hand to his shoulder and put his right on her waist, touching bare skin. He pulled back, eyebrows raised. Susannah managed to give him a smile. His hand slid inside, slowly, tentatively, along her backbone, sending shivers down to her toes.

"I couldn't reach all the buttons."

"So soft." He pressed his mouth to her forehead, nose, lips. He smelled of saleratus from brushing his teeth. His tongue touched her neck, tasting her. She warmed, as if blushing all over. He unbuttoned the rest. Cool air brushed her shoulder blades. Her knees went weak and she clung to him.

"What are you thinking?" he whispered. His warm fingers drew lazy circles on either side of her spine.

"I wish—" She leaned into his shoulder, her heart thundering. She wouldn't insult him by speaking of her fear. "I wish we'd met a long time ago, so we'd be better acquainted."

"Everyone's afraid the first time, no matter how long they know each other." He shot over her prevarication, his accuracy flustering her more than his touch.

"You're afraid?" Hard to believe. Jesse radiated confidence. He was sure of his place in the world, his relationship with God, the future.

"Men talk," he told her in a matter-of-fact tone. "Especially in the army when they're without women for so long. Coarse, rough talk. Short on facts, long on brass." He pulled her tighter, resting his cheek on the crown of her head. "I'm beating around the bush. Yes, I'm afraid. I don't want to hurt you, do anything to make you more shy of me. I'm afraid of doing something wrong, making you think I'm no good."

"I wouldn't know the difference." No, that didn't sound right. "What did you tell me? Forget about the 'shoulds.'"

Jesse cupped her face, his fingers rubbing the back of her head. "Susannah," he said, his voice a gentle rumble. "Yes, I wish we'd met a long time ago too. I've been needing you." He danced her to the lamp and blew out the flame. Moonlight softened his profile. "Wish I weren't so mule-faced, so you'd look me in the eye and know it's me and not some other fellow."

"There is no other fellow."

He made a sound in the back of his throat, like coughing with his mouth closed. Step, step, turn. His breath warmed her cheek and tickled her ear. "Ready?"

She was not ready, perhaps never would be. But refusing him now would only postpone, not cancel, her part in this arrangement. Might as well get it over with.

Not trusting her voice, she nodded. Jesse swept the dress over her head and back into the trunk. He took in a sharp breath. "So beautiful . . ."

He picked her up and laid her on the bed. The new straw of the mattress gave off a fresh, sweet smell.

Concentrate on Jesse, she reminded herself. His nightshirt dropped to the floor, then his weight settled gently on her.

Chapter 44

Hallelujah!

That was it? That was the pain a wife must endure, a woman's lot to suffer? It was hardly worth worrying about. Especially since Jesse seemed to enjoy it. Maybe she could make him happy after all. Susannah lifted his arm from her waist, and her skin caught as if his body heat had adhered them together.

As she slipped into her nightgown for her morning trip to the outhouse, she caught a salty smell, a tang not her own. Jesse left his scent on her. She was a married woman in every sense of the word, no longer a virgin. She took inventory, trying to pinpoint the difference, finding only a vague sense of unwinding, like a pocket watch marking the passage of time.

Cold dawn air sent Susannah hurrying back to the soddy. She shivered by the stove, stirring a dried corncob into the coals.

"I'll warm you." Propped up on one elbow, Jesse turned back the covers.

Susannah closed the oven door. Beside the bed, she found Jesse's nightshirt. She set it beside him. His hand shot out and clasped her wrist.

"No need for shyness anymore."

The strategy she had adopted, focusing on the third button of his shirt, was ill suited for his present state of undress. She stared past him at the tufts of dry grass delineating the sod bricks. He rolled upright, bringing his face directly in front of hers. Susannah glanced down, then with a catch of her breath, back to his face.

"That's one way to get you to look me in the eye." His smile changed to an expression of concern. "Did I hurt you?"

"No." Her shivering increased.

Jesse maneuvered her into bed. Her body, in direct opposition to her mind, relished his warmth, settling into the curve of his body. "I'll make it easy on you; you won't have to look at my ugly mug." He drew the blanket to her chin, tucking it around her goose-bumped arms. "You're still afraid of me."

"No."

"Susannah, I don't mind if you disagree with me—in fact, there's times I wish you would—but we'll do better if we're honest with each other." His cheek rubbed the top of her head.

"Yes."

"Am I that different from Matt? He's pretty easy to be around." He massaged her icy toes with the sole of his foot.

"For you maybe; he's your brother."

He went up on his elbow again. "Matt was always the most outgoing, most sociable of all of us. Made friends like—" Jesse snapped his fingers. "Within a week of the first day of school, he had the teacher eating out of his hand. I took many a licking from schoolmasters who didn't believe little Matt could be any trouble. And secrets! He knew the whole town's business. Had the War gone on any longer, he could have been a spy because everybody confided in him." He tilted his head, trying to peer under her eyelashes. "Everybody except you."

"Yes." She found a new focus point, the cleft of his chin, stubbled with walnut-brown whiskers.

He collapsed onto his pillow. "You've seen a score of pastors come and go. Surely you felt comfortable with one of Matt's predecessors."

"Not really."

"Your gentleman callers?"

"No." There hadn't been any. Time had not erased the hurt of being passed over in the friendship and courting arena.

Jesse stroked her upper arm, making deep circles in her muscles with his fingertips. "What about Ellen? You and Ellen had some good talks. You felt comfortable around her."

Susannah shrugged. "I guess so."

He leaned his chin on her shoulder. "Are you scared of everybody, the whole world?"

"I haven't met everybody."

"All right. Forget everybody and try to make friends with just one person: me. I don't like having my wife shy of me, especially when I've given her no reason."

He was right. He hadn't given her a reason. He'd been gentle and patient. A better husband than she had hoped for. "I'm sorry."

He pulled her closer, dropping his voice to a whisper. "Especially after last night. Oh, woman. I can't even begin to say . . ." He stroked her hair. "Let's do it again, right now."

She caught his hands raising her gown. "In the daytime?"

"Yeah!" Jesse tugged at the ribbons, untying her neckline.

"But it's not—" She stilled his hand.

"Not proper? Who says? Remember, no 'shoulds' out here."

"Not even a 'should' about being on time for church?" Beneath her hand, his fingers flexed, working her buttons loose.

"They'll understand. I had to wait for them last year."

"What about the oxen?"

Jesse exhaled. "Oh, all right. We have all winter to play. One more kiss—"

He dropped his mouth onto hers. One arm wrapped around her shoulders and the other cradled her head. The quick peck lengthened into a full-blown, breath-stopping kiss. He prolonged the kiss and began to touch her in ways that would undoubtedly lead to a reprise of last night. She jabbed him in the ribs and wriggled out of bed.

"Hey, can I help it if I can't get enough of you?"

While Jesse dressed, Susannah concentrated on rolling out sourdough. As he left to picket the oxen, he turned and gave her a long look. "Someday, Susannah, you're going to trust me, you're going to want me to touch you. Hope I live long enough." The door closed with a firm thud.

Was he right? Could she want him?

Susannah hesitated at the top of the bluff.

"Even prettier than last week." Jesse winked.

Heat rose in her cheeks. "Will they know? Will they be able to tell what we've done?" She focused on the yellow leaves dotting the cottonwoods.

"They think we've been enjoying married life ever since you got off the train."

She glanced up. "Yes, but this week you are . . . *grinning.*"

"I never felt so good!" He reached for her, then froze as a wail pierced the morning. "Sara!" Jesse raced for the big tree. Susannah followed as fast as her cumbersome skirts would allow. How could such a loud noise come from such a little person?

Hollow-eyed, Ivar yawned at them. "All night, no sleep."

The baby gasped, then let loose with another long cry. Perspiration stuck her white hair to her beet-red scalp. Even Marta propped her head in her hands.

Handing his guitar to Susannah, Jesse picked up the baby. He kissed her forehead. "No temperature. When did she eat last?" he yelled over the extended howl.

Ivar collapsed onto the blanket, plopping his hat over his eyes. "Not long ago. She refuses more."

Jesse slid his hand under her dress. "Don't slap me for being forward, Sara. Just checking your diaper."

Ivar tossed his hat at Jesse, whacking him on the knee. "Of course she's dry. We half been parents long time. Veterans."

Ignoring the neighbor whose faced flushed as red as his daughter's, Jesse cooed to the infant, "Three months, Sara. You'll never get a job with the Northern Pacific if you stay ahead of schedule. The wine, please."

"Don't you get my baby girl drunk, Mason."

Marta poured a glass of wine and Jesse dipped his little finger in. He swabbed the white nub protruding from her lower gum. The infant blinked, then clamped down. Her crying ceased. Four adults sighed with relief.

"Teething," Jesse explained.

Ivar rolled upright and took his Bible in his hands. "You half a scripture for everything, my friend. What verse for this?"

Jesse cradled Sara on his knee. "Proverbs 31:6."

Ivar flipped the pages, then burst out with a snorting laugh. "'Give wine to those of heavy hearts.'"

When their laughter subsided, Jesse continued, "The real lesson is in the Gospels. People brought their babies to Jesus so He could touch them. Not just see Him, not just hear Him. Not have Him wave a magic wand over us. But touch. We are made to touch and be touched."

Susannah lowered her head to hide her reddening face. He was talking about her, to her.

Jesse looked down at Sara. Her fingers daintily uncurled as her sleep deepened. "There's still power in touch." Jesse nodded at Ivar. "One of the ways Jesus touches us is through His supper."

Ivar conducted the sacrament in Norwegian, handing flatbread and plum wine around their tiny circle. First-century communion must have been like this, Susannah thought, a common cup passed among people who knew each other. Definitely preferable to a church filled with strangers.

The discussion during lunch centered on the upcoming trip to town. Agreeing to meet at dawn Wednesday, they parted.

From the ridge top, Susannah watched Marta and Ivar disappear into the crimson-tinted grass. "How did you figure out she was teething? You knew just what to do."

"Second oldest of ten, an uncle many times over. I've picked up a few tricks."

"Such as pulling a sermon out of thin air?"

He grinned.

"I'm amazed," Susannah said. "Your brother spends his week locked away with a bookcase full of references."

"What's he do that for? He's got plenty of kids to write sermons on." Jesse adjusted his guitar strap and they headed for the homestead. "What'd you think of the message?"

"Good." She slowed, putting space between them.

"Right." He broke off a grass stem, popping the seeds off with his thumb. "I don't know if it's because of the banker or some other reason, but you don't like to be touched."

"I never said that."

"You didn't have to." He turned and reached for her.

Reflexively she stepped back, realizing her mistake a second too late. "I'm sorry."

"Next week's sermon is on apologizing too much." He grabbed her elbow, compelling her to walk with him. "Where do you like to be touched? Are your feet ticklish? Does it feel better if I touch you easy or a little more?"

"I don't know."

"Do you like your kisses wet or dry?"

She lifted her shoulders, more of a jerk than a shrug. How was she supposed to know, when his kisses comprised the full extent of her experience?

"Exploring unknown territory. Lewis and Clark, Stanley and Livingstone, Susannah and Jesse."

Yes, he had the intensity and vision of an explorer. If only he would choose a less personal subject, say British literature or steam engines. But he would not be diverted. He caught her peeking at him. Her words choked out like food gone down the wrong way. "Are you . . . will you tell me . . . what you like?"

"Nope, Sacajawea. Got to blaze our own trail."

The flutter in her chest returned. She crossed her arms over her middle so he wouldn't see it. "What if I do something wrong?"

"Was there a wrong route to the Pacific? No. Different routes, different scenery. First exploration starts now. Do you like to hold hands this way or the other?" He pried her arm away from her body and joined hands, first fingers interlocked, then palms together.

"Either."

"Speak up, girl. Did you say 'neither'?"

"Either, both."

"Both!" Jesse beamed. "Log entry for this day reads: 'Met friendly native.'"

Chapter 12

Your idea about becoming one flesh,
God—it's the best.

A half dozen prairie chickens burst out of the dark green slough grass with a flurry of feathers and squawks.

Jesse grabbed the reins. "Easy there, Pa. Have to remember this place. They tend to feed in the same area."

Susannah pried her fingers from the wagon's seat and watched the birds disappear on the horizon. "Seems like a lot of hunting for so little meat. Could they be tamed? Then you wouldn't have to buy chickens."

Jesse shook his head. "They're wild. Don't worry—we'll see enough from the wheat to get your Rhode Island Reds."

The Sheyenne River meandered under a canopy of bright yellow leaves. The tallest trees were cottonwoods, reaching seventy or eighty feet. Despite their size, Susannah could see why Jesse didn't build his house from them. Before the trunk reached the height of a man, it split into sections that curved too much for use as lumber. Other species, mostly oaks and box elders, grew only a foot or two in diameter.

Jesse set fishing lines, then started chopping. Susannah collected windfall from the underbrush, noting the location of wild grapes, gooseberries, and raspberries for next summer's picking. Next summer. Would she have a baby by then?

When they had collected a cord of wood, Jesse rigged up a block and tackle to a square of canvas. A few yanks on the rope hauled the pile up from the riverbank.

"How did you learn this? Were you an engineer in the army?"

Jesse coiled the rope. "Nope. Pa taught me to take every opportunity to try new things." He hauled in the fishing lines and tossed three trout under the seat, then reached for her. "This warm day could be an opportunity." His finger stroked her lips, down her throat to the neckline of her basque. The top hook popped open.

"Outside? In the middle of the day?"

"Can't think of anything I'd rather do." He unfastened the second hook.

"But the fish will go bad."

He chuckled. "They already have. I saw their reports from school."

The third hook opened, exposing the edge of her corset.

"Jesse!"

He slid his finger into her chemise, pulling her toward him. "This is one of the unique opportunities available in the territory."

"The *Emigrants' Guide* didn't mention it." She pushed his hands away.

"What a waste of a perfect day." He exhaled heavily and lifted her to the seat.

Susannah fastened her bodice with trembling fingers. Never once had she seen her parents touch, much less express affection. A man might escort his wife, her gloved hand on his well-clothed elbow. But more ardent displays of feelings crossed the line of propriety. Kissing in public belonged to the lower classes, foreigners, loose women. Removing one's clothing outdoors was completely unthinkable. And what Jesse suggested was no less than animal behavior. But she couldn't change him, so she would change the subject.

She nodded at a long line of birds migrating below the cirrus wisps. "Could those be pelicans? This far north?"

"Yep." Jesse swung into the seat. "They nest upriver."

"More traffic than Woodward Avenue on a Sunday afternoon."

He aimed the wagon for the soddy. "Tell me, pretty lady. How come you turned down all those city boys? The ones who took you driving up and down Woodward in their cabriolets pulled by fancy trotters?"

"They all went to war."

"None of them came back?"

"Mother took ill in '64. Caring for her kept me busy."

"You needed a sister to help you."

"We tried to hire someone. If her difficulties had been only physical . . . I don't know if it was the apoplexy or losing her only brother in the War, she just wasn't in her right mind. Ellen arranged for ladies from the church to sit with her, but they decided she was possessed. Nothing Reverend Mason said changed their minds."

"Was your pa sick too?"

"He worked himself to death, battling the horse epidemic."

"I read about that. Hit Boston, New York, as far west as Milwaukee."

"It was awful. Detroit lost hundreds of horses, despite everything Father tried. He passed away one morning on a call at the police stables. At least he didn't suffer."

"And there was no one to help you." He shook his head.

"My father was the only member of his family to emigrate. Mother just had the one brother." Mother had drilled into her the principle that girls who talked about themselves were bores. "What did you do in the War?"

"Against the wishes of my folks, my older brother and I volunteered. For God, Country, Glory, and Adventure. We'd all be home by Christmas. But I came home alone, leaving him dead at Gettysburg. Thank God Matt and the rest were too young. Guess that's a big part of my leaving, that empty place at the table. If I could have reloaded faster, stood in his place, taken that bullet . . ."

His spiral into despondency unnerved her. "How did we get started on such a gloomy subject?"

Jesse straightened. "I was trying to figure out how you escaped the clutches of the Detroit bachelors."

"Then let me ask you the same question."

"Don't think Detroit bachelors would be interested in me."

"No, I mean, why didn't you marry before you came here?"

"And miss the adventure of writing off for you?" He tickled her under her chin. "It's embarrassing to admit, but even with the shortage of men caused by the War, no one chose me."

"You mean, no one chose to come out here."

"I might have stayed back east, for the right offer."

"The right offer? New York girls do the asking?"

"Not exactly, but they sure do let a fellow know how his question will be received." He stretched his legs against the footboard. "Truth is, that yearlong binge after the War blew my reputation to smithereens. I got nothing but cold shoulders at my sister's wedding." He turned to look at her. "Did one of those Detroit boys bother you?"

She returned his gaze. "None of them bothered with me at all."

"Their loss, my gain." His eyebrows twitched together. "Anything else you want to ask me?"

Susannah thought a moment. "How many others did you write to?"

"Just you. Ellen said you'd be perfect for me, so no sense wasting money on stamps."

Her heart sank. He hadn't chosen her after all.

Jesse halted the wagon and leaned over to kiss her. "I'm happy with the way it worked out. Hope someday you'll be too."

Happiness, she thought, was too much to expect.

When they had left for their afternoon trip, Susannah had pulled a handful of corn kernels from her apron and scattered them in the grass. Jesse had raised an eyebrow but hadn't interrupted his rendition of "Tenting Tonight." Now, as they returned at dusk, he sat bolt upright.

"Susannah, the prairie chickens are waiting for you! You've tamed them with one meal."

She jumped off the wagon, gathered three docile fowl, and climbed back on.

Jesse inspected her catch. "Still alive but acting mighty strange. What exactly did you feed them?" He stuck his nose into her apron pocket. "Clever girl! You've gotten them drunk! But on what?"

Susannah folded her hands. No one had called her clever before. "They're not inebriated, they're medicated. Simmons Liver Regulator. Ellen packed it."

Jesse hooted. "Have to tell her you've found a new use for her favorite concoction. All right, let's get these birds home before they sober up and figure out they've been shanghaied."

After dinner, Jesse picked out a few notes on his guitar while Susannah mended his socks and shirts. The melody wandered without words from "Battle Hymn of the Republic" into "John Brown's Body," then "Johnny Comes Marching Home." She left him alone in his wartime reminisces to delve into her own.

In this particular memory, seventeen-year-old Susannah Underhill toiled over her schoolwork in preparation for final examinations. The fragrance of hyacinths filled the parlor. Father unfolded the *Detroit Free Press*, tilting it toward the kerosene lamp in the center of the marble-topped table. "An army of secessionists occupied a Federal garrison in South Carolina."

Her literature anthology slipped to the floor with a thud. "Does that mean war?"

Mother stabbed the hem of Susannah's graduation dress with her needle. "Ladies do not talk about such things. Go to your room and remain there."

Six weeks later Susannah was arranging a freshly ironed cloth over the dining room table when Mother appeared in the archway. "You need set only two places this evening. Your father has enlisted."

Jesse slapped his hand against his guitar, returning her to the present. He said, "I hope we have only daughters. No sons."

Susannah let her needle pause. "Most men prefer sons."

"I've seen too much war to want any son of mine—no, that's not right. War hurts women too—refugees, mothers, wives—" His focus reeled in from an unknown distance. He nodded her way. "Daughters, nieces. Thousands of years of so-called civilization and all we got to show for it is killing each other more efficiently. Wonder why God puts up with us. We're not getting any closer to peace." He shook his head. "Men have had their chance. I say, let women run the country."

"Are you saying women could keep the country out of war?"

"Let's say Ellen had been president instead of Lincoln." He stowed his guitar and paced between the bed and the table.

"I can't imagine a woman president."

"Sure you can." He poured a cup of coffee and handed it to her. "What does Ellen do when there's trouble at church?"

Susannah considered the tumult over instrumental music in

the service, the uproar when women's clothing styles became more elaborate, the tensions over support for the Freedmen's Aid Society. "She meets with each person involved, hears them out, then brings them all together to work out a compromise. Of course, she prays a lot." Susannah sipped the coffee. "She has this amazing ability to make the people involved feel ashamed of themselves for the disharmony they've caused. That's when Reverend Mason steps in to bring reconciliation."

"She keeps the church together. It's better than Reconstruction." He took the cup from her and polished off the rest. "I think you may have hit on the answer, or part of it anyway. It's not in men giving up so women can run things but in both working together. Wonder how it's going in Wyoming Territory."

Susannah resumed mending the shoulder seam of Jesse's shirt. "You're in favor of women's suffrage?"

"Absolutely. The women in my family, present company included, are all smarter than us men."

He included her in his family? A lump formed in her throat. She swallowed and regained control. "Reverend Mason is in favor too, but this may be another issue threatening church unity."

Jesse sat and unlaced his boots. "You can call him Matt. He's your brother-in-law now."

"No, I can't. Ellen calls him Reverend."

"She does? What do the children call him?"

"Papa."

Jesse changed into his nightshirt. "Well, I'm not going to solve all the country's problems this week. Come to bed. We're due at Ivar's by dawn."

"I'll be done shortly." She hoped he would be asleep by the time she slipped between the sheets.

He wasn't. And he made her glad of it.

Chapter 13

Lord, please take away these nightmares.
Or make Susannah strong.

G et down!"

A hand slammed into Susannah's shoulder, jolting her from sleep and shoving her to the edge of the bed. "Here they come! No time to reload! Bayonets!"

Susannah dug her fingers into the mattress and braced her feet against the frame. Her heart raced and her eyes strained against the darkness. "What? Who—"

"Reinforcements! Pull back, pull back! Where's James? Hey, anyone seen Lieutenant Mason? All this smoke. What a way to run a war." A hard-soled foot snagged her ankle. "Man down! Stretcher-bearer! Over here! Oh my God! It's James! Don't you die on me! Move it! Out of the way!"

A heavy arm smashed into her back, ejecting her from the bed. Her head glanced off the stove. She landed on hands and knees.

"You got to save him, you got to—" He stopped in mid-yell. "Susannah? What are you doing on the floor?"

She swallowed, trying to get her dry throat to work.

"Come on back to bed now. I know you're excited about seeing Marta and going to the store, but it's not morning yet." He
untangled himself from the quilts, sat on the edge of the bed, and
extended a hand toward her.

She flinched with an involuntary gasp.

Even in the dark he didn't miss her reaction. "What happened?"

"Nightmare," she managed to whimper.

"You had a nightmare?" He gathered her like an infant, pulling
her onto his lap and rubbing her arms. "Hey, you've got the cold
sweats. Poor heart's galloping away. Hush, you're safe. No more bad
dreams. I've got you now."

He pulled her down into the warm curve of his body. Within
minutes his breathing evened to a deep rumble that continued
uninterrupted until sunrise.

Safe here? Hardly.

Clear-eyed, Jesse bounded from bed, gave Susannah a kiss, and hurried out. She rinsed the dirt from her scraped palms and palpated
her skull. A tender spot but no swelling. Seconds later a strangled
yell split the morning. Another nightmare? Insanity? Indians?
Susannah grabbed the Winchester and ran to the stable. The prairie
chickens circled Jesse, diving and squawking. The oxen sliced the
air with their horns. Jake barked and raced among the animals, his
hunting and herding instincts fighting each other for dominance.

Susannah propped the gun against the doorjamb and grabbed
the shovel. She swatted two birds, dazing them. The third made
his escape.

Susannah leaned against the wall and caught her breath as Jesse
dispatched the birds with the ax. "You're bleeding!" She touched
his chin, turning his face toward the sunrise. Scratches crossed his

forehead and ran down one cheek. "I am so sorry. You told me they were wild, but I didn't listen—"

"Nothing to apologize for." Jesse blotted his face with his bandanna. "Army had a few fellows like these prairie chickens, in a *fowl* mood when they're recovering from a drunk."

She smiled at his play on words. "You're not mad at me?"

"How could I be mad at the woman who saved me while wearing only her chemise and drawers?" He waggled his eyebrows. "Medicating the birds is a great idea. We just need to wring their necks while they're still tipsy." He gave her a lopsided grin. "Can't have people in town thinking I'm *henpecked* after only three weeks of married life."

Susannah's smile froze as her fingers caught on a line of glue in the shovel handle.

For once, Jesse didn't make eye contact. "What I'd like to do to that banker." He set the tool against the wall.

Susannah crossed her arms to cover herself and hurried back to the soddy. "I'll wash your wounds."

"Sit beside me." Susannah slipped onto the trunk and pointed to a spot in the sunlight.

"Anytime." Jesse slid in and grinned. "Now I've got you where I want you."

"Hold still." She daubed his head with some sort of medicine. This close, he had a wonderful view. And a wonderful chance to steal a kiss. He leaned forward and she winced.

Why was she still afraid of him?

A memory rushed back: the sharp bite of gunpowder, cannons booming, his rifle grip slick with blood. "The nightmare last night. It was mine, wasn't it?"

She nodded.

He slumped against the cold wall. The scream of the wounded man he'd tripped over, the bugle sounding charge, the smell of the summer sun on the dead. "I thought I was done with that when I stopped drinking."

"I shouldn't have asked you about the War."

"Don't take the blame for my mess." Whose sons had he shot? Whose brother took his bayonet in the gut? Jesse turned toward her and she braced. "What did I do? Did I holler? My sister said I'd wake the whole house."

"Yes."

"Tell me."

She wadded the cotton. "You yelled about your brother."

"Gettysburg, then." He groaned. "What else?"

"You pushed me off the bed."

He gathered her stiff body to his chest. He'd started to make some progress with her and now this. "Did I hurt you?"

"No."

"Here I thought you were the one with the secret." He pried her chin from his shoulder, forcing her to look him in the eye. He had given her a fright. "I am sorry. And if I ever do anything like that again, you have to speak up. Promise me."

She nodded and looked away. Susannah would never keep that promise. She'd bury it—the same as she did with all other pain.

The rising sun outlined the Volds' soddy, sitting in a shallower draw than Jesse's but otherwise its duplicate. Freya and Thor barked their greeting. Ivar hailed them from between his oxen. While Jesse gave him a hand with the harnessing, Susannah knocked on the door to see if Marta needed help.

"Come in!"

"Well said, Marta," Susannah complimented her. She stepped over the threshold and gasped in wonder. "Jesse, look at this!"

"At what?" He joined her in the doorway.

"Look how they've fixed up their house!"

Ivar clapped Jesse on the back. "Nothing like a wife to pry money from your tight fist, old man. Marta coated the walls with plaster; easy as frosting a cake she told me. Sure does make it lighter, not so much hole in ground. And she put cheesecloth on the ceiling. Won't stop the leaks in the spring, but keeps dirt and bugs from falling on us the rest of the year."

Susannah raised a questioning eyebrow at Jesse. Their list of necessities was long already, but perhaps—

Jesse gave Susannah a wink, then turned to Marta. "Looks good, Marta, but I want to see Sara's new tooth."

Ivar interpreted for Marta, who handed him the baby while she boarded the Volds' wagon.

"We're off!" Jesse gave a rousing rendition of "Erie Canal." Holding the reins between his right elbow and his knee, his hands played an imaginary guitar.

"Do you know 'When Morning Gilds the Skies'?" If she could keep him singing, she wouldn't have to talk.

Shifting the reins to his left hand, Jesse kept time with broad sweeps of his right arm.

"'A mighty fortress is our God.'" Hands busy conducting were not touching her. Ahead, in the lead wagon, Ivar and Marta sang alternate verses in Norwegian.

"'My country 'tis of thee.'"

Nearly two hours passed before they descended to the Sheyenne River, shallow this time of year, and approached a cluster of unmarked structures beside the railroad tracks. Grass grew unabated between the buildings; not much traffic here.

Jesse pointed to a boxcar-sized tent with a stovepipe protruding from its peak. "The Western Hotel I told you about. The owner, Mac, used to run a trading post out of there before the Roses built their store." Jesse nodded at the two-story structure next to the siding. Bright yellow pine clapboard showed the store had yet to face a Dakota winter.

"The long building is the railroad section house, and the little square one belongs to the army. Mac's log cabin is on the other side of the river, beyond the water tank. Can't wait to see his face when he finds out I got married. He was wailing a forlorn bachelor song last time I was in town."

Town? What wild-eyed optimist, Susannah wondered, designated these few buildings a town? Where was the post office, dry goods, hardware, drugstore? It didn't even qualify as a crossroads; only one road ran through here, and it was more of a path. "What is . . . does this place have a name?"

"Several of them. Let's see, when I wrote to you, it was Second Crossing of the Sheyenne, or Sheyenne for short. Since then I've heard it called Fifth Siding and Wahpeton. I'm sure Mrs. Rose will tell you which is in use this week."

She groped for something positive to say. "The trees are pleasant."

The entire population turned out for their arrival at the store's loading dock. Overwhelmed, Susannah shrank on the seat.

"Mason. Vold." Mr. Rose peered at Susannah. "Well, look here. Mrs. Rose, you've got another woman to chitchat with."

Mrs. Rose stretched her neck to see over the teams. "This must be—"

Jesse attempted to introduce Susannah as he lifted her down. A whirlwind of barking dogs and yelling children separated them. Ivar busied himself with unloading the wagons.

"Another woman! What a blessing!" Mrs. Rose sighed with self-satisfaction, as if she had single-handedly brought Susannah to Dakota Territory. "You're Miss Susannah Underhill of Detroit, Michigan. Welcome!"

Mr. Rose shook her hand. "We got the telegram about you awhile back. Our son Adam took it. He's our oldest, real smart, knows Morse code."

"We don't get many telegrams out here, you know." Mrs. Rose took her other hand. "Most folks' families are in the old country, like Volds' here. Telegraph line don't run all the way to Norway."

"Like as not Adam will have to mail order himself a bride too, seeing as how there aren't many girls out here," Mr. Rose said. "Can't expect him to wait for the Vold baby to grow up. Not that he'd marry a foreigner, if you know what I mean."

"Sara was born in American territory," Susannah said.

Mrs. Rose's arms flapped, the fringe of her shawl jigging to her words. "The telegram read: 'Miss Susannah Underhill arriving Tuesday.' We couldn't think, for the longest time, whatever a 'miss' would be coming to see Mr. Mason for."

"Then we remembered." Mr. Rose raised his index finger. "Mason had a letter from you last spring and wrote back."

"He must have quite the way with words." Mrs. Rose fluttered her eyelashes, as if playing the ingénue onstage. "Although you lived in the same town as his brother, the parson. Maybe you'd met Mr. Mason before. But I won't pry into anyone else's business. 'Keep to yourself' is my motto."

Mr. Rose's eyes gleamed under bushy brows. "So on that hot fly-swarmin' day, Adam rode all the way out to your place. It ain't easy to find, but the boy's got a good head."

"Did you find a parson to marry you?" Mrs. Rose asked. "If we're short of anything more than females out here, it's parsons. I don't even know if Mr. Vold's properly married to his wife, and they have a baby now. Well, you never know with foreigners. Where are my manners? Come on in and have a cup of tea. Bring Mrs. Vold along too. Feels like winter coming on out here."

While Mr. Rose weighed the harvest, his wife winged her way in, chattering continuously. Susannah leaned against the wagon, her knees rubbery from the verbal barrage. She'd had a sudden attack of panic when Mrs. Rose asked about a parson. Susannah half expected the storekeeper to demand the proxy certificate.

Marta emerged from hiding behind the wagon and honked like a goose. Yes, with her long neck perched on sloping shoulders, her flapping arms, and the way her bustle accentuated her pear-shaped figure, Mrs. Rose did indeed resemble a Canada goose. Susannah giggled, linked arms with her friend, and followed.

Susannah stopped just inside the door. What colors! Yellow-handled tools, red cooking implements, green farm equipment, a rainbow of fabrics, a riot of canned goods. She inhaled and almost choked on the smells: coffee, spices, leather. After the muted hues and silence of the prairie, the store overwhelmed her. She closed her eyes and tried to get her bearings.

Marta squeezed her hand and led her through the maze of barrels and bins to the counter. The storekeeper poured tea into mugs and yelled, "Good day, Mrs. Vold."

"Mrs. Vold is learning English," Susannah said quietly.

"Her husband sure learned fast. I can understand near everything he says."

Susannah suppressed a smile. When had the Roses let Ivar get a word in edgewise?

"How's that baby?" she bellowed at Marta.

Marta unwrapped Sara, who, rather than expressing dismay at the shouting, dazzled Mrs. Rose with a single-tooth smile. After agreeing that this was one of the prettiest babies she had ever seen, the storekeeper began working on Susannah's list.

"Never had any trouble with Mr. Mason when it comes to

money. Won't accept credit. Real careful sort," Mrs. Rose confided. "What nice handwriting you have. Bet you went to one of them fancy ladies' schools out east. School's another thing we're short on here in the territory. Let's see: sugar, cinnamon, raisins, ginger. Sounds like you'll be doing some baking, although it don't look like Mr. Mason has starved cooking for himself. Some men do just fine in the kitchen, you know, like those fellows over to the hotel."

Jesse carried in empty barrels, pulled the list from Mrs. Rose's hand, added three items, and took a sip of Susannah's tea. With a wink, he rolled out full barrels.

Mrs. Rose continued, "I'm checking off molasses and pork. You go ahead and pick out your piece goods, dear. Wool on the top shelf, calico on the second, denim next, flannel on the bottom. Mr. Mason's got some sewing planned for you. Now, what's he want with clothesline, plaster, and cheesecloth?"

Since Mrs. Rose didn't need any response to her soliloquy, Susannah concentrated on choosing fabric and yarn. The blue worsted was a little thick for shirts, but there wasn't anything else suitable. And the red twill had a few defects. Maybe next time. No, the next trip was months away. She set her selections on the counter.

While Marta shopped, Susannah escaped with the sleeping baby. She found Jesse on the platform, teaching the Rose children a singing game. One grimy-faced youngster hung from his shoulders. Three others, street urchins worthy of *Oliver Twist*, circled him. Jesse sang a line, clapping and stomping out the rhythm. When he called their names, the children echoed back, laughing as they bungled the complicated pattern.

"Jesse Mason, me favorite pettifogger!" With the trilled *r* of a Scottish burr on his tongue, a man wearing a mattress-ticking shirt ambled over from the tent hotel. His wavy dark hair lay flat against his skull from a recent wet-combing. The slicked hair accentuated his most prominent feature, ears set perpendicular to his head.

"Thieving bairns," he mumbled, and the children scattered under his gaze.

The man seemed loosely put together. His eyebrows snaked over his forehead and his mouth formed strange shapes as he spoke. When Jesse reached out, hoisted him onto the platform, and shook his hand, Susannah half expected the man's arm to come loose at his shoulder.

"Who are you calling a pettifogger?" Jesse asked him. "Last May you kept me up all night debating Adam's and Eve's navels."

"Since you refuse to drink yourself into oblivion like the rest of us, I must talk you to sleep. Planning to sneak away without stopping in to see me, were you? Well, I can hear you singing clear across town. Sounds like you're sharpening a saw. Abner said you'd roped some lass into—" He caught sight of Susannah. His mouth dropped open, flattening his full beard onto his shirt placket. "And a baby already!" The man slapped Jesse on the back. "It's not been a month. You'll be crediting your fancy springwater, I suppose."

Susannah looked for a place to hide.

"Hey, that's my baby." Ivar hefted a sack into his wagon.

The man leaned forward, peering at baby Sara with his pale blue eyes. Susannah caught the sharp aroma of whiskey on his breath. "I should have recognized your wife's good looks, Ivar."

"Mac, I believe you just insulted my bride."

The hotel proprietor thumped his forehead with his hand. "I'll never be getting married if I cannot talk nice around women. Jesse, yours is ever' bit as bonny as Ivar's. In fact, had I seen her before you, she'd be Mrs. McFadgen now. How'd you slip her by?"

Susannah squirmed. Now she knew how a prize heifer felt at the county fair. Behind her in the store, Mrs. Rose plowed on at full volume. "Nice enough but a mite skinny, if you ask me."

"Had her get off at Fourth Siding. Almost lost her to Abner, though. Susannah, this is Donald McFadgen, former Northern Pacific crew boss, virtuoso of vegetables, and first settler in—what's the name of your town this week?"

"Worthington." He dried his hands on the towel tucked in his waistband, then shook Susannah's. "Morrison and McKinnon will be sorry they missed you."

As Mr. McFadgen bent over her hand, a movement at the corner of the section house caught Susannah's gaze. A large man backed into the shadow, leaving his paunch in the sunlight. Abner Reece. Susannah inched closer to Jesse.

"So, where are your partners in crime?"

"They're off chasing rumor of a buffalo other side of the river. Much as I like haggis from buffalo, with the luck of the Irish, we'll dine on potato soup tonight. Speaking of luck, Jesse Mason—" Mac tipped his head toward Susannah. "Though you'll say she's an answer to prayer."

"You don't know the half of it, Mac. Susannah learned animal doctoring from her pa. She got twins out of my cow."

Mac gave her a head-to-toe looking-over. "Let's see, your homestead is eight miles southeast of here. I'd best make a visit, be sure you're treating her right."

"You do that. Much as I'd like to stay and jaw with you—"

"Aye, lad. Married men have better things to do." He gave her a grin that made her blush, then strolled back to his hotel.

Jesse handed his letters to Mrs. Rose.

"Writing your brother again? Here's his. Best fix that address. He seems to have moved. And here's one from New York. Looks like your sister's penmanship. Give this to the Volds. All the way from Norway. Don't those foreigners write funny?"

Rechecking the arithmetic, Jesse signed off the ledger book. "Ready? This is it 'til spring."

Susannah eyed the section house. "Let's go."

As the wagons crossed the river, Susannah and Marta exchanged glances, then collapsed in a fit of giggles.

"Marta says please, no more English lessons," Ivar interpreted. "She doesn't want to understand the Roses."

"Ask if she will teach me Norwegian. I don't want to understand them either."

The wagons parted, and Susannah waved good-bye as the Volds turned toward their homestead. "Mr. and Mrs. Rose are so lonely."

"They've got each other—no reason to be lonely." Jesse squeezed her knee. "I've got big plans for this winter, plans for coaxing you into talking, maybe even rouse you into an argument if I'm lucky."

"Wives are supposed to respect their husbands, not argue with them."

"That what my brother says?" Eyebrows raised, he handed her an envelope.

"Mail!" She tore it open, finding only one sheet of paper in Reverend Mason's writing. Nothing from Ellen. She'd been counting on hearing from her. Susannah turned away, letting the wind dry her eyes.

Jesse pulled her close and nuzzled her ear. "What's my little brother have to say?"

"'Dear Jesse and Susannah,'" she read. "'Hope this finds you all in good health, and that Susannah arrived in the Dakota Territory without incident.

"'We have been through a time of trials here. The Detroit congregation was reluctant to make the necessary addition to the parsonage. In September, the Bishop assigned us to a station more in keeping with the ever-increasing size of our family. The move was an ordeal for Ellen, leading, I believe, to a difficult confinement. However, we are now settled in Ann Arbor. We welcomed Benjamin James to our family on September 12.'"

"Another nephew I haven't met."

Susannah wished she could have been there to help. But Ellen's resourceful mother and an adept sister or two probably journeyed out from New York. They would have the household running like clockwork. Susannah would have been in the way.

She resumed reading. "'Unfortunately, in our turmoil, I have neglected to execute the Underhill estate. Be assured, dear sister-in-law, I will attend to this matter expeditiously. No further correspondence from the bank has been received.

"'All are well here. Hope to hear the same from you. Your devoted brother, Matthew.'"

"He writes like a pompous fool. Does he talk like that?"

"Maybe he's expanding his vocabulary for the new congregation. Ann Arbor is a college town."

Jesse shrugged. "Not like here, then."

"There's no Mr. and Mrs. Rose."

"At least Mrs. Rose cooks as well as she slings the scuttlebutt."

From the basket, Jesse produced two brown paper packages containing warm meat and potato pies. Susannah bit into the flaky pastry. Ah, seasoned perfectly with onion and pepper. During her first ride in this wagon, the biscuits had sat in her stomach like a lump. But today her appetite had returned. She glanced over her shoulder at the load of ingredients, including laying hens. She looked forward to baking as a pleasure, instead of another item on her list of chores. When they got home—

Home? Was she calling the soddy *home?* Not quite home, perhaps, but no longer a prison. More like an exile.

Her mind formed a picture of her house in Michigan. She still missed her parents and wished the banker hadn't forced her abrupt departure, but the deep sadness had eased. That heavy lump in her chest had been replaced by an odd flickering in the vicinity of her heart. Could it be love?

"I guess I embarrassed you when I introduced you to Mac." He brushed a flake of crust off her skirt.

"I'm sorry I'm not as pretty as Marta."

He peered under the brim of her hat. "Maybe not when you first arrived. But now you've got a little color in your cheeks, meat on your bones." He nodded. "Dakota agrees with you. You agree with me." He stretched his arm across the backrest, snugging her closer.

"Do you think Mr. McFadgen will call on us?"

"He never has before, but then it was just me."

"Have you had callers?"

"I'm sure we'll have more, once you train the parlor maid to receive them properly." Jesse winked. "Let's see. Visitors. Year ago spring, a pair of surveyors came through to tell me I was squatting on the northeast corner of section 8, township 35. We dined on antelope."

He reached for his hat as the wind gusted. "End of May, or early June, Fort Ransom closed. When the boys marched north to Jamestown, they stopped by for a buffalo roast. We stayed up all night. Had a sorry sort of dance without any ladies, but they were in high spirits anyhow. They were looking forward to being on the rail line: regular mail, companions of the female persuasion, better food."

"What's buffalo taste like?"

"Good. Like beef, only more flavor."

"And antelope?"

"You had to ask." Jesse began the motions Susannah now recognized as guitar playing. "The surveyors brought a fiddle and a harmonica. We got so busy swapping songs, we let the beast burn. So I'd have to say it tasted like charcoal. I hoped to shoot another once I bought my Winchester, but they're too quick."

Susannah watched cumulus clouds build into thunderstorms miles to the southwest and considered his visitors. Jesse had family and friends back in the States, a home he was born in and could return to. He was the one who craved company, the congenial host to assorted threshers, soldiers, and surveyors. The exile wasn't hers, it was Jesse's.

The folds of her cape parted as his hand searched for hers. Finding it, he worked his fingers between her glove and cuff, stroking the skin on the inside of her wrist, making her insides shiver. She drew her gaze from the hard white of the clouds back to the man next to her, sparking an eager smile from him.

Susannah had hoped he wouldn't be overly demanding, insisting on fancy meals, requiring a spotless house. Instead, he complimented her for the simple fare she cooked, approved of the linens she'd brought, and didn't ask for much in the way of housekeeping.

No, his demands were of a more frightening nature. He wanted to know her.

The rooftop barrel and stovepipe appeared on the horizon. Jake raced out of the draw. Susannah had just enough time to say "uh-oh" before the dog jumped in the back of the wagon and landed in the midst of six squawking hens. The surprised elkhound bolted over the seat into Susannah's lap. The air filled with feathers and fur.

Jesse brushed down off her shoulder. "You won't have to pluck them for cooking."

"But I'll have to make sweaters for any we want to keep."

Jesse hooted. "Mac's right. I am lucky. Blessed. Thanks for staying."

Chapter 14

Man's not meant to live alone.
You're right, as usual.

A north wind chilled their next woodcutting trip. Susannah tightened her shawl as the wagon crested the hill. "What's that?" She pointed to a smudge beneath a storm cloud.

"Dear Jesus!" Jesse snapped the reins and forced Pa Ox into a trot. "Fire! Lightning's got the grass burning."

Susannah dug her fingers into the seat and braced against the footboard. Behind her, logs clattered as the wagon lurched and bounced. Smoke billowed white against the indigo thundercloud. Antelope streaked toward the river. A white-tailed jackrabbit zigzagged under the wagon, and flocks of goldfinches, ducks, and plovers thrashed the air. Storm and smoke raced to cover the afternoon sun.

By the time the wagon reached the soddy, smoke had won.

Jesse dashed into the shed for an empty flour sack and a pail. "Susannah!" he shouted over the bass notes of the thunder. He grabbed her elbow and pivoted her to look him straight in the eye. "Stay here! If the fire comes close, head for the creek." He scowled at the trickle of water winding beneath the brown leaves of the thicket. "No. It's near dry. Stay inside. If you see flames, get in the root cellar. And pray."

His mouth worked as if he had more to say, but he couldn't organize his racing thoughts into sentences. Lightning streaked overhead, followed by thunder, and Jesse sprinted toward the spring.

"Jake, stay with Susannah," he called back over his shoulder.

Susannah held the door open for him. "Come on, Jake."

Lightning rent the cloud overhead. Thunder shook the shelves and rattled the tinware. Jake barked. Susannah scanned the ceiling, expecting to see flames curling around the rafters. The dog pushed his wet nose into her hand.

"We were told to stay." She studied the root cellar. If she emptied out the food, she and the dog could curl into the dirt cave Jesse had dug into the hill.

Susannah peered through the window. As far as she could see, the prairie was covered with dry grass. The Volds would be hit first; Ivar would be busy trying to save his own place. The next closest neighbors, the half dozen citizens of Worthington, lived too far away to help.

A pair of foxes darted through the yard, ignoring the hens squawking behind the fragile willow fence. She thought about Ma Ox and the calves. If they hadn't run off, smoke would scorch their lungs, hot cinders would burn them. They'd be frantic.

"All right." Susannah's words brought Jake's ears upright again. "We're the only help he's got, you and me. I'm terrified. You'll be brave enough for both of us, won't you?" The dog faced the door. "Find Ma Ox. Go!" Susannah opened the door, gathered her skirts, and raced after the dog.

The scene at the top of the hill stopped her. Flames lined the base of towering smoke clouds, miles closer than before. The smell of burning grass tinged the air. A family of ground squirrels darted and squeaked around her feet. No Jesse.

Were they all going to die?

Jake barked, commanding her to follow. Through the crackling and rumbling, a low moan rose to a screech. Ma Ox stamped in agitated circles around her calves. Susannah yanked the pin. The animals made a beeline for the shed.

Storm clouds brought an early dusk. Susannah filled buckets and wet the roof, drenching herself in the process. With each flash of lightning, she looked up, hoping.

Shouldn't Jesse be back by now?

Ash-laden air swirled through the draw. A live ember landed in the haystack, and stems began to redden and curl. Susannah swung the bucket in an arc, only to have the wind blow the water back in her face. Hot pain knifed through her shoulder blades, but she tried to ignore it as she raced up the slope to position herself behind the haystack. The second bucket hit its mark, directly in the center of the flame. The hay sizzled. But before she could celebrate her victory, opaque smoke enveloped her.

Thunder rumbled again. Flickering light encircled Susannah. It seemed as if the whole world blazed.

"Jesse?" she shouted into the wind. No response except the howling of the storm.

The wind buffeted her, first hot, peppered with sparks, then cold with rain. Fire crackled nearby, popping and snapping. Susannah grabbed the shovel and bent low, searching for breathable air.

What if he's hurt?

She shouldn't have given away the gall salve—it would soothe burns. She hadn't made butter yet, but she did have lard, a passable base for a burn ointment. *If he's alive . . .*

Her feet found the strip of dirt Jesse had plowed to add on to the shed. At the far edge, the fire smoldered, burning itself out.

"Jesse?" Smoke seared her throat. She followed the furrow, stopping every few paces to scoop dirt onto stray flames.

And if he's dead? What then?

She couldn't entertain that possibility.

God? It's about Jesse. I know You're not impressed with me, but please help me find him.

A voice came out of nothingness. "Halt! Who goes there?"

"Jesse!"

"State name, rank, and unit, or I'll bore you full of daylight." A soot-covered face solidified in the vapor. Jesse.

She moved within arm's reach and cleared her throat. Her voice came out in a croak. "Susannah. No rank or unit."

"Woman on the battlefield?" Squinting, Jesse tilted his head. His smoke-darkened face creased into a smile. "Susannah?"

He remembered. She staggered under his weight as he sagged onto her shoulders.

Jesse glanced from the last vestiges of the fire, sizzling in the rain, to Susannah. He touched his fingertips to her cheek. "Yes."

Jake appeared, bumping his master's legs.

Jesse laid his palm on the dog's head. "Yes."

A smattering of freezing rain pelted them. She tucked her hand under Jesse's elbow. Was he all right? What happened to his bucket and flour sack? "I need help putting Pa Ox in the shed."

He nodded. "Rain." He took the shovel so she could raise her skirts out of the mud. Frigid gusts spewed icy water over them. Reaching the soddy, she headed for Pa Ox, still harnessed to the wagon.

"Go inside!" Jesse yelled.

And with a blast of snow, their little valley disappeared.

Susannah stirred the fire, heated milk for cocoa, and changed clothes, but her mind was on Jesse. Tuesday night, talking about the War had set off his nightmare. But today he'd talked about apples: picking with his siblings, pressing cider with his father, scorching his tongue on his mother's fresh-baked pie. Nothing about the War. Had the smoke and danger caused him to hallucinate?

Susannah draped her wet, smoky clothes over the line strung across the corner. The Late Unpleasantness, some called it. Ha. She'd seen that hollow look in her father's eyes. The same expression haunted the man with one leg who swung past the house on his crutches. She'd learned to steer clear of the group loitering outside the produce market, their tattered uniforms staving off efforts to oust them. Even Independence Day picnics and parades carried an underlying current of sadness, not just for those who would not return, but from those who had—the so-called victors.

The door blew open. Jesse stumbled in, dumping an armload of wood beside the stove. Icicles dangled from his hair.

Susannah closed the door and passed him a towel. "Maybe you should grow your beard back."

"Guess I'll have to." He sipped the cocoa she offered.

"Did you get any burns?"

"No, but I gave my guardian angel a good scare."

With shaking hands, she lifted the fragile chimney to light the kerosene lamp. "Is winter always this—"

She hesitated. What could she say? Bad? No, that sounded too judgmental.

"Sometimes it hits all of a sudden, like today. Other winters hold off until October, November. Dakota gets less snow than back east, but more wind. Don't get caught out in it." He grabbed her wrist as she dropped the spill into the stove. "You're hurt."

"It's nothing."

He opened her hands, and his eyes widened at the welts striping her fingers and palms. "What's this? Rope burn?"

"From the picket line."

"And this?"

"The bucket handle." Susannah curled her fingers. "I'm sorry.

118

You told me to stay inside." And pray. Had God answered her prayer, inadequate though it was?

"You saved our home." Jesse brushed his lips over the base of her thumb. "Keep on thinking. I'm counting on you."

Jesse lifted the lantern and searched the shed one more time. Where had that large pail run off to? He'd found the lid on the floor. Then he remembered: he'd filled it with water, taken it to the fields, beaten the flames out with a wet flour sack. He secured the door and returned to the house.

Susannah looked up from scouring the coffeepot. Never seen a woman so dedicated to cleaning something that would just be dirty tomorrow.

"I lost the large pail, the one with the locking lid."

She nodded.

"But I lost more than a tin pail, didn't I? I lost time, went back to the War." He sat on the trunk to take off his brogans.

She nodded again.

"Susannah, I asked you to tell me. You promised."

"I haven't had the opportunity."

"Well, we've got the opportunity now. What did I do?"

"The weather—" She inspected the stove, shelves, and table, but couldn't find anything else to fuss with.

Jesse grabbed her skirt and pulled her between his knees. "I know what the weather did, but I don't know what I did."

He had her at eye level, but she still managed to find something to scrutinize in the sod bricks behind him. "You acted like you were doing sentry duty."

Perdition. "Did I hurt you this time?"

"No. As soon as you saw me, you came back to yourself."

"Maybe I've been having spells all along and there's been no one here to say." He drew her close.

"We've still got the smaller pail."

He leaned back enough that she had to face him. "Susannah, I'm sorry."

"You don't think I'm to blame for the incident with the banker, do you?" She swallowed hard. "I don't think you're to blame for the War."

Jesse grinned. His wife had expressed an opinion. While looking him in the eye. Reckon that might be counted as something of a miracle.

The storm howled through the night. In Detroit, the house had creaked in the wind, shutters banged, branches screeched against the roof. Here in Dakota, the sod house held solid, with only the clanking of the stovepipe to wake Susannah. She slid out of bed, tossed another log on the coals, and plunged back under the covers.

The rope frame of the bed needed tightening, she told herself. She wasn't quite ready to admit she liked sleeping with a six-foot bed warmer. Jesse rolled over, pulling her close. The stovepipe didn't wake her again.

In the morning, Jesse stomped out to tend the animals. He returned just as Susannah removed oat scones from the oven.

"How is it?" She couldn't tell if it was still snowing or if the flakes shooting horizontally across the window had fallen yesterday.

"As mean as it sounds. Good thing we've already been to the store." He grinned. "Guess what I found stuck in the brush by the spring? The pail! God's looking out for us."

Susannah had figured they'd never find it. Could God care enough to blow it back to them?

After breakfast, Jesse brought out his hymnbook, Bible, and guitar.

Fixing her eyes on her folded hands, Susannah took a deep breath. He had been so kind, waiting through half of August and all of September for her, yet she hadn't thanked him for his forbearance. "Before we start, I want to say how much I appreciate your patience with regard to my . . . wifely duties."

Jesse stopped tuning and stared at her. "Wifely duties? You mean it's just a *duty* to you?"

"A wife should—"

"Not another *should*. I know what we're going to study this morning." He laid the guitar on the table. "Go sit on the bed and get comfortable. This could take awhile."

"Pardon me?" She'd hoped for a simple acceptance of her apology. This subject carried enough anxieties without Jesse taking it on another tangent.

"Today's lesson is from the Song of Solomon. I suppose you've heard of the guy."

Nervousness added a vibrato to her voice. "Son of David, known for wisdom."

"Very good. And what do you know about his Song of Songs?" He unfastened her shoes, dropping them off the side of the bed.

"Not much." Truth be told, she'd only read a few verses. It seemed too fleshly, maybe even naughty, to be included in the Bible. Figuring she must be misinterpreting it, she moved on to the equally incomprehensible but less sensual prophets. "Some say it's an allegory of Christ and the church."

Jesse snorted. "Is that what my brother teaches? Let's see if we get something else out of it." He placed the open book in her lap and draped an arm over her shoulders. "Aloud, please, Mrs. Mason."

"'Let him kiss me with the kisses of his mouth—'" Her cheeks burned.

121

"Go on."

"'For thy love is better than wine.'"

Several pages later Susannah closed the Bible, placing it on the shelf. Without meeting his eye, she reached up and unbuttoned Jesse's shirt.

He smiled. "My hot-blooded woman."

Susannah wrinkled her nose, tickled by the curly hair on her husband's chest. She slid down a couple of inches to his belly, where his hair lay flat, mink brown against his ivory skin. Her body stretched across his, as liquid and lazy as the Sheyenne River. "What are you doing to me, Jesse Mason?" she murmured.

His hands continued their circuit down her vertebrae, up her ribs, his fingers pulsing in the motion she recognized as guitar playing. "Rubbing your back. Can't you tell?"

"No, I mean, I feel so . . ."

"Soft, like Jake's ears."

Susannah smiled, hearing the playfulness in his voice. "Are you comparing me to a dog?"

He scratched behind her ears, slowing the motion to massage her scalp. "Maybe you should've married Robert Burns. 'My love is like a red, red rose.'" Jesse pulled her up within kissing range.

"He passed away."

"Ah. Wouldn't be quite so much fun." He nudged her forehead with his chin, trying to turn her face to his. "And you *are* having fun."

If she didn't look at him, perhaps she could maintain this state of relaxation a little longer. She nestled her cheek into the curve of his shoulder and completed the quote. "'My love is like a melody, sweetly played in tune.'"

Chapter 15

Lord, did You have this much fun
making the universe?

F or all its noise, the storm left behind only an inch of snow.
Monday's sun brought melting and the Volds.

"Looks like you make it through the fire about as well as we did." Ivar vaulted off his wagon.

"Thanks to Susannah." Jesse reached for baby Sara. "C'mon in. Coffee's hot."

Susannah had been afraid she wouldn't see her friend for six months. She hurried forward, then stopped. Did Norwegians hug? Susannah backed off and squeezed Marta's hand.

Jesse told a highly embellished story of Susannah saving the homestead, complete with an exhibit of her sore palms. Susannah fidgeted and blushed. How was she supposed to respond to his accolades? Father had never bragged about, praised, or even commented on anything Mother did.

"Half I not said you need a wife? Was I not right?"

"She's the answer to my prayers." Jesse winked.

"Your brother knew you need smart woman to keep your *rumpe* from trouble." As he tipped his head to drain his mug, Ivar noticed the package on the shelf. "Should half known you wouldn't buy enough plaster for the whole house, Jesse Tightfist."

"We won't be living here much longer; no sense wasting green-backs to fix it up."

"Marta brought her plastering tools."

After a discussion on the best use of the small amount, Jesse chose the upper half of the east wall. The men moved the table against the door. Marta directed Susannah in adding water to the powder and mixing it to a pasty consistency. Susannah bit her lip. She had wanted to do this on her own, to make her contribution to the home. But she was grateful for Marta's help.

"We can still reach the coffee." Ivar refilled his mug.

Jesse grabbed a stack of newspapers and sat crosswise on the bed, leaning against the west wall. "Keep drinking that stuff and you'll be needing to reach the outhouse."

"Work fast, girls."

Marta paused in the wetting of the wall and flicked her damp paintbrush at Ivar.

"She says with plaster, fast is the only speed." Ivar joined Jesse, fencing the baby with their legs.

"Hey, good news for a change. Congress says we can file on another section if we plant trees." Jesse read and Ivar translated a month's worth of the *Bismarck Tribune, Fargo Express*, and *Minnesota Pioneer*. Susannah listened while she troweled.

The Dakota papers were weeklies of four pages each. A farmer near Fargo harvested corn twelve feet high. Apparently corn grew in these dry conditions. Would Jesse mind if she planted a few rows? Construction had begun on a schoolhouse and a Methodist church in Moorhead, just across the river from Fargo. How long before civilization reached Worthington?

The front page of the St. Paul paper carried stories from New York City, Washington DC, and Europe. Fire had destroyed parts of Chicago and Philadelphia. Although their prairie fire probably covered more acres, all it did was scorch forage for a half dozen cattle—not important enough to be considered news.

Stories of big business, politics, and royalty seemed as far away as the back side of the moon. Nothing happening in the States could affect this insignificant scattering of dirt houses, far from any path, beaten or unbeaten. Not even reports of the Modoc War alarmed Susannah; she had seen no Indians here, hostile or friendly.

Jesse folded the last issue. Marta, smoothing the topcoat from rafters to chair rail level, asked a question. Ivar translated.

"*Ja.* We missed your lesson yesterday. What did you talk about?"

"Song of Solomon."

Susannah concentrated on cleaning the trowel. Just this once, could the man *not* say what was on his mind?

Ivar interpreted for Marta, the tone of his voice indicating he had a good idea the direction Jesse had taken the lesson. "Sorry we missed it."

"I'm not." Jesse bounded off the bed and stretched on a rafter, looking terribly pleased with himself.

"Here, half your wife take Sara while we move the table back. She needs to get in practice."

Susannah held her arms rigid as Jesse handed her the squirming infant. Sara wiggled, off balance, top heavy. Any moment she might sense Susannah's inexperience and bawl.

"Relax," Jesse whispered. He adjusted her hold to support the child's head.

Ivar stepped back from the table he moved without Jesse's help. "Well, Marta and I will go. You two want to do more Bible study, or is it baby study?"

Jesse looped his neighbor's scarf around his neck, pretending to strangle him. "Next Sunday, your place."

Ivar raised a bushy eyebrow. "If you don't show, I'll know where to find you."

Although humid, vinegary air filled the soddy, the plaster coating worked the way Susannah hoped, multiplying the evening sun and kerosene light.

Jesse returned from milking and nuzzled Susannah's neck to warm his face.

"You're still shaving."

"I'm off on another exploration. Marco Polo to China."

"Marco Polo was clean-shaven?"

He lifted her hand to his lips and kissed each fingertip before answering. "Marco who?" He went back over her fingers again with his tongue. "Which felt better, dry or wet?"

He expected her not only to tolerate his caresses but to talk about the experience too. Her knees trembled.

"Best try again. This time, shut your eyes so you can concentrate."

His lips brushed the ends of her fingers, thumb to pinkie, then back again, this time with a gentle nibbling. Her mind went blank. On the third pass, his tongue flicked each pad. The experience sent her insides into a frenzy.

He steadied her and asked, "Wet or dry?"

Her voice responded before her mind could engage. "Both."

Toward dawn the wind shifted, enveloping the prairie in fog. On their woodcutting trip, the sun broke through, revealing an iridescent fairyland. Glittering white crystals furred every blade of grass and each branch in the plum and chokecherry thicket. Susannah expected an enchanted castle with wizards, elves, and unicorns to materialize on the plains. Overhead, thousands of migrating waterfowl honked and flapped their way south with a singularity of purpose. Best of all, the cold put an end to the torment of mosquitoes and flies.

All week the firewood stacks grew until they completely covered the front and sides of the soddy. Friday, winter returned with another blizzard.

Susannah yawned. "All this darkness makes me feel like hibernating."

"Good idea. Go climb in bed and I'll fix you some cocoa." Jesse adjusted the damper on the stovepipe.

"But I should start the mending—"

"You've got all winter. Go on."

The absence of light at the windows gave no clue to the hour. Susannah inhaled the scent of roast goose.

"Must be working you too hard," Jesse said from the stove. "You've been sleeping like Rip Van Winkle. Ready for supper?"

"Supper? I'm sorry. I didn't get anything done today. And I slept through your cocoa." She splashed her face with ice-cold water from the ewer. "I don't usually take naps. Maybe the change of weather tired me."

Fatigue caught up with her again during Jesse's nightly music session. Susannah struggled to keep her eyes open long enough to knit a stocking.

"You're not going to finish that tonight."

"I've only got a few more rows."

Jesse put away his guitar, then undid Susannah's braid. "My first horse, a bay mare, was this same color. Of course, you're a lot softer."

"Bet she couldn't knit."

"No, but she did like to be curried." He ran the brush through her hair.

Susannah closed her eyes. Warm finger strokes alternated with skimming bristles. Deep inside, a knot loosened in her tightly knit self. With each pass of the brush she unwound, slowly at first, stitch by stitch, then rapidly until her body vibrated with the raveling. Without thinking she said, "I suppose this means you're interested in a little horsing around?"

Jesse's voice rose with surprise and delight. "Giddyup."

By morning the storm subsided, but Susannah's stomach worsened. Queasiness ripened into nausea as she fried the side pork. She opened the door a crack and gulped arctic air to settle her insides, but the sizzle of the eggs brought on the first spasm. She bolted for the corner, spattering the curtain as she wrenched it aside. She knelt on the dirt floor, chamber pot between her knees, as her stomach wrung itself out.

Don't let Jesse see me.

Sweat dripped from her forehead. Another convulsion rolled up her gut to her throat. She braced against the sod wall, the cold invading her body. The curtain pulled back, bringing welcome fresh air and an unwelcome man. "Go away. Please."

"Here, lean against me." He shifted her away from the cold wall, and she slumped against him. "Why didn't you say you had the pukes? And don't you dare apologize." He dried her face with his bandanna. "Maybe it's seasoning fever."

"Your water never bothered me before. Uh-oh. Go. Quick. Please."

He held her head through the next surge. "You don't seem feverish.

You ought to be pretty well cleaned out by now." He brought her water and had her spit in the pot. "Hey, you didn't bring up much. I knew some guys in the army who could—" He paused. "Well, best skip that story and put you to bed. The objective here is to gain weight so you'll be warm for the winter, remember? You rest."

He lifted her, maneuvering slowly, then set her down on the bed and loosened her dress. "Didn't get any on you. You'll be all right while I go spill out this pot. See if you can sleep it off." He tucked the covers around her, stroking her cheek.

Susannah closed her eyes. She couldn't remember the last time she had been sick to her stomach.

Oh yes, she could . . .

One June day when Susannah was four, she had gotten into the neighbor's strawberry patch. Mother sent her to bed early, as punishment more than for illness. Susannah climbed out of bed, pulled to the window by sounds of children. She parted the lace drapery and looked into the yard next door.

The family played, enjoying the extended evening of summer solstice. The father patted his children's shoulders, ruffled their hair, gave rides on his back. He swung the girls in a circle when he tagged them. He tossed the littlest one overhead. Words of caution drifted from the back porch steps where the mother sat, admiring the fireflies her children captured.

Gravel crunched below, signaling the arrival of Susannah's father. The roof of the kitchen cut off her view of the carriage house. Susannah listened, visualizing him unharnessing the gelding, currying him, and feeding him a measure of oats. Father would bring his veterinary bag into the office to replenish his supplies, then come upstairs to say good night.

The footsteps on the stairs were not Father's.

"What are you doing out of bed, young lady? It's an hour past your bedtime." Mother slammed the window, cutting off fresh air and the sound of laughter from next door.

Susannah scrambled back under the sheets.

The little girl forestalled sleep as long as she could, but her father did not come.

Light reflecting off the snow outside awoke Susannah. Jesse sat on the edge of the bed, his hair a ragged nimbus of copper. She had the uncomfortable feeling he had been watching her for some time. His smile widened into a grin.

"You look like a Cheshire cat."

"Welcome to Wonderland, Alice. Have a cracker."

Susannah rolled upright. "Since when are crackers the cure for the grippe?"

"It's not the flu." Jesse could contain himself no longer. He tossed the almanac in the air. "We're going to have a baby!"

"What? A baby?"

Jesse plopped on the bed and scooped her into his lap. "Sleeping a lot, cranky stomach, no poorlies this month. All points to the same thing: hit the bull's-eye on the first shot! Hallelujah!"

Jesse danced a jig around the room and bumped his head on a rafter.

"How did you know?"

"A large family is a schoolhouse for life. Eat up, Ma." He plopped down.

Susannah nibbled a corner of the cracker. "You look awfully proud of yourself."

"And why not? What names do you like?" He grabbed her

hands and closed his eyes. "Dear Lord, grant us a good crop next year so our baby can grow up in a real house."

"Jesse," she whispered. "You can't just ask God for things like that."

"And thank You for our baby."

"Besides, Ivar and Marta are raising Sara in their soddy. She's fine."

"And, Jesus, watch over Susannah, keep her healthy. Help us become the parents You want us to be. In Your name, amen."

"You pray like you know God personally."

"No putting on airs for Someone who knows me inside out."

Susannah leaned against the headboard and finished the cracker. "How did you get to know Him so well? You didn't attend seminary."

"I spend time with Him, talking, listening. Like getting to know you."

Her hands clenched involuntarily, and Jesse noticed. He enclosed her fists in his, stroking her palms with his thumbs. He uncurled her fingers one by one and traced the red marks left by the bucket handle. "I wonder if you open up to God any better than you open up to me." Jesse's look probed her soul. Susannah wanted to hide herself under the covers, except he sat on them. "If I can figure out that you're mad at God, don't you think He knows it too?"

She turned sideways, tilting her head so Jesse couldn't see her face. "I'm not mad at God."

"Maybe *mad* isn't the right word. Disappointed, let down." He brushed her hair behind her ear. "When my brother died, I spit nails at God. How dare He take away the brain, the leader of the family? That made me the oldest. I did my best to show God what a mistake He'd made." He shook his head, the muscles tight in his jaw. "As many times as I'd heard about Jonah and the whale, you'd think I'd know better. God can find us anywhere."

"Even in Dakota Territory?"

His expression softened. "Go ahead and be mad at God, Susannah. He's big enough to take it. Just don't turn your back on Him, don't cut Him out of your life."

Susannah swallowed down a different sort of nausea. She might as well admit it; Jesse saw right through her. "You wrote your brother for a Christian wife and all you got is a spiritual mouse."

"How much faith does a spiritual mouse have? Mustard seed size?" When he kissed her palms, the beginnings of a beard tickled her. He reached for his boots.

"Where are you going?"

"Back to the shed. I've got a cradle to build."

"You've got"—Susannah counted—"eight months. Until June."

He rooted under the bed for his toolbox. "Enough time to do a real fine job. No reason for you to get out of bed."

Susannah tied her apron behind her back. "Since I'm not sick, I may as well get some work done."

"Loosen your waistbands! Knit booties! And little hats!" He pulled her into his arms for a big kiss.

"Are you going to act like this the whole time?"

He grinned. "Nope. I'll probably get worse."

"That's what I'm afraid of." She returned his smile and pushed him out the door. Her hands settled on her abdomen. A baby. She was having a baby!

Chapter 16

Our baby . . .

S usannah rinsed Ma Ox's udder with warm water, then scooted the stool close and began the rolling motion with her fingers. The milk squirted into the bucket with a satisfying rattle. This breed wasn't known for high production, just enough for two people. More importantly, this cow milked easily without kicking, butting, or sidestepping.

"Hey, you're pretty good at that." Jesse shoveled manure out of the bull's stall.

"Father always owned a cow. He had seen too many diseased cattle in commercial dairies."

He paused, leaning on the long handle of the shovel. "What do you think about Mormons?"

His mercurial thought processes continued to unnerve her. "Are you considering polygamy?"

"Can't afford another train ticket."

"What?" Susannah leaned back. He widened his eyes, then grinned. Ah, teasing again. She shot a squirt of milk toward his boot.

He stepped out of range. "I understand they baptize on behalf of their ancestors. Where do you stand on baptism?"

"What do you mean?"

133

"All the controversies: infant or adult, immersion or sprinkling. We're starting a family. Got to figure this out."

"Whatever you decide is fine."

"I'm asking your *opinion*." The shovel clanked on the wheelbarrow.

Susannah rested her forehead against the warm flank of the ox. Except for the domestic sphere of menus, clothing, and household furnishings, women weren't supposed to have opinions, much less express them. "I suppose it depends on when a minister comes through and what he believes."

"We could do it ourselves, like our wedding, and have Matt send the certificate. Should I say, 'In Jesus' name,' or 'In the name of the Father, Son, and Holy Spirit'?"

"Whatever you think is best." Susannah grabbed the milking pail and hurried out into the snowy day.

After the milk had been skimmed and the cream poured into the churn, Jesse caught up with her. He slid onto the trunk, trapping her in the corner. While she pumped the dasher in the stone crock, Jesse launched into a discourse on mankind's efforts to communicate with God, including Mormons and speaking in tongues. When Susannah responded noncommittally, he switched sides, elucidating the opposing viewpoint. "Come on, argue with me." He tickled Susannah's neck with the end of her braid.

"Don't you have work to do?"

He dragged himself back to the woodpile, and Jake sneaked in to check for food.

"What do you think, Jake?" Susannah pressed the butter into its mold. "A woman ought to be the light of the home, a beacon of morality for her husband and children. But how can she guide them if her mind is a blank?"

She sat, and Jake put his head on her knee.

"A wife is supposed to support her husband's opinions, but after

Father's funeral, when Reverend Mason told me to 'count it all joy,' Ellen argued with him. Actually argued with her husband! She said if any situation warrants mourning, it would be the death of a loved one. The Reverend said faith requires a higher level of response than wallowing in anguish. Then Ellen reminded him Jesus cried at Lazarus's funeral."

Susannah found Jake's itchy spot, and the dog's back leg encouraged her efforts. "Could Jesse be right, that it's permissible to discuss issues with one's husband? I wonder."

The dog sniffed her lap and belly.

"No, there's nothing in my apron. Can you smell the baby already? Do you think I'll be a good mother?" Susannah contrasted her mother's distance and disapproval with Ellen's joy and affection. "I hope I'll be like Ellen."

Jake licked her hand and wagged his tail.

"Yes, Ellen gives lots of kisses and hugs." Susannah wrapped her arms around the dog. "And this baby will get plenty from Jesse. He's so full of love. Is it the way he was raised, or does it come from God? And do you think he could love me?"

That evening Jesse interrupted his guitar playing with a loud chord. "I've got it: Darwin!"

Susannah dropped a stitch. "You want to name your baby Darwin?"

He blinked, then burst out laughing. "No! Wouldn't saddle a kid of mine with a moniker like that. I'm asking if you've read *Origin of the Species.*"

Yes, she had read Darwin's treatise. She had been the only girl in her school to study such a controversial work. Her classmates made it known she was lacking in feminine and Christian virtue, and her mother was furious. She suspected Father had been secretly proud of her, but he only smiled and refused to discuss it when she approached him with the book.

Jesse leaned forward patiently, attentively waiting for her answer. He could hardly fault her for something she did before they married. "Yes, I've read it."

"No ducking this time. Tell me where you stand."

Susannah mentally reviewed the stacks of scientific papers in her father's office, the discussions of provident design, lack of intermediate fossil records, geologic imperative for biologic change, natural selection, common ancestors. "Perhaps the best argument against Darwin is found in mathematics: the Law of Probability."

"I'm getting saddle sore," Jesse said between songs the next night. "Don't suppose you could make a cushion for this trunk."

Susannah nodded. "Certainly. Could you please stand for a moment so I can get out my notions box?" She unfurled one of his shirts with half the buttons missing.

"I'll get it." Laying his guitar on the table, he raised the lid. "No wonder this thing is so heavy. It's full of books."

"Medical texts. Father hoped I'd become a physician, but the only doctoring I ever did was for Mother."

Jesse studied her a long moment, his eyes soft. "Guess you did an A-1 job taking care of her."

Susannah remembered the look of reproach in her mother's eyes, asking why her daughter didn't do something: ease her pain, restore her speech, or the unthinkable, end her suffering. If Jesse had known her then, seen how roughly she handled her mother, heard her snappish responses during the endless nights of interrupted sleep, he wouldn't think so highly of her.

He handed her a tin clicking with buttons. "You'd have made a fine doctor. Why didn't you start school after they died?"

Susannah set her mending in her lap. Jesse thought she was smart enough to be a doctor. Amazing. "It seems like a frustrating profession. There's so little you can do to help, beyond sitting up with someone too restless to die."

"Yeah. I had enough of that in the War." Jesse held up a book. "*The Horse and His Diseases* by John E. Potter. Animal doctor, that's you. I'll never forget my little Susannah staring down that burly driver from the threshing crew, all to make four horses more comfortable. You should have gone to veterinary school."

She glanced at him in surprise. No one, not even her father, had ever expressed this much faith in her abilities. "I would have liked to, but the closest veterinary school is in Ontario, and of course, they don't take women."

"Ontario? Your pa trained in Canada?"

"No, that school has only been open ten years or so. Father trained in Edinburgh, before he and Mother emigrated."

"Medical schools take women. Why not vet schools?"

"Look at the trouble I had with the calves. Women aren't strong enough."

"You're smart enough. Seems what you know is more important than the size of your muscles." Jesse rooted in the trunk some more and came up with a knapsack stenciled "Michigan Cavalry." "Your pa's kit." He pulled out a surgical knife, needles and suture thread, a pair of scissors, and several corked bottles. The heavier farrier tools—hoof knives, chisels, and pincers— were rolled in a pouch made from an old pair of denim pants. "He traveled light."

"No fleams or patent medicines. He didn't believe in bleeding, purging, or dosing."

"Bicarbonate of Potash, Black Antimony, Blue Vitriol," he read from the labeled bottles. "Can't say half these names. You know what this stuff does? Ah, here's one I recognize: ginger."

She repacked the bag. "Father was experimenting with herbal remedies in animal practice."

"Hey, what's this?" Jesse pulled a violin case from the trunk. "You've been holding out on me!"

"It's Father's. I don't play well. Ellen packed it."

Holding the instrument on his lap, he tuned it. "Good, full sound. What do you like to play? Did you bring any music with you? Can you play by ear?"

"Jesse, I don't play well," she repeated. He handed her the violin and rosined her bow. "We could try a Christmas carol."

They played "Hark! the Herald Angels Sing" and "O Come, All Ye Faithful," as snowflakes hissed on the stovepipe.

"You're doing great! How about 'Silent Night'?"

Susannah held out her left hand. "It's been so long . . ."

Jesse kissed her reddened fingertips. "So, what do these medical books say about babies?"

"Do you have a specific question?"

"Well . . ." He raised an eyebrow and glanced at the bed. "Is it all right for us to—"

"You know doctors. Some say yes, some say no." Susannah returned the violin to its case. "There's no scientific evidence either way."

"Then"—he grinned—"I'd say let's call it a night!"

"It's not polite to stare. Please stop."

"Never." Jesse sat in his usual position on the trunk, chin in palm, watching her flip pancakes in the iron skillet.

"Then let's have it out right now." Plopping onto the stool,

Susannah returned his stare. Sunlight echoed off the snow outside and the newly plastered wall, lighting the green and gold sparks in his brown eyes.

"Your pancakes are burning, Mrs. Mason," he said without blinking.

"That's your breakfast, Mr. Mason."

Lunging across the table, Jesse kissed her on the nose. "Ha! You blinked!"

"No fair." Susannah loaded his plate, burnt side up.

"Fair or foul, I must have my morning kiss." He scooped butter onto the stack. "Just enough snow for tracking. Not too cold."

Susannah nodded. "Fresh meat would taste good."

"Your appetite's back. Mind if I go hunting?"

She shook her head and tried to hide her relief. At last she'd have some privacy.

Susannah sorted through the mending pile, choosing Jesse's woolen pants. That man. Whenever he came near, her insides fluttered like cottonwood leaves in a breeze. The way he joked and played made her feel like a child.

A child. Susannah rested her hand on her abdomen. She'd been so awkward when she held Ivar and Marta's baby. Would she feel more confident with her own? No sense worrying over that. Babies come regardless of their mother's lack of ability.

Susannah slipped a finger inside her waistband. Her skirts were still loose, but her basques fit tighter. She sensed a heaviness in her body, as if being with child anchored her to Dakota.

Enough woolgathering. If she kept daydreaming, she'd be totally brainless by the time the baby arrived.

As she turned the pants inside out to locate the split seam,

Susannah's mind strayed back to Jesse. He would be a good father, patient and affectionate. No matter how trivial a child's concerns, Jesse would give him his full attention. Perhaps his war memories would stop troubling him, with the baby to focus on. And what a relief it would be to share the limelight with the baby.

It was dusk already and no Jesse. Putting aside the mending, Susannah hefted two buckets of melted snow from the stove and carried them to the stable.

When she raised the first bucket to the water trough, an odd twinge pulled in the small of her back, like a violin string plucked and tightened at the same time. The second bucket tweaked the muscles again. She leaned against the sod wall until the tension eased.

She sank onto the milking stool. The cow lowed and shied away from her cold fingers. "Easy there, Ma Ox. I'm not up to chasing you tonight." The animal settled. Susannah blinked back her fatigue. She wouldn't wait for Jesse; she'd go to bed as soon as she finished.

She pushed up from the low stool and felt the stable tilt and darken. Milk sloshed over her skirt. Susannah steadied herself against the cow and waited until the dizziness passed. Her fingers found the pulse next to her windpipe: rapid but regular. She glanced around the stable. The oxen had enough hay. Mucking could wait, but eggs should be collected before they froze and cracked. One hand on her back, she made a sweep of the nesting boxes. "Three. Good job, ladies."

She stepped into the clear night, searching the line where the stars stopped. No Jesse. No barking Jake. Frosted clouds of her breath vanished in the wind, cold air scoured her throat. Jesse would need a hot meal. She reached to hang the lantern from the end of the roof, and a sharp pain ripped through her lower abdomen.

The baby! No!

Susannah set the milk pail in the snowbank and pulled herself toward the door. The pain clawed at her insides. Just a few more steps and she could lie down. But a black roaring tunnel engulfed her and she dropped to the snow.

The baby . . .

Chapter 17

Please, God, I can't lose her now . . .

S usannah slid, faster and faster, deep into an icy tunnel. Opposing currents rushed at her like a whirlpool, twisting her body in two. A hot blade sliced between her hips. She couldn't breathe. Something soft brushed her cheek.

A flash of maroon and hunter green—the ceiling of the parlor in Detroit. Rough hands grabbed her shoulders and pinned her to the carpet.

Let me go!

She flung herself to one side. A knee punched into her stomach and forced her onto her back. *Leave me alone! You can have the money!*

A hand twisted her apron strings around her neck. The parlor faded to black.

Then from far away, someone else yelled, a shriek of pure rage. A woman. Ellen. The weight lifted from Susannah's stomach; she gasped in a breath. Pain flamed through her, and darkness descended once more.

Then . . . she was in a bed, her body weighted, too heavy to move. Water splashed. Large hands, too large to be her friend's, lifted each leg.

"I'm not sure she's up to—"

"I assure you, with the dose of laudanum she's had, she'll be insensible to the examination. I must determine the extent of her injuries."

"She was fully clothed—"

"Mrs. Mason, we don't want any surprises, say nine months from now, do we? You haven't changed her clothes or bathed her?"

"No. We sent for you immediately."

Cold air prickled her skin as the violation continued. Susannah tried to scream, but no sound came out.

"No blood. Fortunately, Mrs. Mason, you were successful in preventing further damage."

Another man called her name. His voice . . . she couldn't remember. He pleaded, begged, encouraged. She attempted to answer, but the words stuck, thick and useless, in her head.

Help me, please . . .

There was no response. She slid down the tunnel, away, into the silence.

Silver light. Cold dawn. Susannah felt as if she'd been kicked in the stomach by a horse. Her fingers and toes ached with cold. Shivers racked her body. She curled into a ball, finding no warmth in the sheets. Her hand pressed against her empty abdomen.

The baby . . . gone.

Jesse would be angry. He wanted a child so much. Her fingers slid lower. Dry clothes. He'd cleaned her. She couldn't even take care of herself, much less pull her own weight. She had to be strong, to show him—

The door scraped the icy threshold. Susannah turned, sending the room into a jerky orbit. Jesse came into focus. His shoulders drooped, his skin gray, his eyebrows drawn together. He glanced up, meeting her gaze. The grim set of his mouth widened into a smile. His fatigue dropped off with his coat and gloves.

"You're awake. Sweet Susannah, you sure had me worried."

Her tongue stuck to the roof of her mouth, making her words come out garbled. "I lost your baby."

His eyes were haunted and red-rimmed. He still wore his hunting clothes. Had he slept at all? "Afraid I'd lost you too. You're white as the sheets." He lowered himself to the bed and brushed the hair from her face.

"I'm so sorry."

"No, *I'm* sorry. I should have never left you alone. Got a buck and had to rig a travois to drag it back. Made me late. Jake ran on ahead. I knew something was wrong by his bark." He shuddered, covering his face, his voice straining at the words. "So much blood. More than the deer, more than guys shot through with cannon-balls. I couldn't wake you up. Even your medical books didn't say what to do."

"There isn't any-anything you could have d-done." A lady, Mother always said, must be calm. A lady must not get carried away by futile sentiment. "Miscarriage isn't that un-uncommon, especially with first b-babies. There's lots of sup-superstitions, but no one really knows why it h-happens."

Jesse wiped his tears with the heel of his hand. "You're freezing. Stay here." He tucked the covers under her chin, then hustled around the stove.

Men didn't cry—not when their sons went to war, not at funerals, not even when the president was assassinated. But Ellen argued that Jesus cried, so maybe Christians were allowed. Even Jesse? Especially Jesse with the loss of his child.

"Susannah." He held the bowl like an offering plate, its steam rapidly dissipating in the cold room.

She pushed upright against the headboard, but the edges of her vision grayed. "Maybe later." She sank back to the pillows.

"No. Now." He slid in beside her and cradled her head in the crook of his elbow. She opened her mouth to protest, and he spooned in hot cereal. "Most times I'm more than ready to listen to you, but not today. Get your strength back and then we'll talk." Her shivering vibrated his arm. She forced a swallow. "Grandma said oatmeal gives heat to the body. 'Course us kids thought oatmeal was just a reason to get out the maple syrup."

His voice faded. "Susannah? C'mon now, stay awake. This isn't my most interesting story, but it's all my tired head can think of right now. Wish we had some syrup. Wonder if my sister would send some. Probably not. She was always the last to the table in the morning. The good stuff would all be gone by the time she showed up." He held a mug to her lips. "Cocoa? Take a sip. Two more bites. Good girl."

Despite warm food and piles of quilts and blankets, Susannah continued to shiver. Jesse wrapped her wool scarf around her head and spread her cape on the bed. He threw two more logs into the stove. He heated the new sadiron, rolled it in an empty flour sack, and set it by her feet. Studying her, he rubbed his stubbly new beard. "Bootless," he muttered, referring to the ineffectiveness of his efforts. "Bootless." He shifted his gaze to his footwear. In seconds he stripped to his long underwear, slid between the sheets, and curled around her.

She had lost enough blood to make her light-headed, but she was coherent enough to realize Jesse had saved her life. "Thank you for taking such good care of me."

"I love you."

Love? *Love . . .*

Her shivering subsided and she slept.

Susannah rolled over and opened her eyes. Jesse stood at the stove, slicing carrots into the Dutch oven. Late afternoon sun glowed in his hair like a copper halo.

"Smells good. Maybe next year you could cook and I'll work on the threshing machine."

A slow smile widened his mouth. "Crew'd love that."

A sharp bark from the other side of the door interrupted him. Jesse let the dog in with a swirl of snow. Jake raced to the bed. Susannah reached to pet him. He licked her hand.

"I'm not the only one worried about you." Jesse set a tin plate of meat scraps on the floor. Jake gulped his dinner, sniffed Susannah again, then vanished into the snowy dusk.

"I'm not that hungry," Susannah objected when Jesse ladled up a large bowl of stew.

"Got to build you up, get the color back in those pretty cheeks of yours."

"Well, at least I can sit without fainting." Susannah leaned against the headboard.

"Shucks. I was looking forward to feeding you again. Good practice for when I become a pa." Susannah turned away to hide her tears, and Jesse groaned. "I'm sorry."

"I want to be strong, but—" She sniffled.

Sitting beside her, Jesse pulled her head to his chest. "God gave us tears for a reason, Susannah. Go ahead, let out all your sad so you can start to mend." His voice held an odd note of relief. He seemed almost pleased about her crying.

She tried to swallow the lump in her throat. "How can you miss someone you never knew?"

"I don't know, but I feel it too. Like a hole in my heart." His large hand stroked the top of her head down to her back. "Boy or girl, do you suppose? Would have been a year younger than Ivar and Marta's baby. They could have played together. Now he's getting fitted for angel wings."

"More likely taking his first heavenly harp lesson, seeing as how he's your child."

"Eat your dinner, silly girl," he said. And for the first time in days, he smiled.

After cleaning up, Jesse once again shed his boots and climbed into bed. "Ecclesiastes is right."

"Pardon me?" Susannah asked from her sleepy haze.

"Chapter 4, verse 11." He pulled her back against his chest, matching the bend of her legs with his. "'If two lie together, they have heat.'"

The sun shone weakly through the frosted panes, providing a glimmer of light but no warmth. Grains of snow sifted through unseen chinks, forming drifts across the quilt, in the corners, and along the window frames. Another lumberjack-sized meal burbled fragrantly on the stove. Jesse worked through a four-bar phrase on his guitar.

"What day is today?" Susannah levered herself into sitting.

"Thursday. Didn't mean to wake you."

"Oh no! I slept right through your birthday!" One step from the bed, her legs gave out.

"Whoa! Who said you were allowed to get up?" He scooped her off the floor and bundled her back to bed.

"But—" She had planned to surprise him with his favorite dessert, apple pie.

"Just get better, back to your usual lively self. You're all I want for my birthday, this year and all the years to come." He leaned over to rub noses with her, his growing beard tickling her cheeks. "No sad faces."

"You haven't had anyone here to fuss over you, and now—"

"With a family the size of ours, no one ever fussed over me." He dismissed the idea with a swipe of his long hand.

"You didn't celebrate birthdays?"

"Sure. If it was your day, you got served first. Every night at dinner, Ma would look around the table at the ten of us and whatever cousins were visiting and try to remember whose turn it was. We'd all point at the birthday kid—soon as he got his, we'd get ours."

Our baby won't have a birthday, she thought, then pushed the thought away. She had to stop crying and get better. "What else?"

"We'd sing 'For He's a Jolly Good Fellow' and get lots of hugs. How 'bout you Underhills?"

"Mother made spice cake and served it on her best plates. She decorated the table with violets." Susannah received gifts too: hair ribbons, books, watercolors. But she didn't mention it. Maybe Jesse's family couldn't afford presents.

"Good thing you were born in the spring." He patted the covers. "You'll be ready to make a birthday cake by December 25."

"Who has a birthday in December?"

He arched an eyebrow at her. "Whose birth do we celebrate at Christmas?"

"Oh." She felt a flush creep up her neck. "Yes. Of course."

Jesse kissed her forehead. "No more bolting out of bed, now. I'll sing you a lullaby. And, Susannah?" His brows drew together and he looked away, his gaze passing over the stove, the shelves, and the table before coming to rest on his shoes. His jaw clenched. "Never mind. We'll talk when you're better."

"Much as I like spending time with you in bed," Jesse said, "it sure is great to see you up, back to spoiling me rotten." He bit into a Christmas cookie.

Susannah decorated the gingerbread men with raisins. Whatever he'd been worried about had been forgotten, and she'd do her best to keep it that way. "You're overdue for some pampering. I've been more of a burden than a help to you these past few weeks."

"Never a burden, only a joy." He wrapped an arm across her shoulders. "So, what's with all the baking?"

"I always make extra cookies for—" Susannah paused. "I guess we won't have any carolers, any company."

"It's all right. You know I'll eat everything, and you could use the extra food." Jesse's hands circled her waist. He reached over her shoulder for a pan, frowning at his reflection in its shiny surface. "Susannah, don't scrub the tinware. It just gets sooty again. It's not like Mrs. Child is going to show up to judge your housework. Save your energy. And sit for your baking." He maneuvered her to the stool.

Susannah's thoughts circled the possibilities. "What if you replaced the wagon wheels with runners?"

"Sure, a sleigh would be great fun. Matched pair of horses, bells. I'd take you for a long visit with Mr. and Mrs. Rose."

The talkative shopkeepers? Susannah groaned. "Who needs a sleigh? We're fine right here."

Christmas morning dawned clear, a definite improvement over the murky overcast of December in Detroit. Susannah popped the corn the Volds had given them, strung it, and hung the strings from the rafters. She longed for a Christmas tree but didn't mention it. The nearest pine might be hundreds of miles away, and there was no room in the soddy anyway. After a breakfast of cinnamon pancakes, baked apples, and sausage, Jesse read the story of the first Christmas from the gospel of Luke.

When he got to the part about Mary giving birth to Jesus, Susannah struggled to maintain control. *No tears on Christmas.*

From her trunk, Susannah brought out three packages wrapped in brown paper.

"All this?" Jesse leaned over and whispered to the dog curled under the table, "Maybe she *does* like me." He opened the first two: a red woolen stocking cap and a matching scarf. The third package contained one gray knee-length sock, a skein of matching yarn, and a pair of knitting needles.

Susannah explained, "With me getting sick and you spending so much time in the house, I didn't finish the second sock."

Jesse's eyes twinkled. "That's a relief. Figured the first one was a pattern and you expected me to make the second—revenge for me teaching you to play by ear."

"Since it's no longer a surprise, I can work on it now." Susannah reached for the yarn.

"Not so fast." Jesse kissed her hand, then slid a narrow silver band on her ring finger. "Should have given this to you sooner, but I wanted something special for our first Christmas."

Susannah gasped. Jesse, who kept track of every penny, who wouldn't spend more on the soddy than absolutely necessary, who wore his clothes until they fell apart, had bought a wedding ring for her. Tears filled her eyes. "Thank you!"

He grinned. "One more present. Close your eyes."

He rustled and pounded, then said, "Merry Christmas!"

Her mirror stood over the washstand on a hand-carved pine shelf. Jesse had arranged her comb and brush on either side.

"It's wonderful! Merry Christmas to you too." She rose up on tiptoes, aiming for his cheek. He turned and caught her kiss with his lips.

"My sisters fill their houses with doodads and geegaws." He swept the soddy with a grand gesture, almost knocking over the new shelf. "Our house is clean, and there're your trunks, but nothing else of you here. You need to leave a mark, besides the one you've left on my heart."

"I wouldn't want to clutter—"

"Halt right there. None of this practical stuff on Christmas." Pulling on the stocking cap, Jesse posed in front of the mirror. "I am ze famous French fur trader, Pierre Chouteau."

"Joyeux Nöel, Monsieur Chouteau." Susannah curtsied.

"And you are ze first woman I've seen in a decade." He swept her into his arms.

"But, monsieur, I am married." Susannah held up her hand, displaying her new ring.

"You are so beautiful, I cannot restrain myself." He waggled his eyebrows.

"Monsieur!" Susannah giggled as he nuzzled her ear. "Stop! Your beard is ticklish!"

"Stop? What is ze meaning of zat word?"

Susannah dug her fingers into his ribs. Jumping back, Jesse grabbed her wrist. "Ah, I zee you are full of fire."

"Speaking of fire, monsieur, we are nearly out of firewood."

"So, where is zis husband of yours when ze wood bin needs filling?" He kissed the back of her wrist. "Madame, I will embrace you later."

Susannah yanked his hat down. "If you can find me."

"Flat."

Susannah leaned forward, peering at the hymnal. "Where?"

"Not in the music. Your A." Jesse plucked the note.

Susannah drew her bow across her A string.

"Not that A. The one on your E string. It's not the violin, it's you. From the beginning." After three measures, Jesse hit another A. "Now you're sharp! Listen to what you're playing. Double stop it with your open string. Hear that? Again."

Susannah frowned at the passage, willing it to reveal perfect pitch. These unruly high notes, always screeching. Why couldn't composers keep violin music between the lines of the treble staff?

This time Jesse stopped completely. "What's wrong with you? Can't you hear you're sharp?"

Susannah stiffened her back. "Sorry. I don't have frets like some people."

Jesse jabbed his fingers through his hair, nearly impaling her with his elbow. "You don't have frets, but you do have ears. Don't you want to play better?"

"Certainly," she said in the proper British tone her mother used for reprimands. "I must be ready for my Dakota Symphony Orchestra audition next week."

Jesse glared at the rafters. A jaw muscle twitched. He swallowed. "You're right. Music is supposed to be fun. You choose the next song."

"My choice is to listen to you." Susannah tucked the instrument under her arm.

"Think I'd let you off the hook that easily? Come on, 'Soldier's Joy.'"

They ran through the tune three times.

"Much better."

"On that note, I'm done for the night." Susannah cranked the screw on the bow, loosening the horsehair. "You should have told the Reverend to find you a wife at some music school."

"Now that you mention it, I'm thinking of asking him to send a cellist."

"Preferably someone who doesn't mind being yelled at."

"You think I yelled at you?"

"I don't have to think about it." She laid the violin in its case, snapping the latches closed. "I know when I've been yelled at."

"I did not yell at you. You're upset with yourself for not playing well."

"Good night." Susannah shoved the case into the trunk. She yanked the pins out of her hair, changed into her nightgown, and flopped into bed, disappearing with a jerk of the quilts.

She tried, she really did try to please him. But all her efforts fell short. If only she hadn't lost the baby. He hadn't mentioned trying again. Maybe he planned to send her back after all.

Once, a few weeks ago, he said he loved her. And he gave her a ring. She turned it on her finger. Perhaps, in whatever remained of winter, she could become worthy of his love again.

The bed creaked under Jesse's weight. "You awake?"

"No."

"Got it figured out." He uncovered her head, drying her tears with the corner of the flannel sheet. "With my family, no one can hear you unless you talk loud. You're just not used to that, seeing as you're an only child. So I didn't really yell. You can stop being mad."

Susannah opened her eyes. "Why is Jake barking?"

"Don't know." Jesse threw on his greatcoat, slipped his feet into his boots, and grabbed the shotgun. Seconds later he returned and stowed the gun.

"What was it?"

He rolled Susannah up in the quilts and carried her outside.

"Jesse? What is it?"

The answer glowed overhead. The northern lights, a transparent curtain the color of new straw, shimmered across the heavens from east to west. They watched without speaking until the cold drove them back inside.

"I've never seen anything so beautiful," Susannah whispered when Jesse set her back in bed.

"Just for you. To help you forget to be mad at me."

"If you'll forget about the cello player."

"We'll make one of our own." He grinned and pulled her close for a kiss. "Happy New Year."

Chapter 18

Thanks for the light show, Lord.

Susannah glared out the window at the snow-filled draw. The vernal equinox brought low gray clouds across the prairie. As the temperature inched above freezing, icicles dripped from the edge of the roof.

It hardly seemed fair, gaining a few hours of sunlight only to have it blocked by overcast. A headache moved from her forehead to her temples. She had finished Jesse's Christmas sock weeks ago. All his clothes were mended. Her cape had been transformed into a coat. She started a letter to Ellen but set it aside since it could not be mailed for several months. Nothing to do, and nothing to be done about it.

"Just a false spring. We'll get another storm or two before we see the last of this winter." Jesse hefted the 120-pound bag of seed wheat into the soddy.

Susannah clasped her hands around her legs. "There's nothing I can do about the weather."

Jesse set the bag by the table. "Nothing I can do," he repeated slowly. "Heard you say that more than once. That your philosophy of life?"

Susannah lifted a shoulder. "Philosophy? No, it's just the way life is."

Snipping the knot, Jesse pulled the string to open the bag. "There's always something you can do about problems life throws at you."

"For you maybe. You're a man."

"Thanks for noticing." His mouth twitched under his thick mustache. He spread a dipper of seeds on the oilcloth and ran his long fingers through the wheat, picking out weeds and chaff.

"Men hold the reins of power. Women have to wait for men to decide who to court, who to marry, where to live."

He sighed and blew chaff in all directions. "All right. I'll agree men have more choices. But women can turn down a suitor who doesn't please them. Women have some say in a marriage partner."

"I didn't."

Jesse flinched. Before Susannah could utter an apology, he fixed her with a fierce glare. "You may have noticed, around here we share decisions. You have a good head on your shoulders. I'd be a fool to ignore it."

"So you *choose* to share decision making."

He swept culled wheat into a new bag. "What about the power you have from God?"

"The power of prayer?" She'd given up on praying a long time ago. "Lot of good prayer did when my parents died or when your brother was killed."

"Susannah, look at me." His hands, dusty from the wheat, closed around hers. "God hears your every thought, whether you dress it up with 'Thee' and 'Thou' or not. Yes, we stumble through life not understanding much about what's going on, but afterward—" His eyes moved over her face, searching. "I look forward to the time when He'll tell me why sometimes He says yes, other times no, and most often 'Balderdash!'"

The image of a bearded patriarch in pristine white robes booming out slang drew a quick smile from Susannah.

He dipped out another measure. "That's how I know Ellen didn't make a mistake sending you out here."

Susannah nearly fell off the trunk. "What do you mean?"

"I see the doubt in your eyes. You look at me and wonder how Ellen could think of us in the same room, much less married to each other. Was it her usual efficiency, solve two problems with one marriage? No, it's more than that. Mac's right. I prayed for you."

"No, you didn't pray for me. You prayed for a wife."

"And you're the answer."

She dropped her forehead onto her knees so her voice came out muffled. "How can I be? I'm too skinny. I lost your baby. I can't play the violin by ear. I don't debate with you like your family—"

"We're like a two-piece puzzle, Susannah. Different, but fitted together, we're whole."

A yearning grew within her. She *wanted* to be this man's wife, to be the woman he dreamed of. She wanted to love him. And yet it seemed the more she wanted, the more she feared she was incapable of becoming the right woman. "But if the pieces don't fit—"

"They do." He kissed the top of her head, then returned to his sorting job.

Jesse hauled in the morning's firewood and closed the door with his foot. "Looking for something?"

"No." Susannah stared out the window from her spot on the trunk. "I was wondering why you came out here."

"Thought we talked about that."

Susannah rubbed her forehead. "Yes, but why *here?* Weren't there any farms in New York, or Michigan, or even Iowa?"

"You're asking why I picked this miles-from-nowhere place." Jesse poured a cup of coffee and sat beside her. "You read about Lewis and Clark?"

Susannah nodded. "They nearly froze to death in Dakota. Then General Sibley nearly roasted chasing the Sioux through here in 1863."

"Lewis and Clark found this country full of Indian tribes, herds of buffalo, and a whole slew of other animals. Must be a rich land to support all that life. Fertile soil itching for the plow."

She frowned. "You have so many skills—carpentry, music, cooking. I still think you'd be a fine pastor or missionary. How can you fulfill the Great Commission out here where there isn't anyone to disciple? Aren't you hiding your light under a bushel?"

"Yeah, Dakota's a long ways from everyone. Haven't seen my family in years. No doubt they're grateful for the peace and quiet." He gave a little chuckle. "But when I asked what I should do with my life, the answer was always the same: 'I was hungry and you fed me.'"

"From the parable of the sheep and the goats."

"Right. Susannah, this land, from Kansas to Canada, from the Mississippi River to the Rocky Mountains, is going to be the breadbasket of the nation, maybe even the world. This farm alone will feed a hundred people."

"Jesse, you worked the railroad summer before last to keep one person, yourself, from starving."

He shrugged. "Drought and grasshoppers in the same year. It won't happen again."

"So you plan to stay. No matter what."

"Now that you're here, can't see any reason to leave. Imagine it," he said. "A herd of cattle. A team of horses. Acres spreading in every direction. Wait until spring, sweet Susannah. You'll see what Dakota's all about. The War's over, the territory's open for homesteading, the railroad's through. People will come. Families like ours and the Volds' will show everyone what a great place Dakota is. Since we're the first, we'll have a say in how the territory shapes up, the way the laws are written, and how justice is carried out. Dakota will be a better land because we were here to make it so."

And with that he squeezed her knee and headed to the stable.

Susannah unbuttoned Jesse's nightshirt and slid her fingers across his chest. "Would you like to—"

Jesse caught her hand. "Well, of course I want to, but I've been thinking we should hold off. When the train starts running again, I want to take you to Fargo to see a doctor. Make sure you're all right."

"My monthlies are back to normal. I feel fine. What more could a doctor say?"

"I'm not taking any chances with you." He kissed her forehead, then rolled over toward the wall.

Within minutes his snores resonated across the bed. Susannah lay awake, watching the night drag by the four panes of glass above the footboard.

Another day. The dripping off the roof grew louder and more insistent.

The scrape of Jesse's spoon against his bowl set Susannah's teeth on edge. "Might as well muck out the shed while this warm spell lasts."

"Could I help?"

He shook his head. "Stay here and keep warm."

"Do you have any books to read?"

"The Bible."

After Jesse left, Susannah flipped through the Old Testament without reading. A half dozen medical texts lay in her trunk, a reminder of her failure to cure Mother. What she wouldn't give for a stack of dime novels, even the kind falsely promising adventure and excitement on the western frontier. No good wishing for that. Might as well make the bed.

But it was already made. Should she start dinner? No, too soon. Six steps, turn, six steps, turn. The ceiling sagged. The sod walls inched closer. Smells from every winter meal hung in the air, mixed with sour laundry and a used chamber pot.

She had to get out.

Susannah exchanged her slippers for boots and threw on her greatcoat, scarf, and mittens. She opened the door and bumped into Jesse, carrying yet another load of wood.

"You snore," she announced without looking at him. "The walls are closing in, you have nothing to read, and you're almost out of cocoa. You're bossy and too cheap to send me back. I'm leaving."

Susannah stomped past the chickens pecking their feed, past the oxen who stopped chewing to glance up at her, and out of the draw. Each step held for a moment, then broke through the icy surface as she shifted her weight. She raised her arms for balance and slogged through the knee-deep snowpack. Within minutes her face was slick with perspiration and her chest ached.

She tromped along, finding no tracks of humans or animals— nothing that suggested any living being had ever passed through this country.

Which way to the river? Where was she going? The plains were monotonous enough in summer, but the wind-driven snow had obliterated even the faintest landmarks. Sure, people would come, lured by the promise of free land, but they wouldn't live here more than one winter. Dakota would stay empty like Seward's Folly, Alaska.

Her foot slipped and didn't stop. Susannah fell forward, tumbling, sliding. A wall of snow slammed into her face and cut off all air. She windmilled her hands, tried for a breath, and choked on the snow. When her downward motion stopped, she cleared her face, opened her eyes, and found some air.

"Ow." She flexed her arms and legs. Nothing broken. One mitten missing. She tucked her hand into her sleeve. She had dropped into a drift-filled crevasse.

Susannah tried to stand in the snow-cave, only to sink deeper, dragged down by her heavy skirts. Ice crystals trickled under her collar, melting between her shoulder blades. Her fingers and toes cramped. Waves of shivering racked her body.

"You thought you were trapped in the soddy?" she asked aloud. "Well, now you're freezing to death too."

She had to find the bottom and dig out. She kicked again, but the side of the tunnel gave way. A huge slab collapsed and pinned her legs. She grunted and pushed with all her might. The corner of sky above her shrank and turned a deeper shade of gray.

Susannah stifled her tears. She was a fool. She had found a good man, only to run away. Away from love, into the arms of death.

Death. She had seen so much death. Her parents, the baby, and now the end of her own worthless life. How could she be so cruel to Jesse? He'd find her body in the spring, if the wolves didn't find her first. And if they found her while she was still alive . . .

She trembled, imagining their yellow eyes and sharp fangs. All winter they howled to each other from the ridge, drawing deep-throated growls from Jake. Jesse had gone after them with the rifle but found only their tracks.

Jesse. He'd been so kind. He didn't deserve this. Perhaps his next wife would have a dowry so he wouldn't have to worry about money. She would fill his house with children, not blood. And have an ear for music.

Another wife?

"No, I want it to be me," she cried. The pain in her heart hurt worse than the impending frostbite. Icy air scoured her lungs with each gasp. It was so cold. If she just slept a little . . .

"Wake up!" Susannah's movements generated another dousing of snow crystals. "God, I have no right to ask. You saved me from the banker. You saved me from bleeding to death when I lost the baby. For Jesse's sake, could You save me now?"

The patch of clouds darkened for a moment.

It had to be her imagination. He wouldn't come for her, not after the way she had spoken to him.

A thick rope snaked through the hole. Susannah grasped it, but it slid through her stiff fingers. The line jerked up a few feet, then reversed and dropped back down to her. She tried wrapping it around her chest; her frozen fingers couldn't make it knot. The rope wrenched out of her hands and disappeared from the pit.

After a minute or two it reappeared, this time with a loop knotted in it. She shrugged her upper body through the circle. The pressure around her chest increased. She wiggled her legs, an inch, a few more. At last they were free. The rope slackened then tightened, again and again, a rhythm. With one final hard yank, she crashed through the ice to the surface.

She staggered to her feet. Jake greeted her with a wag of his tail. Jesse coiled the rope.

"I'm sorry—"

"Go."

"But—"

He turned her around and gave her a push in the direction of the soddy. "Go. Run. Now!"

Susannah looked up. Another blizzard raced down from the

northwest, headed directly toward them. The wind roared. The temperature plummeted, and all the early melt turned back to ice.

The cold sucked Susannah's breath away; driving snow obscured her vision and scraped her skin. She lowered her head into her scarf. Gusts whipped her skirts around her legs. She tripped and skidded on the ice. Jesse tucked her under his arm, giving her the protection of his body, and somehow guided them into the draw. He opened the door and stood her by the stove.

"*Look at me*," she almost said, then changed her mind and kept silent. She didn't want to see the damage she'd done. The square set of his shoulders and the slant of his head deep in his collar said enough. She wanted to throw herself at his feet, but fear held her back.

"S-s-sorry—" she said between chattering teeth.

The lamp had not been lit. The faint light coming through the ice-covered windows showed the tremor of his hands as he held them over the stove. When he finally spoke, his quiet, deliberate words barely penetrated the storm's noise.

"Toward the end of the War," he said, "we were running short of horses and mules for ambulance duty. We got a shipment of wild ponies from Maryland. On the march, with no time to break them, we teamed each with a harness-broke mule. The ponies'd kick, put up a good fight, then settle down to business for the most part. We had one, though, who fought until she died."

He shoved his hands into his gloves. "Got to feed the stock." He angled past, then paused at the door.

"Susannah, if it's so bad for you, we'll unhitch."

Chapter 19

You hear my heart, even when it's shot to smithereens.

The wind screamed through the door as he jerked it open and slammed it shut behind him.

What had she done?

He planned to send her back. Divorce her.

An emptiness opened up in Susannah's heart, wider and colder than the crevasse into which she had fallen. What would she do without Jesse? Never seeing his playful smile across the table, never feeling his warm body curl around hers on a cold night, never hearing his songs and hymns carried on the prairie wind in his beautiful rich baritone.

A future without Jesse? Unimaginable. A tear stung her scraped cheek as it slid down her face. She had to pull herself together, to patch up this marriage.

With stiff and aching fingers, Susannah lit the lamp and peeled the wool socks from her feet. Her skin prickled with the pain of a thousand needles, but her toes glowed crimson. Good, no frostbite. She changed into dry clothes and started supper.

The blizzard howled, piercing three feet of sod. It carried voices, snatches of music. It rang in her ears like the sound of some lost

Atlantis of the Arctic. If the wind would quiet just a little, Susannah might make out the words. Instead she heard only a torrent of syllables, chords from trumpets or an organ, garbled by the wind.

Susannah clanged the stovepipe with the ladle. That was the culprit. Like blowing over a narrow-necked bottle.

After a long time, Jesse returned. He hung his coat on the peg next to the door, wiped snow from his face, and sat on the trunk to unfasten his boots.

Susannah cleared her throat. "Jesse, please. I'm sorry. I don't know what came over me. I started thinking these thoughts, preposterous, ridiculous thoughts. Then the words slipped out of my mouth, foolish things that aren't true. Please forgive me."

At last he turned. Exhaustion dragged down the corners of his eyes. "Are you all right?"

Susannah exhaled. He was still talking to her. He hadn't given up completely. "Yes. Please forget every word I said this morning. I don't know where all that nonsense came from."

"I do." He jerked his boots off, studiously beating them against the wall to dislodge the caked snow. "This has been my best year ever, so I didn't think how it must seem to you—stuck, no way out. No break from the cold and snow, no entertainment. Some people come unhinged, drown in homesickness, can't think straight. Felt it myself. Changes in weather, like today, seem to fire it up."

"What did you do to get through it?"

He pinched his shoelaces, stripping them of ice. "Stayed busy. I can see now, sparing you from work isn't doing you any favors. Jake is starting his spring shed—you wanted to try something with his fur. You could braid a rug with the scraps you've been saving. If the straw's still good, you can make hats. We can have a dance in the grand ballroom." He rested his fist on the Bible she'd left on the table. "You could read this."

"You're right." Susannah bowed her head. "I need to keep busy."

Jesse continued, ticking off each item with a rap of his knuckles. "Let's plan the garden, sort the potatoes, figure out how much seed to buy. And our house. How big do you want the rooms? How many windows? How many doors?"

He stopped. "You said it. I'm a bossy son-of-a-gun."

"It's all right. I'm getting used to it."

The truth was, his energy terrified her at first. She had never known anyone with his full-throttled, red-hot enthusiasm. Her parents, with their constrained actions set to measured words, were at the opposite end of the scale. Even his brother seemed reserved by comparison, held in check by the responsibilities of his calling.

"So you're not sending me back?"

"If that's what I have to do to keep you alive, we'll go."

Jesse's eyes, more brown than green tonight, glistened in the kerosene's flame. *"We'll go,"* he'd said. He would give up his homestead for her. She slid her arm across the table and rested her fingers on his wrist. His pulse flowed into her fingertips, up her arm, and through her body like a potent elixir. He reached for her other hand. "You sure gave me a fright, sweet Susannah. Second time I almost lost you. Promised God I'd take care of you and I will. Tell me everything, all about your life and what you like. Start from the beginning. Who were you named for? Susannah Wesley?"

Susannah smiled. "Thank you for saving my life."

"Don't change the subject now. Anyone ever call you Susie? What is your middle name?"

"No, you start while I put dinner on. Tell me your middle name and who you were named for."

He slammed both hands on the table, sending her skittering into the corner. "Can't you see—" He thumped his palms against the door. His shoulders heaved with uneven gulping breaths. Angry white huffs exploded from his mouth.

"I'm sorry." Her throat ached with the strain of held-back tears. "I never . . . well, it isn't ladylike to talk about oneself."

Jesse turned until his back rested against the door. "Is that what this is all about? Do you really believe some etiquette rule, written for schoolgirls attending their first social, applies to a marriage?"

Susannah hung on to the shelf for support, rattling the tinware. "But what if I say the wrong thing?"

"The only wrong thing is not talking, not saying what's on your mind. Not just for me, although it's mighty frustrating guessing what you're thinking, filling in the blank spots, talking enough for both of us. You've got to do this for you, Susannah." Jesse frowned. "Why are you so afraid?"

Susannah sidestepped to the stove and served him a bowl of stew. "Please eat." She wouldn't be able to choke down a bite, but at least she'd do her duty to him.

He squinted at her. "Maybe you're hiding some horrible secret in your past. Let's see—you're a member of the James gang? A spy for Jefferson Davis? Raised by wolves in the north woods? What is it?"

"No. You know my secret. You know what happened. There's nothing else. Nothing interesting. You children from large families have all the adventures."

Jesse eased onto the trunk. "Why do you say that, about large families?"

The Russells had had all the fun in her neighborhood: building a tree fort, damming up the creek, pretending to be Daniel Boone and the Indians. Growing up she wanted so much to join their lively pack of two girls and four boys.

"Susannah." Jesse's knuckles rapped the table and brought her back to the present. "Spit it out."

"Large families—well, parents can't keep an eye on all the children all the time."

"On the other hand, there's always someone to tattle on you when you wander off the straight and narrow." He shrugged. "Being an only child must have its advantages. No hand-me-downs, no sharing your bed with a squirmy whelp who forgets he's out of diapers soon as he's asleep."

"You always had someone to play with."

Jesse slurped his stew. "You had school friends."

"Yes."

He leaned back, frowning. "If I've got to suffer for something they did to you, I have the right to know what happened."

"It's silly. It's nothing." She made figure eights with her spoon in the bowl.

"Must be something to twist your face all up."

Susannah pushed a chunk of potato to the bottom of the bowl. She didn't know what brought more embarrassment—the snub or the fact she'd clung to the pain for twelve years. "The spring before we finished school, all the girls in my class went out to Belle Isle for a picnic."

"Sounds like fun. What happened?"

"I wasn't invited. They didn't hide their plans from me. I heard all about whose carriage they were taking, which person was bringing what food. The week after they told me how much fun they had. No one ever said why I wasn't invited. I considered them my best friends, but maybe I'm not good at friendship."

Jesse spoke gently, without the scorn she expected. "I can't imagine it had anything to do with you. Maybe it was religious or political differences. Feelings ran hot during the War. Perhaps they thought you couldn't afford it, or that your ma was too strict to let you go on an outing. What did your folks say?"

Susannah picked her bread into crumbs. "I couldn't tell them. They would have said I was childish or, even worse, demand that

I be included. I am being childish, to remember it after all these years. I should forgive and forget."

She took a deep breath. The wound had been lanced. The pain diminished.

"There, now, you told me something about yourself and the roof didn't fall in. Keep going." Jesse mopped up the last of his stew with the heel of bread. "Why didn't your parents have more children?"

"Father slept on a cot in his office." The words came out in a whisper.

"That's not something you should feel ashamed about. Tell me—"

He tilted his head to one side, studying her, then came around the table and pulled her into his arms. "Don't worry, Susannah. I'll never ask anything more about that bum who attacked you. I know all about it. Well, not all but enough."

"How?" She tried to pull back to see his face, but his embrace tightened.

"When you . . . when we lost our baby, you went through it again." His hands pressed her back as if he were trying to hold her together. "It happens after battles, soldiers fight in their sleep. Like when I pushed you out of bed. And how you fought! Made General Custer look like a leg case, a coward. Susannah, you don't ever have to talk about this again if you don't want to. Promise. So what's all this shaking?"

She leaned into his solid warmth, but the shivering increased. "I'm afraid." She held on to him with her last shreds of strength. He felt safe, like . . . home. "I'm afraid once you get to know me, you won't like me."

Jesse's large hands cradled her face. "Won't like you? Don't you know? I love you."

Reveille echoed in the first light of dawn. Susannah opened one eye to see Jesse blowing on a bugle formed with his two fists. She pulled the covers over her head and rolled into a ball.

"None of that, slugabed." He lifted the quilts from her legs. Air chilled by yesterday's storm hit her feet and she squeaked. He yanked the covers off. "Atten'hut!"

She glared at him. "What rank did you attain?"

"Oh, I've held a number of ranks. Busted out of a few too. This morning I'm your sergeant. Fall in!" He saluted her, then pulled her into his arms. "Soldiers aren't this beautiful to roust. Men look their worst in the morning, a night's growth of beard scabbing their faces, hair sticking up like rabid porcupines."

Susannah snuggled into the curve of his arm. "That so?"

"Whereas women look all soft and lazy in the morning. Especially lazy." He set her upright. "Private Mason, you have stable duty this morning."

Susannah groaned. "I liked you better when your orders were for bed rest."

"Maybe later." He patted her backside. "Now I'll show you why our door opens inward."

A solid wall of snow packed the opening. Susannah filled the biggest pots and set them on the stove to melt, then joined Jesse in shoveling. The sun bounced off the snow in a blinding whiteness.

When they had dug their way to the shed, Susannah paused to let her eyes adjust to the dimness. "So where have the little biddies been hiding eggs lately?"

Jesse shooed the flock off their roost and outside. "These chickens are certifiable geniuses. They never stash their treasure in the same spot twice. You'd think, small as this stable is, they'd run out of hiding places. But no. Every day it's different. Think of this as the quest for the poultry grail." He picked up the buckets and ax and went for water.

Susannah rooted through the straw, discovering one egg in the manger and a second atop the nesting box. Not bad for winter.

Sun warmed the pile of grass in front of the door. She sat to wait for Jesse. Familiar livestock odors formed an undercurrent to the sparkling clean air. A chicken, the one she'd named Victoria after the queen, flapped majestically in the yard. The storm was over.

Lord, if You're listening . . . I want to thank You for Jesse, my husband, my life.

Jesse returned with the buckets. "You all right?" His voice held concern.

"Yes, just enjoying the sun."

He filled the water trough and stood looking down at her. "Remember watching your first hatch? One of the eggs started wiggling. There'd be a little crack. Then a hole. Pretty soon the egg tooth would come through, chip away a little more. I'd get tired of waiting, want to break the egg, let the chick out. Ma would tell me no, I'd hurt the chick. If she hadn't kept an eye on me, I'd have tried it anyway."

His sideways smile showed the headstrong child he'd been. "Sometimes it seemed like the little fellow'd never make it. He'd work awhile, then stop, like the business had worn him out." Jesse closed one eye. "I'd peek in the hole, see how he's doing, try to cheer him on. Pretty soon he'd knuckle down—do chickens have knuckles?—and get back to work. The hole got bigger. I'd want to pull off that sharp triangle of shell, give him a hand. But Ma said working at getting out makes the bird strong. I'd finish my chores, then race back to find the little guy scrabbling free. He'd made it without my help."

Jesse leaned the pitchfork against the wall. The tenderness

in his eyes warmed her more than the sunshine. He squatted in front of her and put his arms around her. "Like you, chipping away at your shell. I know you're in there. I saw you deliver the calves and stand up to the threshing driver. I felt your body answer mine when we joined together. All of that is you, the you I love, the you I want. It's time for you to break out."

He picked up one of the eggs from her lap, rotating it in the sun. The clear light transformed its plain brownness so it glowed like an opal. "That stuff you said yesterday was the most honest you've ever been with me."

How could he love her so much? Susannah shook her head.

"Keep trying, Susannah-girl. If you could talk to me like that every day, without running away, I'd declare you hatched." Jesse put a hand under her elbow and helped her to her feet. "And speaking of breaking some shells, let's have breakfast."

Chapter 20

Lord, she's so different . . . thank You.

The plopping of muddy drips drove Susannah from her sleep. She wiped her face with the corner of the sheet and sat up. Every bucket and cook pot had been assigned a different leak and now sounded discordant notes with each splash. The air hung heavy with dampness. "Now I know why the Chinese use dripping water as a torture method."

Jesse rolled over to nuzzle her neck. "Ah, but the soft April wind in your hair, the warm sun on your back, the prairie bursting into bloom . . ."

Her melancholy dissolved in the flood of his exuberance. "And you're sowing magic fairy dust, not seed wheat."

He pulled on his boots. "Is there a song about that?"

"You compose one while I make pancakes."

He left the door ajar. A fresh breeze carried the honking of migrating waterfowl. Tough as their meat was this time of year, it would be a welcome change from salt pork. Removing the shotgun from its rack, Susannah settled the butt into her right shoulder and braced her feet. Swinging just ahead of the flock, she squeezed the trigger. A duck dropped into the yard. Jake barked in approval.

Jesse burst from behind the apple tree. "You scared the you-know-what out of me, woman!"

"I'm sorry." She pointed. "I thought you might like duck for dinner."

Jesse ran his thumb along her right collarbone and slipped her nightgown off her shoulder. "No bruise. Not even a red mark. You know how to handle a gun. What else haven't you told me?"

She brushed the wisps at his collar. "Did I tell you I have scissors?"

"If you barber as well as you shoot, I'd like a shave too."

"Gladly."

"But first I have a duck to clean before church."

"Do you think they'll come?"

"Nice day like this? I'm sure of it."

Jesse and Susannah hurried through morning chores and breakfast, then went off to the ridge. The wind and sun had firmed the mud. Tomorrow Jesse would worry about adequate rainfall, but today Susannah would enjoy the easy walk through the pasqueflowers.

Without the coverings of grass and snow, the contours of the prairie were visible.

"This is the edge of a glacier." Susannah set down her violin and fought the wind to spread a blanket on the bluff.

Jesse rubbed his freshly shaved chin. "What?"

"A glacier pushed down from Canada, like the scraper used to build the railroad bed. It pushed rocks in front of it into this ridge and pulverized the rocks underneath into soil."

"You can tell all that just by looking?"

"Not me, a geologist named Louis Agassiz. When I received your first letter, I wanted to learn about where you lived. There wasn't much information. Lewis and Clark and Audubon went up the Missouri River, quite a bit west of here. Mr. Agassiz's writings and General Sibley's military account were all I could find about the eastern part of the territory."

"Here's your piece of Dakota history: Sibley's trail."

Susannah leaned her cheek on Jesse's shoulder, sighting down his arm to faint marks of wheel ruts from ten years ago.

He turned west. The Shcyenne River had overrun its banks, streaming around the trees where they'd met the Volds last autumn. "Tell me about this side."

"It's lower, older, formed before the glacier. See how far away the other bank is at this elevation? The Sheyenne used to be a big river, a half mile wide maybe. The banks are steep, terraced, indicating the river level dropped suddenly, probably ice breakup at its outlet. You're right, thanks to the glacier, the soil is bound to be richer east of here. Anyone who farms in the valley will have plenty of rocks to plow around."

"Don't know much, but I do know dirt." He smiled down at her, his hazel eyes bright under the shade of his hat brim. "You're the smart one."

"If I were really smart, I could tell you if we're standing on a drumlin or a moraine."

"Impresses the socks off me either way."

The prairie remained a dull tan, but the area blackened by last October's fires showed a smattering of green.

"Perhaps you should burn the rest of the fields."

Jesse frowned. "Set a fire? Deliberately?"

Susannah straightened her shoulders. He wanted her opinion, she would give it to him. "Where the old grass was burned away, the sun warms the earth faster and new growth sprouts."

Jesse compared the two areas. "Maybe I could round up some help. If it could be done without setting the whole territory on fire, you might be onto something. Sure be easier to plow."

"The old is gone, the new has come. Like my life. Those things that happened in Detroit . . . could God have caused them, to bring me here?"

Jesse gazed at her. "I don't believe God can ever be the source of evil, so no, He didn't cause that banker to attack you. And your folks were getting up in years, so you can't blame their deaths on Him. But God does work all things together for good. And we can learn even from the most difficult circumstances." Jesse grinned. "Want to do the sermon today?"

"No, thank you." Susannah smiled. Jesse thought she had something worthy to say.

A column of smoke to the west caught her attention. "Are there neighbors on the other side of the river?"

Jesse gave her a lopsided smile. "I believe you've already made the acquaintance of Mr. Abner Reece."

Susannah shuddered.

"He's a big galoot. But as long as I'm around, he won't bother you." Jesse stroked his index finger across her cheek, tucking a loose strand of hair behind her ear. The morning sun outlined the strong angle of his nose, the cleft in his chin, the gentle curve of his smile.

Let all our sons look just like him.

The breeze brushed her cheek, soft as cake flour, fragrant with new growth. A flock of goldfinches chased each other in a scalloped flight down the valley. Three people appeared on the northern horizon. "It's them! Look how big Sara's grown!"

"Go on, kick up your heels." Jesse waved her off.

"Susannah!" Marta ran toward them. Susannah hiked her skirt and raced to meet her. The woman embraced her, then touched her flat belly. "Baby?"

Grief caught Susannah in the heart and pulled her under. She had married in August, so her pregnancy should be well along by now. She shook her head. "I had a miscarriage." How, she wondered, could God work that for good?

Ivar joined them. Holding Sara in one arm, he lifted Susannah off the ground with the other. "Sara's catching up to you." Marta asked him a question in Norwegian. He interpreted, "You half no baby?"

Susannah looked at the ground, unable to speak. Jesse stepped up behind her and pulled her close. "We lost the baby, before Christmas."

"I'm so sorry." Ivar interpreted for Marta, who hugged her again.

"Look at this big girl!" Jesse reached for Sara, who beamed at him. "She remembers me! Hey, she's got a full head of hair, a full mouth of teeth. She's a regular little person. Must have doubled her weight over the winter. What have you been feeding her?"

"Good, solid Norwegian food. I'll give you some for your little wife."

"Enough about my weight."

Jesse winked and pointed to the violin. "Well, look what my little wife brought."

"*En fiolin!* Start the music!"

"Do you know 'We Plough the Fields'?"

"Of course." Ivar nodded.

The chorus was one of Susannah's favorites:

> *All good gifts around us*
> *Are sent from heaven above.*
> *Then thank the Lord,*
> *Oh, thank the Lord, for all His love.*

She looked at each person in the circle, and her eyes lingered on Jesse. *Yes, thank the Lord for love.*

Wednesday morning Jesse yoked the oxen for the spring trip to Worthington. He'd reminded Susannah to hold back on purchases, so the shopping list consisted of only a few items, just the absolute necessities. If the Roses would take in trade their eggs and the straw hats Susannah had made, perhaps he could buy a tin of cocoa. And a spool of blue thread. And maybe a cake of soap.

On this first warm day of the year, the morning sun pulled the dew from the grass. Blue, pink, and white flowers danced in the mist. Dakota Territory puffed out its chest with pride. Susannah shrugged out of her coat and bonnet, liberated at last from long underwear, itchy wool socks, and heavy flannel petticoats. She felt so light and free, she thought she might float across the prairie.

Jesse turned his probing gaze her way. "See, it's not so bad here."

"It's beautiful." She returned his smile. "Do you suppose— would you mind teaching me to drive?"

"You know how to drive horses, don't you? Same thing, only easier because the oxen are so slow." He handed her the reins, then rested his arm across her back, tickling her arm with his thumb. "If we had horses, I'd have this whole section in wheat. And we'd be to the store already. We wouldn't have been stuck in the house all winter. But first got to put up a barn."

Horses. Jesse was saving for a team. No wonder he was so careful with his money.

The Sheyenne River sparkled like hidden treasure deep in the prairie. Beneath budding cottonwoods, Worthington had grown by two partially completed frame buildings and several shanties. The

Western Hotel tent had been taken down, but a thin line of smoke issued from Donald McFadgen's cabin. The Roses' pack of dogs and children heralded their arrival at the store. To Susannah's relief, a wagonload of newcomers kept the proprietors busy. Jesse lifted her to the ground.

"Mason." Abner Reece clamped his hand on her husband's shoulder. Where had he come from? And was he wearing exactly the same clothes as when he intercepted her on the train? Her nose confirmed that possibility. He spit toward the hitching post, wiping his mouth on his encrusted sleeve. "Hear your wife knows animal doctoring. Wonder if she'd look at my cow." He jabbed a tobacco-stained thumb over his shoulder at the shorthorn apathetically chewing her cud beside the store.

"Fine with me, Abner. But you'll have to ask her." With a wink to Susannah, he disappeared inside.

Staying upwind, she followed the big farmer across the rutted yard. The cow blinked her listless eyes at their approach. Dried mud and manure covered her legs and belly. A length of twine circled her neck, dragging the ground. Had she found the energy to walk from his claim or had the big man carried her?

"How long have you been homesteading, Mr. Reece?"

"Made it through my first winter. Wish I could say the same for the cow. I's afraid I'd have to shoot her and eat her."

"Not much here to eat," Susannah said, feeling ribs under the matted hide. "What kind of work did you do back in the States?"

"I's a longshoreman, loading and unloading ships in Boston. Can you help this cow?"

So the neglect was due to lack of knowledge rather than intent to harm. Examining the animal's mouth, Susannah launched into a lecture on bovine care and feeding, especially feeding. Mr. Reece listened, asked questions, and in response to her carefully worded request, summarized the plan she outlined for him.

"Thank you kindly for your advice, ma'am." Mr. Reece walked her back to the store. "I'd like to pay you."

Taking money for common knowledge, information every farmer knew, didn't seem right. "How about if you help us with our barn raising? We don't have lumber yet, but—"

He nodded. "Have Jesse come get me when he's ready. He knows where I'm holed up."

Susannah smiled. Mr. Reece's brawn would be an asset to any building project.

He cleared his throat and took a step toward her. "My offer is still open. If it don't work out with Jesse—"

"Thank you, Mr. Reece. It's working out fine with Mr. Mason." *Add this conversation to the list of things that would never happen in Detroit,* she thought. She hurried up the steps into the store.

Just inside the door, Ivar met her with an opened letter. "Must be bad news. After Jesse read it, he dropped it on the floor and ran out. Didn't say a word. Never known him not to talk." Ivar steered her to the bench on the loading dock. "Let us know if we can help."

Susannah scanned the first page, a friendly letter from Ellen. No bad news. She set it aside to savor later.

Reverend Mason's handwriting graced the second page. The execution of the Underhill estate required a lengthy investigation including numerous trips back to Detroit and letters to lawyers and banking officials. Apparently the malefactor who had attacked Susannah had left the state, present whereabouts unknown. His replacement could find no record of a mortgage on the Underhill property.

A search through her father's papers and an audit of his books showed no outstanding debts. The Reverend had visited the largest, most prosperous of her father's accounts and obtained much of the money still owed for veterinary services. The house and its furnishings had been sold to a young veterinary surgeon setting up practice. Delighted to have her father's library, instruments, and client list, he'd paid handsomely for it all. Personal items were in storage, ready for shipment at her request.

Subtracting his expenses, the Reverend had transferred the proceeds to her. He enclosed a slip of paper with "Susannah Underhill Mason" written in flowing Spencerian script. The amount read one thousand nine hundred seventy-seven dollars and two cents.

Susannah sank back against the bench. Nearly two thousand dollars! They could build a house and barn and have money left over for a team, a buggy, trees—

Marta touched her hand, breaking the spell. "Is bad?"

Susannah shook her head. "It's good."

Ivar's eyebrows met over his nose. If Jesse was pulling a joke on her, Ivar was not in on it.

"You're sure it was this letter that upset Jesse? Maybe he didn't like me talking to Mr. Reece for so long."

"No. He seemed proud you could help Abner. Said you could turn him into a farmer and gentleman at the same time."

The essence of Jesse: unpredictability. Folding the pages into the envelope, Susannah stood. "Where did he go?"

"West, up the tracks, but I'm not sure where he is now. Do you want me to go with you?"

"Could you wait for him here, please, in case he comes back from a different direction?" Moving as fast as her skirts allowed, Susannah hurried across the loading dock and down the steps to the tracks. Mr. Reece and his cow were gone. Her feet slipped on the muddy roadbed. Susannah stepped over the rail and walked on the ties. Their irregular placement slowed her pace even more.

What was wrong? The way he watched his money, Jesse should be dancing a jig, swinging her in the air. For him to be speechless about anything was inconceivable. What could send him off by himself? Another memory of the War? Something in the letter?

Susannah tightened her grip on the envelope. Perspiration stuck the paper to her palm. Where was he? Yellow-green shoots of prairie grass rippled in the breeze, too short to hide a man. Ahead of her by ten or fifteen minutes, he might have left the tracks and disappeared into the undergrowth along the river. She watched the grading for footprints. Jake could find him, but he had been left guarding the homestead. The Roses had dogs, but their pack seemed more bark than brain. The eastbound train was due any moment. If she didn't find Jesse soon, she'd have to go back and wait at the store with Mr. and Mrs. Rose. Susannah rubbed her stomach as her dyspepsia reared its ugly head.

He's Yours, Lord. You know where he is.

The midday sun glinted off a straw hat under a trestle.

"Jesse!" She slid down the embankment. He did not look up. Red blotches marked his face, visible even in the shade of his hat. "Jesse, what's wrong? Are you ill?" She knelt before him in the damp grass.

He pitched a cinder into the creek. "Go ahead and take the next train," he said in a flat voice. "I'll ship your trunks to you tomorrow. Just want to say thank you for giving me these eight months. Wish you the best, whether you finish medical school or . . . marry that new vet who's taken over your father's practice."

She leaned close, trying to get him to look at her. "Is there something here besides winter that makes people take leave of their senses? What are you talking about?"

"This." He flicked the letter. "Now you can follow your dreams, make your own choices, do what you want with your life. Leave behind my crazy notions of farming out here." He uprooted a stalk of rough-edged cordgrass and scowled at the dirt clinging to its roots. "It's not your dream. You don't even like it here. Who can blame you? Folks getting off the *Mayflower* had it easier than this. You deserve a better life than I can provide."

He wrapped the grass stalk around his fingers and pulled until it snapped. "Nothing to keep you here. That marriage certificate probably isn't worth the paper Matt wrote it on. I'll just toss it in the stove. Go ahead and keep the ring for all the grief I've caused you this year."

"You think I'd leave you?"

He nodded, examining the broken grass strands in his hands. "Please make it quick. I can't—" He pressed his fist to his mouth and swallowed hard.

"Oh, Jesse," she whispered. "Maybe I don't dream of feeding a hundred people from one farm, but I do dream of feeding a house full of children. Children with their father's ear for music and heart to serve God."

She held up the envelope. "You know what this is? It's the means to accomplish our dreams—*our* dreams, Jesse Mason. A house for those children to grow up in, the barn and animals and machinery you need to really make the farm operate."

His jaw clenched. His chest rose and fell unevenly under his going-to-town shirt. How could he ever think—

Well, of course. She hadn't told him. She'd been so busy worrying over the right words to say, she'd forgotten the most important ones. "I made a commitment before God, Jesse. You're my husband. I wouldn't leave you. I love you."

At last he looked up. "What did you say?"

"I love you."

He pushed his ear forward. The corner of his mouth lifted. "Having a little trouble with my hearing."

Heart soaring, she yelled, "I love you!"

"Well, why didn't you say so?" He reached out for her and she fell into his arms. He flopped onto the grassy slope, holding her on top of him and kissing her hard. Rolling her onto her back, he unfastened her basque.

"Jesse!" Susannah gasped. "We can't! Ivar and Marta are waiting at the store. They're worried about you."

"Until tonight, then." He kissed the hollow of her neck.

"Besides," she said, pulling him up to the tracks and redoing her buttons, "we need to order lumber for the house and barn. Do you remember how much you figured? Perhaps we could ask Ivar to look after the homestead next week so we could take the train into Fargo and buy some horses. Oh, and I told Mr. Reece he could help with the barn raising in exchange for the advice I gave him about his cow. I hope that's all right."

He stopped to kiss her once more. "Everything's all right."

Chapter 24

Jesus, keep teaching me about love.

Ivar's and Marta's expressions changed from worried to puzzled as Jesse and Susannah approached. Behind her hand, Marta said a word to her husband.

Ivar spit out a Norwegian expletive and threw his hat at Jesse. "We worry sick about you, and you're out rolling in the hay."

Blushing, Susannah picked a stalk of grass from the ruffled trim of her overskirt. Jesse dusted off his friend's hat and returned it to his head. "Could you feed our stock while we go to Fargo, old man?"

"Who are you calling old? And what you want with Fargo? First you race off like a troop of trolls is after you, then come back like they crowned you king. You better tell me what's going on."

"Susannah's come into some money, so I thought we'd take a shopping trip. Train should be along pretty soon."

"Today?" Susannah asked. "Dressed like this? We need to pack a bag since the return train doesn't come back until morning. Shouldn't we finish planting?"

"You look fine. It's not like we're going to Chicago. We'll only be there overnight. If you need something, we'll buy it." He turned to the Norwegian man. "Bring you something from town?"

Ivar squinted over Jesse's shoulder. "There's the train now. I'll half Rose keep your oxen and wagon here. Tell me where your calves are picketed."

"Northeast field. Take any eggs you find. Thanks!" Jesse dashed inside, yelling, "Mrs. Rose, two round-trip tickets to Fargo, please."

Susannah frowned. "Why isn't there a passenger car on this run?"

Jesse helped her into the caboose. Above them, a scowling conductor slumped in the cupola. He wore a Northern Pacific jacket over grease-stained trousers. "You could ask that fellow."

"No, thank you." Through clouds of coal smoke, Susannah waved to the Volds, then let the forward motion of the engine push her back into the seat.

Jesse rubbed his finger over the furrow in her brow. "God's blessed us with love and money. Nothing to worry about."

Entirely too persistent and perceptive, this husband of hers. She might as well tell him. Not talking only increased his persistence. "Will we still have friends?"

"Ah." Jesse watched the miles roll by. "Ivar married and started a family, but we're still friends. Tell you what, let's buy them a present. Maybe something for Sara." He handed her a pencil from his pocket. "Start a list. Put 'present' first. Then lumber for the house and barn, windows, doors, nails, roofing felt, shingles, paint. What color do you like?"

"Talk slower so I can write this down. How about red? So we can find our way home in winter."

"You look beautiful in red. A new red dress."

"A dress? Too extravagant. I can make my own clothes."

"All right then, a sewing machine and piece goods. How many yards do you need for a dress?"

"Ten. A sewing machine?"

"Absolutely. Give me the pencil. You're skipping stuff." He paused to add up the costs. "Plenty left over. Let's see a photographer, get our wedding picture taken so I can show you off."

"Dressed like this?"

"Clothing store before photographer. We'll visit the bookstore in Moorhead. Get a matched team of horses, harnesses, saddles. Dinner at the Headquarters Hotel. New shoes for both of us."

"A bookstore!"

The list covered the envelope by the time the train screeched into Fargo. Ten whitewashed buildings, most two stories tall, faced the tracks across Front Street.

Jesse whistled. "When I came through here in '71, it was only a row of tents for the surveyors and a stack of lumber for the hotel. Crossed the river on a ferry. They were calling it Centralia."

Susannah shook her head. "That's funny. I was just thinking it hadn't changed at all since last summer. In fact, it seems quieter. Maybe just the time of day." The late afternoon sun slanted across the rutted mud. Susannah lifted her skirts. "Wonder which one is the bank."

"Let's start at this end of town and work our way east. We'll find it." Jesse grasped her elbow to steady her. "If I'd known they were paving their streets with manure, I'd have brought a load from our stable. Aren't you glad you didn't change into fancy clothes?"

A team of gray coursers pulled a red, white, and blue striped democrat wagon around the corner of the adjacent hotel.

"Welcome to Fargo!" The balding driver guided his team toward them. The horses strained against the firmly held reins. "My team hates this gumbo too. Give them their head and they'd be out of town, rolling in the grass in no time. Can I give you antelopers a ride?" Throwing the brake with his foot, he extended his arm. "Jasper Chapin, proprietor of the Headquarters Hotel."

Jesse shook his hand. "Jesse and Susannah Mason, homesteaders from south of Worthington."

Maybe it was his portly physique or his jovial manner, but Mr. Chapin reminded Susannah of Saint Nicholas—or at least a slightly inebriated Saint Nick.

"If you could point us in the direction of a bank, we'd appreciate it," Jesse said.

"Don't have a bank yet." He nodded at a building across the street. Block letters rising two feet tall above the second story windows proclaimed E. S. Tyler & Co. "Evan's been stuck with the job ever since he bought a safe."

"Much obliged." Jesse stepped away from the wagon.

The heavyset man squinted at Susannah. "I never forget a pretty face. You're the little lady come out from Detroit last summer. Ordered soup for dinner, toast for breakfast. Didn't finish either. Got my cook all worried. I was sure the wind would blow you back to Michigan. Well, you're looking mighty fine. And this must be the lucky bridegroom."

His gaze shifted back to Jesse. "Mason, eh? Take off your hat a minute, son. With a proboscis like yours, you've got to be kin to Shep Mason out of Genesee County, New York."

"That would be my grandfather. Got out of the sheep business. Did better with Holsteins. You from New York?"

"Native of Genesee County. Worked a farm down to Jamestown 'til I left in '52. Tell you what, get your banking done, come back to my hotel. Give me another chance to put on a feed." Mr. Chapin released the brake. The wagon slogged down the road to the rhythm of the horses' sucking hooves.

Jesse clamped her hand between his elbow and his side. Quiet laughter rumbled his rib cage.

"What's an anteloper?" She scraped her shoes on the edge of the wooden sidewalk.

"Someone who eats antelope—a name obviously given by a city dweller who's never tried hunting one." He opened the door and waved her in with a flourish. "Mrs. Mason."

The grocery and dry goods store was the Roses' establishment multiplied ten times. Where the Worthington store had one brand of peaches, Mr. Tyler had three, in a variety of sizes. Mrs. Rose offered dried apples. Mr. Tyler had fresh apples *and* oranges. Bolts of fabric were stacked to the ceiling, in colors from buff to mahogany, lilac to plum. Patterns of plaid, brocade, pinstripes, florals, even florals with stripes. Muslin, grenadine, cambric, poplin, calico, twill. The glass cabinet in front of the shelves displayed a rainbow of ribbons, braids, lace, and buttons. E. S. Tyler stocked not just J. P. Coats thread but Clark's Spool Cotton and Milward's needles. Oh, the dresses she'd make!

"May I help you?" A lanky man wiped his hands on his white apron.

"We were told you could cash this for us." Jesse handed him the transfer paper.

The storekeeper sucked in his upper lip, bristling the hairs of his mustache. He consulted a handwritten list posted over the safe, then turned back to Jesse.

"Afraid I'm the bearer of bad news. This transfer was drawn on one of the banks that closed. It's no good."

"No good? The bank closed?"

The edges of Susannah's vision went dark. Jesse braced her shoulders. "Breathe," he ordered in an undertone.

"Last September Jay Cooke's bank in Philadelphia failed. It threw the railroad into receivership, put people out of work, and closed banks across the country. Newspapers are calling it 'the Panic of '73.' Business has been slow ever since." The storekeeper returned the paper. "If I were you, I'd write Detroit, see if the bank reopened and will issue a new transfer. I'll be glad to give you credit. Your wife looks like she'd take home my entire yard goods department. And you're welcome to a cup of coffee, on the house."

"Thanks, but we'd better find a place to stay the night."

"Try the Sherman House. Less expensive than Chapin's—er, the Headquarters Hotel. Ask for a room in the back; they're a dollar less. Good luck to you."

The door of the store thudded behind them.

Jesse tightened his grip. "Sorry about your shopping trip."

The wooden sidewalk tilted like the deck of a boat. "I feel like our feet have been kicked out from under us. All our dreams. Please write to Matt. Maybe he can find out where our money is. It must be somewhere. How can a bank close like that?"

Jesse shoved the envelope into his pocket. "Guess we'll have to work for our dreams, like we planned."

"I have the money I brought from Michigan, almost four dollars. Do you think it will be enough for a room?"

"Keep your purse closed. I'll take care of it."

They crossed a vacant lot and climbed up on the next section of sidewalk. "Hey, here's a doctor."

Could this day get any worse? Susannah planted her feet. "No."

"Don't be stubborn."

"We can't afford this."

"I can't afford to lose you." Jesse tightened his grip and steered her into the empty waiting room. "Hello!" he hollered.

"Out on a call." Susannah bolted for the door. Jesse blocked her escape.

From the back room came a cough, followed by a cadaverous man with sunken eyes and a sallow complexion. "Homesteaders, I presume."

"I'm Jesse Mason and this is my wife, Susannah. Are you the doctor?"

"Only one in town. You look healthier than the usual dullards around here. What's the problem?"

"Susannah had a miscarriage this winter—"

The doctor interrupted. "Lost a lot of blood, almost died. It was her first pregnancy, and you want to know if you'll ever get any children out of her." He tipped his head back to peer at her through his spectacles. "Needs to gain weight. Silence!" He pinched her wrist in his clammy fingertips and timed her pulse with his pocket watch. With a grunt he dropped her wrist and addressed her for the first time. "Take a seat, Mrs. Mason. Mr. Mason, come with me."

The door to the back room shut in her face. Susannah removed her hat and pressed her ear to the wall. The plaster was paper-thin, and she could hear every word.

"Shouldn't my wife—" Jesse began.

"This isn't a matter for mixed company. Sit down. Women like your wife are totally unsuited for the homesteading life, Mr. Mason, and certainly too frail to bear children. How many did her mother have? Probably died giving birth. You'd best ship her back where she came from and try again with another woman, this time with bigger bones."

A chair scraped. "No."

"Sit down. Don't get hysterical on me. There are some fine organizations in the States looking for homes for orphans. You may be able to adopt some older children to help around the farm, keep your wife alive."

A drawer screeched and, after an interval of coughing, he continued. "Now, about your manly needs. I assume you have been abstaining since the incident. You may certainly continue to do so and be nominated for sainthood. But there are other options. There is some objection to dissemination of this information, but since you're determined to continue this marriage and endanger the life of this woman, I feel an obligation to advise you. This information is confidential. You will not tell anyone where you learned of it."

He cleared his throat and went on, speaking quickly. "First, spilling the seed, leaving before the gospel. Requires optimal timing and self-control. Some object to this based on an obscure passage in the Old Testament. Second, rhythm. Women are most fertile just before they bleed. You'll need a calendar. Third, sponge, size of a green walnut. Fourth, douche. You've got vinegar out in your hovel. Tell her to use it. Fifth, French letter. You were a soldier, so you're already familiar with these. Here's a package to get you started. Stop by whenever you're in town and I'll sell you some more. That will be one dollar."

He coughed again. "None of these methods is entirely reliable. Should an unfortunate accident occur, bring her into town. I'll do what I can. No guarantees."

Two chairs scraped the floor. Susannah tiptoed to the window and pretended to study the hotel down the street. The doctor frowned at her. She glared back, hiding her fists in the folds of her skirt.

"That will be all, Mr. Mason."

Without speaking, Jesse escorted Susannah toward the Sherman House.

When they were out of earshot of the office, he turned to look at her. "You heard?"

"Every word."

"That's a relief. I was afraid I'd have to explain it, and I didn't understand half what he said."

Susannah bristled. Had she ever been so angry? "How dare he speak to us that way! We should have changed clothes. He thinks we're ignorant country yokels he can push around. My father treated animals with more dignity. Where did he go to medical school, anyway? Did he have a certificate on the wall? Jesse?"

Jesse appeared to be inspecting the leaves overhead. The last rays of sun outlined his heaving Adam's apple. "No children. He said we can't have any children." He pulled her to his chest, tipping her hat back and wetting the top of her head with his tears.

"What does he know?"

"He knew you were an only child. Maybe your pa slept in his office because—"

"No, my parents just didn't get along. Mother never mentioned any difficulty giving birth."

"He knew I'd been a soldier."

"You and every other man your age. He can make lucky guesses. That doesn't make him a good doctor. He can't even cure his own cough. Come on, let's go have twelve children and outlive the fool by fifty years."

Jesse blinked. "Twelve children?"

"Not all at once, of course." Susannah dried his face with her handkerchief. "Unless you're going to ship me back."

"Never!" He tightened his hold.

Her anger boiled dry, bringing other emotions to the surface. "In my head, I know men and women all over the world do it," she whispered, "but in my heart, what we do together is special, private, even holy. Is it blasphemous to say that? The way that sawbones talked made it seem so vile."

"He was pretty crude. Probably an army doctor." Jesse pulled the package from his pocket. "Should we give this a try?"

"Jesse Mason, put that away! If someone saw you, who knows what they'd think!" A furious blush heated her face. She glanced around. The stable yard was empty. "Let's go to the hotel."

"What a day." He started toward the entrance, then turned to her. His palm cupped her cheek, holding her as if she were made of glass. "Tell me again," he whispered.

"I love you."

Chapter 22

All right, Lord, as long as Susannah's
by my side, I don't mind.

"W atch it," Ivar warned as Jesse shinned from the wagon onto the roof of Fourth Siding's shed.

"I built it. Guess I know how to stand on it." He balanced on the peak and squinted off to the north.

"Any sign of life?" Susannah stood, more to relieve her sore backside than from hope of seeing anyone. If Jesse ever did get some money, she hoped he would spend it on a buckboard.

Fourth Siding's population remained unchanged since her arrival nine months ago, but the early spring prairie grass held a hopefulness, the promise of good to come.

"They're northeast about half a mile." Jesse swung back into the wagon and Ivar headed the oxen away from the tracks.

Last Sunday Jesse had read aloud the winter's accumulation of newspapers. The *Fargo Express* reported the birth of twins on February 28 to an Irish-American couple at Fourth Siding. At Marta's insistence, the Volds and Masons were attempting to find the family today. As they bounced over the prairie, the Norwegian woman wrapped one arm around Sara and the other around an iron kettle.

A strip of plowed ground gave the first indication of the homestead. The wagon almost ran over the house, dug into a draw.

"Where's their dog?" Susannah asked. "And their cow?"

"Hello the house!"

The door opened a crack, revealing an ancient muzzleloader and two dark eyes.

"We're your neighbors, from the south side of the tracks." Jesse made introductions. "Saw your good news in the paper. Came to offer congratulations."

The hollow-eyed man stepped outside. "I'm Colum Duffy." Dirt-encrusted clothes hung on his skeletal frame. "We're not expecting visitors."

"Food." Marta held up the kettle.

The young man wiped his hand across his scraggly whiskers. "I'll tell Maureen you're here." He disappeared inside. The dugout looked about half the size of Jesse's. Instead of glass, oiled paper covered its lone window. The empty lean-to on the east side needed mucking.

Colum and his wife shuffled out, each holding an infant wrapped in rags. Mrs. Duffy blinked in the sunlight like an animal emerging from hibernation. A rip in her stained dress showed an undergarment made of flour sacks.

Marta stepped forward, issuing instructions. Behind her, Ivar interpreted. "We have a custom in our country of bringing *søt suppe*, sweet soup, for the mother." He paused, listening to his wife. "*Ja. We* also have a custom of bringing a gift of work to celebrate the new babies. If you will come with us, Mr. Duffy, we'll go for firewood while our wives visit with Mrs. Duffy."

Susannah caught Jesse's eye as he handed Sara to her. The plan had been to share the soup, then hurry home for spring planting. He gave her a surreptitious wink.

Mr. Duffy swayed. His wife took the baby from him. "Go on, Colum. I'll be all right."

The men departed for the wooded banks of the Sheyenne. Marta scooted around Mrs. Duffy into the dugout. Susannah peeked at the twins. Tiny pinched faces, no bigger than her palm, slept in the morning sun.

"How old are they now?"

"Five weeks," the dark-haired woman replied. Veins and arteries laced her face and hands beneath translucent skin. "And yours? She's so big."

"No, Sara is Mrs. Vold's baby. She's almost a year old." Sara did look healthy and substantial next to the Duffy infants.

"Dear me!" The young mother hastened inside. "I've not done a lick of work since the babies came and not much before."

Susannah stood in the doorway. If Jesse's house reminded her of a cave, the Duffys' seemed more like a pit. Three walls were hacked out of the embankment. The window emitted a weak, dull glow. A twist of cloth sputtering in a saucer of fat produced a feeble puddle of light, revealing the squalid condition of the dugout. It smelled like an outhouse. Marta set the kettle on the tiny two-lid stove, then rolled up her sleeves.

"I'm sorry about the mess." Mrs. Duffy laid the infants in a canvas hammock slung precariously from the rafters.

Marta motioned for the new mother to sit on the sturdier of the two crates constituting their furniture. She took Sara and sent Susannah for water.

As the washtub of diapers soaked, the women enjoyed their soup, an ambrosia of dried apples, plums, apricots, and raisins. When the babies wanted to nurse, Marta had Mrs. Duffy lie with them on the straw pallet. The exhausted mother looked like a little girl with her dolls, her dark tangle of curls spread over the pillow.

Halfway through the load of threadbare calico, the babies awoke. Marta directed Susannah outside with them. The fussy one turned red and burped wetly on Susannah's shoulder. Before she could call Marta, his complexion and breathing returned to normal. The other regarded her solemnly. The first opened his mouth and rubbed against her.

"You just ate, silly boy." Susannah lifted them to her shoulder. They began to whimper, alternating breaths, so one always sounded the alarm.

"Walk," Marta suggested from the washboard.

Susannah paced up the slope. The hungry infant nuzzled her neck with his mouth, his silken hair tickling her earlobe. Deep inside Susannah, a spark ignited.

A clatter and rumble announced the return of the men. Hearing the babies' cries, the new father jumped up, almost bolting off the wagon.

"Easy, now." Ivar pulled him back onto the seat. "Your sons half to try their windpipes."

Mr. Duffy raised an eyebrow.

"He knows what he's talking about." Jesse clamped the lad on his skinny shoulder. "You've seen his baby."

Susannah followed the wagon back to the dugout, past Marta laying out clean diapers in the sun. Mr. Duffy dashed inside to check on his wife while Ivar and Jesse stacked the wood. The babies' cries waned into sleep.

"Susannah." Ivar wiped his brow. "You half a way with babies. Jesse should give you some of your own."

Jesse broke a dry stick over his friend's head. "As long as they come one at a time." He turned to Susannah. "Colum says at least one's awake and crying ever since they were born. Fellow slept all the way to the river."

"I agree, one at a time." Susannah shifted the babies in her arms, trying to scratch her nose, finally resorting to scrunching her face. "Holding two means you don't have a hand free."

"Well, that could have some advantages." Pulling Susannah, babies and all, into a big hug, Jesse kissed her.

Ivar thumped Jesse across the back of his knees. "I meant, when you get home, make babies."

"You're a regular Simon Legree, Ivar Vold." Jesse returned to the woodpile. "Didn't anyone tell you? Slavery's abolished."

Inside, Susannah laid the babies in the hammock, tucking the crocheted afghan around their tiny bodies. The inner spark kindled into an unfamiliar flame of yearning.

Mrs. Duffy embraced Susannah. The girl's bones poked through her homespun. "Bless you, all of you." The brief nap and soup put a little color in her cheeks. At the stove, Colum scooped the last of the fruit into his mouth. He grunted his agreement.

Susannah wished they could do more. "What are their names?" She nudged the hammock to keep it rocking.

"Liam and Seamus. Liam's a bit larger. Seamus has little red marks between his eyebrows."

"Too bad you couldn't think of Irish names for them," Jesse said. This drew a smile from Maureen Duffy. "It's time we head for home. Hope you'll come visit us next time."

"Bless you, Mr. Mason."

From the wagon, Susannah turned for a last look at the couple waving from the dugout.

"Fifteen and sixteen," Jesse said from the wagon seat.

"What?"

"If you thought they're half our age, you're right. Fifteen and sixteen."

"Do their parents know?"

"Their folks know, all right. In fact, they shipped their children to Dakota when they figured out the girl was in the family way." Jesse thumped Ivar on the arm. "So, how old is this Norwegian custom of cutting wood and washing diapers for new parents?"

Ivar glanced at the sun. "I'd say three, maybe four hours."

Jesse grinned at Marta. "Good custom."

Ivar let the Masons off near their claim. They strolled through the cool spring evening, the fragrant prairie flowers blowing away the odor of the Duffys' squalor.

Jesse squeezed her hand. "Thought I started out with nothing. Colum was so hungry, he ate those raw potatoes Ivar keeps in his grub box. Bit into them like they were Northern Spy apples."

"Compared to them, we live like royalty." Susannah nodded. "Are you jealous?"

"Oh yeah." He swallowed. "Colum and Ivar swapping progeny stories, you bet."

Susannah slid her hand down his back, inside the waistband of his pants at the triangle of space over his backbone. "Shall we take up Ivar's suggestion, then?"

Jesse extracted her hand. "No, but we will take up the doctor's suggestion."

"Which? The doctor's methods or the orphans?"

Jesse's eyebrows peaked. "Both."

She looked up into the face more familiar than her own, its hard lines a disguise for a soft heart. She wanted to lay him down in the spring grass and love him until she was sure of carrying his child. "What size baby would they send?"

The hard lines curved. "Probably bigger than the Duffys'. Never seen babies that small. My guess is they'll be more the size of Sara."

Longing burned her throat and threatened to spill out her eyelids. She could love an adopted baby, certainly. But what she wanted was Jesse's child. Their child.

White puffs of cottonwood seeds danced like lazy snowflakes in the Sunday sun. Jesse continued through the chord progression but stopped singing in the middle of a phrase. "Ivar, how many Indians are behind me?" he asked in a casual tone, his voice just loud enough to be heard over the guitar.

Indians? Where? Heart pounding, Susannah lowered her violin to her lap. She saw only a flock of goldfinches tracing a scalloped course around a thicket of white-blossomed plum trees.

Ivar scanned the wooded riverbanks. "No Indians."

"You didn't happen to bring your rifle today?"

Ivar's blond eyebrows drew together. "You know I don't hunt on Sundays."

"There's an Indian about twenty-five yards south, heading right for us."

A rangy man with shoulder-length black hair hiked down the slope. A prickling sensation ran under Susannah's hat.

Marta, calm in every storm, pulled Sara into her lap. Ivar rooted through the picnic basket, finding a kitchen knife. Jesse kept strumming. Susannah tensed, ready to hit the savage with her violin, poke him with her bow, throw herself between him and the baby. Why were they just sitting there?

The Indian's long steps closed the distance. Midday sun glittered off the beads and quills decorating his buckskins. He stopped a few feet away and opened his palms toward them. *"Pain, s'il vous plaît? Mangez?"*

"Bien sûr. Voulez-vous dîner avec nous?" Susannah responded automatically. He'd asked for bread, and she'd responded with a line straight out of a practice dialogue from school, an invitation for dinner.

Ivar gaped. "Jesse, your wife speaks Indian."

Jesse strummed the final chord. "Unless I miss my guess, it's French they're speaking."

The Indian folded himself onto the grass between the two men. His rapid walking pace had led Susannah to expect a man in his teens or twenties, but his finely creased face belonged to someone in his forties or fifties. He seemed composed of straight lines: horizontal eyebrows and mouth, vertical nose and hair, diagonal jawlines, erect posture. His skin was lighter and not as red as the Indians in paintings, almost the color of the back of Jesse's neck at the end of summer. Although he did not carry a bow and arrows or a gun, a knife stuck out of a brightly decorated scabbard at his waist. Susannah shivered, and cold perspiration dampened her camisole.

Continuing in French, the stranger told her he recognized the violin but not the other instrument. "It's a guitar," she said in a tremulous voice. With a twinkle of amusement in his eyes, he asked why the others were not talking. Susannah explained they spoke English and Norwegian. Mademoiselle Dupont's lessons, preparing young ladies to read menus in Montreal or to tour art museums in Paris, flashed through her memory. She asked the savage where he'd learned French.

"Black Gown, at the end of the river," he replied, pointing northwest.

Jesse cleared his throat. "You might let the rest of us in on this conversation."

Through laborious two- and three-way interpretations, Susannah introduced the group. The stranger's Indian name tripped her tongue. She understood only the first two French words of his name. The Indian made some sign language, but Susannah still couldn't grasp his meaning.

"He's called 'Sees-the-' and I don't recognize the third word, Tatanka. It doesn't sound French."

"Sees? As in 'looks at' or 'grabs'?" Jesse asked without taking his gaze off the man.

"Looks at."

"Sees-the-Tatanka," Jesse repeated. He passed the man a prairie chicken sandwich. "Ask what brings him down the river."

The Indian had traveled alone to a holy place called Standing Rock, one day's journey south. He sought wisdom for his second child, a son. Grinning with pride, he spoke of a grown daughter married a moon ago and a third child who just learned to walk. But this adolescent son—

He pinched dirt between his thumb and forefinger, then let the wind blow it away. Susannah wanted to ask how he had limited his family to only three, with many years between them. Most white families consisted of stair-step children an average of two years apart. But one did not speak of such things.

Marta passed Sees-the-Tatanka a fried pastry. The expression on his face needed no translation. Licking his fingers, he asked if Ivar would sell Marta to him. Susannah shook her head and refused to interpret his offer. The Indian grinned and thudded Ivar on the back. Ah, he knew how to tease, like Jesse. Assuming he asked about the food, Marta gave him the recipe, showing him how to shape the dough with graceful movements of her hands. Enraptured, the Indian sighed.

"He says you are a most fortunate man, Ivar."

The Norwegian grunted.

Sees-the-Tatanka picked up the Bible and noted its similarity to the one "Black Gown" read. Jesse launched into a discussion of the differences between Catholics and Protestants.

Susannah stopped him. "Mademoiselle didn't cover theological terminology. I don't know the French words for sacrament, pope, saints, or half the other things you said. And I'm not sure he's interested."

The Indian's eyes had glazed over, but he brightened as Jesse reached for the guitar.

"All right then, interpret 'Jesus Loves Me.'"

This was the first English hymn Ivar and Marta had learned. All four voices joined in, with percussion provided by Sara's clapping.

Sees-the-Tatanka leaned back on one elbow, grinning. When they finished, he cried, *"Encore! Encore!"* By the third time, the Indian added his bass to the chorus. Lifting his head on the final note, he blurted in French, "If I don't get home before the new moon, my wife will have me sleeping with the dogs." He bounded up the hill, his voice echoing off the riverbanks: "The Bible tells me so."

Susannah collapsed against Marta. "At least he left without our scalps."

"Seemed like a regular fellow." Jesse corked his canteen.

"Regular fellow? Where were you in '62 when his kind massacred hundreds in Minnesota?"

"Another massacre. Antietam."

Ivar grunted, then grabbed his daughter as she tried to crawl away. "The extra sandwich—did you know we'd half a guest today?"

"No. He ate Susannah's." Jesse finally turned from the northern horizon where Sees-the-Tatanka disappeared. "Come on, Sacajawea, let's go home and get some food in you."

Ivar frowned. "Yes. I want to check my stock."

Jesse led the way out of the valley. "If we had the orphanage letter ready, Sees-the-Tatanka could have taken it to town for us. That'd ruffle Mrs. Rose's feathers, an Indian in her store. Give her something to cackle about. Well, better he skirts town. Mac's trapped with Indians, so he's all right. But some of the boys in the section house subscribe to Sheridan's notion: The only good Indian's—"

"Could we please stop a minute? My knees are knocking." Susannah fanned herself with her handkerchief. "I guess once a coward, always a coward."

"Coward? Who?"

"Me. I was terrified." She leaned against Jesse.

He gripped her shoulders, dropping his head low to look her

in the eye. "With the newspapers screaming 'Massacre!' 'Scalping!' every other column, only a fool wouldn't be afraid. Susannah, you're no fool and you're no coward." He hugged her. "Think back to your French class, the girl who sat in front of you."

"Marie Goodman."

"Ah yes, baker's daughter, clotheshorse. What would Mademoiselle Marie say to Sees-the-Tatanka?"

"She'd run. And scream."

"And get her two dozen petticoats caught in the underbrush." Jesse held her hand as they crossed the ridge. "And what about the girl behind you?"

"Elizabeth Van Meter. She would have the vapors. She actually did faint once, when a bee flew into the classroom."

"And the girl between Marie and Elizabeth?"

"Susannah Underhill. She wouldn't have said a thing."

Jesse lifted an eyebrow. "Do I need to preach a second sermon today?"

Chapter 23

Hey, I could use that army of angels about now . . .

Susannah watched her husband cross the partially cut field, vaulting piles of mown oats. Jesse drew energy from the wind, boundless, unpredictable, vigorous energy. His vitality nourished her, strengthened her, opened her to accept his love.

Love. It still amazed her that he thought she was worth loving. And if he loved her, maybe God could love her too.

Jesse tucked his work gloves into his waistband and rolled his sleeves to his elbows. She loved his hands: strong, masculine hands, with dark hair curling over the backs. She liked the angle of his knuckles, the way his palm curved when he held a tool, the sureness in his fingers when he played guitar. And especially, she liked his touch. In his hands she felt treasured, valued.

He removed his hat, letting the breeze dry the sweat from his head. The sun showed the deep lines etched by the War, sculpting a face more interesting than handsome, a face to study for the rest of her life.

His warm smile of greeting froze. He leaned on the long handle of the cradle, studying the cumulus-flecked sky.

"What's wrong?" Susannah set the lunch basket and canteen at the end of the row.

"The air smells funny. I'd say we're in for a storm."

"Maybe that's why the chickens were so noisy this morning." Susannah settled onto the grass and opened the lunch basket. "Hope it holds off a few hours so I can work on the garden. The beans, carrots, and cucumbers are ready for picking."

"You know that's not what we need to talk about." Jesse folded his long legs, bringing his face level with Susannah's.

She met his intense gaze. "Can't we try again? I'm strong enough to carry two buckets from the spring to the house without stopping. I've gained so much weight, I've had to let out my waistbands."

"So to keep you healthy, we're not even going to consider it." He made a circular motion with his sandwich, tallying the drooping heads of grain. Every morning a brief thunderstorm heralded the dawn, keeping the fields well watered. "Even with the drop in prices, the oats alone will bring in enough for the house lumber. We'll buy the barn lumber and a team with the wheat. If we write to the orphanages now, we can have a family before winter. Think of it, Susannah, children around the house for Christmas. Some little girl who's never opened a gift or a boy who's never gotten an orange in his stocking. Maybe a brother and sister. We'll have room."

"Could we get a little one, a playmate for Sara?"

"A little one with an older brother or sister." Jesse uncorked the canteen, washing the dust from his face with a palmful of water. He squinted over Susannah's head, cocking his head toward an unheard sound.

"We can't take an older child. Not until there's a school."

"Plenty of people, most not half as smart as you, teach their own children. Besides, the Roses have a flock of kids and so does that new family north of the tracks. We'll be getting a teacher soon enough."

All the color drained from his face. He didn't breathe for several moments, then his voice came out in a hoarse cry. "Oh perdition! No! Not again!"

The day dimmed with unnatural suddenness, swifter than the darkening of an impending storm. Susannah looked up, expecting to see an eclipse. A huge black insect flew past her face. She swatted it. One landed on her shoulder, another on her arm. Revulsion shuddered down her spine.

"Get the laundry! I'll get the stock!" Jesse shoved the lunch basket at her. "Susannah, now!"

Grasshoppers whirled across the sky, filling the air with their shrill roar.

"The oats?"

"Too late!" Cradle swinging from his shoulder, Jesse sprinted for the stable.

A curtain of black-winged insects dropped over her, clinging to her clothes, tangling in her hair. A scream rose in her throat. Grasshoppers hit her face, beating, clawing, scratching. She couldn't see through the mass of insects. She had to move, get the laundry, get inside. She took a step. Their bodies crunched beneath her shoes. Others crawled up her legs. She swatted, gently at first, not wanting their crushed bodies on hers, then harder, not caring, just wanting the biting, scratching, and crawling to stop.

Susannah fought her way down into the draw. She gave up trying not to step on the hoppers; they left no part of the ground uncovered. Crawling bodies blackened the laundry, too, and clung to the fabric as she gathered it. She shook them off and stumbled into the soddy, slamming the door and collapsing onto the stool.

The crackling and chewing followed her inside. "Not in my house!" She yanked on work gloves, opened one of the stove lids, and began chasing grasshoppers. Shirts, drawers, sheets, and rags were laced with holes and noxious bugs. Something pinched her leg. She shook her skirts, searching through each petticoat. One screeched in her ear. She raked her fingers down her scalp, unraveling her braid, ripping hair from her head. "Ow! You evil monsters! Go away!"

Grasshoppers hit the window and roof like hail and marched in under the door. "Screaming doesn't help. Calm down. Think. Mrs. Child recommends turpentine, but we don't have any. Spearmint repels ants, and marigold works for potato beetles. What works on grasshoppers?" Susannah snatched the saltshaker from the shelf and sprinkled the doorsill. They kept coming. She tried pepper, but they were not impressed. Kerosene was far too risky. But what about . . .

Jake and Jesse arrived in a stampede of insects, knocking Susannah backward as they scrambled through the door.

Jesse sniffed and made a face. "What's going on?"

"Ellen's perfume seems to be repelling the grasshoppers."

He collapsed sideways onto the bed. "We'll have the best-smelling hoppers in the territory," he mumbled.

The dog shook, scattering insects throughout the room. Susannah raced to capture the invaders. "How long will this last?"

"Until they've eaten everything." His words tolled heavy with finality.

"Everything?" The garden? The herbs from the seeds Ellen sent? The flowers?

"Yes, everything." Jesse covered his eyes with his forearm. He sounded hollow, defeated. "How much food do we have left?"

Susannah checked the shelves. "The brine barrel is a quarter full. We have a pound of bacon, one can of peaches, a half pound of coffee beans, almost two pounds of cornmeal, and nearly five pounds of flour. Hey, they're eating through the flour sack! Into the fire with you. The root cellar is pretty empty, just some dried plums." Of course provisions ran low right before harvest. "Is there anything we can do?"

"I'll set fires tonight, but it won't help. Might as well try to fence the wind."

At dawn, Susannah armored herself in her husband's canvas pants, belted with rope and tucked into socks. She pushed her gloves into her sleeves and pinned on a hat with a veil. With a prayer for courage, she stepped into Dakota's version of the Inferno. Despite smoldering piles in every field, the grasshopper population seemed as great as ever. The chirr from millions of chomping jaws and beating wings continued like the noise of a demonic machine. Jesse, his face black with smoke and despair, stood at the edge of what had been his wheat field. His posture sagged; only his clothes and the rake held him upright. Susannah's steps crunched on insect bodies. "Jesse? Are you all right?"

A tremor ran through him. "The field will have to be burned next spring to kill off the eggs. Or planted late, after they hatch."

"We can do that." She slid her palm under his elbow to steady him. "This smell has turned my stomach, but I'll fix breakfast for you. Would you like your grasshoppers poached, fried, or on toast?"

He pulled away. "Susannah, there's nothing funny about this. We're out of food, out of money, and there's no railroad jobs like in '72."

She retreated a step. "Mr. Rose will let you open an account. You're a good customer."

His spine stiffened. "Once a man gets into debt, he never gets out. I've never owed anyone and don't intend to start now."

"There's the egg money and what I brought with me. Maybe ten dollars."

He didn't seem to hear her. "If I can find a buyer for the calves, I'll order grain from Fargo. Grasshoppers haven't hit there yet, so the price should still be low." At last he looked up. "Where did you get that hat?"

"It's my mourning bonnet."

"Funeral for our homestead."

She took his hand. He didn't return her squeeze. "Come on. I'll fix you a bath and even scrub your back."

The next morning, while Jesse slept, Susannah went out to see what she could do for the stock. The chickens seemed content, lethargic even, from feasting on the grasshoppers, but the oxen snorted their agitation.

A bobbing mass of insects clogged the creek. Susannah found a couple of tree branches broken from the weight of the infestation and anchored the ends in the mud on either bank, crossing them in the middle to form a dam. The insects piled up against the sticks, and on the downstream side patches of open water appeared, allowing the oxen to drink.

When she returned to the soddy, she opened the door to find Jesse sitting at the table staring at the kerosene lamp. He seemed to have aged ten years in the past two days. New wrinkles cut a path down the side of his face.

Susannah slid onto the trunk next to him and stroked his back with slow, even pressure, as if he were a wounded animal. "Did you sleep at all?"

Jesse picked up the leather drawstring purse at his elbow and tossed it across the table. It landed with a soft clink on the back page of the *Fargo Express*, the listing of current prices. Penciled calculations covered the newspaper's margins.

"Thought I'd have smooth sailing once I gave up drinking. Thought I could support a wife and children. Thought I was working hard enough, praying hard enough." He reached for the Bible, opening to a place bookmarked by his ledger. "'But if any provide not for his own, and specially for those of his own house, he hath denied the faith, and is worse than an infidel.'"

He slammed the book shut and hit the table with his palm. "I want to take care of my family. What am I doing wrong?"

Susannah clutched her arms against a sudden chill. She had never seen Jesse so beaten down. "Didn't you tell me God would provide? Where's the verse about how He clothes the lilies and feeds the birds?"

"In the same chapter telling us to give alms. But I can't provide for you, much less help the poor. Maybe our Promised Land is somewhere else. Maybe we should do a Prodigal Son, go back to New York, see if my brother-in-law needs a hired hand." He ground his forehead into his fist. "I'm getting too old to start over. Nothing to show for all these years of hard work."

Susannah clenched her hands. If only she had money. "What about selling the calves? Or the chickens? Maybe Matt's found my inheritance."

He wasn't listening. "I'll go to Fargo, see if I can pick up enough work to get us through the winter."

"Fargo? But the animals—"

He pushed past her, almost knocking over the table. "You know more about them than I do."

"Wait. You're leaving me?"

"I don't have a choice. If it's just me, I can sleep in a barn, not pay for a hotel room. You stay here and keep the homestead going, keep the claim jumpers out. Not that anyone'd want this place—"

"There must be another way. Perhaps Mr. McFadgen—"

"I'll write every week, send you all the money I can." He stomped around the soddy, stuffing pants and shirts into his knapsack. "I'll be back soon as I earn enough to get us through."

"What about trapping?"

"I won't let you starve." He reached for her, pulling her to his shoulder. "I'll leave Jake and the shotgun. You'll be all right."

Overnight the wind picked up, taking the grasshoppers with it. The destruction reminded Susannah of Mathew Brady's photographs of the South after the War. No leaf, no plant in the garden had escaped. Not a stalk of wheat or oats remained. Flat clouds covered the sky like a granite slab over a grave.

On their ride to town, Susannah held back from telling Jesse how much she'd miss him. She wouldn't admit how worried she was, wouldn't ask what they'd do if he didn't find work.

Jesse didn't speak until they arrived at the Volds'. "Something's wrong. No smoke from the stovepipe and the oxen aren't picketed."

"Marta? Ivar?" Swarms of flies covered the house, as thick as yesterday's grasshoppers. Ignoring Jesse's warning about disease, Susannah jumped from the wagon and yanked open the door. Just as quickly she shut it, gasping for fresh air. Mastering her stomach and swatting flies, she stepped over the threshold. "Hello?" She threaded her way past a full chamber pot and bucket and a dead animal that on closer inspection turned out to be a pile of used diapers.

"*Ja,*" Ivar answered from the bed. "We half been up all night. Spoiled sausage. New people north of the tracks bring it. Marta and Sara sleep just now." Ivar nodded at the baby curled between him and his wife. "How is it you happen to come?"

"We're on our way to Worthington." Susannah touched his forehead. Cool. "Shall I ask Jesse to order grain for you too?"

Ivar groaned. "The grasshoppers. *Ja,* I need grain."

She found Jesse watering Ivar's oxen. As she had at their own homestead, she built a brush dam upstream to filter the creek of dead grasshoppers.

"Susannah, you're too smart for this life." Jesse nodded toward the soddy. "How are they?"

"It's been a rough night." She filled a bucket with the water, coffee brown from grasshopper excrement. "They're dehydrated, weak. I should stay, make sure they get back on their feet."

For a moment he climbed out of his pain, his hazel eyes studying hers. "Don't catch it. I won't be here to take care of you."

"It's not contagious. It was bad meat." Susannah laid her palm on his cheek, its stubble testifying to Jesse's low spirits. "How can I bear a day apart from you?"

A hint of a smile flickered at the corner of his mouth. "Better to say good-bye here without Mrs. Rose looking on. I'll have one of the boys bring the wagon back." He pulled her to his chest with painful fierceness. "I promise you. It won't be our animals and furniture getting auctioned off, us getting driven into Fargo, begging on the streets. I won't let it."

She watched until the wagon disappeared over the rise. "Hurry home."

The last load of diapers flapped on the clothesline, and Ivar and Marta sat at the table sipping ginger tea, when the wagon rattled into the draw. Susannah tucked the clean sheets around the mattress and went out to meet it. The wagon was empty.

"Bye!"

A hundred yards away a boy, one of the Roses, leaped like a jackrabbit through the big bluestem toward the north. Susannah stretched to peer into the wagon box. Empty. The wind crackled a paper rolled up in the rifle scabbard. She flattened the brown scrap and held the pencil-scribbled words to the sunlight.

Mac says carpenters needed over to Jamestown. —J.M.

She had allowed herself to hope that Jesse wouldn't have to go, that somehow God would come through for them. And now that hope shattered in her chest and pierced her heart.

The wind swirled a dust devil across the empty field. A killdeer crested the hill on its toothpick legs, then flapped away with a plaintive call. She dried a tear she didn't remember crying.

Ivar staggered from the soddy and propped himself on the box of the wagon. "Where is Jesse?"

Susannah focused on the smoke from the stovepipe vanishing into the overcast. She swallowed down the lump in her throat. "Gone to Jamestown. To look for work."

"Grasshoppers. We won't be able to send money to Norway this year. My brother was hoping to emigrate." Ivar launched into Norwegian, a stream of words Susannah didn't understand but knew Marta would have disapproved of. The man raged on, trying to wall off his distress with fury. Finally he ran out of steam and switched back to English. "There's work in Jamestown?"

"He hopes."

Ivar kicked at the dirt. "He ever tell you how he came to Dakota? His little sister married and he decided he wasn't needed at home. So he hopped the train west. Didn't come to his senses until he hit Chicago."

"Sometimes he thinks he's still fighting the War," she said.

Ivar nodded, grim. "That's why so many of us drink."

Alcohol. Something else to worry about. If only she'd brought a dowry, something more than four dollars. If only—

No. Jesse had told her to stop taking the blame for everything. She didn't know who to blame for the grasshoppers, but they weren't her fault.

The sun teased the horizon. This was no time to dissolve into a puddle. Jesse was counting on her. Susannah stomped over to the clothesline and yanked down the laundry. "I'd best be going. Keep Sara on ginger tea for tonight. Sweeten it with honey or white sugar but not brown."

Ivar followed her to the end of the clothesline. "You cannot go back to Jesse's by yourself. You must stay here."

"And learn to swear in Norwegian?" Susannah shoved the stack of diapers at him. Much as she liked the Volds, she had no intention of squeezing in with them. She needed time alone, time to cry and scream and, if possible, think. "I'll bring in your oxen."

"I'm sorry about swearing." Ivar balanced the diapers. "You cannot go. Is not safe for a woman alone. We make room for you."

Susannah jerked up the picket pins and herded Ivar's team to the creek. "I've got cattle, chickens, and a dog to care for."

"You charmed the moccasins off Sees-the-Tatanka, but maybe you not so lucky with the next Indian. What if he doesn't know French? Or won't let you talk before scalping you?"

She stopped at the clear space below her makeshift dam. "Jesse took his Winchester but left me the shotgun."

Ivar watched her shovel out the area upstream. "What's this?" He tapped his boot against the branches.

"I tried it on our creek. The water may not taste better, but at least you don't have to chew it."

He watched a few minutes before turning back to the soddy. "Go back to Jesse's, then. You don't need my help."

When she came in sight of the homestead, Jake appeared and joined Susannah on the wagon seat. She put her arm around the dog's neck. "I'm glad of your company."

The oxen slowed to a stop by the shed. "All right, show me how to unhitch the team," she said to Jake. The dog just grinned at her and panted. "I see. You'd rather sit up here and watch me make mistakes. Sure, you've got the best seat in the house."

Susannah climbed down and unfastened the bows. With a grunt she lifted the yoke, found it too heavy, and returned it to its position. She changed her grip, lugged it over the back of one animal and the horns of the other, and eased the weight onto her shoulder. She stepped into something slippery and her feet shot out from under her. She landed hard. The yoke whacked her ear and thudded onto her shoulder. The world darkened and spun.

"Darn it! Now *I'm* swearing." Susannah rubbed her sore head. "Jesse," she yelled at the setting sun, "you get back here right now! I came out here to marry a safe, dependable farmer, not an itinerant carpenter. This is not fair! You can't leave just as I find I can't live without you."

Despite her best efforts, the tears came. "I can't do this by myself. God, I need help!"

Pa Ox took the opportunity to sneeze on her.

"That's not what I had in mind." She shoved his nose away and rotated her right arm. Nothing broken. Manure caked her skirts and saturated her petticoats; she had slipped on a cow pie.

"Well, oxen, you know where the water is. Go on."

She scrambled to her feet and slapped them on the flanks, then glared at the watching dog. "Next time you unhitch, and I'll sit and laugh."

He wagged his tail.

The land west of Worthington was as empty as Jesse's pockets. The farther the train went, the shorter the grass grew. Homesteading out here would be nigh impossible. Not that it was easy along the Sheyenne. Rotten, stinking grasshoppers.

He got off at Jamestown and waved good-bye to the half dozen greenhorn soldiers heading to Fort Lincoln. "God be with you," he muttered, "because He surely isn't billeting with me."

Whoa. Where'd that thought come from? *Sorry, God. I know You're here. Somewhere . . .*

He swabbed the sweat from his forehead. Now, something for this dry throat.

"Hey!" A man in dire need of a barber crawled out from under the platform. "You seen my wife?"

"No, sir. Just off the train." Jamestown was a handful of buildings facing the tracks. Not many places to hole up.

"You sure?" The man staggered close, bringing with him the familiar miasma of sweated rotgut. No wonder his wife had gone into hiding. "Betsy's her name. Stands 'bout this high." He held up a hand. "Red hair, like yours. You related?"

"No Betsys in my family. If I see her, who should I say is looking for her?" Who should she run from?

"William Stapleton. Her husband." He pointed to a single-story building at the end of the row, almost losing his balance in the effort. "Say, how about a drink?"

"They have coffee? Easier to find her when you're sober."

Stapleton's hands clenched into fists but wouldn't stay closed long enough to throw a punch. "Ya don't know nuthin'."

"I know Who can help you stop drinking."

"No call for that." Stapleton lurched toward the saloon, yelling, "Betsy!" in a tone that would make hogs run and glass break.

Jesse hefted his guitar onto one shoulder and his knapsack to the other. He crossed the stage road and passed a few log buildings at the base of the hill, the start of the fort, then began the long climb in the hot sun.

William Stapleton. What a mess. A real familiar mess. Maybe even a warning sign from God? He paused to drain his canteen. Warm water never tasted so good. *Thank You, Lord.* Now all he needed was work.

A scrawny kid with a carbine stepped out of the guardhouse. "Halt!" he said, his voice breaking.

Jesse held the Winchester so the boy could see it wasn't loaded and introduced himself. "Captain Bates around?"

"Probably in the company office." The boy pointed. "Or officers' quarters."

"Thank you, sir."

The kid startled. Guess no one had ever called him sir.

Jesse crossed the parade grounds under the snapping flag. He'd hate to pull sentry duty out here in the winter. He'd be gone by then, back to Susannah. He hoped.

Jesse knocked on the office door.

The captain held an official-looking correspondence up to the window. "Enter. Double time if you're selling spectacles."

"Sold my last pair to your sentry when he shot me for a hostile."

The captain dropped the letter and smiled. "Mason. You finally decided to accept my invitation. Welcome to Fort Seward."

"Good to see you." Jesse pumped his sweating hand. "I was afraid you'd finished your enlistment or headed for a warmer post."

"It wouldn't be the army if it wasn't awful. What do you think of my new quarters? Drop your load behind my desk and I'll give you a tour." Bates led him out onto the veranda. "How about this view? Miles of nothing."

The land dropped away south to the tracks, east to the James River, west to Pipestem Creek. "No one can sneak up on you."

"But every stick of firewood has to be hauled up the hill," Bates said with a wry smile. "The men often speak of you, the only settler between Ransom and here." Several greeted them as the captain toured Jesse past the barracks, laundresses' quarters, kitchen, mess room, storeroom, washroom, and hospital. The buildings were frame, with tarred paper lining the clapboard and paper plastering boards on the interior. The way Jesse would build for Susannah. If he ever had money.

The place seemed sparsely populated, plenty of room for an extra carpenter. "How many men you got?"

"Fifty-six enlisted and three officers. We have an eight-acre garden on the bottom land. Hunting and grazing are poor, so meat's shipped in. Speaking of which, how about some chow?"

The meal featured corn grown at the fort. "As good as yours?" Bates asked.

"The grasshoppers loved it."

The captain winced. "No way to bell that cat."

Jesse figured he might as well get to the point. "So I'm looking for work."

"Sorry to say, there's no work and no money to pay you if we did. I hear Bismarck's booming. Custer's building his kingdom at Fort Lincoln."

Jesse looked at his plate. He should eat. Who knew when he'd have another meal like this?

Bates slapped him on the shoulder. "Hey, you brought your guitar. Let's have some music this evening, then pass the hat."

That night Jesse sang every song he knew and several he didn't. The hat yielded a brass button, an eagle's feather, and a little over nine dollars, five of which had been provided by Captain Bates.

Nowhere near enough.

Susannah washed the dishes from her first meal alone, yesterday's cornbread and a slice of salt pork. Cooking for one was hardly worth the effort, especially when her shoulder and ear were still sore from the yoke.

As the light changed outside, it threw rose-colored trapeziums on the plastered east wall and blue shadows along the creek. Susannah followed the sunbeam to the rise behind the soddy. The stratus layer pulled away from the western horizon, and the sun painted a band of honey-colored light between the deep violet sky and navy land. It reminded Susannah of the theater, the stage lights glowing beneath the curtain.

If she were onstage, Susannah wished the Playwright would give her a look at the script.

Chapter 24

Jesus, I thought I understood Your plan.
Doesn't make any sense to give me a wife, then
take away my means to provide for her.

Susannah pushed the quilts back. Last night sleep had rolled over her like a locomotive, heavy and unstoppable. She dreamed of warm, calloused fingers working through the layers of her clothes, caressing her tender places. An hour before dawn the wind banged the stovepipe, jerking her awake and reminding her Jesse was gone. Heartache fought fatigue and won.

"Guess that's enough pretending to sleep. How about you?" she asked Jake. Susannah had brought him inside for company. Talking to him seemed slightly more sane than talking to herself.

Jake's triangular ears twitched at her words. He had spent the week on full alert, pacing, listening for his master, following at Susannah's heels even on trips to the outhouse. Now he laid his head on his paws and sighed.

Susannah shuffled to the stove. The empty wood box, evidence of her lethargy, stared back at her. "Jesse's job," she mumbled. Anger stabbed through her sadness.

Susannah tossed a shawl around her shoulders and wandered

out to the depleted woodpile. She inhaled fresh air. The rain had dissipated the grasshopper stench. Or maybe she'd just gotten used to it.

Any minute now Jesse would come striding down the ridge, wind billowing the sky blue shirt she'd sewn for him. She'd run to meet him and he'd catch her up, spinning her in a circle. He would have found a good job, earned enough, and headed for home, never to leave again.

Any minute now . . .

No, probably later in the day. The eastbound train arrived late afternoon, and it would take him hours to walk home, unless he borrowed a horse. But if he was detained by Mrs. Rose, then he might—

Jake pushed his wet nose into her palm. "Yes, I'm at it again, after I promised you I'd stop mooning about." She gathered an armload of sticks, then paused with her hand on the door latch. Jesse would be sitting at the table, an apology and a smile on his lips. But the door swung into an empty room.

"Jake, Sunday morning breakfast should be pancakes and coffee." She poured water into the iron saucepan. "As long as you don't tell anyone, I'm having toast and tea."

Susannah found her shoes in the pile of dirty laundry under the bed. Mixed with the usual smells of perspiration and animal muck was a faint odor of kerosene. "Let's do laundry tomorrow, before these clothes catch fire. That would make a nice blaze, wouldn't it? Throw in the bedding, the bed if I can get it apart, the guitar—" Susannah turned in a circle. "Where is Jesse's guitar? Did he take it with him?"

Jake leaned against her and she rubbed his ears. "No, burning would be wasteful. Jesse built this house and this furniture. I'll take good care of it."

Boiling water burbled in the pan. She poured it over the tea, adding a pinch of ginger, and slid a slice of bread onto the oven grate.

What if he took the guitar intending to earn money with his music? What if he went to a saloon and started drinking? He could be passed out in an alley again. What if he saw all the soldiers from the fort and thought he was back in the War?

She wrenched herself out of the downward spiral and dried her face on her apron.

"So, Jake, what shall we plan for dinner?" she asked with as much cheerfulness as she could muster. "What do you want? What do I want? Jake, do you realize this is the first time in my whole well-ordered life that I've been alone? No parents, no pastor, no husband to tell me what to do? I can do what I want. So, what do I want?"

Sunrise lit up the bed, fortified with her coat to compensate for the loss of Jesse's warmth. His pillow sat in the middle, wadded up where Susannah had held it through the night. "Jesse. That's what I want."

She took the toast from the oven, left half on the table, and joined Jake on the sunny threshold. The first bite formed a pasty lump in her throat. She passed the rest to the dog, who swallowed it in one gulp.

"In stories, the heroine always has some feeling about the hero when he's away. She knows if he's in danger, if he's dead or alive." Susannah gazed out over the yard, past the creek to the horizon, already shimmering with heat waves from the barren fields. "About Jesse, I feel nothing, absolutely nothing. I have no sense of where he is or how he is, if he's eaten breakfast or gone hungry. Maybe we haven't known each other long enough to be connected in that way. Maybe—"

She sipped the tea; the warm liquid slid past the heavy spot in her throat. "Will I ever know him? I've been letting Jesse do the praying for both of us. But he's gone, so here I am, Lord. Please bring him—"

Something rustled and scratched behind her—a mouse! She grabbed the broom and swept it out the door with Jake in hot pursuit.

As Susannah crouched by the shelves to assess the damage to her meager food supplies, she heard a soft plop on the table. She turned and looked straight into a pair of tiny black eyes attached to a long green body.

Susannah jumped, crashed into the stove, and ran out the door. Then she stopped. If she wanted this snake out, if she didn't want him slithering into her bed, she had to do it herself. And quickly, or he'd hide and she'd be up all night hunting him.

"Lord, please give me courage." She took a couple of deep breaths, then went back into the soddy and stretched out the end of the broom toward the table. The snake obligingly wrapped its two-foot length around the tree branch handle. Its tongue flicked and its head swiveled.

Susannah backed through the door and tossed the broom and its rider into the grass.

"I did it!"

The creak of a wagon carried into the draw, and Jake raced up the ridge. But at the crest, the dog's tail uncurled, his head drooped. Not Jesse. Susannah's heart thudded in her chest.

"Susannah!" Marta, her radiance startling against the bleak landscape, jumped off when Ivar stopped. Susannah hugged her.

"She worried all week about you." Ivar climbed down, then retrieved her broom. "Why—" Then he saw the reptile. "Ah! Where is your hoe? I'll kill it for you."

"No. It's just a garter snake, not poisonous. It was chasing the mouse who chewed through my cornmeal sack. I suppose they're eating my food since the grasshoppers ate theirs." Susannah turned toward the soddy. "Come on in. I've got hot water for tea."

"No coffee?" Ivar asked.

"All right, I'll make coffee for you. I've been drinking ginger tea. Must have gotten a touch of the grippe." Susannah emptied ground beans into the pot. "Looks like you've all recovered."

Ivar settled onto the stool, baby Sara on his knee. "Yes, we're over it. But you? This all you eat?" He flicked the toast crust with the back of his broad hand. "You don't look so good."

Marta poured water from the ewer into the basin, wet a cloth, and handed it to Susannah.

"I was going to clean up before meeting you at the river." She washed, then ran damp hands over her unruly hair. When had she last combed it? If Jesse saw her like this—

Marta touched the muslin tacked over the window.

"Empty windows didn't bother me when Jesse was here."

"No eating. No washing. Hanging curtains, against what?" Ivar frowned. "Have you done any work this week?"

"The grasshoppers ate everything. There is no work."

"No?" Ivar thumped his fist on the table, making Susannah jump. His face darkened in various shades of scarlet and crimson. He was heading for an attack of apoplexy if this temper kept up. Speaking slowly as if she might have difficulty understanding English, he said, "Susannah, this is why you should not be alone."

"All right then, tell me." Susannah sat on the trunk next to Marta and hid her shaking hands under the table. "What should I be doing?"

"Have you mucked the stable? You know the cattle's hooves will rot if you don't. The potatoes need to be forked up, also any turnips and carrots the hoppers missed." He shifted his weight. The stool squealed in protest. "This seat needs tightening. Firewood and slough grass must be cut, and there's back setting, plowing under the stubble. It's too much."

"Of course I cleaned the stable. Soon as I shake this—"

"It does not matter how you feel. You are a woman. Not strong enough. Heavy work will cripple you. You won't be able to take care of yourself or the stock. A woman should not homestead alone."

"Jesse thought I could."

"He left you at our place and expected you to stay."

"If I leave, we'll lose the claim with only a year to go."

"The claim? Who cares about the claim? Do you see anyone from the Fargo Land Office out here checking on the claim?" Ivar pounded again, making Susannah wonder if she'd have to add table repair to her list. "If anything should happen to you, you stubborn woman—" He lapsed into Norwegian.

Stubborn? He was calling her stubborn? Ivar, that high-handed despot, could stand in for Napoleon. Why Jesse ever picked him for a friend—

Marta grabbed their hands, lowered her head, and spoke in a calm tone.

Ivar's deep sigh ruffled his mustache. "She's praying from Thessalonians, peace among the brethren."

Susannah added her silent prayer, then apologized to Ivar. "I appreciate your concern, but I really am all right. What if I sold the calves? Maybe Mr. McFadgen or one of the hotels in Fargo would buy them. If I could pay my way, I wouldn't feel like such a burden to you."

Ivar studied her under his eyebrows. "*Ja*, and I wouldn't have to add on to our barn and wouldn't need so much credit for grain. Good."

Susannah opened Jesse's Bible. "Before we start church, do you remember the song Jesse taught us last Sunday? The chorus has been buzzing through my head all week."

Ivar frowned. "It was about a lamp."

"Psalm one-one-nine," Marta said. "Foot lights."

"Footlights?" Susannah turned to the chapter, one of many

with chords written in the margins. "Here it is: 'Thy word is a lamp unto my feet.' So the Bible is the script?"

"Scrip? Like army pay?"

"No, a script as in a play, acting out a story. The script tells the actors what to say and do."

"*Ja*, the Bible tells us what to say and do. Good lesson, Susannah. Much better than the one I'd planned on grasshopper plagues." Ivar snapped his Bible shut. "Before we pray, we half a surprise for you." He set Sara on her feet. She toddled over to Susannah, face glowing, blond tendrils bouncing with each deliberate step.

"You're walking!" Susannah swung her into a hug. "Jesse will be so proud of you!"

"And of you also," Marta said to Susannah.

"Susannah!" Ivar roared. The Volds had said their good-byes, then stopped just out of the draw. Ivar stood in the wagon, one foot propped on the seat, his face a pre-apoplectic red. When Susannah ran up, he pointed to a scorched strip twice the width of the wagon and running parallel to the draw for a hundred feet or so. "You burned firebreak by yourself. That's a job for men, a crew of men. You could half burned the whole territory!"

"You think I set a fire?" she sputtered. "I would never—We nearly lost everything in that big fire last fall. Don't you remember Jesse telling—" Choking with fury, Susannah spun away to inspect the line where singed prairie met unburned bluestem.

"Enough! Come with us. Now!" He flung down the reins and raised his arms, looking every inch a direct descendant of Thor, the god of thunder.

Thunder? The word stirred an idea in Susannah's mind, and she marched over to the cottonwood sapling she'd transplanted from the river. It had been stripped of leaves by the grasshoppers and split in two by . . .

"Lightning." Ivar traced the charred path down the trunk. "The storm Wednesday." He tipped his head back, studying the sky. "God give you a firebreak. So. You're not alone after all. See you next Sunday."

Every step took Jesse farther away from Susannah. He hadn't found any work in Bismarck, so he had no choice but to cross the river to Fort Abraham Lincoln.

"Where's the ferry?" Jesse called to a boy fishing upstream.

The kid stuck his pole into the muddy bank and raced off on bare feet. Jesse sat on a crate and waited. What was Susannah doing today? She'd be all right; she handled lonesome easier than most. And what a farmwife she turned out to be with her animal doctoring. Today was Sunday; she'd be meeting the Volds at the river for church. They were praying for him, he was sure of it. *Lord, keep an eye on them, especially my Susannah.*

About the time he'd swatted his weight in mosquitoes, two bandy-legged men tramped down the bluff. They wore knitted caps and flannel shirts in spite of the heat. "*Allo,* sir. You are in need of the ferry?"

French, Jesse figured, with a healthy dash of Indian. "I'm heading for the fort."

They settled on a price. Their boat turned out to be a buffalo hide stretched across a wicker frame to form a bowl. It looked about as cozy as a coffin and as stable as a pig on ice. The men held the tub for Jesse, then squeezed aboard.

"Bull boat," the one in the blue hat explained, as if having a name made it seaworthy.

Three feet out, the trouble started.

"Eh, where is the paddle?" Red Hat asked.

Blue Hat lifted his feet, then looked under Jesse.

"I'm not sitting on it."

These fools didn't have any way to steer? What had he gotten himself into? This was Jesse's first experience with the Missouri, and everything he'd heard about it was, unfortunately, true.

"Out. Go." Red motioned for Blue to walk the boat back to shore, but the current spun them into midstream.

"No, the boat will tip," Blue said. "It was your turn to bring the paddle."

"Your squaw used it to stir the laundry."

Judging by their stink, the paddle hadn't helped much. The discussion continued in another language or two complete with wild gestures. The boat bucked like an unbroken horse.

"Hey, what's that?" Jesse pointed. The water rippled unevenly around something. And they were headed straight for it.

"Help! *Au secours! A l'aide!*"

The boat slammed into the stump and flung the men into the air. The river came up to swallow them.

No stage curtains graced this sunset. The clear sky glowed with a pearly mix of grayed yellow and pink, like the breast of a mourning dove.

Escorted by Jake, Susannah trudged up the slope and plopped down on a patch of gravel. "So this is Your script." She held up Jesse's Bible. "Two thousand years ago, maybe. But today? We've got railroads, husbands who leave, grasshoppers—"

Wait a minute. Ivar had planned a sermon on grasshopper plagues. An old Sunday school lesson rang in her head like a distant church bell. Moses and locusts.

Susannah lowered her head. "Jesse said You know all my thoughts, Lord. So You know I'm just up here with the Bible hoping to bribe You into bringing Jesse back." The frayed ribbon marked Psalm 119, so she read the next chapter, tilting the book to let the last rays of sun light the page. "'In my distress I cried unto the Lord, and he heard me.' Well, that certainly applies to this week." She read on. "'I lift my eyes unto the hills, from whence cometh my help.'"

She looked up, hoping to see Jesse strolling home along the ridge. Instead, the fading dusk brightened with a shimmering, ethereal light, purer than sunlight. The grasshopper-eaten wasteland vanished, revealing a ripe-for-harvest farmland portioned by a grid of straight gravel roads. Each square contained crops: oats heavy with grain, velvet green wheat, shiny emerald corn, and yelloworange sunflowers. Columns of trees sheltered well-kept frame houses and barns. A steeple and school bell tower reached toward the sky. Cattle grazed on the slope to the north.

The scene blurred. Susannah blinked, bringing her world back into focus. She knew what she'd seen. It was Jesse's vision of the future. God's vision. And now, Susannah's vision too.

Chetan lifted his chin toward the river. "Whites scare away the fish."

Misun watched the bull boat move in circles down the river. "No paddles. No brains."

"But one has a nice rifle." His cousin started his horse down the bluff, braids slapping his back.

Misun clicked to his gray and followed. "Your mother will be mad if you are shot."

"Whites without paddles are too busy to shoot."

"How will you get the rifle?"

"I do not know." The river might be low this time of year, but it was never free of trouble. The boys trailed the boat downstream. They recognized the two with the knit hats, whiskey traders who had been banned from the Standing Rock Agency. The third, with the nice rifle, was unfamiliar.

"Go." Chetan urged his horse into the water. But before he could reach them, the boat slammed into a stump. The men flew out, hit the water, then disappeared. A moment later something white bobbed up downstream.

The boys swam their horses to the floating thing. Chetan grabbed, but the river did not release it. Misun hooked the other side. The stranger hung underneath. Moving in tandem, they hauled him to the riverbank.

Chetan slid off his horse. "He dropped the rifle."

"So would I." Misun squatted beside the drowned man. The floating thing turned out to be a woven bag. Why did it not sink? Inside, he found a hollow object made of polished wood, about as long as a beaver. Wires stretched its length; perhaps useful as snares. When Misun tried to pull them off, they made a noise.

Chetan donned the man's shoes. Too loose. "Maybe they will fit Father."

"Hey." The wires made sounds, each different. "Maybe our mothers will forget about the fish."

"Only food makes me forget hunger."

The man gurgled and coughed, spitting river water. He opened his eyes, looked at Misun, and said, "Tatanka."

"He speaks." Misun introduced himself and his cousin, then held up the wood thing. "What is this called? What does it do?" But the white's eyes closed and he was silent.

"He called you the wrong name." Chetan rooted through the other bag on the man's back, finding clothes, a tin cup, and a small knife.

"Hey." The boy loosened the string holding the man's hat to

his head. An eagle's feather had been woven into the hatband. "Maybe his name is Tatanka. Maybe he has done a great deed."

"Like shoot some Indians?" Chetan opened a metal bottle and tasted water. Cleaner than using a skin; worth saving.

"I want to keep him. He can teach me this." Misun pulled on the wires, making more sounds.

"Now who has no brains?" In the man's pocket, Chetan found a few coins. He saved them for the next time a trader came through.

Misun brought his horse close. The animal snorted, protesting the strange smell of the man.

"Your horse thinks this is a bad idea too. Leave him here. The whites will bury him according to their customs."

Misun shook the white. "Tatanka! Wake up!"

The man was heavy, but he roused enough to stand. The boys flopped him over Misun's horse, bringing up more river water from his belly. They climbed the bluff and headed toward their village.

"If he is not dead now," Chetan said to the sunset, "he will be when we get home."

Susannah kicked the loose dirt. "Ivar says there could be potatoes here. Dogs are good at digging. Why don't you find them?"

Jake flopped at the edge of the garden, panting.

"Not even pointing me in the right direction?" She dragged the potato fork along the furrows. Morning sun warmed her shoulders and evaporated the dew from the row of stubs that had been cornstalks. "All this good food, gone. Lord, Jesse said it was all right to be angry with You, so let me just say, I'm furious! I worked hard on this garden, planting, weeding, watering. And Jake kept it free of rabbits."

The dog stood, scanning for invaders.

"Why? What did we do wrong?" At the far end of the furrow,

she turned over a finger-sized piece of rind, all that remained of her watermelon crop. "You said You'd provide for all our needs. You said ask and we'll receive. I'm pretty sure Jesse asked You to provide for us, so I'm asking again. Please—"

A leafless woody vine marked the former pumpkin patch.

Orienting herself, she guessed the location of the row, stabbed, and levered down on the handle. Up popped a potato. The next forkful brought up three. Then five.

By noon Susannah had filled the root cellar.

She turned her face to the sky. "Thank You, Lord," she said. But in the back of her mind, the truth gnawed at her: Jesse hadn't needed to leave after all.

Susannah? Jesse reached for his wife but felt only grass and hard ground. His lungs burned from coughing and his muscles ached from shivering with the cold. And the smell! Someone had a bad case of Confederate's disease.

He heard a drumbeat, a steady rhythm. People sang but not in English. Somewhere a dog barked. Jesse managed to get his eyes open. The darkness was complete. Had he gone blind? No, the moon shone through an opening in the roof. He felt around. A tent, with leather walls, he guessed. No clothes. A wool blanket lay next to his feet. He covered himself. Water would taste good about now, to get this bitter taste out of his mouth.

Then he remembered. Grasshoppers. Susannah. Money. How long had he been gone? He had to—

An elderly woman leaned over him. He couldn't understand the words, but she gave him a chewing out that would have scared the toughest sergeant in the army. Moonlight caught on the silver circle hanging from her neck.

Another person came into view, a man with straight long hair, an Indian. Sees-the-Tatanka, maybe.

He tried to speak but the effort exhausted him, and he couldn't stay awake to hear what the man would say.

Susannah swung the scythe at the tall slough grass. The blade bounced, cutting only two stems. She tightened her grip, raised the handle over her left shoulder, and put all her weight into the swing. The impact vibrated up her arm to the base of her neck. Three stalks fell. She took the sharpening stone from her apron pocket, ran it along the blade, and tried again. The results were no better.

"I'm just tired from hauling all those potatoes." Susannah stepped on the hub of the wheel, pulled herself into the box, and lay down. "Five-minute nap," she told Jake, "and then you'll see some hay cut."

When Susannah finally stretched and sat up, the shadows angled long against the prairie; her nap had lasted more than a few minutes. "So much for making hay while the sun shines."

Her hands, swollen and tender from the morning's work, burned on the scythe handle. She hacked away, but dented more grass than she cut. During one vigorous swing, she heard a rip and felt cool air on her shoulder blade. Her sleeve had separated from the back of her bodice. She dropped the scythe, grabbed the pitchfork, and stabbed the small pile of grass. Most of it slid off before she reached the wagon. "Forget it," she said aloud. She threw the tools in the wagon and loaded the hay by hand. Four handfuls and done.

"Ivar was right," Susannah told Jake, "this is man's work. I'd have more success using my sewing scissors. Then I'll split firewood with my letter opener. Let's go home."

Jake's low growl broke into her reverie. A man stood in the

shade of the house. As she approached he stepped into the sunlight and lumbered toward the wagon. A plaid shirt, pattern blurred by grime, stretched across the girth of Abner Reece.

"Lord, help," she whispered. Foolish girl, she'd left the gun in the soddy. The pitchfork? No, she'd most likely hurt herself. Halting the oxen just inside the draw, she hurriedly draped her shawl over her ripped dress and jumped down.

"Mr. Reece, it's an honor to have you pay us a call." She side-stepped to stay upwind of him. Since last spring, he had ripened, like a fresh manure pile on the hottest day of summer.

Jake circled the man, then loped off to the creek. Some protection he was.

"Heard you got chickens." The big man reached inside his shirt and scratched. "Been hungry for eggs."

Why hadn't he walked to the store? Then she realized: He had. And Mr. and Mrs. Rose, the town criers, had spread the news of Jesse's departure. Worthington wouldn't need a newspaper as long as they were around.

"Yes, I have eggs. I'll fix a basket for you."

He scratched his beard. "Well, I was wondering if you'd cook them up for me."

All she wanted to do was rest, but she couldn't risk angering him. "How do you prefer them?"

"Scrambled's fine, half dozen or so." He unhitched her team.

Susannah stirred the fire, then cracked six eggs into the skillet. Mr. Reece watered the oxen and stowed the wagon. His heavy steps echoed across the draw. The room darkened and she heard a snuffling sound. His head bobbed under the lintel.

"Mr. Reece, if you'll take a seat in the yard, please. It's awfully close in here."

With a grunt, he lowered himself to the chopping block. Thank heavens he didn't come inside. If he had squeezed through, he would have collapsed anything he sat on and suffocated her with his odor. "Dear Lord," she whispered, "this would be a good time for Jesse to come home."

Susannah heaped the yellow curds into a mixing bowl, stuck a fork in, and filled a coffee mug. Should she carry the gun? Not unless she grew another hand. She slipped her sharpest knife into her apron pocket, for all the good it would do.

"They might have the grasshopper taste still." She couldn't stand here watching him eat. "If you'll excuse me, I'll get that basket."

Nodding, he palmed the fork and dug in.

Susannah collected four new eggs from the shed, padded them with a layer of straw, and added eight more from the root cellar. Mr. Reece watched as she moved between the house and the shed.

"How are you set for potatoes?" She put the basket on the ground beside him.

"Got enough."

Susannah sat on the threshold, within reach of the shotgun. Would it stop this buffalo-sized man?

"Got sisters?"

"I'm an only child."

"Guess you're lonely out here with Jesse gone. I can stay until he gets back."

"I appreciate your concern, but that's really not necessary."

"You could wait over to my place."

"I'm expecting him at any moment."

"Can't find a wife of my own, nor borrow someone else's." A belch reverberated from deep within, echoing off the soddy. "Change your mind, I'm eight miles west of here. Ford the river on the section line."

"Eight miles! You'd best be on your way so you can make it before dark." Susannah took the bowl and mug from him. "Thank you for calling." Inside the soddy she barred the door, leaning against it for support. She watched as Abner Reece ambled up the slope toward the sunset.

And the truth struck her like a blow: Ivar was right. She couldn't stay on the homestead alone.

Chapter 25

Dying is so cold . . . It hurts so bad.

Mrs. Rose flapped out the door like an agitated duck, her russet and umber dress reminiscent of a female mallard's plumage. "Mrs. Mason! Woe is me! Sorrowful times!" Tears dripped off her beaklike nose onto her heaving breast. Susannah could make out only a few words among the sobs. "Gold-field widows . . . regret the day . . . Black Hills . . . scalp-hungry savages . . . trailing your husband."

Susannah frowned. The day's entire agenda depended on whether or not she could drag this woman from the pit of hysteria. Susannah wrapped an arm around the older woman's shoulders and shepherded her into the deserted store. When Mrs. Rose paused to blow her nose, Susannah jumped in. "Mrs. Rose, perhaps you could settle an argument between Mr. Mason and me."

The transformation was instantaneous. The woman's face lit up in anticipation of a recitation of marital discord.

"Mr. Mason thinks your husband runs the store and you merely help him out. I think Mr. Rose is the brawn, but you're the brains behind this emporium." Susannah discarded her mental picture of Mr. Rose, rail-thin and pale, and offered up a brief silent prayer of remorse for the fib.

"Oh, Mrs. Mason, I knew from the moment I first saw you. Smart as a whip, I said, A-1." Mrs. Rose dried her face and wadded her handkerchief into her apron pocket. "Just between us ladies, Mr. Rose isn't much help around here, other than bookkeeping."

With a swish of her bustle, Mrs. Rose resumed her place behind the counter. "What can I do for you, Mrs. Mason? I thought you'd have gone back to Detroit by now, city girl. Surely you don't plan to stay out on that claim by yourself while Mr. Mason goes prospecting?"

"Prospecting? I'm sorry, ma'am, but I believe you're misinformed. Jesse went to Jamestown for carpentry work."

"Ha!" A crumpled slip of paper flapped from the woman's apron. She crossed her arms over her bosom.

"Dearest Susannah," Jesse had scratched on the back of a used ticket. "No work in J'town. Carpenters make $5/day in Bismarck. —J.M."

Her heart sank. He had gone even farther away. "But this says nothing about gold."

"Humph." This time the apron produced the August 12 issue of the *Bismarck Tribune*.

"GOLD!" the headlines shouted. "Expedition Heard From! Gold and Silver in Immense Quantities, Gold Bearing Quartz Crops Out in Every Hill, Custer's Official Report!"

Susannah scanned the front page. "Sounds like there's gold just lying around."

"Hear tell they're bringing out a hundred dollars a day. Which is why our foolish husbands went chasing after it."

"But Jesse's not a miner."

"Neither is Mr. Rose."

And neither was the neighborhood dairyman who left for the Montana gold fields in 1860, or the milliner's husband who lit out for Virginia City in '63. Susannah held her breath. *Don't cry. Don't think. Concentrate on this moment.* "I need to find out if Mr. Mason ordered grain before he left."

"You poor girl, so brave." With a dramatic sniffle, the older woman slapped open an account book. "No grain orders this month. How much do you need?"

"Fifty bushels of middlings, please. Also, do you know where I might sell a steer?"

Mrs. Rose extended her bottom lip sympathetically. "Seems like everyone's trying to sell and no one's buying. That comes to $45, leaving the Mason account with $14.93."

What? Jesse had nearly sixty dollars' credit with the Roses? Susannah handed over her letter to Ellen. "Have I received any *other* mail?" she asked, unable to keep the edge from her voice.

"As a matter of fact, you have." The shopkeeper hefted a large box. "Looks like your sister-in-law sent books for your school."

"What school?"

"Mr. Mason told us, and we told those new people north of here. They're Norwegian, so like as not they didn't understand. I thought for sure you'd want the money, seeing as how Mr. Mason has no income from wheat. We settled on twenty-five cents a week for each child. That would be eight dollars a month, but I doubt we'll have that long before the snow hits. We went ahead and fixed up the army mail station."

Jesse volunteered her to teach? No, more likely Mrs. Rose had run the idea over him like a locomotive. Susannah swallowed. "Army mail station?"

"Before the railroad, the army carried the mail through here. They left the building behind. Nothing fancy, just some benches and a stove, and a loft for you to sleep in. I said we could put you up." She tossed her steely curls in the direction of the family quarters upstairs. "But Mr. Mason insisted you stay at the school."

"Did my husband happen to say what I should do with the livestock?"

"As if I'd have any idea." Mrs. Rose waddled to the back door. "Robert? I know you're out there. Come help your teacher with her books."

The freckle-faced boy who had driven Jesse's wagon back to the Volds' hauled the box across the hard-packed dirt yard, then ran off. After the soddy, the army shanty seemed almost too bright, too loud. Sunlight streamed in through windows on three sides and reflected off whitewashed walls. No musty odors or spiderwebs; the building had been aired and swept recently. Someone had nailed together a couple of pine benches and topped them with a stack of broken slates. A squat two-lid stove, rusty from insufficient blacking, emptied its pipe into the north wall. A ladder led to a loft with a new straw pallet.

Susannah settled on the only chair and studied Jesse's note. He had dashed it off in pencil, probably as the eastbound pulled into the station. How had it gotten here? If one of the men from the section house had brought it, he could tell her if Jesse was in good health and sober. When did it arrive? And what else had Mrs. Rose hidden in her apron?

Susannah pried open the box. On top was a recent issue of the Ann Arbor newspaper with a question mark inked beside an article about the grasshopper plague. The insects had eaten everything from Dakota Territory to Kansas. Their bodies had piled up on the tracks, stopping trains. Perhaps this wasn't a curse from God after all but simply the kind of challenge that comes to both the just and the unjust. She wished Jesse would come home so she could talk to him about it. Or about anything.

The box contained a book of poetry, ten novels, and assorted back issues of *Harper's* and *Leslie's*. Bless Ellen; no materials for teaching but a welcome respite from reality. Her letter shared about their children and new church but no mention of Susannah's inheritance.

Susannah had never taught, not even Sunday school, and never helped with the younger grades, but she had been a student for ten years. How difficult could it be? And the location couldn't be better. She'd be near the railroad when Jesse returned. And far from Abner Reece.

Susannah stood and headed back to the store. She'd need slate pencils, a lamp. A map would be nice—

"Ivar!" Susannah almost bumped into her neighbor.

"Come." He grasped her arm above the elbow and steered her to his wagon. "There's to be a burying. Those people north of here, their baby died. Marta's with them already. Get in."

"But I don't know them."

"No one does. So. Everyone will come." As soon as she took her seat, he shouted and slapped the reins. They climbed the ridge above the river, cutting through unbroken prairie grass.

"They're Norwegian. Perhaps only you and Marta should go."

"What? You think Norway is some puny country where I know everyone?" He made a growling noise in his throat. "They are from Iowa. Marta and I are from Wisconsin."

Susannah's teeth rattled as one wheel jolted through a hole. "Jesse said you didn't speak English when he first met you, so I thought you'd—"

"Just got off the boat?" Ivar finished. "Good storyteller, your husband. No, I left Norway eleven years ago. I was too old for school in America. Served in Wisconsin's Fifteenth Volunteer Regiment, most all Scandinavians. Didn't learn much English until I came out here. Jesse talked like a river in spring flood. I had to learn or drown."

He eased up on the reins and the team settled into a steady walk. "Work all day, talk all night. Everything from how to build outhouse to how to get to heaven. Sometimes laugh, sometimes cry. Why are we born? Why do bad things happen? What kind of woman is best?"

"I disappointed him, didn't I?"

Ivar growled again. "No. Sundays after lunch, while you and Marta walked, Jesse bragged on you. No afternoon nap for me until I heard how smart, how brave, how good you are. I half never seen a man more proud of his wife, or more in love."

"Mrs. Rose thinks Jesse caught gold fever."

Ivar's bushy eyebrows twitched. After a long moment, he conceded, "Maybe, *ja*, the way he is about money."

Susannah's heart sank even further. "But that area's full of Indians. General Custer took hundreds of soldiers for protection. How far away are the Black Hills?"

Ivar shrugged. "Past where the railroad ends, but not so far as California."

Two white shapes broke the horizon line. One became the cover of a heavy wagon, similar to a prairie schooner, the other a tent, pitched in a neat square of cut grass. Their oxen and a Guernsey milk cow grazed with two horses. A chestnut stallion and mare, their sleek conformation more appropriate to racing than farmwork. A breeding pair? These people must be well-to-do.

"Jesse should be here. He would know what to say, what verses to read. These people expect *me* to talk at the grave." Ivar retrieved his Bible from under the seat and shoved it into her hands. "Look up some verses for me."

"I can't read Norwegian."

He snatched the book from her and slapped the reins into her hands. "You drive, then."

"Try Job, the Psalms, Isaiah 49, First Thessalonians."

"The Psalms? There're 150 of them. Which one?"

Susannah parked the wagon so the oxen would be shaded

by the tent. Introductions and directions swirled around her, the unfamiliar names fusing with other incomprehensible words. After a whirl of activity, she found herself alone inside, holding a basin of water and a washrag.

There on the pallet, under a drape of netting, lay the baby. Balancing the basin between clumps of grass, Susannah knelt, touching her finger to the tiny fist already drained of warmth and color.

"So small. You must have been born during their journey." Indignation raced through her. "Couldn't they have waited, stayed in Iowa where your mother wouldn't have had it so hard?"

Susannah dipped the rag into the cool water, wrung it out, and wiped the baby's face, starting with the tears she had dripped onto the tiny forehead.

"I don't even know your name, or if you're a boy or girl." She unwrapped the blanket. "A boy. Little boy, when you get to heaven, you can play with my baby. I can't tell you who to ask for or what my baby looks like. Check the choir."

Susannah washed his round back, the tiny folds at the base of his neck, the creases of his legs. She dressed him in a clean diaper and rewrapped him in the blanket, tucking in his hands and feet, leaving only his pale face visible. She nestled him in her arms and willed some of her body heat into his still form.

The opening of the tent darkened. A man brought in a packing crate, resized to fit. For a second their eyes met, then Susannah looked away, unable to see her pain reflected and amplified in his face.

"I couldn't find any clothes for him," she said, because she couldn't think of anything else to say. She placed the baby in his long pale hands. The first words of his hoarse-voiced reply she recognized as "Thank you," but she lost the rest of his message.

He laid the body in the box and smoothed the blanket around ears smaller than his fingertip. He fitted the lid, then raised his mallet. It landed with a thud and Susannah flinched. The man swallowed, adjusted his grip, and finished the job. Stooping under the ridgepole, he carried the coffin out.

Susannah dried her face, then followed him into the noon sunshine. She blinked. It should be November gloomy, not early September bright.

Ivar handed Sara to her. "Where in Isaiah?"

"Try chapter 49. About mothers remembering their babies." Susannah embraced Sara with both arms. The child was so warm. So wiggly. So alive.

"*Ja.* Here it is." Ivar clamped his hand on her shoulder, then hustled up the slope to join a cluster of mourners.

Susannah trailed behind, pausing to pick some feathery stalks for Sara to hold. The prairie grass shimmered violet, crimson, and bronze in the wind; winter would arrive soon.

Mournful music pulled the group tighter. The dirge emanated not from the violin Susannah expected but from an instrument similar to a bagpipe. It rested on the lap of a curly-haired man with close-set eyes. He pumped the device with movements of his right elbow.

"Uilleann pipes," a voice behind her whispered. "Irish excuse for a bagpipe."

Susannah turned to find the hotel keeper. "Mr. McFadgen. How do you do?"

His apron had been replaced with a frock coat and matching vest. "The musician is my partner, John Morrison. Fool is playing a tune lamenting one of the many defeats of the Irish at the hands of the Vikings. Hope these Norwegians don't recognize the song, just hear the sadness."

He nodded at the group of men removing their hats across the circle. "Appears the whole town has turned out. Saloon must have closed. There's Pat Flood, the section boss, Hendrickson Lee, John Olson, and Pat Burns from the section house. The other Irish is the pumper, Connors, but I can't remember if his given name is Pat or Mike. Colonel Marsh wants to build a mill on the Sheyenne. Frank Wright has a claim north of here. He's from Jesse's neck of the woods."

Donald McFadgen drew a line in the gravel with the toe of his shoe. "Sorry about Jesse. Had I wind of his plans, I'd have appointed myself sheriff and jailed him until he thought better of it."

The music droned to an end. Ivar stepped to the edge of the freshly dug hole and read a psalm. Susannah let the Norwegian words ripple over her while she scanned the mourners behind him. Marta supported a sobbing woman, the mother. The grim-faced man beside her must be the father. The younger man from the tent, who now placed the crate in the ground, would be, perhaps, the baby's uncle. The stair-step children hovering solemnly behind were the baby's brothers and sisters. The family was dressed in new clothes and shoes. The mother and two oldest girls wore gloves. Why would people with money come here?

Ivar concluded and led the congregation in a hymn. The railroad men filled the grave. Susannah turned to a touch at her elbow. Mrs. Rose stood behind her, accompanied by her flock, each hair slicked down, each mouth quiet.

Susannah braced for the onslaught, but the storekeeper drew from a previously untapped well of decorum. "Mrs. Mason, I've got to get back to my store. If you would be so kind as to bring my soup kettle once it's empty." She nodded at the pot over the campfire, then placed a sack in Susannah's free arm. "Here's some bread and cookies for the young'uns."

"I'll have Mrs. Vold tell them it's from you."

Susannah lost track of Marta in the flow of people down the hill. A competent-looking older girl took charge of Sara. Susannah stationed herself at the open fire. Through cow chip smoke, she ladled soup to a blur of faces while mediating the battle between the fire, the wind, and her skirts.

Ivar's familiar voice cut through the hubbub. "Eat. Before it's gone. They can serve themselves."

Susannah filled a bowl, grabbed a chunk of bread, and followed him to a seat on the grass next to the uncle.

"Susannah, the Hansens need to get their soddy up, and quick. It's a wonder it hasn't snowed already. Could they use Jesse's cutting plow?"

"Of course."

"They won't be able to pay rent until their wheat comes in next summer."

"That's hardly necessary."

"Jesse isn't the only man with pride around here."

Susannah contemplated the Hansen man through the steam of her soup. The firm set of his mouth, broad shoulders, eyes that would not meet hers for more than a second. Yes, considerable pride there. "I'll need to board the stock, if I'm to teach. And I could use some help with firewood."

After a quick consultation, Ivar told her, "We'll divide up your stock. He will cut your wood. Saturday next."

"I'm coming back up tomorrow to teach school at the depot. I'll bring the plow then."

A flicker of amusement crossed Mr. Hansen's face. Ivar snorted. "He asks if you are Freya, the Norse goddess, that you can load a plow by yourself."

Susannah closed her eyes. Every day, every conversation brought continued reminders of Jesse's absence. "I haven't thought this through. I'll need help with my trunk too."

This time they pulled the father into the conference.

"Here's what we're going to do. Magnar"—Ivar pointed to the uncle—"and *Mor* Hansen and her little girl will go back to your claim tonight. In the morning, you and Magnar and the plow will come back. *Mor* will stay and take care of your stock."

"But, Ivar, it's just a soddy and a long ways away. Will she be all right out there?"

"It's away from that." Ivar nodded at the grave atop the wind-swept knoll. "Just what she needs."

Despite the frost, Susannah propped the door open. Fresh morning air cleared the soddy of the smells of too many people. Mrs. Hansen and the three-year-old had slept in the bed with Susannah. The uncle had flipped the table upside down onto her trunk and spread his bedroll on the floor.

Why had the uncle come? Maybe the father had stayed to comfort the other children. Or the parents weren't getting along. Or the uncle was in charge of building the Hansen soddy. This morning he'd studied the house and shed. Susannah had shown him Jesse's trick, using a rope with twelve evenly spaced knots to square the corners. She'd written out a list of supplies he'd need from the store. Then he'd left to load the cutting plow.

Mrs. Hansen had taken the little girl, Tove, to do the milking, giving Susannah a welcome moment of solitude. She packed Jesse's army chest with potatoes and a few kitchen supplies. Then she opened her trunks to sort through her clothes. She set aside her father's cavalry knapsack; the medicines and surgical instruments were irreplaceable. Better take long underwear and flannel petticoats.

Her hand paused over a drawstring bag filled with bird's-eye and outing flannel rags. Frowning, she went to the almanac.

What day was today? Not yet this month. Not last month. How could that be? She turned the pages, back before the grasshoppers. Her jaw dropped. "I'm pregnant," she whispered and sank to the bed. "All this queasiness, sleeping so much, bursting out of my clothes. A baby."

When the supply of condoms had run out, she and Jesse had tried one of the other methods. The doctor had said fertility increased closer to menses, so they used days in the middle of her month. And now she was pregnant. Having a baby. "Oh, Lord, thank You."

Her trembling fingers set the almanac in its place under the Bible. She leaned on the doorpost, facing west. "Jesse, you've got to come home. Oh, God, please bring him back." She laced her fingers over her abdomen. "Please, please let me keep this one."

Jake herded Tove back to the soddy. Time to pack for teaching, not think of a baby in front of a woman who had just lost hers.

Chapter 26

Lord, I thought I was doing all right in the faith and trust department. But this is beyond all my efforts.

Magnar swung the wagon around the north side of the army shanty. The ride from the claim had been one long English lesson, with no time to worry about the baby, Jesse, winter, or anything else. The big Norwegian handed her off the seat.

"*Takk,*" Susannah said.

His eyebrows shot up. "T'ank you," he answered with a quick smile. Then he climbed into the wagon box for her luggage.

"Mrs. Mason!" A small-framed man hustled across the grass from the store.

"Mr. Rose, you're back already."

"Who's this?"

Susannah made the introduction and the two men shook hands. "Mr. Hansen will be over soon to purchase supplies."

Mr. Rose waited until the Norwegian man entered the shanty. "Do you have news for me?"

"Sorry, no. Government's not letting anyone into the Black Hills. General Sheridan's orders."

"Did you see Jesse?"

The older man shook his head. "Asked around town, every business and bystander, and over to the fort. No one's seen him. I'm afraid he's gone prospecting."

Susannah slumped onto the steps and closed her eyes. A door creaked and banged shut; Mr. Rose entered his store. Susannah leaned forward and willed herself to breathe. This was no time to cry. There was a job to be done, a baby to think of. But the tears would not be held back.

She did not hear Magnar Hansen step out of the shanty and sit beside her. He pressed a handkerchief into her fist and spoke gentle Norwegian words. She cried harder. His hand cupped her shoulder, slid across her back to her other shoulder, pulled her to his chest. She leaned into him, gathering strength from his warmth, until the storm subsided.

Suddenly she realized she was sitting in public, in broad daylight, in the arms of a man who was not her husband. She got up and stumbled away without thanking him, without even daring to look at him.

"I'm a married woman," she mumbled. He couldn't understand most of the words, but she was saying them as much for her own benefit as for his. "You must not touch me. People will gossip." She headed for the pump to wash her face. "Please send the children to school."

Chetan saw Medicine Mother first and raced off to hide behind Hehaka's tepee. But Misun was studying the white man's wood beaver and did not see Medicine Mother until she grabbed his ear.

"Misun. I talk to you about your captive." She lifted her chin at the tepee behind him.

The boy focused on her Peace Medal and bent to keep from

losing his ear. "Yes, Grandmother. Winona has done as you told her. She pushed food into his mouth and washed his blanket."

"Yet he continues to sleep. He smells like a skunk."

"He opened his eyes yesterday."

"It has been forty-two days."

"And he no longer coughs." Did that mean he was dying or healing? Misun did not have the makings of a medicine man.

"He is a lazy, worthless dog."

And everyone knew what happened to lazy, worthless dogs. "He does not eat much."

"None of us eats much."

"But he said 'Tatanka.' He has an eagle feather."

Medicine Mother had refuted this argument when Misun first brought the white stranger home. She narrowed her eyes and the boy braced to be hit by lightning. "Misun, you should be out hunting and fishing with the men. Instead you waste time waiting for this dog to arise."

"Please, Grandmother. He will wake, teach me to use the wood beaver, then—" Then what? If Misun took him to the fort, he would be shot by the soldiers. Sitting Bull had forbidden any contact with the Standing Rock Agency, so Misun could not take him there. Maybe a trader would come by. Or a boat—except boats did not come until spring filled the river.

"You have until the full moon."

Susannah adjusted the pillow under her head, aligning the knothole in the gable with a star in the southwest sky. "Well, Jesse, you talked to me before I came out here. I guess I can talk to you now. Please come home. Or write. Let me know you're safe in Bismarck or wherever you are. Even if you haven't found work. Just don't go down to the Black Hills, don't go looking for gold."

She steadied herself. She couldn't afford to cry; her tears would freeze. "I found some verses for you and turned them into a prayer. Psalm 91. Lord, because Jesse loves You, please deliver him. When he calls You, please answer him. Be with him in trouble and save him. Amen."

Susannah pulled the quilt under her chin. "I hope you're warm. Living in this shanty makes me appreciate your sod house. Every morning the students bring bags of cow chips and twists of cordgrass for the stove, but the water in the bucket still freezes overnight. The wind finds every crack in the walls, all the gaps between the boards, every knothole. For such a little building, it sure can creak and rattle. Last night I dreamed you were singing to me, but it was only the stovepipe. Maybe it wouldn't be so bad if Jake were here, but he's guarding Mrs. Hansen, Tove, and the animals on the claim."

Swallowing back the lump in her throat, she touched her finger to the icy hole. "You once asked if I thought of you as a handsome prince on a white horse. Tonight I wish you'd dash up on that black steed, the Northern Pacific Railroad, and slay this dragon of a teaching job. Who would have thought eight students could be so difficult? Four don't speak English, the other four can't sit for more than a minute, and none has ever attended school. All I've got is one McGuffey second reader, three slate pencils, and a stack of broken slates. No parsing sentences or spelling bees for this group. Most of my first week's pay has already been spent trying to make this building into a schoolhouse."

She slid her hands to the curve of her abdomen. "I'll need to buy ten yards of wool to make a wrapper. I've let out my waistbands as far as possible. This child of yours is growing like wheat in a spring rain." She turned her head a fraction of an inch to follow the star's path through the night. "If only I could feel your arms around me. Come home, Jesse."

The flap of the tepee opened, admitting the sergeant with the gray braids. She launched into her usual harangue, whipped off Jesse's blanket, and flailed him with something that felt like a porcupine. "Ow. Ow! There are more efficient ways to kill people," he croaked out. "I'd prefer to be shot. Where's my rifle?" The memory returned in a rush. His rifle had sunk to the bottom of the Missouri. Wonder if those two ferrymen made it. No sign of them.

When the beating was finished, the old woman propped him upright on a frame. The tepee swung around and grayed at the edges. Jesse closed his eyes and gulped a breath. A handful of slumgullion filled his mouth.

"Mmph."

The woman held a bowl up. The expression on her face let him know, in no uncertain terms, he would be eating its contents. His taste buds voted no but were overruled by his stomach and the old woman. He reached for the bowl. What was this? Something runny and brown with a bitter taste. Like army food. Better off not knowing. The sergeant continued her lecture until he finished. She yanked the bowl away and gave him a dipper of water. One swallow later, she dragged him out the door. A cold wind sliced whatever skin he had left.

"You, my dear, are no Florence Nightingale."

And she didn't care. She was a head shorter than he, but somehow she managed to get him standing. The ground circled and the world started to go black, but she slapped him a good one and hauled him to the latrine. She waited while he did his business, then dragged his wheezing carcass back to the front of the tepee. "And you're not Clara Barton either."

He ought to worry about being naked, but he was more afraid he'd freeze to death. The old woman, paragon of kindness that she was, threw a blanket at him. When she bent to give him another piece of her mind—how much did she have left?—Jesse got a look at the medal hanging from her neck: Jefferson on one side, clasped hands on the other.

Lewis and Clark had given her a Peace Medal? She looked old enough.

With a final warning that left him wondering what other tortures she might have up her buckskin sleeve, she left.

Jesse looked around and tried to focus. Tepees. More than a dozen, tucked into a fold of a bluff. The grass rippled yellow and brown. He'd been sick a long time. Was he a captive, a slave? Newspapers said they kept women and children but tortured and killed men. With his red-brown hair and light skin, it wasn't like he'd blend in here.

"Anyone here speak English?" he asked. But the wind blew away his feeble voice.

Between the nearest tepees, a woman stretched out a pelt. Another woman pounded grain. She stood, her silhouette showing she was in the family way. *Susannah, I miss our little one.* But what if he had a third mouth he couldn't feed? A trio of small children played in the dirt farther on. A yellow dog nosed through a pile of debris.

No warriors, no guards, no men at all. Even the sergeant had left him alone. He could walk east until he found the river, turn north until he came to Fort Lincoln, borrow clothes and train fare, and go home. Jesse gathered the blanket, brought his feet under himself, and stood. The world around him spun, and he sat down again before he could fall. No need for a prison other than his own body. *Please, God, I've got to get home to Susannah. I promised I'd take care of her.*

Grasshoppers, no work, near drowning, and now captivity. Was there some lesson God was trying to drill through his hard head?

The old woman brought a bucket of corn to pound. Jesse picked up the grinding rock. *Lord, You are my rock, my fortress, my hiding place.*

"Tatanka!" A boy strode toward him carrying his guitar. Something besides him had survived the river. The kid tapped his chest. "Misun."

"Misun? Is that your name?"

An older boy followed, introducing himself as Chetan.

"I need to go home," Jesse told them. "My wife will be worried about me."

The boys responded with a barrage in their language. *God, about that Tower of Babel, different languages thing. Shouldn't we be over that by now?*

Misun passed him the guitar. The back was warped. The glue had loosened in several places. But none of the strings had broken and they all went back in tune, for the moment.

The younger Indian peppered him with questions. "Guitar," Jesse said, touching his instrument. The Indian repeated the word.

"Tuning." Jesse showed him. "Note. Chords. Songs." Jesse tried the first line of the only hymn he could recall, "Jesus Loves Me." His voice came out as a rasp, and the guitar had a rattle to match. Exhaustion slammed him and his hands dropped limp.

As Jesse sank into sleep, Misun took the guitar, and he and Chetan sang the rest of the verse. In English.

No. He must be dreaming.

The tune of the final hymn sounded familiar, perhaps Martin Luther's, but the lyrics were sung in Norwegian and Susannah could not recall the English words. Jesse would know. He'd keep time and tune with his guitar.

Ivar conducted the Sunday service, roped into it after preaching at the burial, he'd grumbled to Susannah. The youngest Rose had stuck his head in at the beginning, then realized the proceedings were conducted in Norwegian and made his escape. Susannah had wanted to follow, but she had nowhere else to go.

Warmed by the sun and the ten people crowding the shanty, she hid a yawn behind her hand. Long fingers reached for her wrist and turned up her palm. It was blistered by the saw handle. Magnar held his up next to hers, a matched set of wounds.

She inched away from him, then smiled at the Hansen children on the adjacent bench. They had transformed yesterday's woodcutting trip into a picnic. They caught fish in a woven willow basket and roasted them over a fire, raced for the wagon with armloads of kindling, sang high harmonies on the return trip. A giant yellow lampshade seemed to cover the sun, turning everything it touched to gold: the noisy yellow cottonwood leaves, the russet stemmed grass, the blond hair of the children.

Her initial impression of Sissel as a typically responsible oldest daughter melted under the girl's fiery sense of humor, usually expressed in a practical joke on her uncle. Disa, the nine-year-old, daydreamed at play just as she did at school. Erik, the rough-and-tumble seven-year-old, wavered between helping his adored Uncle Magnar and scaring the girls with his Indian act. Then there was Rolf, at five her youngest pupil, always looking for a lap to climb into. He'd found Susannah's again today.

Their shyness had vanished. They brought her a bird's nest, wrote their names, last week's lesson, in the packed mud of the riverbank, and hollered, "Teacher!" Magnar echoed their call and brought her a wildflower that had somehow survived the frost. She made the startling discovery that this placid man had dimples when he smiled. This morning he had managed to sit next to her. She wished she could accept his friendship, but all this attention made her uneasy. Hadn't Ivar told him she was married?

He wouldn't be sitting next to her if Jesse were here. But if Jesse were here, she wouldn't have needed Magnar's help. *Lord, bring him home. Soon.*

The song ended. Marta and Mrs. Hansen huddled deep in conversation over the food basket. The two Hansen men and Ivar deliberated some serious matter in the corner. Swallowing a wave of jealousy mixed with loneliness, Susannah picked up the water bucket and followed the children outside.

When she returned from the pump, Magnar took the heavy bucket from her.

"Ask one of the children to do that," Ivar admonished in the parental tone he'd used since Jesse left.

She wouldn't apologize. "I'm just getting some fresh air."

"What did Mr. Rose say?"

Susannah glanced at Magnar. What had he told Ivar? The younger man studied a loose floorboard. "Nothing new. The government's not allowing anyone into the Black Hills."

"Then where is Jesse?"

"I don't know." Susannah stiffened her spine. She would not break down in front of all these people, especially her students. "Excuse me. I need to help with dinner." She slid between the men.

"Mrs. Hansen said you had a visitor. A large, dirty man who spits. He brought a load of hay, read the note you tacked on the door, and left."

She should have warned Mrs. Hansen. "Abner Reece."

Ivar wound up for another swearing session. A hiss from Marta cut him short. He scowled. "Why didn't you tell me?"

"He wants eggs."

"Eggs? For cutting your hay, that's all he wants?"

"It's all he's going to get."

The Hansens left. Susannah had a moment alone with Marta.

"Good news!" She caught her friend's hand, placing it on her waist. "Baby!"

Marta's eyes glistened and she hugged Susannah.

Ivar returned from loading the wagon. "The Hansens half to—"

Susannah shook her head at Marta. Ivar had been in such a foul mood since Jesse left, she couldn't guess how he'd take this news. But Marta missed her cue and revealed the secret. Well, as fast as this baby was growing, the whole territory would know soon.

Ivar lifted Susannah in a bear hug, then set her down gently. "Jesse. Dear God—"

Marta pressed fingertips to his mouth.

"You were alone last week. What if something goes bad, like before? What's the name of that doctor? I half to get you to Fargo."

"Ivar."

He stomped around the shack, boots echoing off the plank walls. "I do not know how those men in Utah stand it, halfing more than one woman to worry about."

"Ivar, I am not your second wife and you are not to worry about me." Three days of teaching had developed her command voice. "I am an adult. I will take care of myself."

"What if—"

"What if I die?" Susannah completed his thought. "I'd rather be out on the claim, in my own home, than in some town where I don't know anyone except that pitiful excuse for a doctor." She looked down at her hands. "I'd give anything for a healthy baby,

office nor my husband's medical practice, has heard of Mr. Jesse Mason. I can state with some degree of certainty that your husband is not in Bismarck at this time.

Several outfits surreptitiously departed for the Black Hills last month. Perhaps he joined one of these groups of unknowns?

You may also want to inquire at Fort Abraham Lincoln.

Best wishes for the return of your beloved,
Linda Slaughter, Postmistress

Susannah tried to hold back her tears. Jesse wasn't in Bismarck, so where was he? Gold prospecting seemed more likely every day. If she wrote to the fort about Jesse, would the soldiers arrest him? Could they find him in all that wilderness? Winter was coming. Soon travel would be impossible.

The door rattled. "Mrs. Mason? Are you all right in there? What's your letter say?"

Susannah folded the heavy stationery into the envelope and leaned against the door with a sigh. A married woman running the post office in Bismarck. What next for this territory?

Jesse had a plan.

The next time the kid crawled into the tepee, Jesse was ready. "Misun. Where are my clothes?" He patted his arms and legs. "I can't sit around in a blanket. It's getting cold." Not as cold as it usually got this time of year, but chilly enough.

The boy said a bunch of stuff, then held out the guitar.

"No." Jesse shook his head. "I want my clothes." The boy motioned for him to lean forward, off the backrest, then he pulled out Jesse's gear. All this time he'd been sitting on it. Jesse pulled on his pants and shirt. If he'd known he'd be out here this late in the year, he'd have brought heavier clothes.

No, if he'd known, he'd have never left home.

"Thank you. Now, where're my shoes?" Jesse pointed to his feet.

The kid shook his head, then handed him the guitar. Too smart. Maybe that was the problem with government Indian policy, underestimating their adversary.

"But, Mrs. Mason, if an Irish family with twin babies lived near here, we'd know about it."

Susannah guided Pa Ox from the Roses' shed. "My point exactly, Mrs. Rose. Since they haven't come to you for supplies, I'd best go check on them." She returned to the shed for Ma Ox.

"Mr. Rose, don't you touch this wagon. Mrs. Mason is not going anywhere, especially all the way to Fourth Siding." The woman planted her hands on her hips and continued talking without taking a breath. "The only foreigners around here are those Norwegians."

"No, my dear. McFadgen has some Irish friends." Mr. Rose stepped around his wife, carrying the heavy yoke. "John Morrison and Richard McKinnon."

"Right. If anyone needs to check on those people, it should be one of their own." Mrs. Rose thrust her face toward Susannah's. "Unless *you're* Irish."

"My parents were English. I'm American." Susannah had just about used up her day's allotment of patience in this first hour of the morning.

"Those boys are busy fur trapping this time of year," Mr. Rose said.

Mrs. Rose shot her husband a look, then continued her assault on Susannah. "What would Mr. Mason say about you gallivanting all the way to Fourth Siding and back?"

"He'd say they're overdue for a visit."

"And the weather?" The woman ignored her. "It can change in a flash. Might look nice now, but we could have a foot of snow on the ground by nightfall. If you're caught out in it—"

"It's a fine day for a drive. Indian summer."

Mrs. Rose jumped on the word. "Indians! You'll run into a tribe of bloodthirsty savages and be scalped for certain."

"Now, Mrs. Rose." Susannah loaded a basket of potatoes into the wagon. "When's the last time you saw an Indian?"

"Actually, we haven't seen any." Her husband fastened the last trace onto the yoke. "Occasional half-breeds is the best we do for Indians around here."

"Well, Lord only knows what evil you'll run into out there. A woman in your delicate condition. You'd better take someone with you. Robert!"

After attempting to teach that rapscallion all week, Susannah certainly didn't plan to spend her Saturday trying to keep him from burning down the territory. She climbed onto the seat. "I'm sure that's not necessary. I have a shotgun and a dog. Mrs. Hansen returned Jake when she moved into her new home."

"Well, I could go with you." The old bird's eyes glittered. "I'll fetch my shawl."

Susannah didn't bother to hide her annoyance. She'd rather be stuck at the schoolhouse. "Thank you, but no."

Mr. Rose herded his wife toward the store. "You go gallivanting off across the prairie, Mrs. Rose, who will help me with inventory?"

Susannah snapped the reins over the backs of the oxen. To Mr. Rose, she smiled and mouthed, *Thank you.* He touched his fingertips to his forehead in salute.

The last word was Mrs. Rose's. "I'll have you know, you're on a wild-goose chase!"

Better than being pecked to death by a domestic goose.

Susannah whistled for Jake. The dog joined her on the seat and dug his black toenails into the wood. The team stepped out, energetic after several days' rest. She guided them onto the narrow ruts of the stage road.

The sun baked the prairie, perfuming the air with the humid smell of grass. The dog retreated to the shade under the seat.

Susannah passed the time thinking of questions for Maureen Duffy. When did this upset stomach pass? It seemed so wasteful to have to eat a second breakfast because the first wouldn't stay down. Susannah had noticed several spots of blood on her toothbrush. Could this be due to the pregnancy or were her teeth giving out? When did Maureen start to feel the baby move? Could she tell hers were twins? The babies would be seven months old now. Would they be sitting up, crawling, sleeping through the night?

Fourth Siding's shed appeared on the eastern horizon. Why didn't the Duffys come to Worthington? Fargo was much farther away. Had someone warned Maureen about the Roses? Were they in good health? Had they been spared the grasshopper damage? Susannah turned the oxen off the road, heading northeast. She reached under the seat to pat Jake. "Almost there."

The wagon tilted, then began a rhythmic bumping.

"Whoa!" Susannah frowned. This strip looked like the Duffys' firebreak, disguised by a summer's growth of wildflowers and prairie grass. A serious oversight this time of year. Didn't Colum remember last autumn's fire?

Jake bolted off in search of water. On their last visit, Mr. Duffy had answered the door with a muzzleloader. He might mistake Jake for a wolf.

"Hello, Duffys!" Susannah called. This was their draw, she

was sure of it, but where was the stovepipe? Perhaps they'd taken it down for cleaning. And the path? A chill grazed her spine. She thought this was the right place, but—

The draw was empty. Grass grew two feet tall where it should have been trampled down. A dark rectangle showed where the door had been. The southeast corner of the dugout had caved in.

"The babies!" She raced to the opening. The soddy was empty. No people. No stove, no packing crate furniture, no hammock. The hole in the roof let in more sunlight than the oiled paper window, enough to see where rain had scooped a dip in the floor. Bird droppings spattered one corner. Susannah stepped on the threshold. The board creaked, tilting the door frame further off plumb.

No need to see more. The Duffys were gone.

Tears blurred her view of the dugout. This wasn't some sudden tragedy. The family had packed thoroughly, carefully. They'd left nothing behind.

Susannah wondered if the babies were all right. There was no way to know. The prairie grass would swallow up graves as quickly as it did paths and fields.

She took one last look around. Nothing plowed. The Duffys must have left shortly after their visit this spring. Where had they gone? Someplace easier, she hoped. She would imagine the four together, because any other image would shatter her.

By this time next year, the dugout would be completely gone, returned to the prairie. Nothing would show a young Irish couple had once tried to homestead here.

Susannah shivered, aware of her isolation. Jake nudged her hand with his wet nose. She knelt and wrapped her arms around the dog's neck. His long pink tongue swabbed her face.

"Watch over them, Lord, wherever they are."

Susannah returned to the wagon and headed the team back

to Worthington. A line of cumulus towered over the western sky, the southernmost forming into an anvil. "Get up, Ma Ox, Pa Ox."

Fourth Siding's shed slid by her left shoulder. Just over a year ago she'd arrived here to begin a new life with Jesse. How long before the prairie took back his claim, before the grass choked their draw and reclaimed his fields? How long before the roof collapsed on their soddy and the rain melted its walls? In less time than it took Jesse to build, it would all be gone.

She would not let that happen.

The wind swung around to the north, driving cold rain, then ice and flurries, into the tepee. Jesse put on his woolen drawers, both pairs of pants, both shirts, jacket, and hat, then wrapped the blanket over all. He crawled to the dry part of the floor and shivered. He should have left yesterday. But he got winded walking to the latrine and back. And he still couldn't find his shoes. Or even an extra pair of moccasins.

He didn't know how far the boat had drifted downriver, or if the tribe had moved the village while he was sick, but he suspected Fort Lincoln was farther than he could walk. The Indians had horses but probably wouldn't take kindly to him borrowing one. Why hadn't they killed him already? For the most part, they ignored him. Except the kid with his big dreams of making music.

Misun crawled into the tepee. Right on time for his lesson, except he didn't have the guitar. The boy didn't look at him; Jesse was always suspicious of anyone who wouldn't meet his eye. Without a word the boy gathered up the backrest and second blanket. Now how was he supposed to stay warm?

Misun grabbed Jesse's elbow and towed him out. If the tribe was moving, they'd probably go farther away from civilization, not closer. Maybe they'd give him his shoes and leave him here.

But all the tepees were standing. The usual people did the usual work. Nobody seemed to be packing.

The boy hauled him over to a bigger tepee, one with smoke coming out the top, and pulled him inside. It was warm here, at least, and he could smell meat cooking.

Misun motioned to a spot beside the door. A spot on the boy's buffalo rug, more comfortable than sitting on the ground. When Jesse's eyes adjusted to the dimness, he saw two others sitting by the fire: a woman who might have been Susannah's age and the young girl who sometimes brought him food. "Your mom and sister? Do you have a dad?"

The woman raised her hands, looked up to the smoke hole, and said a few words before handing out breakfast. Jesse didn't recognize what she said, but it sure looked like saying grace.

Warm habitation, hot food, and best of all: no sign of the sergeant.

Susannah shoved her hands deep into her coat pockets and walked with her back to the wind, stomping her feet on the frozen ground. The train had steamed into town, necessitating a recess. Even if she had been able to teach over the distraction and noise, the children couldn't be seen in the army mail station. If some train-riding officer objected to their use of government property, her students would be out of a school and she'd be out of a job.

Today, the approach of the Northern Pacific coincided with the disappearance of the sun behind a cloud bank. Susannah tightened the wool scarf around her ears. The children and Jake raced around in a bilingual "blindman's bluff," oblivious to the chill. They gave little notice to the passenger whose arrival lengthened their break.

The man got off the train and raised his arm to secure his hat, but even though Susannah couldn't see his face, she knew it wasn't Jesse. This man moved too hesitantly. Besides, Jesse wouldn't come on a westbound train.

The stranger disappeared into the store. Mrs. Rose would give her all the details—and more—this evening.

The engine built up a full head of steam for the climb out of the valley. Opaque white clouds swallowed the locomotive and lapped the platform of the store. The expanding hot metal of the firebox cracked and boomed in the cold air. A whistle blast sent the train westward and signaled the end of recess.

The students raced inside to thaw at the stove before resuming their lessons. Susannah had paired each Hansen child with a Rose. At first it didn't seem fair to burden the English speakers with teaching duties, but the Hansens' thirst for knowledge kept the wild Roses on task. In fact, a bizarre competition developed among the Rose children: "My Norwegian talks better than your Norwegian."

Susannah took a seat between the two oldest for their arithmetic recitations, keeping one ear tuned toward Robert Rose, who had tried to sneak vulgar names for body parts into yesterday's lesson.

"Mrs. Mason?" The passenger, a burly middle-aged man, entered the building. The students went instantly silent. The man doffed his broad-brimmed hat and rearranged strands of faded brown hair over his prominent forehead.

Jake padded over to administer his standard welcome. The stranger's smile froze. Salt-and-pepper wisps of beard quivered on his lower jaw. He backed toward the door, sneezing and wiping his hooked nose.

"May I help you?" Susannah snapped her fingers, ending the dog's circle-and-sniff inspection. The man sighed his relief and unbuttoned his straight-breasted black coat to reveal a white shirt, black vest, and tie of plain black ribbon.

"Good afternoon. I'm John W. Webb." His booming voice rattled the windows. A politician?

"Do you have webbed feet?" asked Robert.

Mr. Webb glared and clenched his fists.

"Quiet, class." Susannah shot the boy a quick frown. "Please excuse the interruption. This is only our third week of school."

"May I speak with you?" One eye on the dog, the big man inched toward the stove.

Susannah consulted her father's pocket watch, pinned to her bodice. "We have a few more minutes of school. Won't you make yourself comfortable while I finish their lessons?"

"I'd be honored to assist."

"Very kind of you to offer. How are you at arithmetic?"

"At the head of my class until geometry."

"Very good, then, if you could listen to Robert and Erik recite—" Susannah indicated the two boys wiggling by the west wall. When Erik yanked off Robert's stocking cap, tufts of hair above his ears had pulled upright, standing like horns. *Well, Mr. Webb,* she thought, *there's a clue as to what to expect from that child.*

Subdued by the presence of the stranger, the children sped through the lessons, then dashed home in the early dusk of the low clouds.

Susannah fed the stove another cow chip and lit the kerosene lantern.

"Mrs. Mason, I'm stunned. A school meeting in a shanty, guarded by a wolf. No books, no paper, no desks. Half the students unable to converse in English."

"Run by a teacher without a certificate." A pregnant teacher, no less. Susannah sat on the opposite bench. "You're from the Territorial Board of Education?"

"Actually, no. I'm a missionary from the Northwest Iowa Methodist Conference. I was told Jesse Mason, brother of a fellow minister, could provide me with accommodations and orientation to the community."

Ah, a preacher. That explained the voice. "Mr. Mason is out of town on business. I expect him back any day."

"Mrs. Rose said he was prospecting?"

"A veritable fount of information, isn't she?"

"Mrs. Mason!" The Reverend's pale eyes opened wide, shocked by Susannah's attitude or Jesse's employment, she couldn't tell. The corner of his mouth twitched with a suppressed smile.

"The Roses can provide you with a bed for the night and a meal, unless you're partial to potatoes."

The mention of food brought him to his feet. "That reminds me—the relief supplies!" With the easy movements of someone accustomed to physical labor, the man carried in several barrels. He pried open the lid on the largest, revealing apples cushioned with straw, and tins of coffee, cocoa, and crackers. "The smaller barrels are salt pork. The newspapers carried the story of the grasshopper plague, so the congregations in the States sent food for the needy. I could use your advice regarding distribution, starting with yourself, of course."

"We lost our wheat crop, but we still have potatoes." Susannah indicated the army crate in the corner.

Reverend Webb tilted his head to the side and placed his hands, fingertips together, in front of his chest, exactly as her brother-in-law did. Must be part of their training, Susannah thought, ministerial posturing.

"Mrs. Mason, how long have you been subsisting on potatoes?"

Although his solemn expression struck her as ludicrous, Susannah's embarrassment at her poverty kept her from laughing. "It's difficult to recall exactly."

"Six weeks? Then your next opportunity for provender other than potatoes would be a minimum of eight, possibly ten months from now."

"Except for fresh meat from hunting."

He ignored her remark as if too outrageous to merit a response. "Mrs. Mason, do you recall Jesus' visit to Jacob's well? His disciples had gone to town for food. He asked a Samaritan woman to give Him a drink of water."

"Yes, I remember." Jesus had asked the woman about her husband, but she didn't have one. Was this sermon about Jesse?

"Our Lord is able to feed thousands from a couple loaves and fishes, yet He accepted water and food from others."

Susannah looked at the barrel and swallowed. This baby seemed to make her hungry all the time. "Reverend Webb, shall we discuss distribution of relief supplies over supper?"

Chapter 28

Lord, I don't have to tell You,
this isn't what I had in mind.

B reath puffing white in the dawn chill, Reverend Webb burst
from the store. "Fine morning for a drive! May I be of assistance?"
"Certainly."

Susannah's heart sank. Last night the Reverend had stated his
intention to accompany her to the claim. He wanted to see more
of the territory and how its people lived. Susannah really needed
time to herself after teaching unruly students and dealing with Mrs.
Rose all week. She informed him that Dakota looked the same from
a wagon as it did from the train. The ride was long, the wagon seat
hard, and laundry was the only objective for the day.

He didn't get the hint but insisted on accompanying her. On
the chance he might be a late sleeper, Susannah woke before sunrise. Apparently he was an early riser too. Might as well put him to
work. "I could use your help with the oxen."

Reverend Webb swung the yoke with a practiced ease. Obviously
he had done more than study Scripture in recent years.

Susannah fastened the bows and threaded the traces through
the loops. "It's really not necessary for you to go with me." Susannah

nodded at Jake seated on the laundry bag. "Between the dog and the shotgun, I'm quite safe."

"It's a privilege." The Reverend joined her on the seat, dashing her last hope that he would think of some other activity for the day. He shot a glance at the store, letting out a shudder.

Susannah shook the reins, guiding the team across the Sheyenne and up to the prairie. "The Roses have that effect on me too."

"And those children," he groaned. "I've seen better manners in barroom brawls. You are to be commended for endeavoring to teach such hoodlums."

"You ministered in saloons, Reverend Webb?"

"It is the sick who need a physician."

Topping a rise, they startled a herd of antelope. Jake leaped off the wagon and gave chase. Susannah grabbed the gun, but the deer bounded out of range before she could raise the butt to her shoulder.

Reverend Webb shivered in stunned silence. For the thousandth time, Susannah wished Jesse were there. He wouldn't have any difficulty keeping the conversation going. And he'd appreciate that the Reverend's nose was larger than his. Now, what could she ask the man to get him talking again? "Saloons. I guess you have quite the testimony."

"Ah, Mrs. Mason. You know just how to warm the heart of an old circuit rider. I shall endeavor to keep it brief."

Out here, the wind took the echo out of his voice and blew away a little of his formality. "I was born in Indiana in 1825. When I was fourteen, an accident involving a runaway team took my mother and sister from this troubled life. My father escaped without a scratch—one of the ironies of drink. The other irony is that rather than putting him on the path of reform, his vile habit worsened. Within the year, he joined his wife and daughter in the grave."

Susannah opened her mouth to express her condolences, but the

Reverend continued on, preaching to a congregation of one. Only fourteen. If her parents had died so early, what would have become of her? Perhaps God had been watching over her all this time, even as she accused Him of abandonment.

"As you may have observed, boys of a certain age grow about a foot a year and seem to have a hollow leg when the dinner bell rings. I took on many jobs to fill my belly: farmwork, digging wells, building barns. When a circus came to town offering a prize to whoever could best their fighter, I figured my muscles would win me an easy meal. But their boy knew his business. He flattened me before the end of the first minute. I followed the circus the rest of the summer, hanging around the boxing ring, watching fights, picking up a few pointers, learning how to work the crowd. A fighter takes part of the bets if he wins. Pays better than farmwork."

Susannah smiled to show him she wasn't scandalized.

"After a while I headed west, arriving in Iowa in '55. I fought my way through the saloons along the Mississippi, keeping myself fed as long as the law looked the other way. One night, after a disputed bout, a gang of river rats jumped me. They tossed my carcass in a graveyard, but I wasn't nearly as dead as they thought. Next morning a preacher came upon me. He conveyed me to the parsonage, where his wife tended my wounds.

"Now, what do you suppose a preacher would do with a captive audience?" He pulled a worn Bible from his coat pocket. "I received healing in body and in spirit."

Head down, tongue lolling from the side of his mouth, Jake trudged out of the next draw and dropped to the ground. Embarrassed about the antelope, he pretended to nap.

"Shall I retrieve your dog?" Reverend Webb offered reluctantly.

"No, he'll be along. You went into the ministry?"

"With a name like John Wesley, what else could I do?"

"What indeed?"

"I promised to keep this short." His mouth curled in a wry smile. "I served as a deacon and elder in Iowa until I got the call to the Northern Pacific Mission. Like the Good Samaritan who rescued me, I've tended many a lost soul. The tragedy of my father's inebriation and my experience with pugilism has been put to good use in the ministry. Do you believe great victories can come from trials and adversity?"

Susannah suspected the Reverend referred to the grasshoppers and Jesse's departure, but she applied his story differently. Her veterinary training, a liability in Detroit, became an asset on the frontier. She'd spoken more French with Sees-the-Tatanka than she had since graduation. She'd played her violin in church. "Yes. Dakota requires everything of you—all your talents, all your skills, all your knowledge." Would the Reverend be up to such a difficult life?

Jake returned. The minister inched forward, keeping his distance. The wind ruffled his peculiar whiskers, reminiscent of a goat's beard. Perhaps it hid a goiter or a prominent Adam's apple. "This country—"

"Awe inspiring, isn't it? In Detroit, between buildings, trees, and smoke, I never saw the sky." She tipped her head back. "It's more beautiful than anything man-made. Sometimes there's lightning like the world's coming to an end, clouds like marble castles, and the stars! It's amazing, Reverend, just amazing."

He gave her a relaxed, almost boyish smile. "My friends call me J.W."

"Call me Susannah." The wagon bumped over a dry creek bed. She braced against the footboard.

"Last night we spoke of the inhabitants of Worthington. This morning I've droned on about myself. Now I'd like to hear about you."

"Our claim starts about here. This is our wheat field, the

firebreak—" An animal moved through the tall grass. "That's not a deer, it's a horse!" A dun-colored pony grazed northeast of the soddy. Pulse racing, Susannah snapped the reins. *Please, Lord, let it be Jesse, let him be home.*

Susannah halted the oxen by the creek. Piles of hay, Mr. Reece's contribution, loomed behind the stable. Magnar had stacked firewood in front. Otherwise the homestead appeared unchanged.

"Jake." Susannah made a circular motion, sending the dog on a reconnaissance of the yard. Reverend Webb marched up and knocked. The door remained closed with the latch string pulled in. One of the curtains was missing, so Susannah cupped a hand around her face and leaned against the glass. The white fabric lay on the table, but the rest of the room was lost in shadows.

"Hello!" she called. "I don't mind your using my house, but I hope you'll let us come in and warm up."

The door opened a crack, and with a flash of bright red hair a young woman peered out. "You're Susannah?" She pointed to the weathered note tacked to the jamb.

"Yes. And this is Jake." The dog pushed past to check out the house. No one could hide from his nose.

"That's Jesse?" The woman nodded at the minister.

The Reverend introduced himself, balancing the laundry bundle under one arm. "May we come in? This wind is mighty fierce."

The woman opened the door wider, then eased onto the stool. She moved carefully, as if recovering from an injury. Jake returned to Susannah's side, his inspection complete.

"Moving will warm you up." Susannah handed the coffee grinder to the shivering minister, then adjusted the stovepipe damper and set water on to heat. She turned to the woman. "I'm sorry I wasn't here when you arrived."

"I don't mind." She resumed stitching the curtain. Something was amiss; the woman still had not introduced herself.

"I don't recall seeing you before. Do you live around here?"

"Other side of the river a bit."

"What store do you use?" Not the Worthington one, or Mrs. Rose would have told her all about this lady.

"Haven't done much shopping lately, on account of the grass-hoppers."

"What brings you out this way?"

"I was heading for Fargo when my pony tuckered out."

"I'll have a look at him after I start the washing." Susannah leaned closer. "What are you working on?"

"I hope you don't mind." She held up the curtain. "I stitched the grasshopper holes into a design using white work. My husband never let me do fancy—" She pressed her lips together.

"You're Betsy Stapleton of Jamestown."

The woman jerked as if she'd been shot.

"Your husband took out an advertisement for you in the Fargo paper."

"Oh no." Betsy seemed to shrink within herself.

Susannah softened her voice. "I remember the ad, because I'm in a similar situation as Mr. Stapleton."

The woman flashed a skeptical glance. "Your husband ran off?"

"Not exactly, but I don't know where he is or when he'll return." Susannah paced the room, stopping to trace the carving on the mirror stand, his gift on their first and only Christmas together. "Not a day, not an hour goes by that I don't think of him, wondering if he's all right, if he's alive. I can't tell you how bad it hurts." Susannah faced the woman with her tears. "Do you suppose your husband is in such pain?"

Reverend Webb recovered his pastoral self. "'What God has joined together, let no man put asunder,'" he quoted. "'Wives, submit to your husband as to the Lord.'" He looked down his nose at her. "Jamestown is one of my preaching points, so it is both my duty and my joy to effect a reconciliation between you and your husband. I would be honored to escort you home this week."

"I can't go back."

"With God, all things are possible."

"Possible, yes. A good idea, no." Betsy turned her back and began to unfasten the top buttons of her dress.

"Mrs. Stapleton!" Reverend Webb gasped and averted his eyes. For someone who had been in the circus and on the boxing circuit, Susannah thought, the man shocked easily.

The morning sunlight lit Betsy's shoulders and revealed her flesh striped with angry red welts and half-healed bruises in shades of purple and yellow.

"Reverend," Susannah said, "you need to see this."

Against his will he looked, then turned a shade of green that was attractive only on celery.

"Why don't you go check the oxen?"

He bolted out before Susannah took her next breath. She eased the collar back around Betsy's neck. "Your husband—" she began, then stopped herself. Any man who would do this didn't deserve the title of *husband*. "Mr. Stapleton did this?"

Closing her eyes, Betsy nodded.

"Let's get you cleaned up, make sure there's no infection."

"Please don't trouble yourself. All I ask is that you don't tell William you've seen me."

"Of course not." Susannah opened her trunk. Why would anyone do this to another human being, someone they pledged to love?

"What about that distinguished minister of yours?"

"I'd say you've given him quite the education today." Susannah set the washbasin and clean rags on the table with a bottle of isopropyl alcohol and a jar of ointment. "He's probably run off, trying to catch the next eastbound train."

"I scared him that bad?"

"You and the whole uncivilized territory." Susannah poured the warm water into the basin. What Stapleton had done to Betsy was wrong. Inexcusable. "Have a seat. How far down—?"

Betsy looked Susannah straight in the eye. "You really are going to help me." Tension ebbed from her face, leaving a childlike openness. "Every place covered by clothes."

Susannah bit her lip to keep from crying. "How long—?"

"Awhile. A good long while. We got married when he came home from the War." Betsy loosened the ties of her blood-flecked chemise. Bruises, welts, and burns covered her torso and arms. She continued in a matter-of-fact tone. "After the War, he seemed all right, telling me how clean and quiet the house was after living in an army camp. He didn't talk much, said the War was over and he had nothing to say about it. We moved to Chicago. For a better job, he said, but sometimes I think he wanted to get away from the other soldiers who'd been in his unit."

Susannah wrung out the cloth. Jesse had been a soldier too, but he never hit her, never touched her in anger. "I've got to wet your chemise. It's scabbed to your back."

"Go ahead, whatever needs to be done." Betsy turned her face away. "At first he enjoyed his work, making deliveries all over the city. Then there were days when he'd sit and stare, like he was in a whole different world, a horrible world. The foreman told him not to come back, seeing as how he wasn't showing up for work more than once a week. That was the first time. He smashed the furniture and me. Next morning he was sweeter than Christmas candy. Said the city made him crazy, so we left the States and took up a homestead."

The alcohol bottle shook in Susannah's hands. "This might sting."

The young woman inhaled through her teeth but motioned for Susannah to continue. "Last year didn't go too bad. He'd slap me every once in a while if dinner wasn't quite to his liking or some such. Then the nightmares started. Like he was fighting the War all over again. I made the mistake of buying him whiskey, thinking he'd sleep through the night. Made him worse than ever."

Susannah warmed the ointment in the hot water and spread it with a feather. Even if Betsy had been the worst cook in the world, she didn't deserve this.

Betsy pulled on her chemise and bodice and stepped out of her skirt and petticoats. "He said I deserved it because I wouldn't give him children. I didn't do anything to stop them, they just never came. Now I'm glad. Probably wouldn't have gotten away with a baby hanging on me."

"Doesn't sound like he'd be a good father." As opposed to Jesse, who would be a terrific father and had never raised a hand against her. Working her way down Betsy's legs, Susannah blinked back tears. No one deserved this. No one.

"Do you have family, somewhere to go? Of course, you can stay here as long as you need to. It's nothing fancy, but—"

"No, it's a wonderful. Your spring, your garden, all those acres broke. Thank you, I'd like to stay a bit." She inched her stockings up.

"I could leave Jake here to keep you company." *To guard you.*

"He's so attached to you." She shook her head. "I have an aunt in St. Paul, but I'd rather be sure of my welcome before I show up."

"I can take your letter when I go back to Worthington."

"I'd appreciate that." Betsy stood and stretched. Her green eyes glowed beneath long auburn lashes. "That's much better, body and soul. It's like a big rock rolled off me. Thank you."

"I'd better check on your pony and bring in the Reverend before he turns into an icicle." Susannah carried the basin of bloody water to the door. "Betsy, no matter what you've done or not done, you didn't deserve this kind of treatment. No one does. He was wrong. The guilt is all his. You're not to blame."

Hadn't Jesse said something like that to Susannah, about the banker?

Betsy was not to blame.

And neither was she.

Chapter 29

Jesus, why am I here?

The students had left for the day, so Susannah opened the door to sweep.

"Mrs. Mason!" Donald McFadgen headed straight for the school. "I've a present for you."

A flash of alarm streaked through her. What if the hotelier, like Abner Reece, intended to court her?

He hefted a huge burlap sack onto the doorstep, then opened it, revealing a dark orange globe more than two feet in diameter.

"A pumpkin!"

"I believe you Americans have Thanksgiving next week."

"You're a remarkable gardener. Will this make the newspaper, like your four-and-a-half-pound cucumber?"

"The publisher was afraid these Irish had rubbed off on me, so I had to send that particular vegetable to the paper. No, Fargo isn't sinking its teeth into this little beauty. It's for you."

"Why, thank you." Susannah grabbed the stem and tipped the pumpkin toward her to estimate its weight, then ran her hands over it. Its smooth skin glistened in the amber light of the setting sun. Unblemished, no soft spots, flesh firm. "If only I had my pie plates."

"Surely, back at the homestead—"

"I wouldn't want to chance freezing this fine specimen."

"You're welcome to the loan of a pie plate."

"That's very kind of you, but I'd also need a rolling pin, spices—"

"I've got everything you'd need, but—" He peered around her, taking in the two-lid stove and army box. "Mrs. Mason, it would be the utmost in foolishness for you to attempt baking in this make-do outfit when I've got a fully equipped kitchen so close."

Susannah glanced at the second-floor window above the store. Lamplight silhouetted a bobbing head at the end of a long neck. Mr. McFadgen followed her gaze. He waved and yelled, "Good evening, dearie." Mrs. Rose vanished.

"Morrison's over. You'll be chaperoned. Those of us who know Jesse wish nothing but good for you."

Susannah returned his smile. "Let's make some pies."

Jake dashed along with them through drifts of leaves to the house. The windows glowed warmly in the frosty twilight.

"I've never been in a log cabin before."

"You're better off in a soddy. Cottonwood logs warp something fierce. I'm forever chinking, yet have more snow to shovel inside than out."

She smiled at the exaggeration. "Are you certain the Irish haven't rubbed off on you?"

"Mrs. Mason!" He grinned in return and pushed open the door. Susannah followed Jake in. The dog found plenty of interesting smells. Stacks of pelts in various stages of processing lined the walls. The odor of furs mingled with the distinct aroma of corned beef and cabbage. Susannah said a quick prayer of thanks that her pregnancy had progressed beyond the early sour-stomach stage.

Triplets of "The Irish Washerwoman" danced in the air.

"Lad. Did I not ask you to tidy up? And change the tune, before Mrs. Mason thinks you're asking her to do laundry."

A curly-haired musician, the man who'd played the uilleann pipes at the baby's funeral, stood beside the stove. "Sure and I did clean. There's enough space in here to hold a dance."

"If you're a leprechaun." Mr. McFadgen turned to Susannah. "Mrs. Mason, may I present John Morrison."

"Happy St. Patrick's Day." He bowed over his tin whistle.

"Closer to Bobby Burns' birthday." The hotelier hung Susannah's coat on a peg as his partner started a new tune. "Now, which spices will you be needing?"

Like the pumpkin, the kitchen was on a grand scale, a holdover from the days of serving as a restaurant for the tent hotel. With Mr. McFadgen's eager help, Susannah soon had three pies in the oven.

She stepped back from the table and wiped her hands dry. "Mr. McFadgen, I believe I've been hornswoggled."

"Pardon me, Mrs. Mason, but I'm not familiar with that particular American word." His face shone with an expression she had seen on her students when they completed an exceptionally difficult computation.

"Bamboozled, tricked." She crossed her arms. "You brought me over here to teach you how to make pumpkin pie."

"Well, you are the teacher." He grinned so hard the corners of his mouth nearly reached his ears. "As an apology, please accept an invitation to supper."

Susannah accepted gladly; her stomach had been anticipating the meal since she arrived.

After gulping down his portion, Morrison returned to his whistle. "Any requests?"

"Aye. Peace and quiet." Mr. McFadgen cleared the table.

"Do you know 'Monymusk'?" Susannah asked.

"Sure and it's a fine Irish tune."

"Nay, lad. 'Tis Scottish."

"English," Susannah stated.

"What?" The dueling pair gaped at her.

"Nothing like a little Anglo-Saxon interference to bring about Celtic unity." She winked. Jesse had taught her well in the fine art of teasing. And oh, she missed him so much. She took her plate and set it in the dishpan.

"Now who's the hornswoggler?" Mr. McFadgen chuckled. "I will not impose cleaning chores on you, especially when I've a professional dishwasher in my employ." He cast a fierce look at Morrison, still piping away. "Mrs. Mason, may I escort you and your lovely pastry back to school?"

"Please call me Susannah." She pulled on her coat and clicked her tongue for Jake.

"Susannah. You share a name with one of the finest women to walk this earth, my mother. You must call me Mac, then."

"Thanks for the fine evening, Mac."

"Aye, lass, you were due for one."

She stepped out and gasped in wonder. Bright spots bracketed the moon like celestial parentheses. "Look! Moondogs!"

"A sign from God."

Textbooks said that moondogs were an optical illusion caused by light rays bending through temperature layers in the atmosphere, but Susannah didn't see why they couldn't be a sign from God too.

The hotelier strolled along, balancing the pie on one palm like a waiter. "I've been wanting to ask a favor of you. Jesse and I had a talk about faith awhile back. I put him off. Figured there was plenty of time when I'm an old man to consider the afterlife. But with the Norwegian baby dying and Jesse disappearing—ach, now I've upset you."

"No more than usual." Susannah blinked away a tear. Even

through the evening's laughter, through the difficult days teaching, and especially through the long nights, grief held her heart. Like the wind, it never stopped, just came at her from different directions.

Mac opened the schoolhouse door for her and Jake, then set the pie on the stove. "If you've a moment, Susannah, would you stand in for Jesse and pray with me?"

Some word of encouragement would be appropriate here, but her throat closed. Every prayer she'd learned, every verse she'd memorized deserted her. But her heart knew, with certainty, that God existed, that He was present. She offered her gloved hands.

Mac clamped them between his mittens. "Well, God, sorry it's taken so long. Here I am. Not much of a life. Hope You can make something of it." He sniffed and cleared his throat. "Now, about Your Jesse Mason. Could You send him back this way? We're missing him."

He stopped. There was silence for a minute or two, then Mac whispered to Susannah, "I've no more to say."

"In Jesus' name, amen."

He pulled a well-worn linen napkin from his pocket to swab his tears. "Thank you, Susannah."

Jesse should be here, Susannah thought, *to harvest the seed he planted.* "You might want to speak with Reverend Webb next time he comes through. Perhaps he could get you a Bible."

"Jesse bought me one the year he worked the railroad. You know how tightfisted he is, must have a Scot back in his family tree. Him spending money on a Bible? I couldn't have been more surprised if Morrison stopped piping." Mac's face glowed in the moonlight. "Yes, it's been a grand evening, lass."

"Welcome to the family of God, Donald McFadgen." *And welcome back to Susannah Underhill Mason.*

287

A quartet of men rode into the draw with a deer they'd shot. The village turned out and worked like a well-oiled machine: boys caring for the horses, girls watching the babies, women preparing the meat and cleaning the hide.

Jesse's mouth watered as the smell of roasting meat spiraled among the tepees. He'd heard Indians lived on buffalo, but this village had been getting by on fish, waterfowl, or prairie chickens. They filled out the menu with corn, some sort of potato, and pumpkin prepared in ways he'd never imagined. Meat would taste good, real good. But one deer among fifteen tepees with an average of three people living in each? He'd better not count on it.

"Tatanka." Misun's mother motioned for him to put away the grinding stones.

One of the hunters spotted Jesse and yelled. Quicker than a last breath, the men fenced his throat with knives. No civilized Indians here; these were warriors. Angry warriors.

Jesse turned his palms up, hoping they got the message of surrender. "Into your hands, Jesus—"

The name of God set off a debate never heard in any Sunday school. Jesse couldn't tell if they were for or against. Misun pushed into the circle, carrying the guitar and voicing his opinion. Jesse hoped they wouldn't kill him as the kid watched.

With a unison grunt of assent, the men stepped back. Jesse swiped a hand across his neck. No blood. Yet. Misun shoved the guitar into his hands.

Was he supposed to sing for his supper? No, sing for his life. His hands shook as he started "Jesus Loves Me" and nodded for Misun to join in. His voice was as shaky as his fingers. Chetan arrived and made it a trio.

When they finished, the Indian men looked at the short, round-headed brave with the leathery skin, apparently the judge and jury in these parts. Shorty studied Jesse, Misun, and Chetan without changing expression. Finally his head moved down half an inch. Misun smiled and started "Blessed Assurance."

Jesse drew in a breath and joined him. Still alive. Alive was good. Alive meant a chance of going home. And playing guitar sure beat carrying water or grinding corn. He grinned and sang louder.

When the warriors moved away, Jesse sank on trembling knees to the cold ground. As the sun set, the temperature plunged. He drew closer to the communal fire and kept the music going until a gray-haired man brought out a drum. With a sigh of relief Jesse ceded the stage and returned to the tepee. Misun's mother slipped him a chunk of meat, then left to watch the singers and dancers.

He tossed more dung on the tepee's fire and propped his feet to thaw. Time was, Jesse didn't care if he lived or died. He knew where he was going and Who was waiting for him. But now he had Susannah to go home for. *Lord, show me the way.*

The sergeant poked her head into the tepee and threw a pile of water skins at him.

"Madam, I sense my recital was not up to your professional standards."

Her only response was a threatening gesture he understood all too well.

Jesse loped to the creek, filled the skins, then looked up and gasped. The moon hung low on the horizon, circled by a thin white line with bright spots at three and nine o'clock. Could Susannah see the moon tonight? Did she remember watching the northern lights with him?

The Indians noticed too and stopped dancing. He wondered if moondogs had a special meaning in their religion. Maybe God telling them to let this white man go free.

Brown cottonwood leaves skittered between Worthington's cluster of buildings. Susannah filled two buckets at the pump, then headed back to the shack, empty at the end of the day. Evenings were a struggle. She caught herself listening for Jesse's voice, singing as he did when work was done. She ached to talk over her students with him, to feel his strong hands rub the back of her neck, to lie close to him and feel his warmth. But she couldn't dwell on it. Melancholy wasn't good for the baby.

Ahead of her, Jake raced off to intercept two men leaving the section house. The first, Donald McFadgen, was familiar, so the dog concentrated his efforts on the stranger. An army officer. Susannah groaned. Would he shut the school down just when her students had started to progress?

The man in the cavalry uniform bent for a closer look at the dog. "Fine-looking fellow." Jake, intent on sniffing, circled. The officer followed, man and animal doing a dance in their efforts to investigate each other. "Yes, a lot to smell on me: horses, saddles, Autie's hounds."

Autie? Wasn't that the nickname of—

"Susannah." Mac took a bucket from her. "May I present Lieutenant Tom Custer, Company L, United States Seventh Cavalry at Fort Abraham Lincoln. He's visiting his old war buddy, Mr. Flood. Mrs. Susannah Mason."

His attention drawn from the dog at last, the officer snapped into a full salute. Susannah's breath caught. She'd seen numerous pictures of his celebrated brother, General George Armstrong Custer, especially during the War. Before her stood a variation on the theme of spare frame, fair skin, and prominent cheekbones. His hair, light brown instead of his brother's famous strawberry blond, showed the distinctive Custer tendency to curl.

Recovering from the salute, he reached as if to shake her hand but grasped the bucket instead. Mac stepped forward to relieve him of the burden only to have the lieutenant take possession of both pails. He marched to the mail shack, setting them neatly on the threshold.

Susannah bit her lip. So. The army had found out about the school and sent the lieutenant to evict her. "I'm sorry, but the mail shack was vacant, and we have no other structure suitable for a school."

Custer did a sharp about-face, turning his back to the building. "Mail shack? Don't believe I recall such a place." Below the tilted brim of his campaign hat, a blue eye winked. "Is this your dog?"

Jake's nose traced the yellow line up the side of Custer's pants. "Yes, I'm sorry. He's usually not so poorly mannered. Jake!" Susannah clapped her gloved hands. The dog sneezed on the lieutenant's polished riding boots, then reluctantly sidled to Susannah. At least he obeyed. He'd been cantankerous since their move to Worthington.

"Autie has thirty or forty dogs but none this well suited for Dakota. Could use one like him at Lincoln."

"He's a Norwegian elkhound. Great for hunting, herding, and guarding. He sheds a lot, especially in the spring. Ivar Vold raises them on his homestead south of here."

"I'd pay handsomely for first pick of the next litter."

"I'll let him know."

Mac cleared his throat. "If you're through swapping dog stories—"

Custer moved from "at ease" to "attention." "Yes, madam. About your husband—"

Susannah glanced at Mac. "Mr. Mason didn't know about General Sheridan's order closing the Black Hills."

The lieutenant took her hands in his. "I'm deeply sorry for your plight. Please understand, the army is doing everything in its power to protect the civilian population of the territory."

Susannah blinked. His formal words resounded with grim finality.

"Are you saying, lad, there's naught to be done?" Mac thudded his fist against his leg. "Perhaps if I went back with you—"

"I'm afraid Bismarck's civilian population is even more mobile than the army's. Likely the trail's cold by now." The lieutenant's sun-streaked mustache quivered. "Write to Autie. I'll brief him when I get back, but your letter will serve as a reminder, keep the situation in the forefront of his mind."

Susannah nodded, unable to speak over the lump in her throat.

"Now, if you'll excuse us, I believe it's starting to rain." Custer touched the brim of his hat. His invitation to Mac for a poker game drifted through the patter of sleet on the dry leaves.

He thought Jesse was dead.

Chapter 30

If You're going to rescue me, Lord—and I'm
praying You will—this would be a good time.

Susannah had been waiting all day for the students to leave so
she could pop the button on her skirt.

"Ahh." She straightened her shoulders, threw on her coat, and
dashed through the cold dusk toward the Roses' store. *Dear Jesus,*
help me endure. What kind of prayer was that, addressed to a
God who made the universe? All right then. *Dear Jesus, help me*
be strong.

The door opened and Mrs. Rose pulled her in. "Mrs. Mason!
How kind of you to visit. I'll put tea on and you tell me how you've
been feeling. When did you realize you're pregnant?"

The wild Rose boys raced through, working off whatever energy
they had left after tormenting their teacher all day. Robert collided
with a shelf. A box of doorknobs crashed to the floor and spiraled
around. Adam took a swing at one or more brothers, knocking over
a stack of bread pans and muffin tins. Susannah covered her ears.
Perhaps praying for temporary deafness would be expedient.

Mrs. Rose didn't let the racket stop her recitation of symptoms.
Susannah certainly would not discuss breast tenderness in front of

her students. She picked out a bolt of wool and said, "Ten yards," holding up fingers.

Suddenly the boys stopped.

Mrs. Rose gasped. The scissors slipped from her hand.

Susannah turned.

Sees-the-Tatanka stood in the doorway, wrapped in a blanket. His face seemed thinner; had the grasshoppers destroyed the Indians' crops too? He smiled at Susannah. *"Bonjour."*

"Bonjour, monsieur. Comment allez-vous?"

"Très bien, merci. Et vous?"

"Bien, aussi."

Mrs. Rose slid to the floor.

"Un moment, s'il vous plaît." Susannah ran her fingers along the inside of the storekeeper's wrist, finding a rapid but regular pulse. The children scurried up the stairs. Blessed peace. If only there was some way the Indian could join her in the schoolhouse.

"Voulez-vous une tasse de thé?" Susannah poured Mrs. Rose's brew and they sat. She inquired after the Indian's family. Sees-the-Tatanka's son was industriously training horses, trying to impress a certain young woman.

Mac had told him of Jesse's departure. The Indian assured Susannah he would search for her husband when he traveled.

"Merci beaucoup."

Sees-the-Tatanka reported he had taught their song to everyone he met. He nodded and sang "Jesus Loves Me" in an elegant baritone. He left with a prayer for Jesse's safe return and a promise to bring a carrier for her baby. *"Au revoir."*

How did he know? Susannah rubbed the small bump of belly, then finished cutting her fabric from the bolt. "Mrs. Rose?"

The woman blinked, then sat up. "Indians! We're all going to be scalped by savages!"

"Your guest left. I gave him a cup of tea."

Mrs. Rose pointed an accusing forefinger. "You talk Indian. Are you one of them?"

With blue eyes, skin as white as flour, and wavy hair? Susannah wouldn't dignify the question with a response. "I left payment for my fabric."

"Did that heathen rob us?"

Susannah raised one eyebrow. The cash box was sitting on the counter, exactly where Mrs. Rose had left it.

"You were not robbed. And for your information, the Indian man is not a heathen. He is a Christian." Susannah made her escape and left Mrs. Rose to mull over the implications.

Back in the mail shack Susannah swept the schoolhouse floor, then unrolled the burgundy wool. "Isn't this beautiful fabric?"

Jake stretched out next to the door. His ears twitched with the meager attention he gave to activities that didn't involve food. "I don't usually wear bright colors, but Jesse likes red. This is the closest Mrs. Rose had."

She knelt at the end to align the selvages. "Betsy's crocheting the trim for me. Can you believe anyone would hurt such a sweet lady? Sounds to me like her husband is beyond redemption, but J.W. plans to pay him a visit when he preaches in Jamestown."

Susannah climbed to the loft for her nightgown, managing the ladder with a sure-footedness generated by three weeks of practice. When she reached the floor again, she found Jake stretched across the middle of the cloth. "Apparently I should have bought dog-hair gray."

She arranged the nightgown on the wool, using it as a pattern. "Some people call this style a 'Mother Hubbard.' No empty cupboards here, so we'll call it a wrapper." She picked up her scissors. "New fabric. I don't want to make a mistake and ruin the whole ten yards. But I can't wait to see how the dress will look when it's done. Fear and anticipation . . . like having a baby, or journeying out to Dakota to marry a stranger."

Given all the effort he put into getting her to talk, Jesse would no doubt be shocked at all the time she spent conversing with a dog. But Jesse was gone, and Jake had become her constant companion.

She cut out the body of the gown, leaving generous allowances for seams and hems. "Where was I? Oh yes, J.W." Susannah grabbed Jake by his feet and flipped him off the fabric. He stalked away and plopped down with his head facing the corner.

"Do I try to steal your coat?" Susannah unrolled another length and repositioned the nightgown. "J.W. can be a bit pompous," she went on, "but he sure knows how to preach. The familiar message of free grace, beautifully told. Did you see how the Rose children hung on every word? No, guess you didn't. He asked you to leave. You make him sneeze."

Susannah cut across the fabric, forming the bottom edge.

"Ivar must have done a good job translating, the way the Hansens shook his hand. Although when they offered him a beer, well, I guess we'll be hearing a lesson on temperance next."

Adding her hand's width for gathers, she cut out the sleeves. The yoke came last.

"If only sewing were as fast." Susannah folded the pieces and stood to stretch her back. "Did you know J.W. offered to pay for my ticket back to Michigan?"

Jake pricked up his ears and turned to stare at her.

"Guess you and I are the only ones who think Jesse's coming home. You still think so, don't you, Jake?"

The dog laid down his head and closed his eyes with a sigh.

Galloping hoofbeats crescendoed in the darkness. A dog barked. A man shouted. Susannah awoke with a start. The banker! Footsteps pounded on the porch. He pummeled the door and it gave way. He had found her, just as he threatened.

She scrambled to hide, but her legs were trapped. She rooted around the pallet, hunting for the shotgun. Her heart raced and her breath came in short gasps. The man's voice echoed, closer. He wasn't speaking English. It was Norwegian.

"Su-sah-nah!"

Light flared in the room below, then rose up the ladder held by a gloved hand. Magnar Hansen's head appeared, covered by a royal blue stocking.

"*Skynde!*" he said. It was a word Susannah recognized, Sissel's after-school admonition to her sister, Disa. *Hurry.*

Magnar rattled off an incomprehensible explanation, followed by more commands in puffs of white in the cold air. She shook her head. "I don't understand."

He disappeared for a moment, returning with a slate. He drew stick figures, labeling the two-legged one "Erik." Pointing to the larger four-legged animal, he whinnied. For the smaller one, he snarled.

"A wild animal attacked Erik and one of the horses. I'm coming." Susannah tried to follow Magnar down, but her shaking legs wouldn't hold her, and her feet slipped off the rungs. The Norwegian caught her and eased her to the floor. Susannah yanked on her boots and threw on her coat. She slung her father's knapsack over her shoulder, whistled for Jake, and reached for the shotgun.

"No." Magnar held up his Winchester. He pulled her outside to the bareback stallion, mounted, then reached for her. Susannah unbuttoned the pleat of her coat. Forget propriety. A boy and a horse needed her care. She hiked her nightgown and climbed on behind him.

The jittery horse tossed his head at her weight. Magnar quieted him with a word. Using his free hand, he tugged her forward and tightened her arms around his waist. With a kick of his heels, they raced across the frozen prairie. Susannah turned her head and rested her cheek between his shoulders to shelter her face from the breath-stealing wind. Stars glittered over the coldest time of the night.

Within minutes, the effortless gallop brought them to the Hansen claim. A substantial soddy, three times the size of Jesse's, loomed before them. Shaped like a U, it boasted a window on each wing, and a window and door in the middle. The stallion stopped and they dismounted.

Mrs. Hansen brought her in to warm by the stove. The bright beam of a lamp bounced off the newly plastered walls, highlighting a boy on a stool.

Sissel told the story. "Erik took the horses to water. Big cat try to eat him."

Erik dropped the blanket to display his emblems of bravery. Four lines of dried blood striped his back, just to the left of his spine. These were surface scratches, already cleaned.

Susannah whistled. "Hate to see your coat."

"*Mor* says horse hurt bad."

With a nod to Mrs. Hansen, Susannah followed the path to the stable. Magnar held the mare's halter, but she reared as soon as she saw Susannah. The young man steadied the animal with a few words, then blindfolded her with his muffler. Staying downwind, Susannah assessed the damage. Claw marks streaked the horse's left flank. A deeper wound ran from hock to fetlock on the same side. Dark circles of blood spattered the frost-hard paddock.

Mr. Hansen produced a bottle of whiskey and a bucket. Susannah shook her head. She knew a better way.

"I'll need rags and hot water." She tried to sound confident; what she really needed was a fully qualified veterinary surgeon and an interpreter.

Magnar frowned and shook his head. He didn't understand. Blood dripped from the wound. No time to run back to the house. Taking a surgical knife from the knapsack, she slashed across the hem of her nightgown. A hard yank peeled off a strip of flannel. She wadded it in her palm and reached for the chloroform, but changed her mind when a shiver rippled the horse's flank. The mare would freeze to death out here. Susannah jammed the stopper back into the bottle.

She pointed at the stable, then rested her cheek on her hand. "Bring her inside. I'm going to put her to sleep."

Mr. Hansen raised a questioning eyebrow, but Magnar stepped to the mare's nose. With a constant stream of encouragement, he led her in to a bed of dry prairie hay along the back wall. The cattle stamped and lowed, agitated by the smell of blood. The stallion trumpeted his distress.

Susannah searched among the harnesses, bridles, and rope arrayed on pegs and found a feedbag. She estimated the horse's weight, poured chloroform onto the rag, and dropped it into the feedbag. The mare tossed her head and backed away. Magnar took the bag in one hand, the horse's ear in the other. Mr. Hansen mirrored him on the left. They forced her nose into the bag. She threw her shoulders sideways, slamming Magnar into the wall. Susannah winced, sure he'd be her third patient of the night, but his calm voice continued. The horse stopped fighting. Her legs buckled, her head lowered. The men eased her onto her side.

Susannah removed the feedbag and showed Magnar the faint movement of the mare's nostrils. "Sit here. Father would tell you that not only the horse's but also the veterinary surgeon's life depends on doing this job well. Sit." She pointed by the animal's neck and slid the chloroform bottle into his coat pocket. Kneeling by the animal's back leg, Susannah assessed the damage. "I need to clean the wound. *L'eau*. No, that's French. What do the children say? *Vann.*" She turned to Mr. Hansen, gesturing for him to leave the lantern.

"*Ja. Vann.*"

The older man returned with a bucket, steaming in the cold air. Susannah ripped another length from her nightgown, rinsed the wounds, then completed antisepsis with Mr. Hansen's whiskey.

"Teacher?"

"Sissel. Good," Susannah said without looking up. "I need more rags, any clean fabric will do." Tucking her coattails under her, Susannah lifted the injured leg onto her lap. "Still asleep?" She glanced at Magnar, who nodded. Susannah probed the wound. "Intact tendons, thank the Lord. No muscle damage. Bleeding's slowed. Low temperature's in our favor, constricts her blood vessels. I've got to work fast, don't want to keep her down too long."

The needle dropped from her slippery gloved fingers. She yanked off her gloves and tried again, but her bare hands cramped. With scissors from her father's kit, Susannah snipped the tips off the index and thumb of the right glove and pushed the knitting up to her knuckles. "Cold constricts my vessels too. Why am I talking so much? It just seems natural, I suppose. Father talked while he operated. He enjoyed teaching. I enjoyed learning. It was the only time—"

She glanced up, wondering what the Norwegian men thought about her monologue. Both were focused on the horse. She showed Mr. Hansen how to blot the wound while she joined the layers of skin. "Short stitches, easier to remove."

The mare stirred. Magnar called out. Susannah flung herself to one side, curling to protect her abdomen. The hoof glanced off her hip.

"More chloroform, please." Susannah pantomimed tipping the bottle into the rag and scrambled back into position. She resumed stitching.

"Rags." Sissel set rags next to Susannah. "Jake are here."

"Jake *is* here. Give him water. Perhaps he can lead your father to the wildcat."

Sissel adjusted the lantern. "Sew horse?"

"I'm sewing her skin together. Not too tight or the skin will pucker. Too loose, it won't heal." She moved up the leg. "It's like hemming in reverse. The knots and thread are on the outside."

"Hurt?"

"No. Your uncle is keeping her asleep. I'll show him how to put medicine on it so it won't hurt when she's awake. Keep her quiet the next few days."

A last snip of the scissors. Another dousing with whiskey. "Done."

Magnar left his place to look at her work. "Good!"

Susannah repacked the kit, then tried to stand. Her feet had gone numb, and her legs wobbled. Magnar caught her, took the bag, and half carried her through the silvery dawn.

"I'm fine," she told him, but he didn't understand those words either.

After the stable, the house smothered her with warmth. The short night, demanding surgery, and even more demanding baby drained her energy. Susannah leaned against the wall. Mrs. Hansen greeted her.

Susannah turned to Disa, who was busy drawing with a fingertip on the frosty window. "Please tell your mother I cannot take off my coat," she said. "I did not have time to dress."

Magnar lifted the hem of her greatcoat, revealing the edge of her nightgown, chopped to an indecent knee length. He held Susannah's arm up, pointing out the cut tips of her glove.

Mrs. Hansen made a clicking noise with her tongue, then guided Susannah into the west alcove, the parents' bedroom. Pulling the curtain closed behind them, Mrs. Hansen opened a large painted trunk and sorted through folded clothes. Then with motherly care she unbuttoned Susannah's coat and eased the gloves off.

Mrs. Hansen shook her head at the bloodstained nightgown and lifted it over Susannah's head. She paused to touch the curve at Susannah's waist. "Baby. Good." She did not make eye contact as she dressed Susannah in a white blouse and blue jumper. They both knew it wasn't good, a baby on the way with her husband who knows where.

Mrs. Hansen slipped out and spoke quietly to Magnar. Susannah heard the word "baby," the same in both languages. But *Mor* wasn't telling him anything new; Magnar had known since he'd helped her down the ladder in the early hours of this morning.

Susannah stepped into the main room. Magnar had his back to them, ladling porridge into red ceramic bowls. He turned. *"Ja!"* He reached for Susannah and escorted her to the table.

"Uncle says you look good Norwegian," Disa reported.

"Wrong color hair." She should have taken the time to redo her windblown, sleep-mussed braid. Too tired. She slid onto the bench at the long table, closed her eyes, and held her hands over the bowl. She could fall asleep right now, face-first into the porridge. Magnar's large hands enfolded hers, massaging the stiffness out with rose water and glycerin.

Every time he touched her, she missed Jesse more.

A clock chimed the hour.

"Thank you. *Takk.*" She pulled her hands out of the man's grasp and picked up the spoon. "I'm late."

Rolf crawled from under the table and clambered onto her lap. "Uncle wagon to school."

Across the table, Magnar devoured his breakfast without taking his eyes from her. What was he staring at? She was straw-dusted, smelled like a horse, and pregnant.

To avoid looking back at him, Susannah surveyed the room.

The house was constructed with milled rafters instead of the peeled logs Jesse had used. The east alcove contained two beds and another brightly painted trunk. Along the west wall sat a bed with a trundle beneath it. It seemed like a lot of furniture until she remembered eight people lived here. Next to the window, Mrs. Hansen uncovered a small black appliance.

"A sewing machine!" This family was prosperous enough for horses, rafters, and a sewing machine? Susannah thought back to the vanished Irish couple with twins at Fourth Siding. Both houses were made of sod, but there the similarities ended.

"*Mor* sew for teacher." Disa stretched to continue her artwork on the top panes. "You sew horse. *Mor* sew dress."

"All right. After school I'll bring my fabric when I check on the mare."

With a death grip on Jesse's ear, the sergeant dragged him into the overcast morning. The north wind sliced through his cotton shirt, and the frozen grass pricked his feet like needles.

"Ever hear of dressing for the weather?" Probably not. Blankets and moccasins seemed to be the only winter wear here.

The woman hauled him to the grassy slope by the creek. She handed him a burlap sack and pointed her whip at a pile of horse apples. Well, someone had to bring in the fuel, and he did enjoy the fire. "Don't suppose you thought to bring gloves?" he muttered.

She might not have understood his words, but she recognized stalling. Another yank on his ear put some hustle in his step. Between pickups, he sneaked a look around. Empty that direction. Same this direction. No sign of life. No sign of the river. Well, the creek probably—

There was a snap, a sting, and Jesse rubbed at his wrist. The

Indian woman twitched her whip. She didn't smile, but Jesse thought he saw a contemptuous laugh in her beady eyes.

"I'm working, I'm working," he said. But not getting paid.

What was Susannah doing for fuel? She wasn't strong enough to cut wood, but the oxen generated plenty of cow pies. He grimaced, imagining his wife's fingers picking up dung. Maybe she could wear work gloves, like she did when she dealt with the grasshoppers.

He filled the bag, but the job wasn't done. He had to empty it beside one tepee, then go back for more. At least frozen-solid horse apples didn't smell.

In camp, one of the younger women helped a pregnant girl to a tepee set by itself. The sergeant joined them.

This was his big opportunity. Jesse worked east, pausing now and then to add to the bag in case anyone watched. He inched closer to the river. Closer to Fort Lincoln. Closer to home.

One chance. If he failed, if he was caught, the tribe would torture and kill him.

He crested the slope and looked up. A huge ash-gray cloud loomed overhead, rolling toward him, already shooting downdrafts of snow.

One chance. But no chance at all.

"Go ahead." Susannah shooed the Hansen children. "I'll be along after I check for mail."

Sissel took the bundle of Susannah's fabric and herded her siblings toward home. By the time Susannah escaped from Mrs. Rose's dire warnings about Indians, grilling on the early morning events, and commentary on Norwegian clothing, the children were specks on the horizon. She trudged after them and glanced at the envelopes as she walked, then shoved them into her pockets. Nothing from Jesse.

Where was he?

Dusk sped into dark. The last few degrees on the thermometer vanished with the sun. The northwest wind pelted her with ice balls and fine grains of dirt. In spite of the scarf over her face, each breath ripped the inside of her nose and scraped her lungs. The cold penetrated her boots and two pairs of socks until she couldn't feel her legs.

She tried to walk faster, but her muscles were sore from riding the stallion and spasmed in protest. A hot pain clawed her side. Susannah crossed her arms, pressing a fist into her ribs. She slowed, twisting to try to ease the cramp, but the throbbing sliced down to her hip and spread to her other side. She turned her back to the wind and sank down on the frozen ground.

Please, God, the baby . . .

"Teacher! Teacher!" Erik dashed up, followed by the other children in the buckboard with their uncle.

"Teacher hurt?" Sissel held a lantern.

"No, just tired." Susannah struggled to stand, but Magnar scooped her off the ground and deposited her on the wagon seat. He tucked a heavy gray blanket around her legs.

"Uncle says sorry wagon late." Rolf climbed over the backrest to snuggle against her, nudging her into Magnar. The pain loosened its grip. Susannah sighed, exhaling a white cloud. *Thank You, Jesus.*

Magnar halted in front of the house and carried her inside.

"Put me down! I can walk! Sissel, tell him!"

The children giggled. They'd be impossible to teach after all this silliness, as naughty as the Rose children. Magnar set her on her feet at the front door. She spun away and headed for the barn.

"I need to see the horse. Sissel, please bring the lantern."

In the stable, Mr. Hansen raised an eyebrow at his snickering offspring. The mare's eyes were calm, her stitches dry and cool. Susannah's meticulous father would have no complaints.

"Did you find the cat?" Susannah curved her hands into claws and growled. Fresh laughter erupted from the doorway. A hint of a smile crossed the face of the usually stolid Mr. Hansen. He led the group around the soddy, where Jake guarded a tawny carcass. Dark blood matted the fur between the cat's ears.

"What are you grinning about?" Susannah asked her panting dog. "You didn't bring him down."

Susannah examined the cougar, the clouded lenses of his eyes, the gray fur sprinkling his muzzle. "He's half blind, missing three of his four canine teeth. This cat's hunting days were over. Probably thought Erik was a colt."

Mrs. Hansen called them to the table. Like Marta, *Mor* Hansen carried herself like a queen and ruled over her family with dignified benevolence. A thick braid circled her head in a crown. But beneath her calm exterior ran a sharp mind, manifested in Sissel's wit, Disa's elaborate dreams, Erik's mischievousness. Without a doubt the children inherited equal attributes from their father, although Mr. Hansen's reserve did not invite social contact. Susannah glanced across the supper table at the quiet head of the household. Did people find her equally difficult to approach?

After the meal, Disa produced a basket of yarn. "I fix teacher mittens."

Susannah reached into her pockets and brought out her gloves and the mail. Good manners dictated that letters be read aloud or saved for when one was alone, but the rule couldn't possibly apply to this situation. Mrs. Hansen pumped away on the sewing machine. Sissel dried the dishes. The men had left for evening chores. And the next moment Susannah was alone, she'd drop off to sleep. She settled little Rolf on her lap and opened the first envelope.

It was from Reverend Webb. He had been unable to locate Susannah's or Betsy's husband in Jamestown, but would continue to search on his next visit. The village on the James River was populated with approximately two hundred souls, many employed at the fort, and all in need of clerical care. God willing, he would leave for Bismarck in the morning. He promised to inquire about Jesse, and he looked forward to seeing her on his return trip.

The next was from Ann Arbor. Reverend Mason had received a letter from a minister in the territory, one John W. Webb. Her brother-in-law expressed distress that Susannah had been reduced to teaching school in a shanty to a gang of ruffians, half of whom were heathen foreigners. She carried a gun and kept a wolf. She was in a "delicate condition" and her diet consisted entirely of potatoes. The Mason homestead, little more than an animal den, housed a woman of questionable reputation. Jesse had apparently taken leave of his senses and abandoned her. Correspondence had been initiated with the War Department; military action in the Black Hills was not expected until spring. She must remove herself from these unfavorable conditions at once, by the next train.

Heathen foreigners? Susannah glanced around the room at the loving Hansen family. Reverend Webb showed a melodramatic bent.

"Teacher?" Rolf held up three train tickets.

Susannah spread them on the table. Fourth Siding to St. Paul, St. Paul to Chicago, Chicago to Ann Arbor.

Magnar and Mr. Hansen returned on a gust of snow flurries. The tickets spun out of Susannah's reach, twirled around the room, and landed by Magnar's boots. He picked them up. His face creased into a frown as he looked from the tickets to Susannah.

"Uncle say you go train?"

Every eye in the house stared at her. She studied the plane marks on the table. Real doctors and pharmacies, coal heat, gas lights. But what if Jesse came home and she wasn't here? "I don't know."

Norwegian fireworks erupted with a cacophony of discussion and argument.

Sissel provided the blow-by-blow interpretation. "Uncle says you are needed here, to teach and doctor horses. *Far* says you cannot stay. *Mor* says you have baby and no husband. How? You need husband to make baby. *Mor* says it is late. You sleep in my bed." Sissel sat next to her. "Teacher, don't go." The rest of the children echoed her cry.

Magnar disappeared into the east alcove, jerking the curtain closed. The sound wasn't as loud as a slamming door, but the emotion came through. Why was he angry? Susannah kept her head down, careful not to make eye contact with either of the parents.

Mrs. Hansen swept the children off to bed.

Susannah pulled her washed and mended nightgown over her long underwear, then climbed in beside Sissel. What was she going to do? But as always, it seemed the decision had been made for her: she would return to civilization, stay with Matt and Ellen until the baby arrived, and hope the army would have some information about Jesse by then. The oxen and chickens were already here at the Hansens. The children adored Jake. Betsy would take the homestead. It was all settled.

But how could she move farther away from Jesse? It would be like giving up.

The stove door squeaked. A log thudded onto the coals. Nightshirt flapping around his long johns, Magnar approached the bed and motioned her to the window. "Come."

"I'm in my nightgown," she whispered. If he wasn't careful, he'd wake his nieces with his unseemly behavior.

"Come."

"Well, all right, you saw it this morning." She sidestepped around the trundle bed.

He exhaled on the middle pane and wiped it with his cuff. She didn't have to look; the glow of the night told the story. The snows had begun.

"Su-sah-nah stay." He smiled.

When Jesse woke, a pair of moccasins sat beside his head with socks tucked inside.

Misun's little sister giggled. Jesse winked at her and she giggled some more. He pulled on the socks and thanked God he hadn't lost a toe or two. Then he opened the flap.

The draw was knee-deep in snow. Moccasins or no moccasins, he wasn't going anywhere. Perhaps for a very long time.

Chapter 34

Tell Susannah I love her, and . . . I'm sorry.

"You're getting the fabric wet," Betsy observed from the stove where she heated glue.

"Silly. I don't know what's wrong with me." Susannah wiped her eyes with Jesse's red bandanna. Magnar had hitched up his sleigh and returned her to the homestead. She had Betsy for company. And she had the baby.

There was much to be thankful for, she knew, and yet she was barely hanging on. Constant prayer was the only thing that kept her from falling apart completely.

"My aunt boo-hooed through all eight of her confinements. I'll fix you a cup of tea." Betsy filled the tin coffeepot from the pail of melting snow on the stove. "If it bothers you so much to cut that up—"

On the table lay Jesse's disassembled shirt. Using a dress of Sara's for a pattern, Susannah was sewing a layette from Jesse's old clothes.

"No. The fabric's still good, soft from all the washings. I just feel sorry for the baby." She stroked her melon-shaped abdomen. "His mother can't afford new fabric for his clothes. And without a father—"

"I expect that will change soon." Betsy filled the tea ball with leaves. The ball and curling iron were the only household implements Betsy had taken from her old home; William didn't drink tea and his hair curled on its own. "The only question is, who will the lucky bridegroom be? You pick one and I'll take the other."

"Ridiculous thing for two married women to discuss."

"Don't tell me you haven't thought of it." Using a chicken feather, Betsy applied glue to the mortise and tenon, then pushed the joint back together. "When your husband smashes furniture, you learn to make repairs."

Susannah snipped the knot and pulled out the thread holding the sleeve together. "After what you went through, I'm surprised you're not shy of men."

"On the contrary, dear Susannah," Betsy said with a sweeping gesture. "I'm ready to show the world what an excellent wife I really am. Prove my snake-in-the-grass husband wrong. I'm ready for someone who will cherish me, tell me I'm pretty, treat me like a lady. I want someone to look in my eyes and say I'm the best thing that ever happened to him. I'm ready for love, fairy-tale, happily-ever-after love." She went quiet for a moment, staring off into her dream world.

Could Betsy find a beloved? Someone like Jesse, who would treat her tenderly, gently, hold her through the night? Another tear made a dark circle on the cotton.

"Now, who would make the best husband?" Betsy asked. "The Reverend or that Norwegian bachelor?"

"Can't imagine." Susannah didn't want to imagine anyone other than Jesse walking through the door. "Dear Lord, please bring Jesse home."

"Amen." Betsy poured the tea. "Susannah, you're a beautiful lady, one of those enviable women who looks radiant when she's expecting. You're a survivor, fighting off that banker in Detroit.

Hey, I read in the St. Paul paper that some guy posed as an insurance agent to procure young girls. Wonder if it was the same fellow."

Telling her story to Betsy last week had drained Susannah, but it was a good fatigue, as if she had tackled some particularly onerous spring-cleaning chore and defeated it.

Betsy continued. "You're intelligent. You know everything about the Bible. No wonder Reverend Webb's interested. Married to you, he'll never have to open his concordance."

Susannah spoke slowly, basting her thoughts together. "If it hadn't been for Jesse, no man would have looked at me twice. I don't mean just geography, bringing me out to empty Dakota. His love made me feel free to let other people know me. Because Jesse loves me, even though he knows me, I grew to believe in God's love for me." She hid her face in the steam rising from the mug. "I'm sounding moonstruck."

"All you talk about is Jesse," Betsy said. "No living husband can compete with a departed saint."

"I wish we'd had our picture taken when we were in Fargo. I'm starting to forget how he looked."

"Your baby needs a father. So, who—"

"Shh." Susannah lifted her head. Last night the ridge west of the soddy had echoed with two yips and a long howl. "That coyote's trying for a chicken dinner." She grabbed the shotgun and slipped out to the gray dusk. Icy wind pelted her with tiny beads of snow, but she didn't have time to put on her coat.

By the corner of the stable, Jake and a coyote circled and growled. The wild dog stood a few inches taller but thinner than the elkhound.

"Jake, come!" Susannah could not get a clear shot unless the two separated. Instead they lunged. In the writhing mass of legs, teeth, and fur, Susannah couldn't tell which animal had the upper hand. Jake went under the coyote, reaching for the throat. The wild animal snapped at the dog's withers, twisting away with a mouthful of gray fur.

Susannah wished she had a rifle, but the shotgun was the best she could do. She aimed over them and pulled the trigger. The gun's report had no effect on the two fighters. Now she had only one shot left and her eyes watered from black powder smoke. Blood flecked the snow. Which animal?

"Hold your fire!" A blur passed on her left. Dashing into the fray, Betsy doused the animals with a bucket of melted snow. The coyote rolled off, shaking his head, backing up. Betsy flung the bucket and he skittered away. Jake regained his legs. Betsy grabbed the scruff of his neck. Scrabbling after the intruder, the dog yanked her off her feet. She hit the snow still holding on. "Oof!"

Susannah fired her last shell at the retreating coyote. A sideways jump interrupted his stride. He had run too far out of range for the shot to penetrate his winter coat.

"Are you all right? You could have been bitten." Susannah helped Betsy to her feet, then ran her hands over Jake. No blood; the coyote had missed.

The dog shook himself, spraying them with ice droplets.

"The only thing wrong with me is I smell like wet dog. Ugh." Betsy retrieved the bucket and the brass shells, then peeked into the shed. "You chickens go back to laying. Susannah's on guard. Let's go in; it must be ten below out here."

"That was the most courageous—"

"No braver than marrying a man you've never met, talking French to a wild Indian, or facing down a herd of bachelors in rut." Grinning, Betsy raised their joined hands. "Bravest women in the West!"

Susannah held the gun overhead. "Thanks be to God, yes, we are!"

"I hear sleigh bells!" Betsy danced around Susannah. "Let me take a look at you. Your wrapper is marvelous, thanks to my skill with the crochet hook. Now, don't smash your curls under your scarf."

"And waste a sleepless night with my hair in rags?" Rubbing a porthole in the frosty window, Susannah glimpsed the Hansens' wagon, its wheels replaced by runners. She loosened the bow and strings of her violin and closed the case. "Are you packed? Can't let the horse wait in this cold. Cookies, presents, dog—"

Magnar burst through the door, gathering both women in a hearty embrace. Icicles hung from his beard and mustache. He smelled fresh, like the air after a storm. *"Gledelig Jul!"*

"Merry Christmas to you!" Betsy winked at Susannah. "No wonder you weren't interested in the preacher. Look at the shoulders on this one!"

"Betsy!" She blushed. "Please give him the last cup of coffee."

"His dimples could cure frostbite."

"Honestly. I'll hitch your pony, if you'll bank the fire. Where's the note for Jesse?"

"Dear heart. Do you really think he'll come home in winter?"

Susannah rubbed the silver band on her finger, holding last Christmas close. "I don't think anymore, just pray."

"Jingle bells, jingle bells," Betsy sang. "Come on, my friend, every soprano needs her alto." She prodded Susannah with an elbow.

"Ha. I can't feel your pointy elbows through all these layers." Susannah burrowed under the pile of blankets in the wagon box. "It's far too cold to sing."

"Cold? It must be nearly 20 degrees, positively balmy, and sunny too." Betsy flapped a mitten at the feeble sun.

From the driver's seat, Magnar started a song. He faced the wind without shivering, his ruddy cheeks the only indication of the low temperature.

"Ooh, he sings like an angel. Very smooth and on key. Imagine waking up every morning to that voice."

"Jesse's a baritone."

"Don't start getting all gushy-slushy on me. Tears will freeze on your face. The next song will be sung by the Sweet Springs Duet, on their first tour of Dakota Territory."

"Why do I put up with her?" Susannah asked Jake, who lay panting at their feet.

"So you won't have to squeeze in with the neighbors. Although I wouldn't mind squeezing in with this one." Betsy flashed a smile in Magnar's direction.

"You are incorrigible."

"Me, incorrigible? Why, I didn't even finish school. Our turn. Jingle bells, jingle bells . . ."

Betsy's shaggy pony cantered behind them, his nostrils frosted, head bobbing. Seeming to enjoy his release from the confines of the shed, he kept the pace set by the longer-legged stallion.

The solstice sun, low in the pale sky, washed the snow with indigo shadows. The northwest wind polished away the lines of the runners, as if offended by marks other than its own. At some point the train tracks passed beneath them, unrecognizable in the drifts. The prairie stretched lifeless in all directions, except for a flock of birds circling on the northern horizon. The chirping sparrows were attracted to the sheaf of wheat fastened to the ridgepole of the Hansens' house.

"Gledelig Jul! God Jul!"

Susannah greeted the Hansens and the Volds and introduced

Betsy. The Norwegians had not absorbed the American prohibition against mentioning pregnancy. Expressions of concern for her health mixed with comments on her shape and correlative speculation as to the gender of the child.

Betsy reassured them of the adequacy of their diet and divulged that the baby had begun to kick. To escape from their palpations, Susannah slid onto the bench at the candlelit table. She pulled Sara onto her lap and Rolf wiggled in next to her. Just as deliberately it seemed, Betsy positioned herself at Magnar's side.

Erik strode into the house, followed by John W. Webb. "Look!"

"Just in time to say blessing." Sissel set another place.

"Bag any wayward husbands, Reverend?" Betsy asked.

"Not this trip." He frowned at Susannah. "Why aren't you in Michigan?"

"In Norway we half peace on Christmas Eve." Ivar helped him out of his coat. "You'll half to save your fight for another day."

"There's a seat here, Reverend." Betsy patted the bench to her right.

When the blessing was finished, Mrs. Hansen sent bowls of rice porridge down the table.

"We hide a nut in one to bring good luck for the next year."

Betsy swirled her spoon through the preacher's bowl. "You don't need luck. You've got God."

Susannah tensed for a sermon on the presence of God within each of us or a lecture on appropriate conduct for married women, but J.W. laughed, charmed out of his bad mood by Christmas personified in her green dress and red curls. The children had also dressed for the holiday in brightly patterned sweaters. Straw figures hung from the rafters, dancing on air.

Susannah asked Sissel, "Who made the decorations?"

"Disa. I wash house, wash people, make cookies."

"Betsy and I baked too."

"Cookies? How many?"

"Four different kinds."

"And the ten *Mor* make is fourteen. We'll all have good luck this year."

Erik pulled an almond from his bowl. "Look!" Had he learned only one word in four weeks of school?

"Apparently I'm sitting with the wrong man." Betsy batted her lashes at the boy, sending giggles around the table.

Betsy had drawn all the men in the room into her orbit by the time Mrs. Hansen served the fish. When Susannah was in school, it seemed every year one girl developed an entourage through quick wit and a crystal-bell laugh. Susannah had coveted the part but never attained it. Twenty years and a thousand miles later, she accepted that the limelight would always belong to someone else. Tonight Betsy held the role, with all its attendant accolades.

"Would you like some help?" Susannah asked Rolf. She put her hands over his to cut the pork.

"You eat now." Marta transferred Sara from Susannah to her husband.

"She needs to practice holding a squirmy baby during meals," Ivar said.

Marta patted Susannah's belly. "No room."

"Say, Susannah." Ivar fed Sara a bite of his meat. "Magnar half a plan for you."

"Oooh?" Betsy hooted. Susannah concentrated on serving mashed potatoes to Rolf and refused to look in her direction.

"It's about your yearlings. He half offer to buy them."

"Splendid. You'll have money for train fare," J.W. said.

Susannah wouldn't look at him either. "Buy? The Hansens have earned them after boarding them all winter."

"He says you're paid up, because of—what's this about his horse?" Negotiations were postponed for the telling of the cougar story.

Now the attention swung her way and Susannah squirmed. "Please tell Magnar that Milking Devons are usually fertile, but the female of any twin set might be sterile. I've examined her, and—"

J.W. choked, turned red, and sprayed coffee down his white shirt. Betsy fussed over him, patting him on the back.

"I'd like to see your sewing job, Susannah." Ivar stood. "Shall we wish the animals good yule?"

Herded by Jake, the entire group bundled up and trooped to the barn. Mr. Hansen raised the lantern, and Magnar parted the mare's winter coat so all could see the flat white lines of scar tissue. The Norwegians were unanimous in their praise of Susannah's work.

"Amazing . . . stitching on a live animal, in the dark and cold. All that blood," Betsy whispered.

J.W. frowned. "How dreadful for a lady like yourself to be exposed to such—"

"Reverend, you're a bit green around the gills." Betsy took his arm and led the group inside.

The preacher recovered quickly and read the Christmas story as they thawed with hot cocoa. Closing his Bible after the angels and shepherds, J.W. produced an envelope of peppermint sticks for the children. From Ellen's latest book box, Susannah handed out Norwegian-English dictionaries to the Hansens and Volds, *Little Women* to Sissel, and picture books for the rest of the children. She gave Betsy a paper of needles and five spools of colored thread. She and Betsy had knitted J.W. a muffler and mittens in a clerical shade of medium blue. The Volds presented Susannah with a tin of cocoa; apparently Jesse had told them of her love of chocolate.

Magnar arranged the Hansen children around Susannah. What was he up to? And could she stop him from making a scene?

"Look!" Erik held up a pair of boots made of fur the color of clover honey.

"For teacher!"

"From the cougar!"

"Try them on!"

Magnar knelt by the bench, unlaced her worn black boots, and slid the new ones on. He tied the royal blue braiding just below her knees. Susannah pressed her petticoats down in a futile attempt to maintain modesty.

"Doesn't this remind you of Cinderella and the prince, Reverend?" Betsy asked. "Will Susannah turn into a princess?"

"A Norwegian," Ivar suggested with a sly grin.

"A woman with warm feet," Susannah corrected, although how much warmth came from the soft rabbit-fur lining and how much from Magnar's attention, she could not say. "*Takk.* Thank you for this most wonderful gift."

Magnar, still kneeling at her feet, whispered something, but his words were lost in the chatter of the children.

Disa set the violin case on the table, opened it, and traced the instrument's shape with her finger. Susannah propped the hymn-book against chunks of firewood and tuned the strings. Where was Jesse tonight? He should be here to lead the music. If he were here, Magnar would stop giving her so much unwelcome attention, the Reverend wouldn't send her back, and Ivar wouldn't try to move her off the homestead.

"Betsy, you have perfect pitch. Sing me an A."

Next to Betsy, J.W. sat with the shocked expression of someone who'd had a snowball dropped down his pants.

"Would you lead the singing, Reverend Webb? I think everyone knows 'Adeste Fidelis.'"

J.W. snapped back into his ministerial mode. English carols alternated with Norwegian hymns. Some, like "Silent Night," had words in both languages. Others were unfamiliar and Susannah labored to follow the tune.

As the children dropped off to sleep, they were rolled into

blankets and nestled into the straw. The clock chimed midnight. The Norwegian men left for a last check of the stock. Blinking with fatigue, Susannah returned the violin to its case.

"I must speak with you." Carrying a candle, J.W. directed her into the east alcove, out of earshot of the women washing dishes at the table. "You've done so well with Mrs. Stapleton. She seems completely recovered."

"The credit goes to your spiritual guidance. I merely provided Betsy with a place to stay while she healed." Susannah stepped around him to the window, shivering in the chill this far from the stove. "She's been a good friend."

"I'd hoped Reverend Mason would send train tickets for you."

"Please, J.W., I'm too tired to argue." Her back ached, her eyes felt parched. Susannah polished the frost from the pane. Stars glittered in the still night. The temperature would drop far below zero. "The snow came."

"There's a stage to Fargo. Surely the Roses told you." He sat on the edge of Magnar's bed, leaning forward with his large hands pressed together. "If you wait much longer, it will be inadvisable for you to travel."

A star guided the wise men to Bethlehem. Could God send a star to guide Jesse? *But no,* she thought. *He doesn't need a star. He knows the way home.*

J.W. cleared his throat. "If you feel the need for an escort, I'd be glad to serve in that capacity."

Jesse knew the way, so why wasn't he here?

"Susannah." The small increase in volume required no effort for a voice trained in preaching. She turned to face him. Candlelight showed new lines around his eyes. White-knuckled hands clasped his knees. "The living conditions here are so harsh, you'll be old before your time. You'll work yourself to the bone."

"Old? I'm seventeen years younger than you." She caught his

wince and apologized. "Last winter I tried to talk Jesse into leaving. Not anymore. I've grown to cherish the freedom, the openness of this land, the wall I plastered, the trees I planted. I can see God using me. Homesteading, building a community with people I care about—people you've labeled as heathens. What basis do you have for that judgment? And telling Reverend Mason I live in a cave—"

He had the decency to look embarrassed. "You'd be more comfortable in Michigan."

Susannah leaned on the trunk opposite him, tracing the bird design painted on the lid. "You know how meager clerical salaries are. You know what a burden another person—soon two extra people—would be to Reverend Mason."

"He'd gladly welcome you."

"I've no doubt of his hospitality. He's obligated. But I want to be more than someone's obligation, an added number the food must be divided by, the reason his children have to share a bedroom."

"You could teach in Michigan."

"With a child? Without a teaching certificate? No. I won't even be able to teach here once the Territorial government gets organized." She rubbed her head, determined to break through to him. "There are so few veterinary surgeons—"

"That's hardly work for a lady."

"Don't you feel called to preach?"

"You feel *called* to doctor animals?"

"Maybe not a calling like yours, but it's what I know, what I'm good at. It's a way I can help."

He dismissed her comments with a wave of his hand. "What about Mr. Mason's family in New York?"

She shook her head. "Jesse told me to wait for him."

The ropes of the bed creaked as J.W. stood. "I have a letter for you from General Custer. I'm sorry."

Hands trembling, he held the paper out. When she made no

move to accept it, he left it on the trunk next to the candle and returned to the main room.

Susannah scanned the letter, struggling to understand it in the onrushing flood of exhaustion. *Regret to inform you . . . two bodies, believed to be white men . . . to establish identity . . . any previous fractures or missing teeth . . . military operations recommence in the spring . . . father, Sergeant Major Underhill, remembered for his humane treatment of my horses.*

No, Lord. Please, no.

"Susannah, Mrs. Hansen fixed a bed for us. You'd better not fall asleep before you tell me what the Reverend said. Now, what's got you all weepy?"

Before Susannah could stop her, Betsy whisked the letter off to the main room. She should get up, keep her from reading it out loud, let Magnar have his room back. Her body fused into the sod wall behind her: cold, hard, immobile. She could not feel her heart beat. She did not know if she still breathed. Her eyelids outweighed her body. Only the tears slipping down her cheeks connected her with life.

Magnar entered the room and lifted her. His napped wool coat smelled faintly of horses and sweet hay.

Then the world went black.

Chapter 32

*How am I supposed to tell these people about
You, Jesus, when we don't speak the same
language? And tell Susannah . . . well, I'm not
having a Merry Christmas without her.*

The aroma of hot coffee and the rumble of male voices woke
Susannah. She pried open her eyelids, stiff with dried tears.

Her mind went to the letter, to Jesse. She had never felt more
alone in her life. If Jesse was gone, was God gone too?

With every breath, she had asked God to bring her husband
back. Jesse said God always listened but sometimes answered no.
How could she live with that answer? A flutter stirred low within
her, and Susannah put her hand over the baby. *Help me be strong,
Jesus.*

Morning's weak light showed a basin of steaming water and
a clean cloth on the trunk. Susannah wiped her face and tried to
coax her hair into some semblance of order. She put on her red
dress and new boots.

When she pulled back the curtain, all conversation stopped
and all eyes looked at her. She had always wanted a large family, a community of people who cared about her. Unfortunately,

caring came with strong opinions. Ivar and J.W. and Magnar and Betsy all seemed to be certain they knew what was right for her, how she should live her life. Without Jesse, who would speak up for her?

And then, with a flash of insight, she knew. Knew what Jesse would say, knew what she had to do. For her own sake and the sake of his child, she had to find the courage to speak up for herself.

She straightened and stepped into the room.

"Susannah. Mrs. Mason." Reverend Webb left the table and hurried to her side. "I must speak with you."

But Susannah had more urgent needs than listening to him. The position of the baby made it necessary for her to get to the outhouse. Immediately. With a brief smile, Susannah hurried into her coat. "I'll be back in a moment."

J.W. glanced at the crowd around the table, then lowered his voice. "Let me accompany you, so we may speak in private."

Did he really expect her to listen to him over the demands of her bladder? Susannah whipped the scarf around her head and threw his favorite word back at him. "That's hardly *appropriate*," she said.

"Given the nature of the environs, populated with wild animals and Indians, perhaps an escort is in order."

She shoved her hands into mittens and pushed through the door. By the time he got his coat on, she'd be back. Unfortunately, she heard footsteps pounding the snow behind her.

"If you're determined to stay in the territory—"

"Please go back inside." She rounded the corner, heading into the teeth of the wind. "You'll catch your death of cold."

He took hold of her arm, and she saw that he'd snagged his coat on the way out. "How would you feel about living in Jamestown? I've made the case to the conference to locate there, in the middle of the territory. With the pass the railroad issued me, I can develop east and west circuits. I've rented a set of rooms over the furniture store. There's an alcove with a south-facing window that could be a passable nursery."

He continued, his words jumbled by shivering. "You could put your teaching skills to work starting Sunday schools in all the preaching points. Use your gift of music—"

She gave him the fiercest expression she'd ever used on her students. "Excuse me," she said and bolted for the outhouse.

She completed her business and emerged from the privy to find him sheltering in the doorway of the barn, hands in his armpits and face red. Apparently he wasn't going to quit until he had his say, even if he froze to death in the process.

"I promise to care for the child as if it were my own and never discriminate between it and children of my own issue." A cold hand touched her cheek, trying to turn her to face him. "Marry me, Susannah. I regret the abruptness of my proposal, but the exigencies of frontier life prevent me from properly courting you. Your confinement is near, so I must speak frankly."

She blurted out the first thing that came to mind. "But that would be bigamy!"

The minister rolled his head from side to side, his tuft of beard dragging across his chest. "If Mr. Mason were still alive."

Susannah could take no more. She fled from him and stumbled inside.

Marta met her, taking her coat and guiding her to *Mor*'s chair at the head of the table. Ivar sat on one side, J.W. on the other. Would he ever let her be?

"I'm so sorry," Betsy whispered. The rest murmured their sympathies.

Sissel filled a plate and coffee mug for her. "*Mor* says you eat. For baby," she added with a raised eyebrow at J.W.

Ham, eggs, and a potato pancake. The potatoes seemed easiest to manage with a dozen pairs of eyes watching. She choked down one bite before Ivar started in.

"Yes, you think of baby. You cannot stay alone on the claim. Jesse told me what happened last winter."

Jesse told him? She'd have the man's hide, soon as he returned.

"I'm not alone. Betsy's there."

Her redheaded friend shrank behind the Reverend.

"Mrs. Stapleton also received mail," J.W. said. "She has an offer of employment as a seamstress's assistant in St. Paul."

Susannah mustered a smile. "It's the job you were hoping for. Congratulations."

"No. I won't leave you."

"You can't pass up the opportunity."

Ivar thumped the table, earning a hiss from Marta. "Susannah, it's too much. Chopping wood, plowing, diapers—*uff da!* the diapers!—cooking, mucking the ox pen, gardening. More work, less sleep, no money."

"I exchanged the train tickets for lumber for beehives. Honey will bring in cash. There was an article in the Bismarck paper about sunflowers as a crop, so I bought sunflower seeds too."

"You already bought seed? You half to let your fields go fallow. Susannah, you think you can do everything, but plowing is the heaviest work a farmer does all year. And it will half to be done just after the baby comes. Impossible." He leaned closer. "Magnar wants to start a livery in Worthington. Horses and oxen. Your animal doctoring would be a big help to him."

Susannah had felt the young man's blue eyes watching her all morning. She met his gaze. "Good idea. Homesteaders arriving by train will need teams. This is excellent grazing land. Your biggest problem will be keeping your stock from running off. Picketing takes time and fencing takes money."

"See. You know the business. You would be a big help to

him. Teach him English too. You could live out here or build a house in town. Norwegians are good people. Dependable, treat their women well—"

The Reverend cleared his throat. "I've asked Mrs. Mason for her hand."

Blood seemed to pound in her ears, but it was only Ivar pounding the table. "But Magnar wants to marry her!"

The table erupted in bilingual warfare. Sissel, who had been translating for her mother, clanged a spoon on a pot. "*Mor* says not good for the baby, this fighting. All men to the barn. Now."

The Reverend, Mr. Hansen, and Magnar gathered their coats and headed out. Ivar paused next to her shoulder. "That preacher, he'd move you away from us."

She rubbed her forehead. "When he's around, I always say the wrong thing."

"It's not you. I half the same trouble. Now, Magnar, you'll find, speaks plain."

Susannah whispered, "We don't even speak the same language, Ivar. I don't know anything about him."

"What is there to know? He's a fine man from a good family, all fond of you, by the way. He's strong, works hard, knows farming."

"Sounds like I'd insult the entire Norwegian race if I turned him down."

Ivar waved his arms. "Why say no?"

Susannah finally looked up at him. "Ivar, I can't. Marrying again is admitting Jesse's not coming back. I can't believe he's—" She couldn't even say the word.

A warm tear slid down her cheek. He was coming. He had to be. But it was Christmas. He'd already be here if he could.

"In the States, you might wait. But here—" He hurried his words as Marta tugged him toward the door. "Susannah, be a little selfish. Baby needs father. You need husband."

Mor rested her hand on Susannah's shoulder. Sissel interpreted. "You are welcome to stay here. You don't have to marry Magnar."

"Takk." Here? But the Hansens were already crowded. And living in close proximity to Magnar would be awkward, to say the least.

Betsy slid next to her. "Two proposals in one day!"

"The Reverend would marry out of a warped sense of duty. Magnar, I don't know what he wants—free veterinary services, perhaps." Susannah took a bite of ham. "You should snatch him up. He'd be better off with someone who thinks he makes the sun rise."

"If only I could sew horses." Betsy sighed, but her eyes twinkled. "You have more choices than anyone I know."

Susannah blinked. "Strange, isn't it? I came out here without any choices at all."

Well, if it was her choice, she knew exactly what to do. *Lord, give me wisdom*, she thought. *Help me do right by this new life.*

"So, how long have I been here? Anyone know the date?" Jesse asked when Misun's family gathered around the fire. "If I could just explain. I need to get home to my wife. Her name is Susannah. You'd like her. She's—" He choked up and had to stop.

The family ignored him and continued murmuring in their language. Misun's mother used Jesse's knife to chop a root into the cook pot. Had Susannah found something to eat? She must be frantic with worry. *Lord, give her Your daily bread.*

The sun moved low along the horizon and didn't stay up long, like maybe they were close to the solstice. Which meant he'd passed his birthday picking up horse apples. And meant today could be Jesus' birthday. "So, how do you celebrate Christmas here?"

No answer.

How could he tell them about Christmas? All he had was his guitar. Jesse taught Misun "The First Noel." The family was good with music, singing in tune and imitating words they didn't understand. Jesse struggled through "Hark! the Herald Angels Sing" as memories of Susannah playing it on her violin overwhelmed him. Then, in case they were keeping him alive only until the kid finished his lessons, he added his masterpiece, an instrumental of "Greensleeves."

The storm changed direction, blowing in a fresh batch of snow, as if they didn't have enough already, and threatening to put out the fire. Misun's mother adjusted the smoke hole to block the wind. Ingenious, really. Who called these people primitive?

Jesse continued, "I didn't cook up a fancy meal, or make you cookies, or bring you any presents. But if I could, my deepest prayer, right after going home to my wife, would be to tell you about the best present of all, Jesus."

Behind him a voice said in English, "I can tell them."

Chapter 33

One foot in front of the other. So far to go . . .

Accccording to the almanac, another month of winter could be expected. In defiance of that prediction, a southwesterly breeze melted the snow off the roof. The evening air beckoned with softness.

Susannah did not stop to put away the violin she'd been practicing. She climbed out of the draw, stepping on dry patches carved by the wind. Dusk found her on the ridge overlooking the Sheyenne River. From "Petronella," a lively dance tune to celebrate a warm day in early March, she slid into the more contemplative "Skye Boat Song." Then her fingers searched out a long-forgotten melody in a minor key. Rhythm established by the lower notes, the tune surged into passages of high notes, then ebbed back to the rumbling G string.

Jake rushed past her to greet Ivar. The neighbor strolled along, hands in the pockets of his coat. He looked her over, checking to see how she'd weathered the winter, then, satisfied, faced the sunset.

Susannah ended the lament with a double-stop.

"Sad song. What's it called?"

"I don't remember. Father learned several in Edinburgh, at

school, but I can never match the titles to the tunes." She tucked the violin under her right elbow. "How's Marta? And Sara?"

"That child is running us ragged. When it warms, we're moving her in with the dogs. And your baby?"

Susannah rubbed her belly. "No Methodist here. He's up dancing all night."

"I will come for you in two days. Before the next storm."

"No hurry. The baby isn't due for a month or so."

"And if you need help, what? You send Jake to get me?"

"Jake, go get Ivar."

The dog looked from one to the other, then sighed. He'd already sniffed the man. Ivar didn't have any food on him, so he didn't merit further consideration.

"He heard you say Sara's going to the dogs. He doesn't want to deal with babies any sooner than necessary." Susannah pressed her knuckles into the small of her back, trying to ease the pulling weight.

"The Hansens half your oxen?"

"And Betsy's pony. She doesn't need it in St. Paul. Will your chickens mind a few guests?"

"Any that squawk, we'll eat." His mouth twitched behind his whiskers.

The sky changed to magenta and gold. Beneath the black lace of cottonwoods, the river lay frozen, silent, a periwinkle ribbon.

"Ivar, I think we have a sickness in this nation. A contagious disease of leaving. We leave the old country for the new, the states for the territories. Men go off to war or the gold fields. Horace Greeley advises young men to go west. But no one tells them to go home."

"You wish for someone to tell Jesse to go home."

The baby stretched, pushing against her ribs. "You're right. Give me a day to pack."

"Marta will be glad of your company." Ivar let out his breath. "Perhaps Magnar will pay us a call."

"He's been a regular visitor. He brought Disa to keep me company in January, then Sissel in February." Susannah turned the screw on the bow, loosening the horsehair. "The truth is, as fine a man as Magnar is, he's not Jesse. Hard act to follow, that Jesse Mason."

"*Ja.* True. Like a brother to me."

She smiled at her red-cheeked neighbor. "Ivar Vold, you've been a brother to me these past seven months. Thank you."

As he turned to walk back to his claim, Susannah heard him say, "A real brother would half sent you back to Michigan already."

The English-speaking voice was Matthew, Misun's older brother, known west of the Missouri as Mato. He had attended school at the Santee Mission and came home to find himself cast in the role of interpreter. To begin with, he informed his family the white man's name was Jesse, not Tatanka, their word for "buffalo." Together he and Jesse spent the winter sharing the Good News with the village. And in turn, the village educated Jesse on their history. Like white men, Sitting Bull's Lakota wanted to provide for their families.

Today, the first break in the weather, Matthew put on his clerical garb, including a silver cross the size of his hand. "So the soldiers will hold their fire."

"They won't shoot a guy with red hair and beard." Jesse turned to the family, his Indian family. "God be with you, Winona, Cansasa, Misun."

The boy blinked away tears and handed him the canvas bag.

"When you come to the Mission, to school, little brother, I will buy you a guitar," Matthew promised.

"Well, if you won't take my guitar, you must take this." Jesse pulled the eagle's feather from his hatband. "For bravery."

Misun smiled and, for a moment, looked him in the eye.

"Could we pray?" Jesse got nods. "Lord, thank You for sending Misun to save me from the river. Thank You for the healing care of him and Winona and—" What was the sergeant's, er, medicine woman's name? "And all their family. Watch over them, keep them safe, and help them tell about You to everyone they meet. And help me tell the Indians' story to everyone I meet."

Matthew interpreted, adding prayers for the safe return of Jesse to his wife. The family said, "Amen."

The evangelist mounted a roan, and Jesse climbed on Misun's gray. Or tried to. The hard winter had sapped his energy, and Misun had to give him a boost. They both laughed, and he clapped the young man on the shoulder. "Good-bye, my friend."

He had been trying to get away all winter, and now that he was going, he had a lump in his throat and watery eyes. Blame it on the wind.

Matthew led him on a couple hours' fast ride, along high places the wind had cleared of snow. Good thing the old woman had kept him in camp all winter. He would have gotten lost and died in the snow. Now he was going home. Home to Susannah.

At last they came in sight of the fort, where the American flag waved in the clear sky overhead.

"They see us." Matthew reined in, then reached toward Jesse. "God be with you."

"And also with you, my brother." Jesse clasped his friend's arm, then slid to the ground. He handed the gray to the evangelist, adjusted his knapsack and guitar, then walked up the hill singing "Amazing Grace."

Would he be welcome? Would Susannah understand why he'd been gone six, almost seven months? He'd had no way to send word; it was possible she counted him dead. He shouldn't be surprised if she'd found another husband. He would have to set aside his selfish feelings and be glad she hadn't been alone, but it would tear him to pieces.

By the time he reached the sentry post, a whole company of soldiers had gathered. Jesse guessed he was the first visitor of 1875, certainly the first approaching from the west. A scruffy long-legged dog ran out to sniff him.

"Good morning. I'm Jesse Mason." This crowd had no problem maintaining eye contact.

A grinning lieutenant stepped out of the crowd and reached for his hand.

"Mr. Mason. Your wife's looking for you."

Chapter 34

Once again, I could use some fancy talking, Lord.

Susannah paused just outside the door, surveying the misted bubble of her world. A chickadee chirped near the creek, its voice soft in the morning fog. The wind seemed to be picking up.

Humming "Shenandoah," she managed the morning chores: scattering wood ashes on the path, shoveling out the shed, watering and feeding the chickens. *Lord, hurry spring; I'm down to the last bag of cracked corn.* A search of the nesting boxes yielded a single egg, plenty for one person.

Jake padded out of the mist, sure-footed with his long toenails.

"Always in time for breakfast. After you, my dear." Susannah let him inside. The dog dined on pork scraps while his mistress ate fried potatoes.

After breakfast, Susannah sorted through the provisions for her move to the Volds'. Bless Ivar and Marta for their gift of cocoa. She opened the tin. Enough for a small chocolate cake. Perfect use for the egg.

"We're low on wood. Come on, Jake. I don't trust you alone with cake batter."

Always jumpy around wood chopping, the dog disappeared

immediately. A brisk southern wind shredded the fog, allowing the sunlight to nudge its way to earth. Ice turned to slush.

After a noon meal, with warm chocolate cake as the highlight, Susannah curled up for a nap. The somersaulting baby woke her moments later. "Yes, yes." She patted her belly. "Back to work."

Susannah pushed the wheelbarrow to the garden. "Pumpkins, watermelons, cucumbers, potatoes." With each shovelful of manure, she planned the layout and prayed: *Lord, hurry spring; I'm ready to plant.* She rubbed her taut belly. *Ready to burst.*

Despite Ivar's concern, she felt strong, sure of her body. She started to return to the soddy, then headed the other direction, up to the ridge. Ivar's footprints from yesterday melted deeper into the snow. The ratio of open land to covered tilted slightly in favor of open. Fog hid the riverbed. Travel would be risky.

What was she thinking? Was she worried about Ivar coming tomorrow? No, it was hope, the painful hope that had been with her every day since the day Jesse left. Would she ever stop watching for him, missing him, longing for him?

Jake leaned into her leg and Susannah bent over the best she could to scratch his ears. With one last look westward, she followed the dog down the slope. In a sun-warmed spot beside the spring, a pasqueflower sent up a purple bud. Even the land was ready for winter's end.

At dusk, the sun surrendered to the fog and the chickens returned to their roost. Susannah ate potato soup by lamplight. The kerosene was running low; she dimmed the lamp to stretch the supply. For her last night of privacy, she heated water for a bath. Then she dragged the remaining potatoes from the root cellar to sort for planting. If she was going to bathe, she might as well be good and dirty.

Jake paced, stopped to listen, then gave his sharp "out" bark.

"All right. Just remember, no porcupines, no skunks."

The dog's ears twitched with impatience. He dashed out at a

full gallop. All four legs slid in different directions. He skidded, then disappeared into the fog.

"Silly dog."

Susannah returned to the table. The stool sank under her weight. A couple of weeks ago Betsy's repair of the rungs had loosened. "Watch over her, Lord." All the nails and glue had been used to build beehives, so Susannah had tried to hold it together with rope. The makeshift repair stretched, lowering the seat until she was eye to eye with the potatoes.

Eyes. She thought about the sky-blue of Magnar Hansen's eyes, the pale blue-gray of J.W. Webb's. What should she do? Was last fall's teaching job God's way of preparing her to start Sunday schools? But four weeks in the classroom hadn't wiped out a life-long desire to care for animals. Jamestown had a school. Would Worthington have one by the time her baby was ready? Sissel would be old enough to teach by then. The girl adored her uncle. He was gentle and playful with all the children. J.W. would be stricter, more serious. If a man knew a child from birth, gave him his name, would he accept him as his own?

What name would Jesse choose?

Absently rubbing her abdomen, she tried to imagine herself repeating marriage vows to Magnar. No, not possible. Could she see herself moving to Jamestown as the Reverend Mrs. Webb? Even more unlikely.

She looked up at the rafters. *I'm listening. I know You hear me. Just help me know what to do. I know You love the baby and me. I know You're working for good in our lives.*

The wind shifted. The roof creaked. Four winters without sags or gaps. Jesse had built a sturdy house. It held heat in winter and stayed cooler in summer than frame houses. The windows and doors fit snugly. The garden, the fields, the freshwater spring: all of this was home. How could she leave?

Something scraped out in the yard, loud in the fog-hushed darkness. Susannah froze, listening hard. The sound repeated. Ivar? No, not after sunset. Jake? Susannah placed her palms on the table to push herself up.

The door opened an inch. A man. A jolt shot through her.

She should have barred the door. Instead she had let a man walk in, just like in Detroit. Only now there was no Ellen, no one to hear her scream.

The door swung wide, bringing her a whiff of wild animal pelts. Not smelly enough or large enough to be Abner Reece. The man stepped across the threshold. Beads and quills decorated his shirt. Fringe dangled from his buckskins. An Indian! Indians walked into people's houses without knocking.

And slit their throats.

He stepped between her and the shotgun. Maybe he just wanted food. She'd give him the rest of the cake. And anything else he wanted. Anything, as long as the baby was safe.

"You're here. You're still here."

He spoke English. His voice was hoarse but familiar.

"Jesse?"

Without taking his eyes from her, he pulled a wide strap over his head, setting down not a quiver but his guitar. "Susannah. You look so good."

"You're alive?" The kerosene light flickered as she sagged against the table.

Jesse's tentative smile revealed new wrinkles. "Ghosts don't stink."

Susannah inhaled the smoke of wood fires, the tang of cooked wild game, the sour smell of his unwashed body. *It's Jesse! It's really him. Oh, thank You, God. Thank You.*

He glanced around the room. "Anyone else here?" His hair,

clotted with grease and dirt, grazed the top of his shoulders. His beard straggled to his chest like panicles of wild oats.

"What? Anyone else? No, of course not." She wanted to run to him, grab hold of him, but breathing took all her energy.

"If you thought I was dead—"

He'd lost weight. The beard couldn't disguise his thin cheeks. Had he been ill?

Curiosity fought with elation. "Where have you been? Not a word from you in months. The bodies of two white men—"

He nodded. "Ferrymen without paddles. Mind if I sit? It's been a long walk." He wiped his palms on his pants, then sank onto the trunk.

"You're back. You're alive."

"Don't sound so disappointed," he teased. He looked around a second time. "The place is in good shape. Woodpile, haymow, firebreak. Did you do this all by yourself?"

She shook her head. "The firebreak was a gift from God, a lightning strike followed by a downpour. I rented your cutting plow to the new neighbors in exchange for the wood and traded eggs for the hay." And soon as she got her thoughts in order, he would hear about leaving her at the mercy of Abner Reece.

"And the potatoes?"

"From my garden." She hesitated, but he didn't react to her taking ownership. "I sold a few, gave some away, ate a lot, and still have enough to plant."

"You've been living on potatoes?"

"And prairie chickens. I taught school to buy necessities. A circuit rider brought grasshopper relief supplies from churches back in the States." No, she hadn't hungered for food.

"You managed without me. The city girl conquered Dakota." He slumped against the wall, studying her under fatigue-heavy eyes. "Susannah, I can't tell you how sorry I am for leaving, for staying away, for coming home empty-handed. I was a fool. If you've found someone else, I'll understand. Deserting you all this time, I wouldn't blame you."

His hand circled the air, then flopped down. "Thinking I was dead, of course you'd, a fine woman like you—well, every bachelor in the territory—" He stuttered to a halt on, "A better man than me . . ."

Finally he shrugged, defeated. "I'll just go. No one will have to know I was back. I rehearsed this speech the whole walk home and still made a mess of it."

"You're not the only one who's been practicing a speech." Susannah took his hands, squeezing until he met her gaze. "Back before the War, some hunters wounded an eagle over by Lake St. Clair, a little north of Detroit. They kept her in a chicken-wire cage, feeding her crackers and seed, trying to get her to talk and do tricks like a parrot. The bird wouldn't eat, became lethargic. Word got around to Father. The hunters had lost interest, so they let him take her. Father removed the lead shot from her wings, fed her meat scraps. The eagle grew strong again, squawking and fighting to get loose. So Father took her back to the lake and set her free. Next spring we saw a nest that might have been hers."

Jesse frowned.

Her grip softened into a caress. "I'm not the storyteller you are, but I've felt like that bird. You patched me up, helped me grow strong, brought me to a place where I could fly and build a home." She held his gaze. "Yes, I do have more options now. I have choices. I choose you."

He exhaled a pent-up breath.

"Wait a minute, Jesse." She searched his hazel eyes. "The question is, are you going to want me? I've found my wings. I've been running this homestead by myself, earning and spending money, making my own decisions, expressing my opinions, standing up for what I believe. I'm not the same woman you married."

He closed his eyes and touched her fingers to his lips. His whiskers tickled. She shivered. "From your first day here, from your first letter to me, I felt you fighting that cage. I'd catch a glimpse of who you really are when you talked to Jake, when you delivered the calves. So I worked at the cage door trying to set you free. Yes, I want you. I want to see you fly, to fly with you if you'll let me."

He opened his eyes, and the tension in his face ebbed away. "Still, I'm surprised you're here."

"You thought I'd go back to Michigan? Back to the cage?"

"No, I thought you'd be over at Ivar's."

"So did he."

"Did I miss a fight?"

"A discussion. Well, several heated discussions."

"Which you won." Jesse grinned, deepening the creases on either side of his nose. "I was half afraid I'd find Abner Reece camped out here."

She glared at him. "He offered."

"I'm sorrier than I can say. And who else? Circuit riders are usually bachelors. Bull's-eye. I got home just in time."

"In more ways than one." Susannah pushed aside thoughts of Magnar. "You still haven't told me why you were gone so long. Have you been mining all this time?"

"No, not mining. I crossed the Missouri last fall, going to see Custer about a job. The ferrymen dunked us. A Lakota boy pulled me out. He was interested in my guitar. By the time I recovered from drowning, winter had set in. When I get rested up, I'll tell you the whole story and you can tell me yours."

His back straightened and his shoulders lifted. A little of the old Jesse returned. "Listen, I've got to go to Washington. I need to talk to the president and Congress, tell them not to violate the treaty with—"

Susannah slapped her hand on the table. "No."

"—the Sioux." He stopped, his mouth open. Then he squinted and cocked his head. "Susannah, did I hear you right? Did you say, 'No'?"

"I most certainly did."

"I always wanted you to argue with me." He flashed a grin. "But you see, I have to tell the president—"

"God listens to me and you will too. You just got home and you're planning to leave again? How dare you!" A flash of anger, a remnant of the anxieties of the past months, heated her blood and raised her voice. "Do I have to nail your boots to the floor?"

"You can't do that." He lifted his foot to show her a moccasin. "Susannah, I don't ever want to spend another day without you." He winked. "Or another night. Come with me."

"You will have to put your thoughts to the president in a letter. I'm not traveling this spring. And neither are you." She pushed herself upright. "I told you I'm not the same woman you married. Remember last August, the Perseids meteor shower? Up on the hill, when we—"

Jesse rose, sidestepping around the table. "I thought of it every night."

She rose and came around the table.

"Oh, Lord." His eyes widened and filled with tears. He reached for her, shaping the dress to her belly. "Susannah, can you ever forgive me?"

"Are you here to stay?"

"Wild ponies couldn't drag me away." His hands stroked what used to be her waist. "Got home just in time."

"I calculate six more weeks. Of course, if the child takes after his father, who knows when he'll make an appearance."

Jesse winced. "I deserved that. Hey, he's moving."

"Just wait until tonight." Susannah guided his fingers. "Here's his head, back, and keep your hand here, you'll feel more kicking."

"Have you seen a doctor?"

"When the nearest one doesn't know a 'safe day' from a wet rock?"

"If I didn't smell like a polecat, I'd—" Jesse nodded at the pails on the stove. "Don't suppose you'd scrub my back?"

Susannah took his face in her hands and kissed him. "Not just your back. Welcome home."

Reading Group Guide

1. Susannah and Jesse marry after exchanging a few letters. How long were you in a relationship before committing? What discoveries did you make after committing? Are there any surprises left for long-time couples?

2. Susannah is intimidated by Dakota's emptiness. What frightens you when you travel?

3. Susannah wants privacy, but Jesse craves intimacy. How do couples work this out?

4. Jesse refers to their marriage as a two-piece puzzle—different, but fitted into a whole. Is he right? Do opposites attract? Do you believe there's someone for everyone?

5. Susannah wants to confide in Marta. How important are girlfriends? What can you say to a girlfriend that you wouldn't discuss with your spouse?

6. Victorian culture blamed women if they were attacked. In what ways does today's culture blame victims? What should our stance as Christians be toward victims?

7. Jesse tells Susannah to forget the "shoulds." What "shoulds" does today's culture impose on us? Do "shoulds" point to a more Christ-like life or restrict our freedom in Christ?

8. Jesse's expectations for his wife don't include fancy meals or a spotless house—he wants to know her. How do expectations affect relationships? How do expectations change over the years?

9. Jesse keeps trying to coax Susannah into expressing her opinion,

debating with him. On what issues should couples agree? And where are differences of opinion acceptable?

10. Susannah stopped praying when God didn't give her what she wanted. What other ways do people react to disappointment with God? Have you had a similar experience with unanswered prayers?

11. Jesse thinks the grasshopper invasion is a lesson or punishment from God. When Susannah learns the extent of the plague, she remembers Matthew 5:45, which says that God "sendeth rain on the just and on the unjust." Who is right? In your life, which problems do you attribute to God's discipline and which are "just life"? Are some problems both?

12. Susannah renegotiates her marriage. Have you had to do this? How did it work out?

13. When Susannah has to make a decision, she struggles to hear God amid advice from friends. What role should friends have in discerning God's will?

14. Jesse's love for Susannah opens her to believe God loves her. Who in your life has helped you understand God's love? How can our actions show God's love?

Acknowledgments

T hank you to everyone who helped on this long journey, especially:

Nebraska Novelists, who expertly critiqued numerous revisions, read the best writing I've heard all week, and didn't let me quit.

Omaha Public Library's Connie Ashford, who deserves a microfilm-reel tiara for her interlibrary loan expertise.

My family, who joined me on research trips. All your friends went to Disney World, so we had North Dakota to ourselves!

Sandra Bishop, who tracked me down as I vacationed without my laptop and revised this proposal while taking her son to the doctor. That ACFW Agent of the Year Award is well earned.

Editor Amanda Bostic and the Thomas Nelson team for believing in this story.

> Now unto him that is able to do exceeding abundantly above all that we ask or think, according to the power that worketh in us, unto him be glory in the church by Christ Jesus throughout all ages, world without end. Amen.
>
> Ephesians 3:20–21

About the Author

Catherine Richmond was focused on her career as an occupational therapist until a special song planted a story idea in her mind. That idea would ultimately become *Spring for Susannah*, her first novel. She is also a founder and moderator of Nebraska Novelists critique group and lives in Nebraska with her husband.